MITZY MOON MYSTERIES BOOKS 16-18

PARANORMAL COZY MYSTERY

Carols & Yule Perils

TRIXIE SILVERTALE

Sittin' On A Goldmine
Productions L.L.C.

CHAPTER 1

Never in all my Arizona-born days did I imagine myself trudging through knee-deep snow in almost-Canada to cut down my very own Christmas tree! But, as I prepare to celebrate my second Christmas in Pin Cherry Harbor, the place I now call home, I'm distracted by my job as a human snowplow.

To be honest, I've grown to love this place in a way I never thought possible, but I'm still not a huge fan of snow.

However, this hike does have an upside. The view!

Leading the way toward Birch County's secret stash of perfect Christmas trees is Sheriff Erick Harper.

He's marching along as though he was born to it, and he makes wading through two feet of snow with a chainsaw look like a Paris runway during fashion week.

As my newly acquired boots break through the crust of snow and sink into the powder beneath, the distance between my warm-hearted boyfriend and me grows with each step.

He stops, glances over his shoulder, and his sky-blue eyes dance with mischief. "You okay back there, Moon?"

"Don't get smart, Sheriff. I don't have quite as many years of experience hiking through the snow as you do."

I feel like a snowwoman suddenly exposed to the direct heat of the sun when his lips curve in an enticing grin. "Are you calling me an old man?"

While Erick may be five years older than me, he's far from an old man. His broad shoulders tower above me and a swath of his beautiful blond bangs slips out from beneath his beanie.

"Not old. Let's call it seasoned." I smirk and shrug.

He howls with laughter and strides off toward a stand of prized balsam fir. "You should've tried the snowshoes. I'm telling you, it's ten times easier."

Easier! He thinks that strapping some contraptions that look like tennis rackets to the feet of a naturally clumsy person, and then sending that person into the wild to trip over their own *feet-*

rackets is somehow a solution. You gotta love this guy.

As I continue slogging through the deep drifts, the antique mood ring on my left hand sizzles out a warning. Pretending to stop and tie my snow boots —not sure if that's even a thing—I slip off my mitten and sneak a peek. Something red—

Erick comes to a sudden halt, drops the chainsaw, and shouts, "Stay where you are, Moon."

It's so cute that he thinks he can command me. I dig deep into my young but uncooperative body and *run* to his side.

He shakes his head in dismay and raises a finger to his lips.

Before he has a chance to bring me up to speed, I whisper, "Is that blood in the snow?"

He nods. "I think it is. Probably a wounded animal. Hopefully a rabbit or fox, but if it's a wolf, that could be dangerous. I'm gonna hustle back to the cruiser and grab my sidearm."

"10-4."

Erick ignores my attempt to play deputy. "Stay still and quiet."

While he lopes away as though he's traversing a grassy meadow rather than plowing through months of snowfall, a sudden realization hits me.

I'm alone in the woods!

Sure, I have a chainsaw, but I don't know how

to use it. There's probably an injured timber wolf stalking me at this very moment. Goodbye, Sweet Erick. Who knows what might've been?

The once inviting forest shifts, as the leafless birch trees take on the appearance of skeletons clawing into the air, and the green of the dark pines becomes an ominous black.

Sitting in the profound silence, my brain kicks into overdrive with operation: Distract Mitzy from Sudden Death.

Somehow the thick layer of snow sucks all sound from the air. It's like the world's best sound-dampening blanket. If I could figure out a way to manufacture something with this level of sound absorption, maybe I could turn my clichéd film-school dropout story into an inspirational inventor's TED talk.

The sharp call of a reddish-pink bird with grey wings echoes through the forest, and my clairaudience unfortunately deciphers the song.

Death. Death. Death.

Before I can scream with the ferocity of a horror-movie scream queen, Erick's tramping return snaps me out of my psychic panic.

He takes one look at my face, draws his weapon, and cocks it. "Did you see a wolf?"

I have to tell him . . . And I pray he doesn't ask

too many questions. "It's not a wolf. I think it might be a human."

His head tilts to one side. "One of your hunches?"

I nod.

Adopting a tactical crouch, he follows the blood trail.

Plodding along behind, I'm hoping the freezing temperatures have thrown my extrasensory perceptions off and all we find is an injured, but still alive, bunny.

No such luck.

Twenty feet ahead of us, on the rough trail, is a crumpled pile of winter gear and boots. I know there's a human in there somewhere.

He holsters his weapon and rushes forward.

The stark pool of red in the alabaster snow is all I need to see. My clairsentience gives me an additional punch in the gut, whether or not I want it.

She's dead.

Erick rolls her over, and from a tiny hole in the front of her neon-blue jacket . . . blooms red death.

You'd think I'd be used to it by now, but it gets me every time. I run off the trail, grip the black-and-white scarred trunk of a birch, and unload my breakfast in a most unladylike fashion.

When I return to the trail, Erick is on the phone, trying to call for backup deputies and the medical examiner. "I can't get a solid signal out here. I should run back to the cruiser and call this in. Do you want to stay or go?"

Keeping my distance, I avert my gaze and blow out a shaky breath.

"I'm not sure what to say, Moon. I know I tease you about being a corpse magnet, but this is uncanny."

I hate when he uses the word uncanny. It's easy to sense he has suspicions about my hunches. While he knows I can see ghosts, I haven't been completely honest with him about my psychic powers. "Why is it so *uncanny*?"

"Well, you know, we parked at Twiggy's cabin and she gave us permission to cut a tree or two on her property, and this woman—"

"Is it Twiggy? It can't be. She was at the bookshop when we left." My extrasensory perceptions have completely checked out. No help at all. I can't afford to lose my one and only employee! Especially not one who works for nothing but front-row seats to my unavoidable klutzdom!

"It's not Twiggy. It's Carol Olsen."

I look at Erick as though he's crazy and throw my hands in the air. "Is that name supposed to mean something to me?"

He steps away from the body and exhales as he

approaches me. "You know the guy Twiggy's on-again/off-again dating?"

Swallowing loudly, I struggle to find my voice. "Wayne?"

Erick jerks a thumb over his shoulder toward the body. "That's his ex-wife."

CHAPTER 2

Now THAT WE have stumbled upon a crime scene, Erick is hesitant to leave the body unattended. Being an amazing girlfriend, I step up to the plate and offer to head back to the cabin and call the station.

A few hours earlier, I would've thought nothing about wandering alone through this idyllic winter wonderland. Of course, after our discovery, my mind works overtime playing tricks on me, and I think I'm seeing a murderer behind every tree.

When I approach the lone cabin in the woods, the "Gone Fishing" doormat peeks out from under a layer of snow and strikes me as a sad epitaph for the recently departed Carol Olsen. The two-bedroom clapboard structure sits quietly amidst the deep drifts of the long winter pressing against its lake-facing side. Of course, said lake is a frozen tundra at present.

Luckily, I've been to Twiggy's woodland outpost once before. If I needed to psychically replay the memory of how to light pilot lights and open fireplace flues to set up the cabin for habitation, I could. But I only need to ignore the musty abandoned smell, and make a couple of phone calls.

First: Call the station to request backup, and tell them to get the medical examiner into the office on a Sunday.

Second: Call my dad. Not because I need comfort or anything like that. I simply want a ride home.

If Erick had driven his personal vehicle out here, he might've let me drive it back, but there's absolutely no way he's handing over the keys to his county-issued vehicle to a civilian.

Both calls go off without a hitch, and I promise to fill my dad in on all the details on our drive back to Pin Cherry.

The deputies are the first to arrive, lights flashing and sirens blaring. While there isn't exactly an emergency, they don't see a lot of action in our tiny town, so any excuse to put the pedal to the metal is eagerly accepted.

My father, Jacob Duncan, fruit of the loins of

my grandmother's third marriage, arrives a few minutes later. "Hey, Dad."

As a reformed felon who did hard time, he's a quick study. He glances at the two patrol cars and runs a worried hand through his white-blond hair. Intelligent grey eyes, which are a mirror of my own, widen, and one corner of his mouth tugs upward. "I'm gonna go out on a limb here. Is it a body?"

Playfully pushing him back toward his 1950s Ford pickup truck, I grumble under my breath. "Between you and Erick, I've had about all the wisecracks I can take for one day. I can't help it if I happened to be walking through an area where a crime was committed. It's not my fault. Certainly not my choice. And it's definitely not uncanny!"

Jacob opens the door for me and pats me on the back as I climb in. "And I'm the Queen of Sheba." He slams the door and his shoulders shake with laughter as he walks to the driver's side.

I cross my arms and pretend to pout while he powers through the deep snow and heads toward the main road.

"So, am I gonna have to pry this story out of you with french fries, or are you gonna volunteer it?"

My stomach is still a little swirly from the *discovery*. Despite my love of—some would say obsession with—fries, the thought does not sit well. "I'll tell you anything you want to know. Just don't make me eat."

Concern fills his gaze, and he eases off the gas. "Do you need to go to the hospital? I didn't mean to poke fun if you're really not feeling well."

"No. No, you're fine. I tossed my cookies earlier when we found—"

"So it is a body?"

I nod, yank my stocking hat off my head, and wipe the clammy sweat from my brow. "Yeah. We were headed out to cut a Christmas tree for the bookshop and one for Erick's house— Shoot! Now he's not gonna have a tree."

My dad reaches his strong hand toward me and pats my knee. "Don't you think he'd rather spend Christmas with us? Last week you told me his mother was heading to Florida to visit her sister for the holidays. Even if he has a tree, Christmas all by himself doesn't sound too great. You know Amaryllis and Stellen would love to have him at our place."

I stack my mittened hand on top of my father's and my heart swells with love. "Thanks. That's a much better idea. And trust me when I tell you, Grams will be thrilled we didn't get a tree!"

My dad guffaws so loudly he temporarily loses control of the truck.

I grip the dashboard in terror. "Hey! One dead

body today is enough. Watch where you're going, buddy."

"Sorry. But if memory serves, Isadora is adamant about which tree is displayed for her proper holiday."

I twist my torso toward him, lean my head back, and open my mouth in mock awe. "So you're telling me she was bossy in real life, too?"

We both laugh at that comment.

"Even though I can't see or hear her like you, Mitzy, I can assure you the cold hand of death could not change my mother. If her ghost is anything like her human form, you will display that silver tinsel tree and you'll like it."

Pressing a hand to my unsettled tummy, I try to stifle my laughter. "Stop. My stomach is still upset. But that quote was almost verbatim. She made me dig that thing out of some storage closet and, once I unpacked the atrocity, I asked her if she wanted me to throw it away, and she flew into a ghost rage! I thought she was going to try to possess me!"

Jacob snickers. "So where did you put it up?"

"Nice. I like that you assume I had to put it up. Which I did. Complete with hand-strung garlands of popcorn and cranberry. But I argued to keep it inside the apartment, where it'll have the least exposure."

He grabs the steering wheel with both hands

and his frivolous mood turns somber. "Did she tell you the story?"

"Yeah. She said after her second husband Max was killed in the accident in Europe, and she lost a kidney, she had to turn her life around. I've heard that part before, but not the part about how much money Max had left her. She put herself in rehab, and when she got sober, the first thing she bought with the money from Max was that tree. And celebrating her first sober Christmas—alone—made her swear never to forget what she sacrificed for her sobriety."

Jacob nods. "It's a pretty sobering story—"

My dark humor jumps at the chance to lighten the mood. "No pun intended!"

He shakes his head. "It was accidental. But the story even convinced your grandpa Cal to let her put up the 'ex-husband tree,' as he called it. He was pretty upset about it the first year, but eventually it became part of our family tradition. I know it's nothing to look at, but it has deep meaning for all of us. I'm sure you've heard one or two stories about Isadora's—or I guess I should say Myrtle's—drunken days."

"Why do you think she started going by her second name after she got sober?"

"Honestly, I don't think it had anything to do with sobriety. Myrtle was the name she associated with Odell. They opened the diner together, named it after her, and then things went south. I have a feeling she dropped her first name as a way to erase some of the pain associated with losing him."

"But Grams said they repaired their friendship at the end, when she was sick. She said he was at her bedside every day."

His eyes drift to the rearview mirror. "Sure, at the end. Think about it, honey. If something happened that prevented you from being with Erick, but you had to live in the same town with him your whole life and he never remarried, because he never got over you, wouldn't you try to put any kind of distance between your heart and that memory?"

A hideous chill washes over my whole body. "I don't ever want that to happen, Dad."

He bites his lower lip and nods. "Your grandmother compromised a lot to make Cal happy. She always used to say it was worth it because she got me out of the bargain, but sometimes I wonder . . ."

We ride in silence for a few minutes as we both ponder the mistakes and losses in our lives.

As the city-limit sign comes into view, he taps one of his hands on the steering wheel. "Hey, I interrupted the story about the body. Did Erick know who it was?"

"He did. It's Wayne Olsen's ex-wife, Carol."

My father draws a sharp breath through his

teeth and shakes his head. "I'd say 'ex-wife' is generous. I know she moved out a long time ago, but it's my understanding she never granted him a divorce. She was Canadian and needed the marriage to give her free access across the border."

Something about the way he says free access prickles my psychic senses. "And why exactly would she need that?"

"Oh, you'll hear about Carol Olsen's many questionable ventures soon enough. Her latest endeavor was something called Carol's Canadian Maple, if I'm remembering correctly. She was either an *importer* or an *exporter* of pure Canadian Maple syrup, depending on who you ask."

"Why do you say it with that look on your face? Do you dislike maple syrup?"

He leans back as though I've offended him. "Listen, you don't grow up this far north without a deep, abiding respect for maple syrup. What I dislike are Carol's underhanded practices."

"So you don't think Twiggy killed her?"

Jacob stomps the brakes, and the truck fishtails wildly. He calmly counter steers and gets the vehicle under control at the side of the road, or as close to the side as he can get without driving into the huge snowbank. "Twiggy? Why on earth would Twiggy kill her? Does Erick think she's a suspect?"

"He seemed a little concerned when we first

found the body. I reminded him that Twiggy was at the bookshop when we left, but, as Wayne's girl-friend, I think they'll put her on the suspect list."

My father scoffs darkly. "Speaking from experi-ence, I hope she has a rock-solid alibi."

"Do you think an entitled cat and a sassy ghost can testify in court?"

Chuckles abound as he turns down the al-leyway between our two buildings and pulls into his garage.

"Hey, I'm serious about inviting Erick. He's more than welcome for Christmas Eve supper across the way." Jacob gestures over his shoulder and grins. We continue our walk toward the metal side door of my bookshop and I wrap my arms around his huge barrel chest and squeeze. "Thanks for coming to get me, Dad. I really needed to get out of there. You know?"

He returns the hug and kisses the top of my snow-white head. "The way I see it, I have twenty-plus years of fathering to make up for. You call me for a rescue any time—day or night."

Pulling back, I look up into his eyes and smirk. "You remember who you're talking to, right?"

He laughs and musses my hair as though I'm still a kid. "Yeah, I might be in for more than I bar-gained for, eh?"

"See ya later!" I call out.

He waves as he slips into the side door of the Duncan Restorative Justice Foundation.

I'm eager to race up the wrought-iron circular staircase to share the big news with Grams, but a sense of duty compels me to fill in Twiggy first.

I can barely see the top of her grey pixie cut peeking above the dilapidated rolly chair as she types our weekly order into the vintage computer.

"Twiggy, you got a minute?"

She slowly rotates the chair toward me, her countenance a textbook image of exasperation. "I don't see a tree, kid. Even you can't be that blind. They're all over the place out there."

She kicks the heel of one of her biker-boot-clad feet onto the opposite knee and slaps her hand on her dungarees as she cackles.

Swallowing hard, I tiptoe toward the unsettling news. "Unfortunately, there was also a body up there."

Her normally sarcastic expression melts away, and she leans forward with concern. "Anybody I know?"

"I'm afraid so. Erick said it was Carol Olsen."

Now the color truly drains from her skin, like the fading glow of an old CRT television screen as it powers down. "Carol? Was he sure?"

"I guess. I didn't take that close of a look. Plus, I don't know what she looks like."

"Does Wayne know?"

I cross my arms and hug them around my stomach. "You better hope not."

Twiggy gets to her feet and rakes a hand through her short bangs. "It was murder?"

"Definitely. Shot through the gut. One bullet. Dead center. Too precise to be an accident."

She leans forward, glances both directions, and whispers, "You gettin' any leads? You know, psychic stuff?"

My shoulders shrug involuntarily. "I got the hit about there being a body, but nothing else—yet."

She rubs a hand across her chin and reaches for her cell phone. "I should call Wayne."

Putting my hand on her arm, I shake my head. "I know you want to break it to him gently, but I think it would be better if he shows genuine surprise when Erick gives him the news."

Twiggy slowly lowers her hand and drops the phone on the desk. "Good point." Her eyes snap into focus and she tilts her head back. "Boy, lucky for us you're on the side of the good guys, doll."

"Gee, thanks." Eager to change the subject, I dive into the mundane. "Did you feed Pyewacket this morning, or am I going to get scolded when I walk into the apartment?"

"I haven't seen him. And I sure as sunshine didn't feed him, but who's to say what Isadora might've done." She angles her body away from me, but I can still see the smirk on her sarcastic little face as she pokes fun at my complete lack of control over my ghost roommate's activities.

I check the floor for any evidence of a bowl, and shrug. "I suppose I'll head up there and take what's coming to me."

She sighs and returns to her duties. "Everyone thinks I work for you at the Bell, Book & Candle, but, truth be told, we all work for his royal furriness!"

"Ain't that the truth!" I call out in solidarity.

Carefully stepping over the "No Admittance" chain at the bottom of the spiral staircase, I climb the treads and slowly make my way across the Rare Books Loft. The oak reading tables sit in neat rows like model students, and each one holds a brass lamp with a green-glass shade. The scent of mystery and possibility hangs in the air.

The last scholarly "open reading" session was the previous weekend, so we'll have the loft to ourselves until the New Year.

When I first came here, I didn't understand the true value of this collection. Twiggy and I still fight about whether the chain needs to be hooked all the time, but I finally understand what's at stake. More than once someone has stolen a book from this collection, and both times it ended badly. But that's another story.

Right now, I have to face the potential wrath of a spoiled caracal, and get Ghost-ma to help me set up the murder wall.

CHAPTER 3

THE SECRET BOOKCASE door whooshes closed behind me and the apartment appears empty. Isadora could be on the third floor of the adjacent printing museum, working on her memoirs, but I have no idea what's happened to the furry tan terror.

"Grams? Pyewacket?"

Nothing.

The fiendish feline has all kinds of mysterious ways to come and go as he pleases, so his absence is of little concern. However, I strongly suspect that Ghost-ma is still having a pout over our holiday-tree discussion. Luckily, I know the one thing her ghost finds irresistible.

Pushing the large, rolling corkboard into the center of the room, I clear my throat dramatically.

"Oh well, looks like I'll have to set up the murder wall all by myself!"

Twiggy purchased this corkboard for me, and keeps me supplied with tacks, 3 x 5 cards, and green yarn. I'm not allowed to put tacks into the authentic lath and plaster walls, and I'm also not allowed to use red yarn, because it gives my resident ghost the heebie-jeebies.

"Since nobody wants to hear my juicy gossip, I suppose I'll head over to the diner and grab some lunch."

Turning to leave the apartment, I run smack dab into a translucent wall of vintage burgundy Marchesa silk and tulle.

"Did you say gossip? And murder?"

"Like a moth to the flame." I cross my arms and offer a smug grin while she fully materializes. It really does take all the fun out of it when she's so predictable.

"Listen to me, young lady, don't you pretend to know the first thing about me—"

"Hold on!" I wag my finger back and forth at her shimmering form. "We have a rule in this bookshop. If these lips aren't moving, you don't get to comment. No thought-dropping. No exceptions."

She places a bejeweled fist on her hip and rolls her ghostly eyes. "There have been exceptions. Sometimes you're in danger, and the only way we can communicate is telepathically. Or when you're trying to hide things from Erick, or when—"

"All right. Point made. But this wasn't one of those times. Now, do you want to hear my tale or not?"

At the mention of a tale, Pyewacket saunters out of my massive walk-in closet as though he owns the place. He flicks his thick tan tail and twitches his black-tufted ears.

I've nicknamed the home for a seemingly limitless supply of couture the *Sex and the City* meets *Confessions of a Shopaholic* closet, and it's the place where my grandmother made a physical manifestation of her love for me. Before she died, she carefully packed the closet with precious vintage items from her own illustrious collection, as well as a gargantuan supply of updated items she thought I'd need. My tendency to fall back on jeans and snarky T-shirts is a bit of a bone of contention between us.

"Bone of contention!" Isadora arches a perfectly drawn brow.

"Grams! What did we just talk about?"

She clutches one of her strands of pearls and sighs. "I'm sorry, dear. That was an honest mistake. I'm telling you, it's all jumbled together for me. I'm never sure if you've said it out loud or just thought it."

Taking a deep breath, I point a finger toward

my lips, but before I can chant the mantra, she steals my thunder.

"I know, I know. If those lips aren't moving, blah blah blah." She swirls toward the coffee table, snatches up the pen, and floats it above the stack of 3 x 5 cards. "Let's get on with this murder investigation, shall we?"

I peel off my winter layers and collapse onto the overstuffed settee. "We shall." Quickly bringing her up to speed on the corpse in the forest, I offer the short list of potential suspects.

Her ethereal head is shaking firmly before I finish the list. "Twiggy? Do you really want me to make a card for Twiggy? You said yourself, she was here at the bookshop when Erick picked you up for the outing."

"True, but we don't have time of death yet. She could've been out at the cabin early this morning and made it back to town, before Erick picked me up."

"Reeeee-ow." A warning from the caracal.

"Pshaw! You can't possibly believe that."

The tag-team of opposition irks me, and I stubbornly cross my arms. "Look, one thing I've learned since these psychic powers clicked on is that everyone's a suspect until they're not. So make a card for Twiggy, or I'll get a new assistant."

Right on cue, Pye jumps onto the coffee table

and pushes the stack of 3 x 5 cards onto the floor with his large paw.

Grams and I both crack up.

"Sorry, dear. I didn't mean to lose my temper. Twiggy's been my best friend for more years than either of us would like to count, and I absolutely know in my heart of hearts that she could never kill someone."

"Copy that. But since you don't actually have a heart, we're going to make a card for her and see where it takes us. To be fair, I don't think she's guilty, but I also wouldn't want to be on the wrong side of an argument with her, if you know what I mean?"

Grams giggles. "Oh Mitzy, you're too much."

Approaching the vast empty corkboard, I tack a card for Twiggy, one for Wayne, and, in the center, a card for our victim—Carol. The green yarn connects them all and that's not a good thing.

As I stare at the unhelpful index cards and tap my finger on my chapped lips, the face of my lawyer and alchemical mentor pops into my head. "Oh brother! I was supposed to meet Silas for an early lunch at the diner!"

Running into the closet, I wiggle out of my tree-cutting outfit and shout for my otherworldly stylist. "I'm supposed to go to some kind of solstice thing at his house. What do I wear to a solstice thing?"

Grams phases through the wall, flickering with excitement. "Is he having the full coven?"

"The what now?"

"Well, back when I was a practicing witch, Silas used to host the winter solstice celebration every year for our coven."

"Spoiler alert, I'm not a witch, Grams. And I'm also not in the coven." Lowering myself to the padded mahogany bench in the middle of fashion central, I wait for further details.

"Oh, I know, honey. But with your psychic gifts, and the transmutations Silas has taught you, you've got more talent in your pinky finger than most of those old biddies."

I wiggle my left hand toward her, brandishing my mood ring. "I think you mean in my ring finger."

She giggles, whooshes through me, and dives into the clothes. "You'll need something warm, for the part where you go outside to light the Yule Log — Unless he's doing that inside this year? It also needs to say celebration, with a hint of winter and . . ."

Yawning loudly, I glance at an imaginary watch. "Is this outfit gonna materialize anytime soon, Isadora?"

"I'll have three, or maybe two, options in about ten minutes. You better text Silas that you'll be running late for lunch. And whatever you do, don't go into that cave!"

"Pretty sure there's not a cave at the diner." Maybe she's going ghost crazy.

"I'm not— Never mind. I'm talking about that cave in the cliffs out at Silas's mansion. You told me you went down and explored it? Am I misremembering?"

She's right. I know exactly which cliffs she's talking about now. "No way! That cave is located down a treacherous set of steps that aren't easy to climb in the summer. I certainly won't be following him down that death slide in the winter. After all, what would be the point?"

Grams presses her hands to her chest and sighs with melancholy. "Silas takes his solar holidays very seriously. The entire coven used to build a large bonfire in the cave and sleep there overnight, keeping the fire burning brightly as we each took our shift urging the sun to be reborn on solstice morning. Earth-based traditions believe in honoring nature's cycles. Planting cycles, solar cycles, lunar cycles . . . You get the idea."

I really didn't get the idea, but I understood the concept of sleeping in a cold cave in the middle of winter, and I knew for certain I wouldn't be doing it. "Well, let's hope that item has been removed from the ceremonial agenda. It sounds awful."

Ghost-ma suddenly ceases her rifling through the clothes and drifts toward the well-lit ceiling. "I'm not describing it right. It was truly magical. A group of women, feasting and celebrating together, is heartwarming. The night-long vigil brought us all together. We had to rely on the person keeping watch to build up the fire and keep us all warm. Emerging from the cave at sunrise and feeling like our modest effort somehow insured the new dawn— It's indescribable."

The emotion in her voice almost makes me reconsider my stance on cave camping, but not entirely. "It sounds lovely, Grams. I'm going to try to do something with my hair, and throw on a little makeup. Which should make you happy. When I get back, there better be an outfit waiting."

She claps her hands together with glee at the mention of makeup. "Don't you worry. I will not disappoint you, sweetie."

Splashing warm water on my face in the bathroom, I can hear the hangers sliding back and forth in the closet. It's actually a little eerie to know that I'm technically alone in the apartment, and yet there's something in my closet. One of the many conundrums of living with an earthbound spirit.

Makeup has never come easy with me, and whenever I get stressed about which things to apply in which order, or feel like giving up altogether, I think back to the precious moments I was able to spend with my mother before she was taken from me too soon.

Memories of sitting on various counters in the bathrooms of the different places we called home, watching her "put on her face," wash over me. With my developing psychic skills, I'm able to replay the memory in more detail. I can hear her comforting voice explain each step to me as though she were sitting beside me.

"This is called foundation, and it covers up any imperfections so I look ready to conquer the world."

The sound of her voice echoing through time makes me feel invincible.

"The blush gives my cheeks a little color so no one can tell I'm running on four hours' sleep."

I had forgotten how hard she worked to keep a roof over our heads. Time erases so much.

"This cinnamon mocha lip tint gives me a confident smile, but keeps it professional."

My lips are the picture of hers. My smile is a link to her love.

"A gentle application of smoky shadow gives my eyes depth and intelligence. Not that I'm not intelligent; this just confirms their suspicions."

I may share my eye color with my dad, but I know I get my smarts from my brilliant mother.

"Always give the eyebrows a light nudge with a pencil, so you look like you mean business."

Then she would apply a little mascara to my lashes before she coated her own and say, "Dark lashes give you a finished look. Serious but mysterious." And she would kiss the tip of my nose, every single morning until—

As I twist the mascara wand back into the tube, I have to blink back the tears welling up in my eyes.

"I wish I could've known your mother, Mitzy." Grams' face pushes through the wall from the closet, and glistening ghost-tears trickle down her cheeks.

"Me too. Maybe next year Silas will teach me how to run a proper séance and we can both talk to her." Our eyes meet in the mirror and she nods before slipping back to her wardrobe duties.

"I'll be there in a minute. Just need to do some hair zhuzhing." My skill with the styling wand has improved at least a thousand percent since my arrival in almost-Canada. I never would've expected a ghost to be the one to teach me the ropes, but, truth be told, Grams is rather amazing.

My eyes shimmer with unshed tears and I touch the dream catcher necklace around my neck as I whisper to my mother. "I love you, Mama. I'll never forget you. Thank you for being my mom, even if it was only for a short time. You gave me everything I needed to survive. I wish you could see me now."

Blast it! A couple of those unshed little buggers manage to trickle down my freshly blushed cheeks. Grabbing a tissue, I carefully dab at the moisture on my face and head to the closet to take my medicine.

"Well, what are we looking at? Is there any way I can avoid a four-inch heel in this weather?"

Ghost-ma ignores my taunt and gestures with her arm in a wide arc toward the two outfits she's selected.

One involves an extravagant wrap-around cape that I can't even begin to understand how to deploy, and the other seems a good compromise. Lovely black slacks with enough stretch to be comfortable for a feast, and a soft red sweater, with an appropriate neckline.

"I'm sure you already guessed, but I'm choosing the sweater."

"It's fine. It's the time of year for generosity, so I'll let it slide. I even selected a smart shearling-lined boot with barely a two-inch heel!"

I fan myself as I pretend to faint. "Oh, my stars! The little Christmas elves are smiling down on me."

Grams giggles. "Don't you mean smiling *up* at you?"

"Good one. I set you up for it, but still—"

She whirls around the closet grabbing jewelry

and other accessories, while I suit up for my lunch and the evening's solstice party.

"Am I supposed to take anything? Like a host gift or something for the ceremony?"

She stops so suddenly she appears as a single frozen frame from an old-fashioned cartoon reel. But before the heat of the bulb can bubble the cellulose, the film picks up speed. "You're supposed to take two things. You need to have something that represents a bad habit or memory that you want to release from the past year, and then you need to offer something that represents a positive thing you want to achieve or incorporate in your life in the coming year."

"That sounds kind of complicated. I don't have any ideas, do you?"

Pyewacket struts into the closet, pushes past me with his powerful left shoulder, and rises on his hind legs to thwack a drawer with his paw.

"Seems like you're trying to tell me something, is that right?"

"Reow." Can confirm.

I step toward the drawer and, as I pull it open, my extra senses pick up the word "gun." "You want me to get rid of my only means of protection, son? Are you crazy?"

"Ree-OW!" A warning punctuated by a threat.

Grams floats toward me and hovers at eye level.

"Maybe you should listen to Mr. Cuddlekins, dear. He has a sixth sense about these things. That gun has definitely done more harm than good. You have so many other skills. Skills that only you can wield. Think about it."

Far be it from me to question this ghost/cat onslaught any further. Reaching into the back of the drawer, I pull out the firearm and slip it into the red-and-grey velvet evening bag I've been instructed to carry. "I'll see what Silas has to say. Now what's the 'good thing'?"

Both Grams and I look at Pyewacket to see if the wise feline has any additional information. He picks that exact moment to rock back on his haunches and take care of some personal hygiene.

Just when you think you're in the presence of true genius!

Grams laughs so hard she snorts.

"You're no help at all." When I'm tempted to give up on the "good thing," inspiration strikes. "I know! I'm going to print out one of the pictures of Erick and me from my phone. That's something I could use more of in the coming year."

Grams lifts her glimmering fist into the air and cheers. "Hear! Hear! Bright solstice blessings to that!" Under her breath, she mumbles, "About time."

"Hey, don't judge me because I want to get it

right the first time. Not all of us are interested in having a laundry list of ex-husbands, Myrtle Isadora Johnson Linder Duncan Willamet Rogers."

"Touché." She taps a perfectly manicured finger on her pursed coral lips while I print out the best pic.

Erick was holding my phone high in the air, and my head was snuggled against his broad chest as we both smiled with genuine joy. I think we took that one out on Fish Hawk Island, right before—

My phone rings, and I glance down in horror. "I forgot to text Silas!"

Grams shakes her head and offers a tsk tsk.

Answering the call on the second ring, I slap on my very best manners. "Good afternoon, Mr. Willoughby. Please allow me to apologize for my tardiness. Isadora took an extra long time selecting my outfit. But I'm all set and I have my items for the ceremony. I'll be at the diner in three minutes or less."

CHAPTER 4

CUT TO—

Myrtle's Diner is bustling with holiday activity. Tally has outdone herself with the beautiful home-spun decorations. I have no idea where she finds the time to crochet after a long day on her feet, but her elves and snowmen are stellar. There are even tinsel garlands tacked to the walls and some beautiful holiday-themed vinyl decals on the black-and-white checkered floor. That modern addition has to be the brainchild of Tally's hard-working daughter, Tatum.

I see a familiar face at the counter and wave happily at Quincy Knudsen, former star photographer of the one and only local newspaper. Quince, as his friends call him, was the first recipient of the newly established journalism scholarship at the local high school, and he has helped me on more than one case. But I don't have time for those stories.

Pointing frantically to the corner booth, I shiver with mock worry. Quince takes one look at Silas, widens his eyes, and nods. He's a man of few words on most days, so I'd say that was a bang-up conversation.

As I slide into the booth, I offer an additional series of apologies.

Silas uncharacteristically waves away my concern, and a smile lifts his sagging jowls.

Boy, this holiday spirit thing must be contagious. "Did you already order?"

This question brings back the familiar look of consternation. His bushy eyebrows squeeze together, and he harrumphs as he adjusts his ever-present fusty tweed coat and unusually patterned bowtie. "Such a question must indicate a severe lack of focus. What troubles you?"

Bonus points to the lawyer/secret alchemist. "Erick and I discovered a body this morning when we were supposed to be out cutting Christmas trees."

Surprisingly, this revelation results in a large belly laugh from my mentor, rather than the expected somber nod. He presses his hands on his round paunch, and his jolly cheeks jiggle until they're bright red. He leans forward to brace himself on the table, and the top of his bald head shines like the star on O *Tannenbaum*.

"I'm not sure what I said to give you such a fit of giggles, Mr. Willoughby."

He leans back and takes a deep breath, but before he can launch into a reply, which most certainly mentions my tendency to attract disaster—

The owner, my surrogate grandfather Odell, approaches the table. "Good afternoon, Mitzy. I heard you got yourself into a little trouble this morning."

As usual, news of my exploits has catapulted through the person-to-person wireless in Pin Cherry Harbor. "If you're referring to the incident near Twiggy's cabin, I'll have you know that the sheriff was also present. And I didn't get *myself* into any trouble. I happened to stumble upon the trouble someone else left."

This defensive argument causes another round of laughter from both lawyer and stand-in grandpa.

Odell slides a beautifully cooked cheeseburger and golden-brown french fries in front of me, and a sensible chicken salad sandwich with a house side salad in front of my lunch date.

"Thanks. This looks delicious." I carefully place a napkin in my lap and grab a few extra from the dispenser at the end of the table next to the carefully stacked jams and the salt and pepper.

Silas nods his approval. "You'd do well to protect that sweater. I'd hate for you to suffer the wrath of—"

"Tanya? At the dry cleaner? She can be a real stickler for stains." I lift an eyebrow and stare at Silas in shock. How is it that he was about to mention the ghost of my dearly departed grandmother in front of one of her ex-husbands? It's not like him to make such an amateur mistake. That's my territory.

Silas folds his hands in his lap and nods. "Indeed. She's never forgiven me for the damage I did to this shirt."

Odell and I glance at the mystery stain on the off-white shirt, but neither of us dare to ask. The cook is more interested in my holiday plans. "You and the sheriff have big plans for Christmas?"

"Not exactly. His mom is visiting her sister in Florida, as I'm sure you already know, so I think I'm going to invite him to my dad's. What do you think?"

Odell's coffee-brown eyes glisten with emotion, and he rakes a hand through his all-business grey buzz cut. "It's good to be around family this time of year. Makes you appreciate what's important." Before either Silas or I can respond, he raps his knuckles on the silver-flecked white Formica table and returns to his duties behind the grill.

"Perhaps you should invite Mr. Johnson to your celebration, Mizithra."

Uh oh. Formal name territory. Now I know Silas means business. "I'll check with Amaryllis. She seems to enjoy entertaining, so I'm sure it won't be a problem. Do you think he'd want to hang out with us?"

Silas steeples his fingers and carefully bounces his thick chin on the tip of his pointers.

I've come to recognize this signal as a brewing lesson about to be served. Something that I've said or done has triggered his need to create a teachable moment out of my mistake. If I'm going to get a lecture, I may as well hear it with something delicious in my belly. I snatch up a handful of golden-fried potato perfection and shove it in my mouth.

His milky-blue eyes seem to bore through my forehead directly into my grey matter.

"All right. I hear what you're not saying. If I focus and use my gifts appropriately, I'll be able to sense whether Odell made his comment because he was feeling lonely or whether it's just something he likes to say to all his patrons during the holiday season."

I take a long sip of my soda, or, as they call it up north, pop, and swallow. "Here goes." I press my hands against the soft wool on my thighs, close my eyes, and replay the recent conversation with Odell. As I relax and let my extrasensory perception fill in the details, my chest squeezes tight with emotion.

"He's terribly lonely, Silas. He throws himself into his work to try to forget, but he's thinking about Isadora—Myrtle—more often than he's not thinking about her. It breaks my heart."

Silas lowers his interlocked fingers and nods once. "Loss affects us all quite differently. For some, their attachments are many and fleeting. When someone leaves their life for whatever reason, they take a deep breath and move on. Hardly missing a beat. For others, the connections are few and deep. For those individuals, each loss seems to steal a sliver of their soul. A finite resource, which cannot be replaced. As the losses stack up, the soul diminishes. I truly feel that for these rare folks, death is not a result of illness, age, or any other tangible factor. At some point, they simply run out of slices, and at that point they leave us."

I'm not sure why I bothered to put on makeup, since everyone is bringing me to tears and inevitably ruining my hard work. Grabbing another napkin from the dispenser, I dab at my cheeks and wipe carefully under each eye. "Odell's one of the people with the soul connections, right?"

Silas glances through the red-Formica-trimmed

orders-up window and watches the man who makes every plate with love. "He is. And I fear he gave more than one sliver to your grandmother. I don't have your gifts, but I've always sensed a piece of him is hollow. I am certain that would be precisely where your grandmother used to interlock."

Desperate to avoid the intense feels, I grasp at anything to change the subject. "Either tell me about the ceremony or ask me about the dead body."

Silas harrumphs, but nods in understanding. "You may proceed first. What did you discover in the deep, dark woods?"

As I look up to speak, the images of the morning replay in rapid succession. My throat feels dry. Taking another sip of my beverage, I swallow and tell my tale. "So, did you know Carol Olsen? When she was married to Wayne, or maybe after?"

He sighs and gazes into the distance. "I believe I met her once at a function your grandmother held. However, I know little of her, other than the standard rumors that drift about a town like this."

"Erick said she and Wayne were divorced, but my dad said that wasn't the case. He said Carol wouldn't give Wayne a divorce, because she needed free access across the border."

Silas smooths his mustache with a thumb and forefinger. "That may be. As I said, I know little about her. Perhaps I am more familiar with Wayne, socially, at least. He strikes me as an honest man struggling under the burden of doing the right thing."

"Which is?"

"Well, he's always been quite interested in our dear Twiggy. However, unable to move things to the next level with her, they frequently part ways before things can become too entangled."

Leaning toward him, I lower my voice. "I hate to ask this. Do you think—?"

His hunched shoulders seem to unfold before my eyes, and the doddering old man that once sat across from me in our booth now embodies the mighty alchemist lurking within. "I think no such thing. And neither should you."

"Copy that."

His voice is quiet, yet carries immense power. There's no room for argument.

Here's me officially taking Twiggy off my suspect list, whether or not Erick likes it.

CHAPTER 5

ONCE INSIDE THE mothball-scented 1908 Model
T, Silas offers me several horsehair blankets. "I recall you being a touch sensitive to the cold. These
should do nicely."

If by *nicely* he means scratch like a bag of
stinging nettle, then yes. They're fantastic.

We make stops at the dry cleaner, the Piggly
Wiggly, and the post office as Silas completes his
weekly errands and prepares for a houseguest. Me.
At long last, we head out of town toward his remote
estate.

As we curve down the meandering drive
leading to Mr. Willoughby's brooding mansion, I
feel as though I may have literally driven back in
time. The narrow private road leading to Silas's

home winds through a beautiful birch forest; trees wrapped in black-and-white bark as far as the eye can see.

When the dwelling in the forest looms into view, its perfect eccentricity still enchants me. An awe-inspiring Gothic structure, with three haunting stories and small dormers in the roof, which indicate a possibly usable attic space. Sharply pointed turrets accent the corners, and intricate stained-glass windows catch the late afternoon sun. The home is not in disrepair, but it has clearly waged a lengthy battle with time and has given up a little ground with each passing year. A grey stone wall, higher than my head, encloses the property.

On my first visit, I entered through the black iron gate, bearing a faintly familiar sigil, which aligns with the once-grand front entrance of the home. Today we venture down another route.

Silas takes a hidden turn to our right and slips around behind the hulking home, pulls into the garage that was once a carriage house, and leads me through the servants' entrance.

"Even though we didn't come through the impressive front door, this place still reminds me of a fairytale castle."

"One doesn't think of one's home in those terms. I simply enjoy the isolation this location provides." He shuffles toward the kitchen. "I shall put the kettle on and bring you a nice hot chocolate in the drawing room."

I'd love to point out that most simple homes don't have chandeliers and drawing rooms, but my teeth are chattering so hard I'm worried I might bite off my own tongue if I attempt to form more words. Rubbing my arms furiously, I search for any indication of warmth.

"You'll come upon a rich bed of coals glowing in the hearth. Feed them some strips of birchbark and layer the split wood on the resulting flames. You shall find yourself as toasty as a marshmallow in moments."

Doubtful, but the promise of fire brings me hope. When I see the glowing pile of embers, I have to stop myself from jumping into the fireplace.

With shaky hands, I perch on the split-rock hearth and follow his instructions. The papery birchbark feels like a cross between leather and tissue paper. If I weren't so cold, I'd spend more time admiring it and less time tossing it into the fire.

A hearty crackle and the aroma of burning wood reward my efforts. Slowly heat seeps into my bones, and my shivering shoulders relax.

The view in the solstice-eve light is breathtaking. The mansion sits atop a bluff overlooking the great lake, frozen in the grip of winter's icy hand and painted pinkish-gold. For a moment it's as though I've been transported to the Arctic Circle.

By the time Silas joins me, flames are roaring, and I've had to slip back to a footstool. I'm starting to feel my fingers and toes again.

He offers me the cocoa, and I gratefully slurp down the warm liquid. The alcoholic afterburn surprises me. "Whoa! You forgot to mention it was fully *leaded* cocoa."

He chuckles and wipes some whipped cream from his mustache as he lowers himself into an ancient leather recliner. "It's a celebration."

His mention of festivities reminds me. "Grams asked if the entire coven would be here. Will they?"

Silas draws a deep, slow breath and presses his tonsured head against a worn spot on the chair. "Ah, yes. The coven. I fear that once your grandmother passed, I broke ties with the remaining women."

"What happened? Did you lose interest?"

He harrumphs and smooths his bushy mustache with thumb and forefinger. "Truth be told, I never had much interest. My involvement primarily revolved around assisting your grandmother to expand her knowledge and get closer to her true goal."

"Did she want to be high priestess?" A bit of

whipped cream sticks to my lip and I lick it off with a satisfied hum.

He sighs and shakes his head. "Have you learned nothing since you arrived?"

My cheeks flush and I move closer to the fire to hide my embarrassment. "Oh, right. You mean her goal of staying on this side of the veil."

"Indeed. It was a complicated stratagem that required a certain level of expertise on both parts. Your grandmother did a great deal of work to gain the opportunity to meet you, Mizithra."

Holding my hands around the warm mug, I turn toward Silas. "I'm not sure I can ever express how truly grateful I am for the gift that she gave me, and the help that you gave her. Growing up without a family left a hole in my heart. I guess I didn't realize how big that hole was until I arrived here and filled it with Ghost-ma, Jacob, Pyewacket—"

Silas chuckles and sips his hot chocolate.

"And you! Present company included."

He waves off my delayed addition. "I have no concern for my name being listed, my dear. I had someone else in mind."

The heat on my cheeks is definitely cherry-red now. "Oh, you mean Erick?"

He smiles with satisfaction. "The two of you make a lovely team. I'm glad you chose to remain with us. The town, and indeed I, are better for it."

I set my empty mug on the hearth and wring my hands as I ask my pressing question. "If it's just you and me, do we have to sleep in the cave?"

Unfortunately, Silas has taken a sip of his cocoa, but he's forced to spit it into his thinning handkerchief, as he's unable to stifle the guffaw my question prompts.

"What? Grams is the one who couldn't stop talking about the cave! How do I know?"

He wipes his mouth and gets to his feet. "I must get this kerchief into some cold water immediately. Good chocolate can leave a dastardly stain."

As he shuffles toward the kitchen, I call out, "You didn't answer my question."

He pauses and replies without turning. "We shall enjoy a lovely feast for two, and you and I will light the Yule Log in the library fireplace. There will be no sleeping in caves, my dear."

My anxious shoulders drop as I exhale, and he's still chuckling under his breath all the way to the sink.

A surprisingly cheerful voice beckons me. "Mizithra, can you lend a hand?"

When I enter the kitchen, he's pulling a succulent ham from the oven, and the aroma brings an audible growl from my stomach. "That looks delicious."

He nods proudly and gestures toward the casserole dish still inside. "Select a potholder, and follow me to the dining room."

Sixteen chairs surround the massive cherry-wood table spanning the formal dining room. Three candelabras grace the red tablecloth, and between each is an array of poinsettias, pine boughs, and red-beribboned bundles of mistletoe.

For a moment I wonder if we'll be playing out a scene from *Beauty and the Beast*, with me sitting at one end of the ridiculously long table, and Silas at the other, but I see the two places are laid across from each other on the left.

The silverware is polished to a glistening sheen, and gold chargers are each layered with a plate and delicately folded gold napkin. There are two pieces of etched crystal above the plate, a water glass and a champagne coupe.

"Wow! What a beautiful place setting. Is there anything else I need to grab from the kitchen?"

"I shall retrieve the bread, and we will discuss the meaning of solstice while the meat rests."

Leave it to Silas to invent a way to delay gratification even further. Placing the casserole dish on a marble trivet next to the ham, I take my seat and fill my glass with water.

Suddenly overcome with a fit of manners, I hop

up and fill his water glass too. I don't see any open wine or champagne, and even I know it would be rude to poke around.

As I return to my seat, Silas enters bearing a beautiful crusty loaf of bread that has been scored to look like an actual log.

"That's so cool. Did you do that?"

He shakes his head and places the bread on the table. "While I am more than capable of making bread, the credit for this well-designed loaf goes to cook. She enjoys putting special touches on the holiday menus."

Silas retrieves a large leather-bound book from a side table, takes his seat, and carefully thumbs through the pages until he finds what he's looking for.

I inhale and open my mouth, but Mr. Willoughby's stern look silences my snoopy nature.

"Our forebears relied on the seasons to guide them. A late frost could kill delicate buds on life-giving fruit trees, a pestilence during the growing season could decimate crops, and disease in the livestock could mean death for hungry villagers. In this modern age, we are fortunate to have plenty, but that false sense of security separates us from the important cycles of nature." He turns a thin sheet and runs his finger down the page.

I know better than to open my mouth.

"Winter solstice is a time to celebrate the return of the sun. For each day after this will bring more hours of sunlight, culminating at the summer solstice.

"Our meal this evening consists of cured meats, root vegetables, and our all-important grains. The bounty of the harvests is behind us, and more hard months of winter lie ahead. The sun will grow in strength, and next year our crops will surely prosper. Let us eat this feast with gratitude and remember the precious gift of each day."

Nodding my head, I swallow my emotion. Working at my minimum wage barista job back in Arizona, when I couldn't even pay my bills, life didn't seem very precious. But if I'd given up then, I never would've had this amazing experience in almost-Canada. "Every day is precious, Silas. Thank you for reminding me."

He turns and pulls a bottle of champagne from a bucket of ice that I swear to you did not exist a moment ago. In a flash, he takes the carving knife from the ham platter, and, with one swift motion, slices the cork into the air as he intones, "Bright solstice blessings!"

Silas pours the bubbly into our glasses, clinks his coupe to mine, and, for the first time I can remember, downs his entire serving of champagne in one unceremonious gulp.

"Cheers to that!" I add before following his lead.

He rises and serves the honeyed ham and some glorious dish he calls dauphinoise potatoes.

After two servings of potatoes, a healthy slab of ham, and an overly buttered slice of thick, warm bread, I'm worried I won't be able to move. The stretch in these wool pants is barely getting me by.

"We shall take our wassail in the library. Come with me."

After briefly returning to the kitchen to ladle up two steaming mugs of spiced wassail, he leads the way to the library.

The polished marble floor boasts an impressive collection of rugs. A sturdy oak-legged table in the center is being tested to its limits with the massive selection of tomes lying open on its surface. The arcane collection in this room surely rivals the Rare Books Loft.

Silas guides me to a vintage wing-back chair with tufted sage-green upholstery and dark cherry-wood framing.

Once I'm seated next to the roaring fire, he snaps his fingers, and the room falls into inky darkness. "Silas? Is that supposed to happen?"

"The light of the sun is a powerful resource. Yet, somehow we never miss the light until it is gone."

Oh, this must be part of the ceremony. Probably best if I keep quiet and don't move.

Some rustling in the fireplace confirms my suspicions. Having worked with torn pieces of birchbark earlier, I recognize the distinct papery crinkle. Some twigs are snapped, some logs are stacked, and the alchemist takes a seat in the matching chair next to mine.

"When the light returns, all will be made well." He claps his hands together, and sparks sizzle from the fireplace.

Silver, blue, green, purple, and red flickers of light dance over the pile of logs like miniature fairies.

"Welcome, returning sun. We are grateful for your light, your warmth, and the life you share."

The logs burst into flame, and I watch as the beautifully decorated limb of oak sitting atop the pyre slowly feeds its ribbons, pinecones, and cranberries to the flame.

Silas reaches a hand out in the firelight and pats my arm. "I understand Robin Pyewacket Goodfellow's concern regarding your firearm. However, the solstice flames are not a place to dispose of such an item. You are a complicated woman, with an impressive and expanding skillset in the psychic and alchemical realms. I should leave it to your judgment whether that item remains with you or finds its way to some other. In contrast, I believe the item you wish to place in the bonfire which represents your hopes for the coming year is more appropriate."

I won't even ask how he knows what he knows. He claims he possesses no psychic powers, but as I sit across the marble-topped walnut side table, I think I'm starting to understand why Erick uses the word uncanny so often. I reach into my purse and pull out the photograph.

Silas smiles and nods.

Moving toward the crackling flames, my heart swells with hope. I want to share more with Erick in the coming year. I'm glad we're taking things slow, but I want to pick up the pace—a little. Here's to the coming year, Erick Harper.

With a light kiss, I toss the photo into the fire and feel a tingle of warmth circle my spine.

Glancing toward Silas, I'm about to ask after the next phase of the ritual, but his eyes are closed, and there's a light snoring ruffling his mustache and wiggling his jowls.

Maybe that was enough. Maybe simply being in

the here and now is what I've been missing all these years.

Tomorrow I'll be back on the case, working with Sheriff Too-Hot-To-Handle to keep my cantankerous employee's boyfriend out of jail. But tonight, I can stare into the flames, rub my full belly, and be happy.

CHAPTER 6

Morning at the mansion is eerily quiet. I walk toward the heavily draped window to see if my efforts have recharged the sun. As I slide the thick brocade to the side, a magical scene unfolds.

Thick flakes of snow are fluttering downward like tiny angels bringing messages to earth. Beyond the sleeping terraced gardens, a large buck feasts on an offering of grains and vegetables that Silas must've placed in the yard before the sun came up.

Hastily dressing in yesterday's wardrobe, I descend the wide staircase as the welcome aroma of coffee wafts upward and envelops me.

"The coffee smells delicious, Silas."

When I enter the kitchen, he pours me a mug and slides a porcelain, cow-shaped creamer toward me. "Will you be joining me for breakfast?"

"Erick asked me to meet him at the diner, but—"

"Certainly. I will be but a moment, then I can ferry you into town."

The last thing in the world I want right now is another subzero ride in his ridiculous excuse for a car. "That's super nice of you, but Erick said he would pick me up. Should I tell him to come around to the back?"

A mischievous grin curls the corners of the alchemist's mouth.

"What's so funny?"

"He will be unable to see the turn, my dear."

"What? Why not? I mean, I know it's kind of on a blind curve, but it's not that hard to see."

Silas strokes his mustache twice and refills his mug. "You can see the turn, because you possess a rare set of gifts. You are but one of three, only two living, who can detect the turn."

"Did you use magic—sorry, alchemy—to hide it? Could Grams see it?"

"Yes, to both. Perception is not fixed. Our eyes can play tricks on us. Using those tricks to create a camouflage is simpler than it sounds. Your grandmother could not always see the turn, but she reached a point in her studies—"

A sudden crack in his voice catches me off guard, and I set my coffee cup on the counter and move to his side. "What is it? What were you going to say?"

"I am certain your grandmother has told you how her relentless pursuit of magical knowledge led to her illness."

"She did. Grams said the doctors chalked it up to liver failure and her early abuses of alcohol. She always believed that delving too deeply into the magical arts ultimately sealed her fate. I don't think there's any way to prove that."

A flash of guilt darts across his wizened face. "There are ways. I know the ways, but instead of discouraging her and putting her health first—"

"What are you saying? You're not responsible for her obsessions. It's very common for addicts to replace one addiction with another. Maybe Alcoholics Anonymous helped her get sober, but they couldn't keep her from magic."

A light of hope flickers in his eyes, and he grips my hand with both of his. A warm, grateful energy floats up my arm. "Thank you, Mizithra. I never truly forgave myself for encouraging your grandmother's wish to tether her spirit. A great burden of responsibility for her choices weighed on me. I could've dissuaded her. For that matter, I could've concealed certain facts, perhaps even convinced her the dream was impossible. A small part of me, certainly vanity, wanted to test the boundaries between dimensions. Your kind words have given me some relief, and, in the end, I helped her achieve something wonderful."

I place an arm around his shoulder and squeeze. "And you gave me an unbelievable opportunity. Getting to know Isadora has changed my life in ways I can't even explain."

Before things can get any mushier, my phone pings with a text.

"Here. Gate locked."

"Erick's here. I know you're not big on crowds, but you're more than welcome to come to my dad's place for Christmas Eve supper."

"I shall consider the invitation. It is most kind."

Grabbing my jacket and purse, I head toward the marble entrance and its sparkling chandelier. "Can you unlock the gate?"

For a moment, I sense a current of electricity in the air.

"It is done." He announces the transmutation as though he's handed me an everyday paper napkin.

"Solstice blessings, Silas!"

His chuckle follows me out the door and is lost in the lovely snow.

Erick pushes through the gate and trudges toward me. "Do you think I should shovel his walk?"

Sweetness overload. It's not as though I can tell him that an alchemist rarely needs help transmuting snow to water or steam, or whatever Silas does. "I think he has someone for that. Thanks for offering."

Erick scoops an arm around my waist and holds me tighter than necessary.

"That's some grip, Sheriff. Did you miss me?"

"Of course I missed you. I've also seen you fall on your backside in the snow more than once. Let's call it a safety precaution."

As we wind toward the main highway, Erick makes small talk. "I thought I remembered there being a back way into his place, but I must've missed the turn."

Looks like Silas was right about the hidden nature of that alternate entrance. Not that it should surprise me. "Yeah, it's a tricky one. Any news about the case?"

He comically hangs his head and chuckles. "Hold your horses. Why don't you tell me about your Yule solstice first?"

"Hey, I'm no *Ben-Hur*. I'm just a curious gal."

I don't appreciate his mocking gasp.

"Since you asked, I believe it's winter solstice or Yule. I don't think you can cram them all together like supercalifragilisticexpialidocious."

Erick taps his thumb on the steering wheel and sings, "Even though the sound of it—"

"Oh brother. Forget I mentioned it."

"Good food, though?"

Pressing a hand to my belly, I sigh in remembrance. "Always. I would kill for that potato recipe. Dolphin something or other . . . It was creamy potato goodness!"

Chuckling, he offers unsolicited commentary. "You have a real strange relationship with root vegetables, Moon."

"Rude. Not root *vegetables*, plural. I happen to enjoy the potato. Many people admire Earth's most perfect food."

He laughs loudly, then rubs a thumb under his eye. "I'm not sure that's scientifically proven, but they are delicious. Was it dauphinoise potatoes?"

My head turns with the ratcheting lag of an animatronic mannequin. "How's that? Are you a secret chef?"

He grips the steering wheel with both hands and eases back into his seat. "Not even close. Since the macular degeneration prevents my mother from reading her cookbooks, she runs all the cooking shows on television, and attempts to re-create the recipes by paying attention to the ingredients they mention on air, or occasionally through online video supplements. She's made that dish a couple of times, and, under duress, I'd be forced to agree that it was—what's that word you're so fond of using? —divine."

"Wow, you're really sticking it to me today, Sheriff. Did you have an espresso this morning?"

He shakes his head. "Nah, I'm running on empty. Maybe I've got some low-blood-sugar-related snark."

"Yeah. We need to get some food in you, stat."

He grins, and his heavenly-blue eyes sweep toward the passenger seat. As they scan over me, I feel my temperature rising. "Can you turn your heater down?"

He glances at the dash, looks at me funny, and arches his eyebrow. "It's already on low. What's happening over there, Moon? Something got you hot under the collar?"

The tingly flush rising from my tummy reaches my cheeks, and I press my face against the window. "It's probably a combination of this ridiculous sweater and the thick winter coat. Nothing for you to be concerned about."

He smirks in a way that makes my stomach flutter as though it's housing a swarm of butterflies.

Attempting to ignore my dry mouth and difficulty swallowing, I move the conversation toward trees. "So, um, since we didn't get a tree—"

"We can head back out there. The crime scene has been processed, and I'm sure the recent snowfall has erased the rest of the unsightly event. Is that what you were going to say?"

"Not exactly." Let's see if I can come at this greased pig of a conversation from a different angle. "Since your mom's in Florida, I was wondering . . . I mean, it seems like maybe—"

"Geez, Moon. I've never seen you so flustered. Should I pull over? Do you need some fresh air?"

His teasing does the trick. I straighten my spine, gulp down some stale car air, and screw my courage to the sticking place, Lady Macbeth style. "I was wondering if you'd like to come to my dad's for Christmas Eve supper." There. I spit the words out in machine-gun rapid-fire, completing the question before I have the chance to lose my courage.

His eyes sparkle and his jaw muscles flex. "Boy, family dinner, and during a holiday, no less. This sounds quite serious. Are you planning some kind of big reveal?" He chuckles as soon as he finishes the sentence, and it's easy to see that he's amusing himself at my expense.

Well, two can play that game. "I didn't want to spoil the surprise, but, yes."

His strong jaw drops, and he turns toward me as the color drains from his face. "You don't— You're not—"

"Oh, keep your eyes on the road, Sheriff. I'm just messing with you. Tit for tat, they say."

He gasps for air and pats his chest. "Okay, you

win. No more games, please. We've got a good thing going. There's no need to tempt fate."

My throat tightens, but I manage to squeak out a response. "You're not wrong."

He parks the cruiser at his spot in front of the sheriff's station and we walk into the diner to a chorus of Merry Christmases, good mornings, and the standard spatula salute from Odell. The weekend crowd has thinned minutely, but we're still fortunate to find an empty booth.

My favorite waitress, Tally, hustles over with a pot of coffee and two empty mugs. Her tightly wound, flame-red bun bobs as she pours our liquid alert and presses for a gossip update. "Gosh, Sheriff, that Carol Olsen case is a real humdinger. Any leads?"

Erick smiles his work smile, which doesn't quite reach his eyes. "You know I can't discuss an ongoing investigation, Tally. You tell the coffee klatch we're looking into a number of possibilities."

She smiles like the cat that swallowed the canary and hustles off.

"Erick! You know better than to give her any ammunition. By the time she shares that with her cronies, she'll have twisted it into a series of arrests and possibly an anonymous out-of-town stranger."

Sliding his hands around his mug of coffee, he nods. "If she doesn't start the rumor, someone else will. As long as they stay away from the facts, I don't much care about the gossip rolling through town."

So levelheaded and methodical. No wonder it takes him so long to get to the truth. "Now that we've talked about my celebration, it's time for you to ante up. Do you have a time of death?"

"I do."

"And? Does it clear Twiggy?"

"Unfortunately, it does not. And to make matters worse, the shot was too precise to be an accident. The bullet didn't pass through the heart, but it was a highly targeted gutshot, meant to allow the victim to bleed out slowly."

I shiver uncontrollably. "Twiggy would never do something like that. That's diabolical. That's an assassin's move, or someone trying to get information."

He walks his fingers across the table and turns his palm upward. As I lay my hand on his, he rubs his thumb across the back of my fingers. "Would it surprise you to know that I agree? The thing is, Twiggy holds three statewide sharpshooter titles. I can't rule her out until I question her, see if she has an alibi, and, if so, confirm it. But in my heart, I don't believe she could do something like this. We're looking into Carol's maple syrup trafficking, but the sugar makers are a tight-knit group. They're not being forthcoming with information."

"Do you want me to go undercover? I can be a confidential informant."

"Settle down, Moon. I don't want you to do anything of the kind. The maple syrup mafia might sound humorous, but it's a dangerous organization protecting a multi-million-dollar syrup trade."

I pull my hand back and place both in the air like a stickup. "Get out of here! Maple syrup mafia? Multi-million-dollar *maple syrup*?"

He shrugs. "I'm sorry to be the one to tell you, but a barrel of maple syrup is worth twenty to thirty times more than a barrel of crude oil."

"Shut the front door!"

Odell slides our irresistible breakfasts onto the table and nods. "I've seen the price go as high as twenty-three dollars for eight ounces of pure Canadian Amber. Those barrel rollers are no joke. If Carol was messing with them, I wouldn't be near as shocked about what happened to her." He lifts his hand to rap his knuckles, but I reach out and grip his arm.

"Odell, would you like to come to my dad's for Christmas Eve supper?"

His face remains stoic, but where my hand touches his skin, I receive a clairsentient flash. A tightly wound ball of emotion. Heartache, wrapped in longing, nearly strangled by loneliness.

"I'll check my schedule." He turns and slides his wrist from my slack grip. No double tap with the knuckles, no parting wisdom.

He doesn't return to the grill. He must've headed straight out the back door of the kitchen. "I'll be right back."

Erick nods and digs into his pancakes without delay.

Pushing open the kitchen door that leads into the alley beside the diner, I find Odell with a tattered cigarette in the corner of his mouth. The first time I witnessed this, I waited for him to light the thing, but I've since learned that he quit smoking over fifteen years ago. He keeps an old cigarette in the pocket of his faded denim shirt to remind him of his struggle with tobacco, and his mother that passed from lung cancer.

The corners of his eyes are wet with tears.

"Hey, I don't mean to intrude."

He waves a hand in the air and shakes his head. "It's not your fault. It's a tough time of year. I appreciate the invitation, but it's best if I keep to myself. No point in bringing everyone down during the holidays."

"Look, I respect everyone's traditions. Before I came here, I used to spend Christmas watching

FailArmy videos on my phone, and stuffing my face with leftover pizza, or Chinese food. And that was only the years when I had a phone plan that was paid up. Sometimes it was just the pizza and a blank wall."

He looks toward me, and the ache in his eyes is palpable.

I hurried outside without my coat, and the windchill from the great lake nestled in our harbor is starting to work its way through my sweater. "I know I told you this before, but I absolutely think of you as my surrogate grandfather. We would love to have you at the family dinner, but no pressure. Seriously. Think it over. There's always room for you at our table."

He struggles to swallow, can't find the words, and nods sharply.

It doesn't take a psychic to see that the man needs some privacy. Squeezing his shoulder once, I return to the booth to enjoy my scrambled eggs with chorizo, and my dashing breakfast date.

CHAPTER 7

ERICK OFFERS to walk me back to the bookshop, to keep me from any snow- or ice-related disasters. However, as we get nearer to the Bell, Book & Candle, I sense a rising tension in my escort. "Is there something you're not telling me about this door-to-door service, Sheriff?"

Shaking his head, he mutters, "You and your hunches."

"Spare me. Just answer the question." I elbow him playfully in the side.

"I was hoping if I talked to Twiggy in familiar, neutral territory, she'd be more likely to cooperate."

"Thanks a lot."

He pulls his arm close to his side and my arm gets squeezed between his powerful bicep and taut abdomen. "Ah, don't be like that. You know Twiggy is a tough nut to crack. Anything I can do to keep her from getting defensive is in her own best interest."

"Copy that. If you want to stay on her good side, don't accuse her of anything. She's smart enough to know she's a suspect, but if she thinks you're actually considering her, she's likely to lock up tighter than Fort Knox."

"Thanks, Moon. And if I didn't say so earlier, I'd be honored to come to the dinner at Jacob's. Thanks for asking."

My breath catches in my throat. I busy myself with door-opening duties and rush inside before he can say anything more sentimental.

"Twiggy? Twiggy, are you here?"

She leans over the thick balustrade, which curves in a large semi-circle along the edge of the second-floor loft. "Up here, doll. I'm shelving some of the new collection."

Erick and I head up to the Rare Books Loft, and Twiggy walks toward us, with arms firmly crossed and her mouth pinched in a fine line.

My brain flips through possible opening lines, and I keep coming up empty. Thankfully, Erick strides past me and reaches out his hand in a friendly gesture. "I'm sure you know why I'm here, Twiggy. I thought it would be better if we had an informal chat, rather than making things official down at the station."

She taps her toe impatiently and does not take his outstretched hand. "Ask me anything you like, Sheriff. I've got nothing to hide."

"Can you tell me where you were Saturday evening between 8:00 p.m. and midnight?"

"I can." She offers nothing further.

Erick nods politely. "And where were you?"

"I was at home, in my own bed, like all good citizens of Pin Cherry."

"Understood. Can anyone confirm that?"

For the first time, Twiggy's confidence wavers, and she breaks eye contact.

Stepping forward, I offer my two cents. "You're not really a suspect. He just needs your alibi. Isn't there anything you can tell him?"

Her energy shifts suddenly, as though she's had a bolt of inspiration. She glances at Erick, and the corners of her mouth turn up for a split second. "I had a guest. I'm sure he can vouch for me."

For the first time in my life, I sense she might not be offering us a completely forthright answer.

He jots a couple of notes on his pad. "Can you give us this person's name, please?"

Twiggy lifts her chin. "Wayne Olsen."

Erick's pen comes to a halt on the paper, and he

narrows his gaze. "Wayne Olsen spent the night at your house? What time did he arrive?"

She uncrosses her arms and shoves one hand in the pocket of her dungarees. "He came for supper, about 5:30."

"Okay. And what time did he leave?"

She hesitates for a moment and looks up to the right. "He left when I headed to the bookshop. So, that was around 8:30 a.m."

Erick finishes his notes, replaces the notepad and pen in his pocket, and offers a perfunctory smile. "Thank you. I'll be in touch if I have any further questions. I appreciate your cooperation today."

She shrugs. "No problem. I told you, I have nothing to hide." Turning, she grabs a book from her cart and climbs up the large ladder that spans almost two stories of shelving.

Remaining neutral and silent, I follow Erick down to the first floor.

"I'll be heading back to the station. I'll let you know if the medical examiner comes up with any additional details. I know it's pointless to ask, but I really wish you'd stay out of this one, Mitzy."

Oh boy, he's using my first name. This is a serious request. "You know I can't. Twiggy is like family. I have to find out who actually did this."

He leans close, as though he's going to kiss my

cheek, but whispers, "I don't think she's being completely above board with her alibi. But I think you already know that."

I kiss him on the cheek instead, and smile too brightly. "I'll let you know what I find out, Sheriff."

He exhales loudly and heads out of the bookshop.

Staring at Twiggy's back, high above on the ladder, I can easily tell she's in no mood for further conversation. Time to tap my ghostly resource for details of Pin Cherry's past. Grams was a wealthy and influential woman. She knew everyone worth knowing and probably plenty who swam in lower circles, but possessed useful information.

As the bookcase door slides open, Pyewacket leaps off the bed, dragging something in his mouth. When he gets closer, I see it's one of the strands of popcorn and cranberry that hung on the tinsel tree. However, it's obvious he's eaten all the popcorn, and the strand only contains cranberries.

"It's not going to be a very festive Christmas if you eat all the decorations, Pye." I pick up the badly battered strand of garland and turn toward the trash can. Before I can make it a single stride, the familiar thwack of a powerful caracal paw assaults my ankle.

He kindly left his needlelike claws retracted, so I know it's only a warning. "Message received. I will hang on to this disgusting piece of trash and see how it fits into our puzzle at a later date." Holding the gross, slobber-wet thread in one hand, I retrieve a tack and add Pyewacket's *evidence* to the murder board.

CHAPTER 8

AFTER SEVERAL UNSUCCESSFUL attempts at summoning the ghost of Isadora, I'm on the hunt.

It's not as exciting as it sounds. If she's not following me around snooping in my love life or telling me what to wear, she's usually in the adjacent printing museum.

I push through the "Employees Only" door from the bookshop, and the smell of ink, metal, and history hits me as I walk across the polished concrete floor.

The space is only half the size of the bookshop, but it has an entire second floor rather than balconies and a mezzanine. The ground floor houses large equipment and a variety of historical displays, including an authentic Gutenberg press.

Trudging up the steps to the third floor, I pause

and take in the scene.

My new stepbrother, Stellen, is home on winter break from his freshman year in college. Last year when his father was killed, we discovered that Stellen could see ghosts. And in that department, he's actually got me beat. Not only can he see the ghosts of humans, but he can also see animal ghosts. He can't hear Isadora, but he can see her, and when she's got enough energy to pick up a pen and write messages, they have lovely conversations.

Currently, he's looking over her memoirs and explaining the process of scanning her handwritten pages to convert them into editable files through character recognition software.

As you might've guessed, Isadora isn't picking up much of what he's laying down.

"Stellen! I was wondering when I was going to get a chance to see you."

He drops the stack of sheets he's sorting and strides past the antique photo-engraving display to give me a hug.

"I hate to be this big sister, but you've grown like a foot!"

He blushes, and his bright-green eyes avoid mine as he smooths a lock of long, black, wavy hair behind his ear. "It's only like six inches. No big deal."

Giving him another one-armed hug, I press him

for details. "All right, so you grew six inches, your hair also grew six inches, and you're home for two or three weeks. What are you doing hanging out with Ghost-ma? Why aren't you at your girlfriend's?"

He pulls away and chews his bottom lip. "Yolo and I are taking a break."

"What? Why? Did something happen?"

"No. Nothing bad. She's got a really intense schedule at MIT, and I need to finish at the top of my class if I want a scholarship for veterinary school."

Reaching out, I grab his nervous hand and squeeze. "Hey, college is about experiences too, not just grades. And you know there'll always be a Duncan-Moon scholarship for you." I offer him a giant wink, and point foolishly at my eye as I repeat the wink multiple times.

He leans back and attempts a scowl. "Something wrong with your eye, sis? You should get that checked out."

I punch him playfully on the shoulder. "Now there's the little brother I missed." I walk past him, but as I approach the task Grams is working on she opens a drawer and scoops her memoirs into it.

"That's pretty *su-spish*, Isadora. You got something to hide?"

She crosses her arms over her full figure and

shakes her head. "I'm an artist, dear. I don't like people looking at my work until it's finished."

"He's looking at it." I gesture toward Stellen. "Why does he get to look at it, and I don't?" I kick out a hip and plant my fist on it.

"Because he's helping me with technical issues. I need to get the first five chapters to the publisher by mid-January."

Glancing at Stellen, I give him a thumbs-up. "That's great. I'm so happy you found a publisher who's interested in it, Grams. But, I'm family. Don't you think I should get the opportunity to read it before it's published?"

Stellen snickers, but quickly puts a hand over his mouth.

I narrow my gaze and stare each of them down in turn. "I smell a rat. Or some other nefarious creature. You two are in league, and I don't like it."

Grams floats toward me and waves her hand dismissively. "Oh, don't be so dramatic, sweetie. There's nothing for you to be concerned about. I'm only asking for a little privacy while I'm creating."

Crossing my arms, I tilt my head and click my tongue. "Oh, it's privacy you want? Because you're so good at returning the favor, right?"

All three of us crack up at that statement, and Grams lifts her ethereal arms in the air. "Mea culpa. Mea culpa."

Taking a quick breath, I return to the original purpose of my ghost hunt. "I'm actually glad you're both here. I'm in the middle of this case, and it never hurts to get another perspective on new info."

Stellen's eyes brighten. "Is it a ghost?"

"Not yet. But I've learned to never say never with the spirit world. Here's what we know so far—"

I bring them up to speed on the latest in the Carol Olsen case, and then I ask Grams the question that led me to the third floor. "So, I was wondering if you know anyone in the maple syrup trade? Either here, or in Canada, but here would be better. I need to get some more information on what kind of business Carol was running, and if she really was in league with, or poaching from, the maple syrup mafia."

Stellen laughs again. "Sorry, can't help it. It just sounds like some kind of oxymoron. Like the teddy-bear hit squad, or the cuddly-kitten assassins."

Grams and I stare at him with somber expressions.

He gulps and takes a step back.

"Gotcha!" We share a giggle at his expense.

"Well, dear, I was very well connected. However, most of my contacts were the upper echelon of Pin Cherry Harbor society. Can't say I was acquainted with anyone illegally importing Québec's finest."

"What makes you say, Québec?"

Her shimmering eyes widen. "Everyone knows the best maple syrup on the planet comes from Québec."

My eyes dance. "The best maple syrup on the planet?"

Stellen clears his throat. "Arguably."

She zooms toward him, and he puts up his hands in surrender. "Whatever you said is right."

"Easy, Ghost-ma. Don't intimidate my source. Stellen, do you know of some better maple syrup?"

He sidesteps away from the angry ghost and sidles up next to me. "There was a guy who really had a thing for trapping and stuffing skunks. He brought my dad a lot of business when we ran the taxidermy, you know—"

Placing a comforting hand on his shoulder, I nod. "I remember. You don't have to talk about it."

Stellen inhales sharply. "Thanks. So, this guy brought my dad a lot of business, but he rarely paid in cash. We had enough maple syrup to host a pancake breakfast every month for probably five years. But it was, as my dad used to say, 'without peer.'"

"This guy's local? Do you think he's still in the business?"

He scoffs at my lack of experience. "Mitzy,

people don't dabble in maple syrup. It runs in their veins. Once they're in, they're in for life."

My jaw slackens. "It sort of is like the mafia." I lift my chin in an attempt to do a Marlon Brando riff, and growl, "You got a name for me, kid?"

Stellen chuckles at my weak attempt at a Mafioso impression. "Yeah. Ezekiel Elhard."

"Wow, that's a heck of a name. I'm surprised—"

My ringing phone interrupts us, and when I see the name of Silas Willoughby on the screen, I quickly answer. "Good morning, Mr. Willoughby. How may I help—?"

Mr. Willoughby's voice is unusually excited. He doesn't even wait for me to finish my official greeting before he launches into his announcement. I manage to get in one "yes" and two "mmhmms" before he ends the call.

"That was weird."

Grams swirls toward me and places her partially corporeal hand on my shoulder. "You should know better than to say that within these walls, dear."

"Touché. That was Silas. He'd suddenly remembered a local contact that might be able to help us out in the Carol Olsen homicide investigation."

Stellen, Grams, and I all lock eyes. In unison we shout, "Ezekiel Elhard!"

This is the kind of psychic moment that's become everyday grist for the mill in my new life.

"I'm gonna hop in the Jeep and head out to his place as soon as I figure out where that is. You in?" I point to my little brother.

He shrugs. "I don't think I can go. I promised I'd help Isadora today. Amaryllis has a bunch of stuff scheduled this week, so today is really the only day I have to work on this. Um, maybe you should take Erick. Ezekiel is a little out there. Not exactly dangerous, but, you know, out there."

A loud groan escapes. "Fine. I'll text him. But if he's too busy, I'm going by myself. This ain't my first rodeo, son."

Stellen shakes his head. "Nope, not a fan of that expression." He stifles a chuckle and returns to the desk with the ghost of my memoir-obsessed grandmother.

Tromping down the stairs on a return trip to the bookshop, I fire off a text to the sheriff. "I got a lead. Ezekiel Elhard. Change into your civvies. I'll pick you up in five."

There. I've offered him two likely insurmountable obstacles. I'm sure he doesn't have his civilian clothes at work, and I'm positive he won't be able to find a way to free himself from duty in five minutes.

My phone pings, and I look down in satisfaction. The smug grin is instantly wiped off my face as I read, "You're on!"

Blerg.

Changing into skinny jeans, warm boots, and a cable-knit sweater, I stuff mittens into the pocket of my winter coat and tuck it under my arm as I head to the Jeep.

When I pull out of the alley, I encounter a patch of ice. Even though I was a bit of a brat at the time, I'm now grateful that my father insisted on snow tires.

Checking my watch, I'm right on schedule. I figure I'll give Erick thirty seconds leeway and then hit the road on my own.

Unfortunately for me, the fully changed, ready-for-action sheriff is waiting at the curb as I pull up.

He hops onto the passenger seat and the stench of champion wafts throughout my vehicle.

"Fine. You win."

He throws his shoulders back and grins. "Was there ever any doubt, Moon?"

I choose to mumble my response under my breath. "I've created a monster."

He casually glances at his phone, but slips it into his coat pocket. "So, you know the way to Ezekiel's sugar shack?"

Choking on my laughter, I cough to clear my throat. "Did you say sugar shack? Are we in a B52's music video?"

He shakes his head and crosses his arms in that

yummy way that makes his biceps bulge. "You got a lot to learn about the sugar bush industry."

Laughter grips me, and I have to force myself to keep my eyes open and watch the road. "You're just making stuff up now. But, no, I don't know the way to Ezekiel's sugar shack. Why don't you enlighten me, Sheriff?"

Erick becomes my personal GPS and guides me turn by turn to the sugar maker's remote property.

We knock on the front door of the farmhouse, but there's no response. Erick steps off the screened porch and heads toward the woods.

My stomach roils with unwanted memory of the recent corpse in the forest, and I stand my ground.

"You comin'? I know the way to the sugar shack. There was a fire out there a couple years ago."

Oh, what I wouldn't give to have recorded that soundbite. I cannot begin to explain to you how many times I would replay the deep rumbling voice of Erick Harper saying, "I know the way to the sugar shack!" Who needs a winter coat with this kind of heat?

"Coming." Hopping off the last step, I jog toward my own sugar maker. And an embarrassed schoolgirl giggle sucks all the cool straight out of me.

"Come on. It's through this stand of sugar bush."

Glancing at the leafless trees, I shrug. "I'm going to go out on a limb. Is sugar bush another name for maple trees?"

"Pretty much. Technically, it refers to two specific species which are the best for sap production and make the sweetest syrup, particularly trees like sugar maple and silver maple."

"Copy that." As we come to the other side of the leafless brown stand of maple, an ominous building looms into view. The creepy wooden shack could easily be the location of several heart-pounding 80s horror movies. "Yikes. *The Evil Dead* much?"

Erick chuckles. "You only think that because they're not in a production cycle. When you walk through the trees and smell that sap bubbling away, it changes your whole perspective. There's absolutely nothing like a craft stick or hockey stick handle wrapped in fresh Jack wax."

I stop and place one hand on my thigh as I recover from a round of belly laughs. "Seriously, you have to stop. You're killing me."

The door of the sugar shack opens, and a giant of a man strides out with an equally massive rifle—aimed directly at the intruders.

To be clear, we are the intruders.

"You're trespassing, you know. You best hightail

it while you have the chance, eh? This blunderbuss ain't for show."

Erick immediately raises his hands in the air, and I follow suit. "Hey, Ezekiel, it's Sheriff Harper. I came in civilian clothes because this isn't an official visit." He gestures toward me. "This here is Mitzy Moon. She's—"

"I'm a friend of Silas Willoughby's. He actually gave me your name. And my stepbrother Stellen Jablonski—his dad used to stuff skunks for you."

Ezekiel lowers the huge firearm and guffaws loudly. "Heck, those are two of my favorite people in the whole world, dontcha know. Come on over. Any friend of Silas or those Jablonskis is a friend of mine."

We close the distance to the cabin and he ushers us inside.

"Sorry, I ain't got any sap on the boil, but I'm cooking down a bit of syrup to make some maple hard candies."

Taking a step forward, I mean to start my interrogation, but Erick grips my arm and offers a nearly imperceptible headshake.

I'm not pleased, but I comply.

"So, how'd the sap run for you last year?"

Ezekiel looks directly at Erick and tilts the large pot of syrup to check something—I have no idea what.

"The first run was a mite disappointing. But I know what I am, you know. I'm not here to compete with the big boys north of the border. I got a nice little business here, and I got no problem with keeping it local, eh?"

Erick rubs a thumb along his jaw and nods as though he's been in the maple syrup business all his life. "Sounds about right. You ever run into Carol Olsen?"

Ezekiel narrows his gaze and strokes his thick salt-and-pepper beard. "You accusing me of something, Sheriff?"

"Absolutely not, Mr. Elhard. As I said, this is not an official visit. I'm sure you heard about the discovery Sunday morning. Miss Moon was the one who found the body."

Once again, I watch the man's expression soften like melting ice. "Well, I sure am sorry to hear that, Miss. Although, I can't say as Carol didn't get what was coming to her."

Erick nods. "What makes you say that?"

"Well, this is the time o' year all the barrel rollers set up their contracts with sugar makers. Now, I don't get involved, mind you, 'cuz I run my own operation. Less hands in the pot, less hands in the till."

The sheriff smiles and nods exuberantly. "Ain't that the truth."

This *hick-afied,* man-of-the-people Erick is really tickling my funny bone.

"That there Carol Olsen didn't see things that way. She was always clawing her way up the tree, you know? She thought she could get some contracts up Québec way, but the big boys didn't like her tapping into their sugar bush. If you know what I mean?"

Erick nods as though he knows exactly what Ezekiel means, while I've only managed to puzzle together bits and pieces.

The key point seems to be that Carol was sticking her nose where it didn't belong, and some powerful maple syrup titans took her out.

Sheriff Harper glances toward the pot. "Looks like you hit the sweet spot."

Ezekiel strokes his beard and glances into the pot. "Good eye, Sheriff. If that lawman thing doesn't work out for ya, there's always a place for you in my sugar shack."

Erick thumps him hard on the back and smiles. "Sure do appreciate that. Let me know if you think of anything else."

"You betcha."

We turn to head out of the shack, and Ezekiel calls after us. "Hold on. It's not gonna be as good as a real sugar off, but you may as well get yourself a little taste while you're here, Miss Moon."

He takes the large stainless steel pot off the fire and scoops a ladle in, then squeezes past Erick and me to pour an arc of hot, thick syrup in the snow. Returning to the hut, he hands us each a tongue-depressor-size craft stick. "Dig in."

Erick shows me the simple technique of rolling the cooling maple syrup mixture onto a stick. He pops it in his mouth and smiles like a child at a carnival. "Wow, Ezekiel. There's no question in my mind why Odell won't serve anything but Sweet Harbor Maple at the diner."

The flavor is rich, caramelly, mapley, brown sugary, and maybe even a little vanilla-y. It's beyond delicious. "Thank you. It's really a treat."

He smiles and nods his thanks. As we head back toward the stand of maple, he calls out, "Keep an eye out for that bear on your way back. She tends to come runnin' when she smells the maple."

I stop with my stick of maple sugar goodness in my mouth and stare at Erick in terror.

He shakes his head. "Ignore him. He's just messing with you. Bears hibernate in the winter, Mitzy. We're safe."

Of course. I know bears hibernate in the winter. Even an Arizona girl like me knows that. There's no time to feel like an idiot though, because I'm too busy lapping every last drop of deliciousness off my little wooden stick.

CHAPTER 9

ON THE WAY back to the station, Erick places a call to dispatch. "Yeah, see if you can get Clermont on the phone and send Johnson to pick up Wayne Olsen for questioning. 10-4."

"Who's Clermont?"

He grins as he taps end on his cell. "Would you believe he's a Canadian Mountie?"

I offer a slow clap as my response.

He glances at the road ahead, turns and offers me a quizzical stare. "Why am I getting the slow clap?"

"Because, in all the time I've known you, I've secretly imagined you as *Dudley Do-Right*. It makes perfect sense that you would have connections with the Canadian Mounties." Tapping my thumb on the steering wheel, I click my tongue. "It's kismet."

He rolls his shoulders back and sighs. "Look, I don't have Canadian Mountie friends. I have a single friend, who I've known since I was a teenager, who happens to be a Mountie. Him and his dad used to go hunting with me and Odell. When you're hunting moose through dense forest, sometimes you lose track of borders. It was always nice to have a tag that was valid in the US and one that was valid in Canada."

"True confessions of a juvenile delinquent." My heart warms with imagined memories of Erick and Odell's adventures. "You were lucky to have Odell in your life. Do you think it was his influence that pushed you toward joining the Army?"

Erick's gaze flows toward the horizon, and his mouth opens twice before words come out. "I don't think so. I was proud to serve my country— But who's to say? He was probably the strongest male role model in my life. He made sure my mom got an occasional break, and he definitely taught me the value of a hard day's work."

"Did you ever work at the diner?" I can't explain what popped into my head and shot that question out of my mouth, but the expression on Erick's face practically screams—

"Uncanny, Moon. I suppose that was one of your random hunches." He shakes his head and mumbles another "uncanny" under his breath.

"So, that's a yes?"

Erick nods. "Yeah, I was no good at waiting tables, but I was a rock star in the pot shack." His laughter is easy and soft.

"Um, what's a pot shack?"

"Sorry, Army jargon. It's where the dishes get scrubbed."

"Copy that."

At the intersection, he points toward the station. "You want to drop me at the station, or are you coming in?"

Smiling broadly, I tilt my head and nod. "You know, Sheriff, you're really starting to get the hang of this partnership. When you muscled your way into my sugar shack shenanigans, I thought I'd lost control of this investigation. It's nice to see that I'm still at the helm."

"I'm not inviting you to run the investigation, Moon. I'm inviting you into the station, to sit in my office while I place a phone call. If history has taught me anything, when I step into the interrogation room to talk to Wayne Olsen, I don't have a lot of control over who comes and goes from the observation room."

"You're not wrong." I park on the street and enter the station behind him. He heads off to change back into his uniform, while I take a moment to greet the deputy at the front desk, whom

I've nicknamed "Furious Monkeys" due to her obsession with said app on her phone.

True to form, she is lost in coconut combat.

"Hey, Baird. How's that game treating you?"

"The new levels are definitely getting harder. They've added blue bananas, which may or may not explode, depending on how you pick them up."

I'm not going to touch that information with a ten-foot pole. "Copy that. What level are you?"

"306. First one in my region to get there. Treehopper17 is hot on my tail, though. I'll probably lose the number-one rank by tonight."

I have no idea how to respond to that tidbit of information, so I smile and sashay through the crooked wooden gate. As it swings closed behind me, the lone deputy in the bullpen looks up.

Shoot. I was sincerely hoping to avoid a confrontation with schoolyard bully, Deputy Paulsen.

She pushes back from her dented metal desk and gets to her feet. The position doesn't increase her height a great deal, since she's a short, squat individual. Her right hand is poised on her gun handle, as per usual. "Ran across another body, eh, Moon?"

The woman gets under my skin. I just can't help it. "Looks like it. Someone's got to do your job."

Before she can access a snappy response, I hustle into Erick's office.

He's behind the desk, exchanging pleasantries with his childhood hunting buddy, Clermont.

"Hey CC, I want to put you on speakerphone. She just walked in." Erick gestures to one of the uncomfortable wooden guest chairs. "Mitzy Moon, I'd like you to meet Charles Clermont, CC for short."

"Bonjour, mademoiselle."

My heart unexpectedly skips a beat. "Hi. I thought Erick said you were Canadian? Are you from France?"

His lyrical French accent sings from the cracked plastic speaker on Erick's desk phone. "No, mademoiselle. I am French Canadian, from Québec. I understand you are dipping your fingers in our syrup. Pray they do not get bitten off by these maple badgers."

I want to respond, but the hum of his beautiful accent has completely thrown me off my game.

Erick leans back and his fingers tap rhythmically on his wooden desk. "Looks like she's having a little trouble with the accent, CC. Dial 'er back a notch, eh?"

"No problem, Harper. What do you need?" The Mountie's thick French accent is reduced by easily fifty percent.

The sheriff looks at me and nods with satisfaction. His momentary flash of jealousy evaporates. "Clermont neglected to mention that he's married to a very nice American woman. They lived in the states for five years and he was with me on one of my tours in Afghanistan. When he returned, they settled in Canada and he joined the Mounted Police."

"Thank you for your service, Mr. Clermont."

He chuckles warmly. "Call me CC."

"Copy that, CC."

Erick fills him in on the recent homicide and the victim's suspected involvement in less-than-legal maple syrup trade. "So, we were wondering if you could look into Carol Olsen's passport history and give us a timeline for the last couple of weeks. If you have any CCTV information or other leads that might explain her whereabouts prior to the murder, I'd sincerely appreciate it."

Clermont chuckles. "Would you consider it a personal favor, Harper?"

Erick points to the phone and shakes his head. "Listen, CC, I saved your bacon more than once over in the wasteland. Don't make me remind you about the details."

"Yes sir, Harper, sir."

"Knock it off. How soon can you get the info?"

"End of day, latest."

There's a brief pause and I give Erick a lame thumbs-up. Not sure why.

"You and your—"

"Girlfriend, CC. She's my girlfriend."

"Excellent. You should come up to Québec for a weekend getaway."

I lock eyes with Erick, and, sadly, we both laugh out loud. I field the question. "Yeah, we've tried the getaway thing, but Harper thinks I'm a corpse magnet. You probably don't want that kind of trouble in your country."

CC chuckles. "This isn't your first—what do you Americans say?—rodeo?"

"It is not. If I were to use maple syrup terms, I'd say you could label me Grade A sleuth material."

He laughs warmly. "I do look forward to meeting you one day, mademoiselle." The accent kicks into overdrive on that last word.

Erick rolls his eyes and picks up the receiver. "That's enough flirting with my gal for today, Clermont. Update me as soon as you can."

The call ends and he drops the receiver into the cradle.

"He seems nice."

Sheriff Harper stands and scoffs. "You'd be surprised how many ladies have uttered that phrase in my presence. CC is a hopeless flirt, but he's one hundred percent faithful to his wife."

The comment seems to impugn my honor, so I jump to my feet. "What exactly is that supposed to mean?"

"Nothing. Trust me, I wasn't saying anything about you. I've never been suave, or whatever. I suppose I was always a little jealous of his 'game.'"

Placing my hands on my hips, I offer a hula-girl swirl and then gesture from my head to my toes. "Well, I don't care how much 'game' he has. He didn't land all this, did he?"

Erick laughs and tenderly scoops me into his arms. Before he can plant a kiss on my ready lips—

Loud exhale. "Johnson put Wayne in room two, Sheriff." Paulsen groans as she waddles back to the pen.

"I feel like I have to say, 'wait here, please.' I'll see you after I finish this interview." Erick stands in the door and smiles down at me. His big blue eyes are full of affection, with a hint of exasperation.

"And, I feel like I have to say, 'copy that.'"

He steps across the hall and the door to Interrogation Room Two clicks open and softly closes.

Creeping toward the doorway, I check that the coast is clear.

All clear.

I slip across the hall, step into the observation room, and click the silver toggle on the speaker.

Erick sits calmly across from Wayne Olsen. If the setting were anything other than an interrogation room at a police station, you'd think the two friends were enjoying a beer and discussing sports.

Unfortunately, this is a murder investigation and Erick has to ask his old friend some tough questions.

"Wayne, we've known each other a long time and you are more familiar than most with police procedure. I've got to ask these questions, and I need you to answer to the best of your ability."

"I understand, Harper. No hard feelings."

"Where were you Saturday evening between 8:00 p.m. and midnight?"

"I was at Twiggy's for supper and a nightcap."

"Did you leave the house at any point before morning?"

Wayne shakes his head. "It's impolite to kiss and tell, but I left shortly after breakfast. Probably around 8:15. Maybe a little later."

"Were you aware that Carol Olsen was in the area this weekend?"

Wayne leans back and his hands grip the edge of the table. He swallows hard and takes a deep breath. "I know how this next part is going to sound, Harper, but you asked me to answer honestly, and that's what I intend to do."

"Much appreciated, Wayne. Continue."

"As you know, I've made more than one attempt to divorce cagey Carol. She's contested at every turn, and dragged things out for years. Saturday, she showed up at my place suddenly willing to sign papers."

For a moment Erick forgets he's the sheriff conducting an investigation and reacts like a good friend. "That's great news. I know you've been trying to move that forward for over five years."

Wayne nods and presses his lips together with regret. "I wish it were that simple. She had conditions."

Erick's spine straightens. "Go on."

"Not sure if you keep up to date with my old man, but his health has been failing rapidly. My mother finally convinced him to take early retirement, and they made the big announcement Friday at a small gathering out at their place. Everyone was relieved, and even my father looked the picture of health as the burden was lifted."

The sheriff nods encouragingly.

"The problem is, that burden goes straight from his shoulders to mine. I wasn't exactly eager to take over. I never wanted the crown, and I've been telling him as much for years. He tried to sell the business a few times, but never got an offer for what he thought it was worth. The current medical situation kinda forced my hand."

"Well, I'm sorry to hear that. Are you going to try to run it?"

Wayne shakes his head and shrugs simultaneously. "I can't even wrap my head around that right now, Harper. This whole thing with Carol has really knocked me off balance."

Erick steers the interrogation back on track. "You mentioned conditions. So Carol showed up, willing to move forward with the divorce, but she had conditions. Can you elaborate?"

"Absolutely. She told me that this is what she'd been waiting for. Now that I had officially inherited the business, she'd happily grant me a divorce for half."

The sheriff leans forward, and I can easily imagine the shock on his face, even though he's seated with his back to me. "Half? She wanted half of a business she had nothing to do with?"

Wayne's shoulders sag. "That was just her opening move. What she really wanted was for me to buy her half out. For some reason, she thought my father was loaded. She assumed I'd inherited the business and a mountain of cash. Carol always was a misinformed dreamer. Dangerous combination."

Erick leans away from the table and exhales. "You're right. This does look bad. Your ex-wife shows up, attempts to extort a sizeable chunk of cash from you, and winds up dead within twenty-four hours. I really hope your alibi holds up under scrutiny."

Wayne's jaw drops and his kind eyes widen.

"What are you saying, Harper? It's the truth. I was with Twiggy. I know it may not make me sound less guilty to admit I technically spent the night with my mistress while my wife was being murdered, but you know the situation with Carol."

Erick nods and pushes his chair back. "Thanks for coming in today, Wayne. We'll follow up on the details of your story, and I'll be in touch." He steps out of the room, and Wayne's head drops into his hands.

From where I'm sitting, every bit of his story rang true. He and his wife had been separated for years, and if he'd actually had anything to do with her death, it's unlikely he would've shared the details of a private conversation. No one knew about Carol's attempt to extort money from Wayne, except him and the deceased. The fact that he shared that detail with Erick goes a long way toward supporting my belief that he's innocent.

Back in the sheriff's office, I can tell this case isn't sitting well with my boyfriend. "You don't think Wayne's guilty, do you?"

He tips back in his dilapidated office chair and laces his fingers together behind his head.

Old habits die hard, and my gaze darts toward his abdomen, in the hopes that his shirt may come untucked and I'll get a peek at those washboard abs.

My compulsion offers a little comic relief, and

he winks at me lovingly. "Thanks for being here. It's tough to separate my friendship with Wayne from my duty, but I have to. If it were anyone else, that story would absolutely make him look more guilty. But his alibi seems to line up with Twiggy's, and he had no reason to tell me that story about Carol trying to get money. I don't think a guilty man would give me that kind of ammunition."

Leaning forward, I put my elbows on the desk and nod in agreement. "That's exactly what I was thinking. Him and Carol were the only ones who knew about the conversation. If he was guilty, it would be foolish to share that detail."

Erick leans in, reaches across the desk, and grips my hand. "Thanks. Something just doesn't sit right, though. I can't quite put my finger on it."

"Go on now, Sheriff. Don't be trying to steal my *hunch* thunder."

He laughs and rubs his thumb along the back of my hand as he quietly ponders the case.

True to form, a thought pops into my head, and I blurt it out. "Wayne mentioned his dad retiring and not wanting to take over the business. What kind of business is it?"

"The Olsens are the founders of Crimson Crest."

I scrunch my shoulders up and tilt my head. "And?"

"Oh right, some 'locals only' knowledge. Crimson Crest Cranberry Farms is a locally owned grower and processing operation. Folks say they have the best bogs in the north."

As soon as he utters the word cranberry, I lean back in my chair and try to ignore the circle of heat emanating from the mood ring on my left hand. I don't have to look at it to know that it's going to show me an image of the garland tacked to my murder board.

"I know that look, Moon. Spill."

"I thought it was nothing. Pyewacket stole a strand of homemade garland from Isadora's tree. He chewed up all the popcorn pieces and only left the cranberries. Then he brought it to me and attacked me when I tried to throw it in the trash."

Erick crosses his arms, momentarily distracting me. "That cat is as uncanny as you. What do you think it means?"

"Well, we know Carol wasn't killed by cranberries. But maybe we're looking at this from the wrong angle. Maybe it wasn't a maple syrup connection."

His jaw muscles flex as he grinds his teeth. "I'm afraid that only makes things worse for Wayne."

"Accurate."

CHAPTER 10

When I return to the bookshop, Stellen is waiting outside the front entrance, carefully examining the intricate carvings on the antique wooden door. The look on his face is all too familiar. "What do you think? Is it Pyewacket?"

He glances up from where his fingers are tracing the outline of a fiendish feline and grins. He walks me through the details of the ornate vignettes. "This one is Chiron and Hippodamia. This is Pegasus with a nod to Selene, and here is Pan and the gift of Aphrodite." When his hand reaches the carving of the wildcat, he crouches and leans his face close to the timber. "This looks like a caracal. It actually looks a lot like Pyewacket. Seems like there are even scratches over the left eye. Do you think it could've been added later?"

"By whom? Supposedly Silas found this door in San Miguel de Allende, Mexico, and had it shipped to Isadora as a grand opening gift. Maybe he bribed the carver to make changes or additions?"

Stellen chews the inside of his cheek and shakes his head. "Everything displays the same degree of weathering. There's honestly nothing that shows any of the carving was done at a different time. Puzzling."

Nodding my head, I slip the hefty, one-of-a-kind brass key out from under my shirt and tug the chain over my head. Inserting the triangular barrel into the cleverly concealed plug, I spin the key three times and feel the lovely sensation of, not just the lock, but also the entire store opening to my touch.

"Speaking of puzzles, come on up to the apartment. This case is turning into a real doozy, and I could use your genius brainpower to my advantage."

"The Carol Olsen murder?" He frowns.

"The very one." I hope working on the case won't stir up unpleasant memories for him.

Stellen holds the door for me. His mother, who died too young of an aggressive cancer, raised him right.

Grams joins us in the apartment, and I serve as afterlife interpreter, while she writes up additional cards for me, and fires off questions about Stellen's freshman year at college.

When all is said and done, the addition of the cranberry inheritance has tied way too many green strands of yarn between Wayne and Carol.

"Far be it from me to question the great and powerful Robin Pyewacket Goodfellow, but I'm having a problem understanding how a woman who's trading in possible black-market maple syrup is murdered by something to do with cranberries?"

Grams hovers above the stack of index cards and nods in agreement. Stellen lies stretched out on his stomach on the floor, scratching rhythmically between Pyewacket's tufted ears. "Did you mess up this time, buddy? Is a cranberry just a cranberry?"

"Ree-ow." Soft but condescending.

Stellen looks at me and shakes his head. "You know him better than I do, Mitzy. Sounds like he's doubling down on his cranberry clue."

The alliteration makes me giggle. Ghost-ma and Stellen stare at me in confusion.

"Cranberry clue? You guys didn't find that funny? Maybe it's just me and my desperate need to deflect with humor."

Stellen tilts his head to the side and scrunches up his face. "Doesn't really seem that hilarious to me, but maybe you have to be older."

I squeeze my eyes to slits and stare daggers at

the little smart aleck. "Are you calling me old? I'm maybe five years older than you, if that. Be careful who you're calling old, punk."

He rolls over on his back, and Pyewacket immediately takes the opportunity to lie across his chest and pin him playfully to the ground.

"Traitor." I scoff and shake my finger at the spoiled cat.

Grams floats toward the murder wall and examines each name and tidbit of evidence carefully. "I'm sure Wayne didn't do it, dear. Although, I have to admit the evidence is piling up against him."

Striding toward the board, I pluck one of the strands of green yarn like the string on a cello. "That's exactly how I know he didn't do it."

Stellen lifts his head and stares at me over the tan lump of his master. "Can you break it down for me, sis? That doesn't make sense."

"No problem. As an expert in film and television, I've watched far more footage than anyone has a right to. The first thing you learn about mysteries of any kind is that the suspect who looks the most guilty by the second act is never—I should say extremely rarely—the guilty party. So, I know things are piling up against Wayne, but I'm not going to fall for it. I know that the update from Erick's Canadian Mountie contact is going to shed new light on this."

No one chimes in to praise my clever sleuthing.

"And I'll apologize in advance to Pyewacket, but I just don't think it has anything to do with the cranberry connection."

Stellen laughs so hard it disturbs his royal furriness, and Pyewacket is forced to seek solace within the thick down comforter on my antique four-poster bed.

"Now what's so funny?"

"Cranberry connection! I get it. I hear it now. It is funny."

Rolling my eyes, I flop onto the settee and stare at my phone. Willing it to ring.

When the phone actually rings, all three of us, including the ghost, jump with fright.

"It worked! I made the phone ring."

Stellen stares at me and swirls his hand in a "get on with it" motion. "Good for you. Now answer it."

"Right." It's Erick, and he has an update from CC. "Great. I'm going to put you on speakerphone so Grams and Stellen can hear the news. We're all in my apartment working on the murder wall." I tap the speakerphone icon and Erick's voice fills the room.

"Of course you are. Why would I believe for even a split second that this investigation was solely in the hands of the Pin Cherry Harbor Sheriff's Department?"

"It's so cute when you think you're in charge. Now, dish."

Grams floats toward the phone and Stellen sits up straight.

"CC checked with the Border Services' records and noted seven crossings for Carol Olsen in the last two weeks."

"So she was definitely doing something in Canada. Was he able to get any leads on who she was meeting or why?"

"He was. There was some CCTV footage of her meeting with a man known as Antoine Berg-eron, a notorious barrel roller who is way up the food chain. CC said the footage didn't have any au-dio, but it looked like a heated argument. Maybe she was working for Bergeron, or maybe she was poaching in his territory."

Grams glows expectantly. "That sounds good, sweetie. Is it?"

Nodding, I continue. "Grams thinks that's promising. What about this Antoine guy? Was there any evidence that he came into the United States?"

Erick clicks his tongue and sighs. "Unfortu-nately, a man like Bergeron doesn't do his own dirty work. If he sent someone to take out Carol, we'd have to comb through two weeks of Border Services' records to find the lead, and that's assuming the assassin bothered to enter by legal means. You know what that border is like. He or she could've snuck across anywhere."

"I suppose. Do you have a picture of this Bergeron guy?"

There's a pause on the other end of the line. The tapping of fingers on a keyboard is the only sound. "I took a screenshot of the CCTV footage. It'll be a little blurry, but that's all we have."

"All right. We'll keep looking at our end. I know Wayne's innocent. There's got to be something we're missing. Stellen and I are going to head over to the diner to fuel up for an all-nighter. Can you meet us?"

I gesture to Stellen, and he jumps up, confirming my suspicion that teenage boys are always hungry.

"I can't get away right now, Moon. Say hi to Odell for me and let me know if either of you get any *hunches*."

Ending the call to the sound of Erick's laughter, Stellen and I head for the diner.

ONCE INSIDE MY home away from home, we grab the booth in the corner, and Tally hops over with her standard-issue grin in place. "What can I getcha?"

"I'd like a mug of hot chocolate and . . . a cinnamon sticky bun."

Her eyes widen. "No fries?"

I tilt my head and ponder the question. "No. No fries."

Glancing back at the kitchen, I take note of Odell's smug grin and the lack of bubbling oil in the fryer. He knew! How does he always know?

Stellen orders hot chocolate and a slice of pin cherry pie à la mode.

As Tally gets our order together, Odell saunters out. "How's the case going?"

"Not great. The more we dig, the more evidence we find that makes Wayne look guilty. I wish we could find one thing that would put him in the clear."

Odell tilts his head. "Did his alibi check out?"

"Hard to say. Twiggy is his alibi. As much as I hate to say it, she could be covering for him. I know I'd cover for someone I cared about."

He turns without a response, retrieves the *Pin Cherry Harbor Post* from the counter, and slaps it on our table. "This may not put Twiggy in the best light, but it oughta clear Wayne." Pointing to the large photo above the fold, he taps in the center.

There, in the middle of the Northern Lights Yuletide Extravaganza, which took place Saturday night, is Wayne Olsen lighting the tree in the central square.

"What time is the tree lighting?"

"It's usually at nine o'clock every year."

"Well, if he was in the town square, lighting the town Christmas tree at 9:00 p.m., he certainly wasn't having dinner at Twiggy's place."

Stellen stares at the picture and shakes his head. "You're right, Odell, this might clear Wayne, but now Twiggy doesn't have an alibi."

Odell shakes his head and raps his knuckles on the Formica twice before returning to the kitchen.

We finish our sugar power-ups in silence and

head straight out of the diner, make a right-hand turn, and trudge into the sheriff's station.

No one is manning the front desk, so we help ourselves through the gate and head back to Erick's office.

He looks up and smiles. "Hey, guys. How's college treating you, Stellen?"

My stepbrother mumbles, "Not too bad."

Erick gets to his feet and comes around to meet us. "You two look pretty forlorn. Is this a hunch, or worse?"

"Worse." I shove the Sunday paper into his hands and point at the photo. "Correct me if I'm wrong, but that looks a lot like Wayne Olsen, lighting the tree at 9:00 p.m. sharp on Saturday night."

The sheriff looks at the photo, tilts the paper back and forth in the light, and chews his bottom lip. "It does look like Wayne. It's not a clear picture of him, though. The tree seems to be the thing in focus."

Nodding, I cross my arms and step back. "That's the artistic eye of Quince Knudsen for you. I know for a fact he takes multiple exposures of every shot. Maybe he changed the focus on some, too. Stellen and I will head over to the newspaper office and see if he has any other shots."

Erick nods. "You know how bad this makes Twiggy look, right?"

"Yeah. We thought of that. I mean, all kinds of folks at the Extravaganza will be able to vouch for Wayne." Attempting to employ my feminine wiles, I step closer to Erick and place my hand on his arm. "Don't do anything until we talk to Quince, all right?"

My clairsentience instantly informs me of his increase in heart rate. Looks like I've still got it.

The sheriff nods. "You have one hour."

"That's fair."

Stellen and I beat a hasty retreat before I can say anything to ruin our brief reprieve.

On the way to the newspaper office, I have to call Twiggy. She may be rough around the edges, but she's the only employee I have, and she knows a hundred times more about running that bookshop than I ever will. "Hey, I'm sure you're busy, but I thought I owed you a warning."

She makes one of her usual wisecracks, which I ignore in favor of giving her a heads-up about the alibi avalanche headed her way. "So, now that the picture of Wayne has surfaced, the sheriff is going to be calling your alibi into question, and that puts you back on the suspect list. Not to mention poten-tial charges for impeding an investigation."

I'll spare you the details of her swearing a blue

streak. The true meat of her argument is that she didn't lie. Wayne was at her house for dinner and did spend the night.

"All right. Fine. I wanted you to know what was going on. We're headed over to the newspaper office now to see if I can get a better picture for Sheriff Harper. I want to help you out, Twiggy. Are you telling me I should lose the negatives?"

When I mention losing the negatives, Stellen twitches in his seat. Sure, I've pulled some questionable moves in his presence in the past, but I did promise Silas to keep it on the up and up around my little brother. I'm supposed to be setting a good example, not teaching him how to be a better delinquent. Apparently, I had a temporary backslide. Not to worry. Twiggy immediately refuses my offer and tells me to do whatever I think I need to do. She's got nothing to hide.

Ending the call, I glance at Stellen. "She's so exasperating! I wasn't actually going to destroy evidence, though. You know that, right?"

He nods, but his face says he seriously doubts my backpedaling.

The great lake that dominates our region commands its own intricate weather system. When we step out of the Jeep and head across the street to the home office of the *Pin Cherry Harbor Post,* an icy wind whips through town and sends the tempera-

ture plunging an easy twenty degrees in the negative. The moisture in my eyes creates tiny icicles on
my eyelashes in the space of seconds.

Lucky for us, the front doors are open. Stellen
and I burst inside, desperate for shelter.

Despite the progress that visits the rest of the
world, nothing has changed in this town that tech
forgot. The birch-clad reception counter still displays an antique silver bell and a sign instructing
visitors to ring for service.

However, this isn't my first visit to Pin Cherry's
fourth estate. I slip behind the counter and walk
through the doorway into the office area. Stellen
follows silently.

Photojournalist, and possibly friend, Quince
Knudsen, isn't at the desk. He must be in the
darkroom.

Like a lot of things in this town, he's clinging to
the past with his 35mm film, photo enlargement
apparatus, and tried-and-true developing methods.
The proof is in the pudding, though. The national
wire services have picked up his amazing images a
multitude of times, and his impressive portfolio certainly helped him get accepted into Columbia Uni-
versity.

Stepping into the black metal cylinder, I motion
for Stellen to wait as I disappear inside the magical
tube and rotate the door around me. A sliver of red

light expands to fill the barrel as the powerful odor of acids and ammonia hits me. "Quince, you in here?"

"Yah."

I'm not sure what he's learned at the impressive college, but it certainly wasn't conversational skills. Quince has a talent for monosyllabic responses, and it appears today won't be anything out of the ordinary. "I need to buy some prints off you."

"Cool."

He's the best. Easily motivated by financial incentive, Quince has helped me out more than once. When I figured out that his currency was literally currency, it was easy to make arrangements that served both of us nicely.

"Yeah, cool. I need to know if you have other angles from the Christmas tree lighting Saturday night. I'm willing to look through some contact sheets if you have them."

He makes some adjustments on the enlarger he's working with, sets the timer, hits a button, and steps back as light passes through the negative and exposes a piece of photographic paper beneath. "Nope."

"Nope, as in you don't have a contact sheet? Or nope, as in you don't have any other angles? Or nope, as in—"

"Dude. Nope, as in no photos."

I almost consider this pile of words a soliloquy, but I still find the message confusing. "Look, Quince, I'm not here to cause trouble. If you're trying to protect Wayne, Erick will have to get a warrant and press charges for impeding an investigation. I know you have photos. I saw one above the fold in Sunday's edition."

Taking the photo paper from the enlarger, he slides it into the first chemical bath of the three trays set up in his stainless steel developing run. He taps the timer on his phone and turns toward me with an unreadable gaze. "I didn't take pictures."

"Oh, all right. Does your dad take digital photos or does he use a film camera like you?"

Quince's phone beeps, and he turns back toward the developing process. Grabbing a pair of rubber-tipped tongs, he pulls the sheet of paper out of the first solution and slips it into the second, tapping another timer on his phone.

"Neither."

"Quince, I know this song and dance is part of our thing, but I really need a better picture of Wayne Olsen lighting the Extravaganza Christmas tree. Can you help me or not?"

He crosses his arms and flicks his long sandy-brown bangs backward with a jerk of his head. "There was a snowstorm in Chicago. My flight was delayed. Dad was putting the edition together and counted on me to get the pictures."

I hesitate to interrupt his abnormal flow of words, but curiosity gets the better of me. "You said you didn't take photos."

"Right. We had to run last year's picture. You know how everything stays the same around here. Same people, same clothes, same everything. No one noticed. Until now."

Stellen grips my arm and I nearly jump out of my skin. I was so absorbed in extracting information from Quince that I didn't realize my stepbrother had followed me into the darkroom. "Yeesh! You're too quiet for your own good."

For some reason, that makes Quince chuckle, which makes Stellen chuckle, because Quince was always one of the cool kids at school and Stellen certainly wasn't.

Stellen's extra brainpower and early graduation were a blessing in disguise. He's definitely hitting his stride at college, and he's going to make an amazing veterinarian. "You two know each other, right?"

Quince bobs his chin. "Hey."

Young Stellen tries to play it cool. "Hey."

I roll my eyes in the semi-darkness. "Anyway, what's on your mind?"

He smiles, and his teeth look pinkish-red in the

light. "That means Twiggy was telling the truth. And so was Wayne. The photo was from last year, so their alibis still hold up."

I throw my arms around him and squeeze his scrawny shoulders. "And that's one more for the genius! Those of you keeping score at home, be sure to mark that down."

Stellen looks at the ground, shrugs, and heads back to the cylindrical door.

I turn to follow.

A hesitant voice calls out. "Hey, you need those prints then?"

Classic Quince. I'm getting hustled, and this kid is as good as Emma Stone in *Easy A*. Reaching into my pocket, I grab a couple of twenties and lay them on the counter next to the enlarger. "Thanks for your time, *dude*."

He walks toward the crumpled bills, and when I step into the cylinder to spin my way out, I hear him utter, "Sweet," as he pockets the cash.

CHAPTER 12

BEFORE RETURNING to the station to share my update with the sheriff, I drop Stellen at the bookshop. "Update Grams, and, if it's not too much trouble, you can apologize to Twiggy for me."

Stellen shakes his head and steps back to close the passenger door.

Ducking so he can see my face through the closed window, I press my palms together and plead.

He shakes his head again, this time with more conviction, and dusts his hands to show he's taking no part in my possible feud with Twiggy.

Oh well. It was worth a try. I'll take my lumps when I get back.

Activity has picked up inside the station, and Paulsen is barking orders like she runs the place. To be clear, she has run for sheriff in Birch County twice, but my handsome, over-qualified boyfriend defeated her soundly both times.

My suspicion that the team is pulling together in hopes of finding a break in the case is confirmed when I see Furious Monkeys fielding phone calls and taking copious notes. If Paulsen found a way to get Deputy Baird to put down her cell, things must be serious.

Taking advantage of the portly Paulsen's preoccupation . . . I won't even try to say that five times fast. I slip into Erick's office and grin mischievously.

He looks up from the report on his desk and frowns. "I don't like that look. You're up to something. Do I want to know what?"

"I have some good news. Not that it helps our case, but it helps our friends."

He crosses his arms over his powerful chest and takes a deep breath. "Oh, it's *our* case now, is it? You must need a favor."

"Rude." Scoffing, I wave away his insult with a flick of my wrist. "I thought you would appreciate the fact that I was making an effort to work together. But if you want me to keep my intel to myself, I'm happy to do so, Sheriff."

"We've come too far, Moon. You're in the inner circle now. Whether you were invited or not is a topic we can debate at a later time."

I roll my eyes and plunk onto the open chair. "You may be interested to know that Quince Knudsen did not take pictures Saturday night."

Erick runs a hand along his jaw and furrows his brow. "Please tell me there's more to the story."

"Oh, there is. No one took pictures Saturday night. The elder Knudsen was at the newspaper office putting the edition together, and Quince's flight was delayed. They had to run a shot from last year. Last year! So, Wayne wasn't at the extravaganza this year, he was at Twiggy's, like they both said."

Erick smiles briefly and smacks an open hand down on his desk. "I knew it. I knew Wayne would never lie to me. Thanks, Moon."

"No problem. I'm as relieved as you are. I was making all kinds of justifications for Twiggy's dishonesty, but, the truth is, it didn't sit well."

He nods, picks up a pen, and taps the end rhythmically on his desk. "I'm gonna call CC and find out if he's had any luck locating Antoine Bergeron."

"Yeah, I don't like the look of that wily-eyed Bergeron rascal. He has one of those creepy grins that shows too many teeth and pushes his cheeks up like two baked potatoes. I'm sure he has something to do with this."

"What is it with you and potatoes?" Erick picks

up his phone and dials the Canadian Mounted Patrol. "Sit tight."

I wait calmly in the uncomfortable chair, but under no circumstances am I sitting tight. I don't even know how to sit tight. What a foolish expression.

"Hey, CC. It's Harper. Is it okay if I put you on speakerphone again?"

The Mountie must've consented, because Erick taps the button and the sultry voice of the French-Canadian spills from the speaker. "Bonjour, mademoiselle."

Without meaning to, I immediately take on a terrible French accent and respond. "Bonjour, monsieur."

CC laughs louder than I feel is necessary. "Not bad, Mademoiselle Moon. But you really must come to Québec and put in the proper amount of practice if you want to improve that accent."

Erick offers me a stern look, and I sit back in my chair like a chastised child.

"We're running out of suspects down here, CC. As we go down the list and confirm alibis, it's looking more like this may have been the work of an assassin hired by somebody on your side of the border."

"If Madame Olsen fell afoul of maple syrup law, then you could be right. However, I have tapped my contacts to the limit, and I can find no concrete evidence that she made any inroads. I have confirmed meetings, I have confirmed arguments, and I have images of her at various sugar makers. What I do not have is a shred of evidence that any of those sugar makers signed a contract with Madame Olsen. Perhaps she was, how do you say, shaking the trees? But I fear nothing fell from those bare branches."

The mood ring on my left hand turns to ice, and I glance down in time to see a hand twisting a silencer onto a gun barrel. "Um, CC, do you know if Antoine Bergeron owns a gun with a silencer?"

He ignores my question and immediately addresses Erick. "Harper, have you recovered the murder weapon?"

Erick raises one brow and eyes me suspiciously. "We have not. However, I've learned to give Miss Moon's hunches fair credence. Do any of the images you have of this Antoine character show him with firearms?"

CC makes a sound that is a cross between blowing a raspberry and outright spitting. "The man is no amateur. He would never brandish a firearm. And, as I mentioned, it is quite likely he would hire someone to do his dirty deeds. He hasn't worked his way to the top of this food chain to take unnecessary risks."

"10-4. Thanks for the interdepartmental cooperation, buddy."

"Not a problem, Harper. I think it's my turn to take the moose, no?"

Erick laughs and leans toward the phone. "The rules haven't changed, CC. I can't help it if I'm a better marksman than you." Erick ends the call, leans back, and continues to tap his pen in frustration.

"You said the shot was too precise to be an amateur or an accident. What if you're wrong? What if Carol and someone were out in the woods to find a Christmas tree, just like us? Maybe the person with her brought a gun for protection, from wolves or whatever, and maybe it went off by accident."

He drops his pen, pushes his chair back, and gets to his feet. "That's as good as any other theory we have right now. I'll get the deputies to round up any of her acquaintances or people she might've had dealings with in the last couple of weeks." He takes a step toward the door.

My blurt button trips and I ask, "Did Wayne say what his father was suffering from?"

Erick's eyes dart back and forth as he scans through his memory of the interview. "No. He just mentioned a progressive medical condition, and his father's need to retire. I don't remember any details about the diagnosis."

Slowly getting to my feet, I tap a finger on my lips as I toy with my next move. "Maybe we should talk to his father. I know it's not really anything to go on, but it's all I can think of right now."

Sheriff Harper nods. "I think Johnson's on that side of town. I'll ask dispatch to pass along the request."

By the time Deputy Johnson returns to the station, I've talked myself out of Wayne, or his family, having any connection to Carol's murder. However, I'll be keeping my doubts to myself. Erick stuck his neck out by bringing a man in for questioning based on a feeling I had when I couldn't think of anything else. The last thing I'm going to do is leave him holding an empty bag.

I'm posted up in the observation room with an ice-cold can of caffeinated pop and a bag of tortilla chips. Nothing would complete this snack better than some freshly made salsa, but what passes for Mexican food at this northern latitude hardly fits the bill.

Erick opens the door for Mr. Olsen, and an elderly man with thick white hair hobbles in, supporting most of his weight with a four-pronged cane. He eases himself into the chair facing the observation room, and Erick takes a seat with his back to me.

"Mr. Olsen, I appreciate you cooperating with our investigation."

"Nonsense. Anything to help our local law enforcement. And call me Niklas."

"Of course. I'm sure you've heard about the passing of your daughter-in-law, Carol. I hope you understand, we're speaking to everyone who knew the victim, just to rule them out. You're not a suspect. I hope you will be forthcoming with your responses."

Niklas Olsen considers the speech carefully and nods. One hand rests in his lap, the other still grips the knob atop his sturdy cane. "She was my daughter-in-law by technicality only. You know how many times Wayne tried to untie that knot. I'm sorry she met with a violent end, but I'm not sorry she's gone."

Setting down my bag of chips, I lean forward and take several deep breaths. There was something in that phrase, something that triggered a spark in my extrasensory perceptions. It's time for me to stop snacking and pay attention.

"I appreciate your honesty, Niklas. Were you aware that Carol had entered the country from Canada several times in the last two weeks?"

He looks directly at Erick as he answers. "I was not."

Erick makes a note on his pad and continues. "When did you decide to retire?"

"I made the announcement Friday night, out at the old compound, as Norma calls it."

"Yes, sir. I understand you had a family gathering Friday evening. What I'm asking is when did you make the decision to retire? A man in your position can't have taken a move like that lightly. I know how hard you worked to expand your business and remain independent from the big conglomerates. Transitioning things to a new company president would take time to organize. What I'm asking you is how long has Wayne known about your plans to retire?"

Niklas grips the top of his cane and adjusts his position in his chair. His gaze narrows. "My boy had nothing to do with this, Sheriff. If you brought me in here in some sort of underhanded attempt to get me to incriminate my son, you've made a grave mistake."

Erick places his notepad and pen on the table and glances across at the elder Olsen. "Niklas, you know I think the world of Wayne. I don't think he had anything to do with this, but if the information has been public knowledge for several months, other people may have found out about your plans.

Someone could've been blackmailing Carol, knowing she'd have access to the Crimson Cranberry coffers."

To his credit, Niklas Olsen doesn't laugh. I can't say the same. Alliteration amuses. I've giggled at accidental alliteration since I was a kid.

Niklas lifts his hand from his lap and places it on the table. I note a slight tremor.

"Sheriff, the decision was more sudden than I care to admit."

I sense Erick's desire to make a note in his notepad, but he admirably resists. "May I ask about your diagnosis?"

"Why not? Everyone will know soon enough. I have Lou Gehrig's disease. I'm on a whole slew of medications, and I'm working with a physical therapist to preserve my diminishing muscle strength for as long as I can. But for all their degrees and certificates, the doctors can't tell me anything definite. There's not much peace of mind in being told you're suffering from a progressive disease with a time horizon that could span anywhere from a couple of months to five or ten years."

Erick leans back and exhales. "I'm so sorry. I had no idea. Is that why Norma pushed for your retirement? For your health?"

The energy in the room shifts, and an odd spark of light twinkles in the old man's eye. "Boy, I've read the stories in the papers about some of the cases you solve. But sitting right here, across from you, and watching that fine mind of yours at work— Well, it's a real treat, Sheriff."

From my vantage point in the observation room, I'd say that was a movie-trope-classic deflection.

Luckily, Erick is easily as smart as he looks. "I appreciate the compliment, Niklas. But I need you to answer the question."

The elderly gentleman chuckles and nods in defeat. "Norma did insist on the retirement, but the medical issues were only half the reason." He lifts his proud chin, stares Erick in the face, and refuses to break eye contact.

I have the advantage of my psychic senses to pluck the word *affair* out of the ethers, but I have no explanation for Erick's genius.

"I know the business was doing well financially, and that only leaves me with one solid option. Were you involved with someone at work?"

Niklas Olsen's jaw drops and, despite his condition, his hand claps loudly on the tabletop. "Well, I'll be—"

"Was Wayne aware of this . . . indiscretion?"

The light in Mr. Olsen's eyes fades and his shoulders droop. "He was not. And out of respect for my family, I'd appreciate that it stays that way, Sheriff."

Erick nods once. "If it's not pertinent to the investigation, Niklas, I see no reason to make it public. Can you tell me the woman's name?"

Niklas Olsen eases his chair back, re-grips his cane, and struggles to his feet. "I cannot. My apologies, Sheriff. Some things just need to stay between a man and his wife."

As Niklas reaches for the door handle, Erick tries for one more piece of information. "How long, Mr. Olsen?"

The defeated man turns. "What are we talking about? The affair or the retirement?"

Erick slowly gets to his feet. "I'd like to know both."

"The affair has been going on, in one form or another, for almost ten years. The retirement was planned hastily, about two weeks ago at the most. Wayne only found out Friday night."

Mr. Olsen turns the handle and opens the door. As he shuffles out, Erick thanks him for his time.

My head is buzzing with questions.

Erick taps on the one-way glass and points toward his office.

CHAPTER 13

AFTER I NOD MY HEAD, it occurs to me he can't actually see me, so I scoot across the hall and take my seat in one of the visitor's chairs.

"Any hunches, Moon?"

The question catches me off guard. "Hunches? What are you talking about? There's no way that old guy hiked into the woods, in knee-deep snow, and shot someone."

He brushes away my distracted thinking. "No, of course not. I was referring to the woman he was having an affair with."

"Oh, that." I rub my hands on the thighs of my skinny jeans, close my eyes, and take a deep breath.

Erick attempts to slip quietly into his ancient office chair, but it squeaks mercilessly under his weight.

Focus. Focus. Focus. I coach myself into a state of semi-calm and a name pops into my head. I angrily dismiss it and try again.

Same name.

Throwing my hands up in exasperation, I blow a raspberry and lean against the chair. "It's no use. I just keep getting the name Carol. And unless there's something really strange going on in that family, I don't think there's any way Niklas Olsen was having an affair with his daughter-in-law."

Sheriff Harper grabs a pen and doodles on the back of a piece of paper. His wheels are turning, my wheels are turning, but we seem to be stuck in the Bog of Eternal Stench. Nothing like a good *Labyrinth* reference to lift my spirits. "I have an idea."

Erick's pen stops before he lifts his gaze, but, when our eyes meet, I can already see his objection. "I'm pretty sure I'm not gonna like this, but I'm also rather familiar with my inability to stop you, Moon. Might as well tell me. Forewarned is forearmed."

"I'm working off the theory that there's no better way to catch up on company gossip than working at said company. So, I'm gonna run home and slip into one of my business suits, snatch a pseudonym from thin air, and apply for a job at Crimson Crest Cranberry Farms. Whaddya think?"

"I don't know what to think. Sounds like a bad idea, but I've seen you get out of stickier situations."

"Great." I slap my knee enthusiastically. "So, we're all in agreement. I'll check in tonight at dinner. My place or yours?"

He launches to his feet and closes the distance between us. Strong arms circle around my back and pull me close.

My tummy tumbles all over itself.

"May as well take advantage of my mom being in Florida. Why don't you head over to my house tonight and let me cook you dinner?"

"Clearly, you know the way to my heart, Sheriff."

He bends down so that his lips are brushing against mine as he whispers, "I'm hoping to find my way somewhere else."

And I'm dead.

Thankfully, his strong arms keep me from collapsing as my knees turn to jellyfish beneath me. I offer him a quick peck on the cheek and race out the door before he can observe the crimson cranberry red of my cheeks!

The door of the bookshop closes behind me with a hollow echo.

"Grams? Grams, where are you?"

Twiggy stomps out of the back room and holds her hands up in a frozen "shrug emoji" pose. "Are you seriously yelling to the ghost of your dead grandmother? What if there were customers?"

I take a hesitant glance between the stacks. "Are there?"

"No, I'm just sayin'."

"Point taken. Also, you're one hundred percent off the suspect list. In case you're wondering."

Twiggy crosses her arms and shakes her grey pixie cut. "No. I wasn't wondering at all."

"Fair enough. I'm headed out to apply for a job at Crimson Crest Cranberry Farms, so if you've got any tips on how to pick up gossip . . . You didn't hear it from me, but apparently Wayne's old man has been having an affair for about a decade. He wouldn't name the woman, and—"

Twiggy turns to tromp her biker boots out of sight, but calls over her shoulder, "And you couldn't resist an opportunity to snoop. You're not gonna find anything out there. But, a word of warning, stay out of the sights of Miss Tremblay. She may only hold the title of executive secretary, but she acts like she runs the darn place."

"Thanks for the tip." I lift my leg to climb over the chain at the bottom of the spiral staircase as Grams rockets through the wall from the printing museum in a delayed response to my summons. Her sudden appearance throws me off balance, and I tumble from my precarious perch onto my ample backside. "Perfect timing, Grams."

Twiggy's cackle echoes from the back room. Apparently she's seen me fall handle over spout enough times that just the sound of impact is enough to tickle her fancy.

"What's so urgent, sweetie?"

"I'm going undercover." I offer her a pair of finger guns and she rolls her translucent eyes.

"Is it dangerous?"

Easing myself over the chain, I fill her in as I climb the treads and saunter across the Rare Books Loft.

"I'm not surprised to hear about the father's affair. The son, Wayne, is a doll, but have you met his mother?"

"No. I only learned her name today. Do you and Norma have a history?" I chuckle mischievously, because I honestly can't think of anyone in town that doesn't have a history with one of the many incarnations of my busybody grandmother.

"I'm not a busybody, Mizithra. I have good ideas and the courage to share them."

"And the audacity to never stop eavesdropping. Get out of my head, woman!"

We proceed directly into the massive closet, and Grams grabs the tried-and-true standard. Charcoal-grey Donna Karan pantsuit, but this time she pairs it with a cranberry-red silk blouse.

I gesture to the outfit. "I see what you did there. Nice touch. Is that some kind of subtle, subconscious color manipulation?"

She spins away from the shoe rack and gazes at the outfit in confusion. "What?"

"The cranberry-red silk blouse. Is that some kind of subconscious visual manipulation? Like, I'm wearing the color of their company, so I seem like a good hire?"

She scoffs. "I hadn't drawn the connection. Apparently I'm getting so good at this stylist career, I'm unconsciously competent."

"Oh brother." Donning the interview pantsuit, I head toward the exit.

"Do you have your secret identity?"

"For the record, it's a cover story, not a secret identity. I'm a snoop, not a superhero. And yes, Darcy Bergeron."

"I'd say you're beating a dead horse re-using that 'Darcy' moniker again, but I suppose the two names work nicely together. Do you have your resume?"

"My resume? The one that would simply have a list of coffee shops I worked at, and was fired from?"

"You're going for a job interview, Mitzy. Most people would take a resume."

"Well, I'm not most people, and I don't actually want a job. I'll make up some story about how I, Darcy Bergeron, just moved to the area, and haven't had time to get my printer set up." I flourish my fingers and take a shallow bow.

Grams claps her hands together gleefully. "You really are good on your feet, dear. Such an admirable trait."

I walk toward the intercom and press the plaster ivy medallion that opens my secret bookcase door from inside the apartment, chuckling as I leave. I think my grandmother just complimented me for being a good liar.

Crimson Crest Cranberry Farms is a much larger operation than their quaint, hand-painted wooden sign would imply.

The main office building is a sprawling ranch-style, which calls up images of the 1960s. Between the parking lot and the building stands a ten-foot-high decorative latticed-brick wall. They framed the windows with plain aluminum frames, and the only difference between this building and some vintage architecture in the Southwest is the peaked roof. I've learned a great deal about the weight of snow since I arrived in almost-Canada, and improperly reinforced flat roofs can be a real disaster under two or six feet of snow.

The sidewalk leading up to the main entrance has been shoveled and salted. Lucky for me! I may only be wearing a two-inch heel, but my severe lack of coordination wouldn't survive an icy patch, even in tennis shoes. The double doors are painted red, and the left one seems to be secured.

Taking a deep breath, I grab the handle of the right-hand door and review my backstory.

Darcy Bergeron. Just arrived in town from—Québec! Thunderbolt and lightning. I love it. I'll be a French-Canadian. I'm fairly confident I can mimic CC's accent well enough to make it through a fake job interview.

Confidently opening the door, I walk toward the reception area on my right.

No modern birch and steel here. There's a large glass window with a small hole for conversation, and a scooped cutout at the base where she slides the clipboard through. "Please sign in here, and indicate who you're here to see."

The receptionist has a youthful face, with wide-set eyes. Unfortunately, her overly back-combed hairdo ages her prematurely.

French accent engaged. "But of course. I am here to complete the job application. This would be human resources?"

She's not impressed with my French flair. "Do you have an appointment?"

"Sadly, no. This was not possible. I must get a new chip for the local phone service."

She exhales and lifts the receiver of her large tan desk phone. "Have a seat. I'll see if Edith can squeeze you in."

Dropping into one of the faded blue vinyl chairs, I kick myself mentally for choosing a French backstory as I grab a magazine to distract myself.

The privacy glass may prevent someone who's hard of hearing from picking up on the patronizing tone in the receptionist's voice, but me and my extra senses can hear it clear as day.

The woman is not a fan of people who don't follow the rules. However, based on the hint of disappointment as she ends the call, I'd say that Edith has found a way to shoehorn me into her schedule.

The thick wooden door leading from the lobby into the bowels of the establishment opens with a loud click. A wisp of a woman with a jet-black bob and cat-eye glasses on a chain peers into the waiting area. "Ms. Bergeron?"

Swallowing my snarky instinct to point at myself in shock and look to the empty chairs on the left and right, I turn on the accent and reply. "Yes. Thank you so much for agreeing to see me."

She presses her frail body against the door, and,

for a moment, I worry she may lose the battle and be knocked off her feet. "Right this way."

I walk past her and pause on the threadbare blue carpet in the hallway.

Edith closes the door and heads left down the hall. Just before she's about to pass through a doorway that T's into another hall, she makes a sudden left and steps up into the human resources office.

I follow her and she gestures to a chair much like those in the lobby, but less faded.

She takes a seat in her brand-new ergonomic office chair, and for a moment I can't get over how out of place it seems in the historic setting.

"Ms. Bergeron?"

Whoops. I've heard that tone before. I must've zoned out and missed her first, or possibly even her second, query.

What's the French word for sorry? "Pardon."

"I was saying we'll conduct the interview first, and then if I think you might be a good fit, you can fill out the paperwork. That'll save both of us some time. What do you say?"

"Oui, this is wonderful."

"So, did you move here from France?"

"No, no, Québec."

The look on Edith's face shocks me. I'm certain Québec is an interesting town, but I seriously doubt

it's worth the shock and awe I'm currently wit-
nessing.

"You're French-Canadian?"

I nod and smile, just like my mama taught me.
"Oui."

"Oh, gosh. I know this is unorthodox, but you
just have to meet someone. Follow me. It will only
take a minute."

Who am I to argue with a woman who may
offer me a job at this fine establishment?

We retrace our steps under the harsh fluores-
cent lighting, and the worn carpet seems to be-
grudge the visit. As she passes the door to the lobby,
I glance into an office on our left and stifle a gasp
when a massive painting of a creepy, possessed boy
in a sailor suit looms into view. Finally, she makes a
left-hand turn down a wide carpeted hallway. The
quality of the floor covering here is an obvious step
up from the main walkway.

We pass two setups, each with a secretary's
desk on the left and a large office on the right.
We've clearly entered the executive area of the
Crimson Cranberry.

As we reach the end of the spacious hall, an at-
tractive blonde in her mid to late forties walks out of
the large office and pinches her lips together with
irritation.

Edith appears suddenly flustered. "Oh, Miss

Tremblay, I'm so sorry to bother you. Darcy is French-Canadian! Just like you. I thought you'd like to meet."

Miss Tremblay crosses her arms and strums perfectly manicured fingernails on her right bicep. "We don't all know each other, Edith. Is this woman selling something?"

Before Edith can answer, Miss Tremblay pushes her way past us and takes a seat at her desk.

The mumbled response from Edith as she struggles to cool Miss Tremblay's wrath fades away as though I've suddenly slipped below the surface of a bath. All sound is muffled when my eyes lock onto the golden nameplate on the executive secretary's desk.

Carol Tremblay. Carol! That's the name that kept popping into my head in Erick's office, and now I know precisely why.

There's no more decisive exit than intestinal disorder. I grab my stomach with both hands, lurch forward, and cry out, "Sacré bleu!"

Beating a hasty retreat, I grab the handle on the large door leading to the lobby and run out through the exit before the cranky receptionist has time to formulate a question.

CHAPTER 14

TEARING out of the Crimson Crest parking lot, my old Jeep fishtails and I struggle to employ the counter steering method my dad taught me. I finally get the vehicle under control, but barely.

I'm so excited about my discovery! I'll never make it back to town with my secret intact. Pulling to the side of the road, I nudge into the six-foot drift left by the snowplow and text Erick the news. "I know the woman's name."

The electric thrill of uncovering the critical clue tingles through my veins as I wait for my phone to ping with a response.

Instead, I'm gifted with an actual phone call.

I put the call on speaker and look over my shoulder to pull back onto the rural highway. "Hey, are you as excited as I am?"

My lead foot is the wrong method for moving oneself out of a snowbank, and my tire spins.

"Um, do you have any tips for getting out of the ditch?"

Erick chuckles. "You need to ease off the gas pedal. Work your tires back and forth in a zigzag, and once you get a little traction give it some gas."

I follow his instructions and, just as my tire grips the road, a white Land Rover rips past me at a totally unsafe speed. "Holy *Fast and Furious*, Batman!"

Erick's voice instantly fills with concern. "What happened? Are you all right?"

"Yeah, luckily I didn't lurch too far into the roadway. Some insane person just blasted past me at about a hundred miles an hour."

His breathing is uneven. "Are you sure you don't want me to send a tow truck?"

The tires finally grip the salted roadway like they mean it, and the Jeep swings back onto the plowed road. "I got it. It's all good. Sorry for the unnecessary segue. Are you ready to hear my news?"

He laughs. "Yeah, I've been ready. Some say, I was born ready."

"Well, that's debatable. Here are the highlights." I bring him up to speed on the undercover operation and the sudden need to be French, and he scoffs unnecessarily. "What? I can do a passable

French accent." In case he doesn't believe me, I treat him to a sampling. "Bonjour, monsieur."

"Get to the point, Moon."

"Right. It's a good thing I decided to be French, because as soon as the human resources lady heard my accent and discovered I was French-Canadian, she had to introduce me to someone. That someone turned out to be Niklas Olsen's executive secretary."

"And . . ."

"And, besides the fact that she's a real 'B,' would you like to guess her name?"

He pushes a loud breath through his teeth, and I can tell he's nearing the end of his patience. Time to put a bow on this story.

"Her name is Miss Tremblay, also French-Canadian. And her first name is—wait for it —Carol!"

The shouts of praise and the standing ovation I expect do not follow.

"Did you hear me? Her name is Carol."

"I'm not following."

"Yeesh! Remember in your office, when I was trying to see if I had any hunches about the woman Niklas was having an affair with?"

"Oh, right. Looks like your hunch was spot on, Moon."

"This is what I'm saying. She seems super

sketchy. I think you should bring her in for questioning."

"On what grounds?"

"I don't know. I'm not trying to tell you how to do your job."

This comment brings gut-busting laugh-out-loud hilarity from the normally sedate sheriff. "Oh, is that right? What exactly are you telling me to do?"

"Well, if I was the sheriff, and this was my investigation, I guess I'd bring in Miss Tremblay to see if she had any additional information about—"

"Mmhmm. I'm waiting, Moon."

At last, the bolt of psychic inspiration hits. "About his retirement! He claims he only decided to retire in the last two weeks. If that's true, his executive secretary would absolutely be able to confirm, or deny."

"Excellent work. I'll send Paulsen out to pick her up."

"Paulsen? Why would you pick her?"

I can hear the smile in his voice. "Well, you said this Carol Tremblay is a real 'B.' So, I figure we fight fire with fire."

I have to cover my mouth to keep the laughter from bursting his eardrums. "Erick! I don't think you're supposed to talk about your employees that way!"

"Easy, Moon. I only said it to get a rise out of you. Paulsen may be a handful, but she is one of the most effective deputies on my force. I'll take high-spirited over unmotivated any day."

I sense his comment refers to present company, not just his star deputy. "I'll take that as a compliment."

"Are you coming into the station, or headed back to the bookshop?"

"Back to the bookshop to get changed. Plus, I have to update Grams and the murder board. When you get Carol in the interrogation room, fire off a text."

"10-4."

Back at the bookshop, Grams is thrilled to hear the not very lurid details of Niklas Olsen's affair. She eagerly fills out a 3 x 5 card for Carol Tremblay and I tack her on the board, completing the update by running the yarn from Wayne to Niklas to Carol Tremblay. I have no way of knowing if Carol Tremblay was acquainted with Carol Olsen, so we leave that link off the board for now.

But Grams makes a question mark card that I tack between the two Carols.

Glancing at my phone, I make a rough calculation for how long it would take Deputy Paulsen to drive out to the cranberry farm and back. "They should have her by now. I don't understand why Erick hasn't texted."

"You're a modern woman, dear. You can always text him."

"How avant-garde."

We both giggle, and I type up a simple text requesting an update.

For the second time today, my text results in a phone call. I'm not thrilled with this repeat break in protocol, but I do love the sound of his voice. "Hey, Erick. You're on speakerphone with me and Grams. What's up?"

"That vehicle that sped past you . . . Is there any chance it was a white Land Rover?"

I look at Grams and send her a quick telepathic message. *Do you think he's psychic?*

Grams giggles and rolls her eyes.

"It was. How would you know that?"

"Because, when Paulsen got to the farm, Carol Tremblay was nowhere to be found. We ran her name through the motor vehicle database to uncover the make and model of her vehicle. The receptionist said that Carol left suddenly with no explanation. I just put two and two together. Trouble is, we have no idea where she is now."

"You've checked her house or apartment?"

"Moon, not my first day on the job."

"Sorry, of course you did. How can I help?"

There's a pause and click in the background that may be a door closing. He lowers his voice and whispers into the phone, "Can you do your pendulum thing?"

"Oh, sure." I look at Grams and shrug while she grins maniacally and claps her hands. "Give me a few minutes to get set up, and I'll call you back when I have a location."

"Thanks. And this is just between us, right?"

"Who am I gonna tell?"

He chuckles and ends our call.

"Battle stations, Grams."

I push the secret panel beneath one section of the built-in wall of bookcases in my apartment, and a large drawer pops open. As I'm digging around to find the pendulum, the corner of a manila file folder catches my attention and brings a surge of guilt. It happens that I permanently borrowed Isadora's medical file from the records room at the local hospital one time when I worked undercover. My fingers curve around the pendulum and interrupt my remorse.

"Grams, I know I apologized once, but I'm sure it doesn't hurt to offer another one. I'm not exactly sorry I stole the records, but I am sorry I looked at them without your permission."

Her disinterest seems an act. "It's fine, dear."

She generally doesn't use such a short, clipped

tone with me. "Grams, I'm so sorry you and Odell lost your baby. It must've been a lot to deal with in such a new marriage."

She busies herself, straightening her strands of pearls and adjusting the many rings on her fingers. "Yes, it was difficult when we lost that one."

"What did you say? What do you mean, 'that one'?"

She zooms toward me, grabs the Birch County map from the drawer, and whizzes toward the coffee table. "The deadline, young lady. There'll be time to discuss family matters later."

When she mentions *Family Matters*, all my psychic abilities fly out the window as I put on my best Urkel impression. "Did I do that?"

Her laughter is halfhearted. She doesn't even look at me. All her attention is focused on smoothing the map out as perfectly as possible on the coffee table.

Seems like this is one of those times when it's best to let sleeping dogs lie. I shake the pendulum, letting it twist back and forth and sort itself out as I approach the map. "Do you think there's anything special I need to ask, or just where is Carol Tremblay?"

Grams taps one of her ring-ensconced fingers on her coral lip. "I think you're going to have to be more specific. You know how Silas gets."

"Boy, do I!"

As Grams and I huddle over the map, Pyewacket becomes spellbound by our actions.

He approaches the map, reaches a needle-clad paw toward the edge, and attempts to yank it onto the floor.

"Pye! This isn't a game. I'm trying to find someone."

He makes another, more determined attempt, and to my surprise Grams swirls toward him with uncharacteristic ire. "Robin Pyewacket Goodfellow! You stop it this instant. You are spoiled absolutely rotten!"

Wow. I've never seen her talk to the cat that way. "All right. Everyone calm down. I need to focus to make this work."

Pyewacket sulks into the closet, and Grams hovers opposite me.

Inhaling deeply, I attempt to clear my head. I extend my arm over the map and let the chain settle. Once the room is quiet, and everything inside my head is still, I focus my energy and ask my question. "Show me the current location of Carol Tremblay and/or the woman who drove past me in the white Land Rover this morning."

This version of the question seems to please the powers that be. The pendulum starts slowly, but quickly spins in larger circles, like the chair-swing ride at a carnival.

On previous occasions, when I watched Silas, the pendulum made two or three arcs and then pulled toward a specific location on the map. This time, the arcs seem to get wider and wider. It's almost as though the pendulum is reaching—

Grams speaks my thoughts out loud before I have a chance to formulate them. "I think you need to move it closer to the edge of the map, Mitzy. It seems to be trying to reach farther than the current radius."

I move my hand slowly in the direction that feels right, but the pendulum continues to circle wider, stretching farther.

I move my hand a little more.

Still pulling.

I move my hand a little farther.

The tip of the conical stone jerks toward the far edge of the map. As it hits the paper, it pulls even farther. Staring at the compass symbol, I'm mesmerized by the letter "N."

Grams and I lock eyes and shout in unison, "She's headed for Canada!"

Grabbing my phone, I call Erick and give him an update.

The news invigorates his investigation. "Thanks. Gotta go. Gotta call CC."

I collapse against the thickly padded back of the settee and exhale. "That was crazy. I've never felt the thing pull like that. There's so much to learn about my powers, and alchemy, and the energies in the universe . . ."

Grams floats toward the map like a feather on a gentle breeze. Her ethereal arm stretches out and one shimmering finger points to the edge of the map where the pendulum hit and dragged.

I lean forward and both of us giggle at the same moment. There, right on the northern border between Birch County and Canada, is a hole and a tear. The kind of hole made rather recently by a caracal's claw.

"Come out, come out, wherever you are, Pye. You're a genius. I'm a stupid human. All hail Pyewacket the wise."

And, as if on cue, he struts out of the closet with his tufted ears held high. He glances at the ghost of Grams, which we've both decided he can see, and then his gaze settles on me. To say that it's the smug look of an overlord gazing upon his subjects would be frighteningly accurate.

I raise both my hands in the air and mockingly bow down to the amazing Pyewacket. After three or four bows, he seems to accept my apology.

"Re-ow." Thank you.

Now that our urgent business has been handled, my grandmother's earlier comment has to be addressed. "Grams, I know you really don't want to talk about it, but I think you should. What did you mean by 'that one,' when we were talking about the child you miscarried?"

She freeze-frames and flickers like the tracking lines on an old paused videotape.

"Grams?"

A moment later, she pops out of the visual spectrum.

"Oh no you don't! You don't get to avoid this conversation, Isadora."

Having learned her weak spots in the past, I head into the closet to threaten her precious couture.

Inside the hallowed walls, I make my threat. "Myrtle Isadora Johnson Linder Duncan Willamet Rogers, you're acting like a human child. If you don't pop into this room immediately, I'm going to start a small designer label bonfire."

She rockets into the room with such force, I fall backward onto the padded mahogany bench. "Yikes! Take it easy."

Ghost-ma swirls toward me, filled with compassion. "Are you okay? I'm so sorry, dear. I know the clothes aren't important. In my heart, I know relationships are more valuable than fashion, but there's still a tiny part of me that can't let go of the glamor of haute couture."

"I'm fine, Grams. As you know, we Duncan women are well padded."

We share a chuckle, but the bright glow of love emanating from her fades as sadness shrouds her energy.

"You can tell me anything, Isadora. I know we tease each other, but I would never judge you. I've done plenty of things I'm not proud of in my short lifetime. Please, trust me with the truth."

She slowly circles the large closet, running her ghostly fingers along the lush array of fabrics. "Odell was my first true love. I had plenty of crushes before him, and there was an undeniable attraction to Cal, but I believe Cal was far more sure about the future of our relationship than I was. Before I could make a decision, they both enlisted in the Army, and Odell came back first."

"Are you saying it was more convenient?"

She hesitates and touches a simple gold band on her left ring finger. "I'm saying it was fate. Fate sent Odell to me, and we were blissfully happy. When Cal came back, things just turned so awful, so fast. He and Odell were fighting, and I mean fisticuffs, not just words. I tried to escape it all in a haze of whatever bottle was in the cupboard."

"So you divorced Odell and left the country?"

"Not exactly. I just left the country. Odell filed for divorce a few months later."

"Oh. And when did you meet Max?"

"I met Max the moment my plane landed in Paris. He was waiting for someone in the terminal, and either they didn't show up or maybe their flight was delayed. I took one look at him, dressed to the nines, European good looks, and an aura that screamed money—"

"Geez. That's a heckuva change from down-to-earth, small-town Odell."

She sighs. "I tend toward the dramatic, dear. I thought I could erase him through grand gestures and over-the-top behavior. Max was the perfect fit. We jet-setted all over Europe, married a month later, and drank our way from Latvia to the Greek Isles. It wasn't until that fateful car crash that either of us ever took our foot off the gas."

Emotions are swirling, and my inappropriate humor takes over. "No pun intended, I'm sure."

She looks away from the Oscar de la Renta, tilts her head, and offers a wan smile. "Oh, I didn't realize what I said."

"Sorry, Grams. You know how I get. Continue."

Her head droops. "Well, you know most of the rest of the story. Once I sobered up, I came back to Pin Cherry Harbor. I was determined to set things right with Odell and send Cal packing. But I came back to a completely different situation."

Her story draws me in, and I lean toward her.

"Odell had pushed the divorce through in my absence and wouldn't speak to me. Cal was eager to pick up where we had left off before his stint in the Army. Mostly, I was lonely and confused."

"So you married Cal and started a family. Why do I get the feeling there's a huge piece of the story I'm missing?"

"Because there is." Her shimmering ghostly eyes seem to look through a portal into the past. Designer-clad shoulders sag, and ghost tears spring to the corners of her eyes. "I couldn't let go of Odell. I had to make one enormous last attempt."

The hairs on the back of my neck are tingling, and an icy chill from my mood ring tempts me. I'm not going to dive into my psychic powers to uncover her secret. It's important that she tells me herself. "It's all right, Grams. You can tell me."

She drifts toward the padded bench and the hum of her energy brushes my skin. "I got pretty drunk. I made sure Odell did as well."

Uh oh. I've heard one too many stories that started like this. In fact, I've had a starring role in a few.

"We spent the night together, and, in the morning, I thought it would be easy to convince him to give me another chance."

"Why wouldn't he? It's obvious how much he loves you. He never remarried."

"He blamed himself for my relapse. Odell said we just weren't meant to be, and he never forgave himself for betraying his best friend. He and Cal had been best friends, before and during their days in the Army. Of course, all that changed after."

"So things didn't work out with Odell, and you ended up marrying Cal. It wasn't terrible, was it? You said your days with Cal and Jacob were some of the happiest of your life. Wasn't that true?"

"It was true, mostly. I made the best of a tricky situation. I maintained my sobriety, by living a lie."

The hairs on the back of my neck are stiffly on end, and my mood ring screams to be acknowledged. Taking a deep breath, I hold her gaze. "What was the lie?"

"Cal wasn't Jacob's father."

The room seems to be shrinking. I feel dizzy and I can't swallow.

She wraps her ghostly arm around my shoulders and tries to shake me. The connection with the intense emotion of the situation robs her of the ability to take corporeal form. "Mitzy? Mitzy, are you okay?"

"Are you saying what I think you're saying?"

"Probably. What do you think I'm saying?" Her luminous eyes look toward the plush carpet and tears spill over her cheeks.

"Odell is Jacob's father? Odell isn't my surrogate grandfather. He's my actual grandfather?"

The weight of what she's telling me is almost too much. I curve toward Ghost-ma, and reach out to comfort her, but she vanishes from the visual spectrum.

Sliding down to the floor like maple syrup pouring over the edge of a table, I lie against the soft carpet and stare up at the cedar-lined ceiling.

Thoughts, images, and emotions race through my body. What should I do first? Should I go talk to Odell? Should I tell my dad that the man he grew up thinking was his father isn't? It's all too much.

I squeeze my eyes closed and dream of escape. Unfortunately, the ringing cell phone in my pocket has other plans.

WHEN ERICK's name pops up on the caller ID, for the first time I can remember, I don't want to answer.

In the end, my insane sleuthing gene takes over, and I answer the call on speakerphone. The mobile rests on my stomach, and my eyes gaze aimlessly at the ceiling as I mumble, "Hello."

"Mitzy, we got her. Are you in?"

"What? You got who?"

There's a pause, and Erick's voice softens. "Hey, are you okay? You sound weird, and you're also not telling me what to do. Should I call the paramedics?"

His gentle teasing reaches my wounded inner child, and I roll onto my side, sliding the phone closer to my face. "Um, I'm in a pretty weird place.

I can't really get into it. It's hella complicated! Maybe you should take this one without me."

The soft tone vanishes from my boyfriend's voice as he embodies the sheriff he truly is. "Listen up, Moon. I'll be there to pick you up in two minutes, and you are to accompany me to the border to recover the fugitive. Your tip led to this capture, and I refuse to let you miss out on your moment of victory because you're having a pity party. Suit up. I'm on my way."

He ends the call without giving me a chance to whine, complain, or cry.

Sitting up in confusion, I shove my feet into a pair of shearling-lined boots, grab a thick puffy jacket, and march downstairs, ready to give him a piece of my mind face-to-face.

The tires crunching over the icy snow in the alleyway alert me to his arrival, and I step outside. I'm working hard to shove my emotions down as I rest an impudent fist on my hip.

He steps out of the car, takes one look at me, and jogs toward me. A moment later, his muscular arms wrap around me like a snuggly blanket and he's kissing the top of my head. "I don't know what happened, but we've got a little drive ahead of us and I'm all ears."

Why did he have to be nice to me? That's the worst. Big salty tears plummet down my cheeks.

He kisses my lips and escorts me to the passenger side. Carefully placing me inside and securing my seatbelt, he hustles around to the driver's side and backs out of the alley.

As we drive past Pancake Rock, I get my silent tears under control. The gorgeous crests, curves, and caves in the ice floes on the shore of our great lake take my mind off my family drama for a moment.

"Hey, Mitzy, whatever happened, you can tell me."

His hand is on my knee and I reach out and grip his fingers as though they're a life raft on a raging ocean. "Erick, I don't want to tell you. I don't think I want to tell anyone."

His thumb caresses the side of my finger and his voice is tender. "You do. Trust me, Moon. Shoving it all down inside is the worst possible option. I tried that when I worked my way across the country, writing the names of fallen soldiers on the back of those green-and-white population signs at the edge of their hometowns. Sure, it kept me moving, and it kept the demons at bay, but it wasn't until I actually talked to someone about the pain I was going through that I found my way out. So, talk to me. It's what couples do."

He squeezes my knee as he utters that last phrase.

Deep down, I know he's being painfully honest. "All right, but I'm telling you this as my boyfriend. There's some stuff you might not approve of, and I don't want to get a lecture from Sheriff Harper in the middle of pouring out my heart. Deal?"

He nods. "Deal."

I race through the bit about me removing medical records from the hospital, and, to his credit, the only sign of disapproval is the flexing muscle of his clenched jaw. When I get up to today's conversation, a fresh sob temporarily interrupts my tale.

His large hand gently rubs my knee. "Go ahead. I'm listening. Finish your story."

Admitting Odell is likely my actual grandfather, and Jacob's biological father, is harder than I imagined. I get choked up a couple of times, and encouraging words and kind smiles from Erick are the only things that pull me through to the end of my story. "So, she just dropped that on me today, and vanished."

His bright-blue eyes fill with concern. "She crossed over? Permanently?"

I shake my head furiously at the thought. "No. I mean, I hope not. She just vanished out of the visible spectrum. Grams does that sometimes when she's mad, or, I suppose in this case, ashamed."

He puts both hands back on the steering wheel and gazes off toward the horizon point. "I never knew my biological dad. And me and my mother were okay with that. When you showed up in Pin Cherry, you met a father who you'd thought was dead. Look how things turned out for you and Jacob. I think it would be a mistake to keep this from him. Or Odell. But I'm no expert. Maybe you should talk to Silas."

"Yeah. Silas. That's a fantastic idea, Erick. Thanks for listening. Dagnabbit, my family is messed up."

He chuckles softly. "No more than anyone else's, Moon. You can only play the cards you're dealt. Talk to Silas. Then do whatever you think is best, and let's hope everyone can be an adult about this. Right?"

"Copy that."

I refuse to admit to Erick that his "talking about it" idea actually helped. But now that the emotional fallout has been sifted through, my snoopy nature is eager to hear more about Carol Tremblay's capture.

"So, did they stop her at the border?"

Erick smiles proudly. "I can't wait for you to meet CC. He pulled off a miracle today. There are a whole lot of people crossing the border during the holidays, and the Canadian government generally loosens restrictions, inspections, and stopping cars in general during these last two weeks of December. He had to move heaven and earth to reinstate the stop every vehicle policy. But it paid off! By the time he got down there with additional mounted patrols, the border services agents had detained three white Land Rovers, and secured Tremblay."

"Three! I had no idea that was such a popular car. And in white? What are the odds?"

He shrugs. "I guess the odds are about three in however many cars crossed the border today."

"Touché."

Erick reaches out his hand and I slip my fingers into his grasp. It's a strange sensation to be riding in a sheriff's vehicle, with a shotgun between us locked into the dashboard, and police chatter spilling over the radio, as we embrace this new level of bonding in our relationship.

Buildings, manned gates, and red and green lights loom into view.

"There's the border. We'll pull into this parking lot and let CC know we've arrived." Grabbing his phone, he calls the Canadian Mountie. "Hey, buddy. We're in the eastern lot, south of gate three." Erick listens intently. "10-4. We'll be right in."

He slides out of the cruiser, circles in front, and opens my door. "This isn't Pin Cherry, Moon. Please mind your manners, and act like you've been in the room before."

I take the offered assistance of his hand, step out of the vehicle, and toss my hair like every movie star removing a helmet in every movie you've ever seen. "So, no mention of breaking and entering, stealing evidence, and, I'm assuming, no accents?"

To his credit, he resists rolling his eyes. "Hang on to me. There's a solid layer of ice under this snow."

I'm not sure if his words are a generous offer to keep me from falling, or a thinly veiled threat. Maybe if I don't play nice, he'll let me fend for myself on the frozen tundra. I'm pretty sure I wouldn't last two minutes. Clutching his arm, I let a helpful mantra echo through my grey matter: Play nice. Play nice. Play nice.

The wind whips up and offers me a face full of chilly Canadian snow as we approach the office building.

Erick holds the door for me. Once inside, I stomp excess snow off my boots onto the industrial floor mat and swipe at my cheeks.

CC waves from a hallway and motions us through. "It's all right, officer, they're with me."

The woman, who looked as though she was about to mid-field tackle us, returns to her chair.

The tall, dark, and handsome man walks toward us. He's almost too good looking. In fact, he wouldn't look out of place on the cover of *Vogue*. His close-cropped dark hair and deep brown eyes complement his lithe form. Although, something about the way he carries himself indicates he can handle himself in a fight. Not because of brute strength, but lightning-fast reflexes.

CC nods to Erick and steps toe-to-toe with me. He grips my right hand, removes my mitten, and presses the back of my fingers to his perfectly curved lips.

Erick smacks him on the arm. "Simmer down, Clermont."

CC purposefully ignores his old friend, hands me my mitten, and slips my arm through the crook of his elbow as he escorts me down the hall. "Bonjour, mademoiselle."

I know I promised Erick, but there's something about accents—I can't control myself. "Bonjour, monsieur."

His playful eyes light up, and he nods his head in approval. The striking red jacket of the Mountie uniform is so much more impressive in person than it was in the old *Dudley Do-Right* cartoons. I'm honestly disappointed CC isn't wearing his Mountie hat. But, as I understand it, you don't wear those indoors.

He opens a door on the left-hand side of the hallway and leads Erick and me inside.

Erick glances around the small space. "Where's Tremblay?"

"Oh, she pulled the Canadian citizen card,

which dumped an extra ton of paperwork in our lap. Can I get you two some coffee while you wait?"

The mesmerizing lilt of CC's French-Canadian voice distracts me from his actual question.

Sheriff Harper pokes at me and shakes his head. "You in there, Moon? Don't be drawn in by his accent. He's married, and he's laying it on extra thick just to stick it to me."

Mentally smacking myself on the forehead, I attempt to follow orders. Right. Get it together, Moon. Sitting up straighter in my chair, I clear my throat. "I'd love some go-go juice, and a doughnut if you've got any floating around."

CC bows his head and steps out of the room.

Erick slides his arm around my shoulders, and I'm not entirely sure if it's for my comfort or to mark his territory. He tilts his head toward mine and whispers, "Do you want to step outside and call Silas?"

"Um, no."

He leans back as though I've offended him. "Sorry. I was trying to help."

"I didn't mean that as harshly as it sounded. It's a fine suggestion. But there's no way I'm stepping outside until it's time to run directly to the car. Which, if you love me as much as you say you do, you'll go out first and pre-warm."

He rolls his eyes dramatically and smirks. "Boy, talk about your Arizona desert princess!"

Crossing my arms, I turn away and pretend to be offended.

That's the exact moment CC chooses to return. "Oh, dear, this looks like a lover's quarrel."

Erick squeezes me a little tighter, and I snuggle into him for effect. The hum of his deep voice makes my skin tingle. "It's called a sense of humor, Clermont. Maybe you should get one."

CC and Erick share a chuckle, and I eagerly accept my black gold and a maple-glazed doughnut.

"I hope they made this glaze from real Canadian maple syrup. I'm told to accept no substitutes."

My quip catches CC off guard, and his comeback sticks in his throat.

My boyfriend smiles proudly. "Good one, Moon."

The Canadian Mountie recovers. "Let me check on the paperwork. We should have you squared away in five or ten minutes."

Erick and I enjoy our java and sugary treats in silence.

CC returns as I'm licking the sticky glaze off my fingers.

He smiles. "It is *that* good. And speaking of good, they're prepping her for transport now. I'll escort her to your cruiser, you'll sign the appropriate form, and the alleged murderer Carol Tremblay will be all yours."

Erick stands up as though CC has simply announced the time of day, but his phrasing catches my attention.

"Murderer? Did you find evidence she was responsible for Carol Olsen's murder?"

CC shrugs. "There was a weapon in her vehicle, which we bagged along with the other items, and you'll have to run ballistics, but she claims she's ready to confess it all. I hate to make your job too easy, Harper, but it looks like this killer is about to plead guilty."

Erick hands me his phone. "When we get her in the cruiser, I'll Mirandize her, and you hit record on the phone. If she's going to spill her guts on the ride home, I want a fully legal recording in our possession. We have no idea what her real involvement, or motivation, is. She may be cooperating in an attempt to stay in Canada. Once she's back in the good old US of A, she may change her story. Anyway, you've got my back, right, Moon?"

"Always and forever." The phrase leaps out of my mouth before I truly comprehend its meaning.

Both Erick and CC gaze at me with the same intensity.

The Canadian Mountie speaks first. "That sounds serious, my friend. I don't see a ring—"

I lift my left hand and display the antique mood ring bequeathed to me by my grandmother.

CC widens his eyes and stutters as he searches for an appropriate response. "That's, some— Well, it's— How . . . unusual."

A broad grin spreads across Sheriff Harper's face, and he offers me a sharp salute. "You are one in a million. Excellent work."

The Mountie gazes back and forth, and I put him out of his misery. "It was a gift from my grandmother. I wear it for the nostalgia. Although, I'm not exactly sure I'm willing to take it off, or replace it with something else. I've grown rather fond of it."

Now it's Erick's turn to look surprised, and CC's chance at a revenge chuckle.

"You two head to the cruiser. I'll bring Tremblay out in a flash."

Making our way through the swirling snow, I voice my concern. "What if she recognizes me from the fake interview?"

Erick pats my mittened hand as though he's comforting a child. "What if she doesn't? Why don't you let me handle things and focus on getting a clean recording of her confession? Sound good?"

It sounds ludicrous, but I keep that thought to myself. "Whatever you say, dear."

He groans and shakes his head.

Serves him right. You mess with the bull, you

get the horns. I mean, I'll try to behave, but my fourth foster dad always told me, "You play how you practice!" Of course, the joke was on him, because I always skipped basketball practice and I never played. Wait, maybe the joke's on me? Since it would appear I played exactly as I practiced—not at all.

CHAPTER 16

A GUST of wind pushes Carol Tremblay and a soupçon of snowflakes into the backseat. Erick and CC wrap up their business, shake hands, and give each other the infamous one-armed bro hug.

Carol sniffles and cries softly in the backseat. She hasn't noticed me yet, and for that I'm grateful.

Sheriff Harper hops into the driver's seat and signals me to start the recording on his phone.

He runs her through the standard Miranda warning, and I jockey the phone into position for the best sound capture. Flashes of the old days in film school, straining to hold a boom pole over my head as all feeling drained from my arms, bring a wistful grin to my face.

"Who is she?" Miss Tremblay leans forward

and, when she gets a better look at me, she gasps. "I saw you! You were at— Why—?"

My mouth opens, but the voice that fills the cabin of the police cruiser is Erick's. "Miss Tremblay, this is Mitzy Moon. She's a confidential informant for the Birch County Sheriff's Department."

My eyes widen, and I nod in appreciation. This Harper fellow is going places.

Carol presses against the backseat, but the panicked tone and rapid breathing continues. "But she's French-Canadian. What is a Canadian doing working for a United States sheriff's department?"

My lips can only stay locked for so long. It's blurting time, and I'm the one to do it. "My apologies for the subterfuge, Miss Tremblay. I'm not actually French-Canadian."

As the clipped words in my wholly American accent penetrate the grating between the front seat and the rear, Carol's weeping increases in intensity.

Glancing at Erick, I shrug. If anything, I would've thought my admission would have consoled her.

Erick ignores her tears and launches into questioning. "Miss Tremblay, is it true that you were having an affair with Niklas Olsen?"

Her tears stop abruptly and she gasps. "Yes, I guess, but how could you possibly know that?"

"I'm not at liberty to reveal our sources. Were you acquainted with the deceased, Carol Olsen?"

The mere mention of the name triggers a fresh set of sobs. Between the choking and gasping, she fits her reply. "We were friends in primary school. She was from Québec, too."

Erick nods, and I stare at my mood ring, hoping for a bolt of inspiration.

No such luck.

"And when was the last time you saw Carol Olsen?"

An over-the-top wail, and both hands cover her face.

Rolling my eyes, I exhale. She smells about as guilty as they come. This false remorse isn't fooling anyone. I hope.

"Miss Tremblay, I need you to answer these questions truthfully. You're a suspect in a homicide. If ballistics match your gun to the bullet recovered from the scene—"

"NO!" Carol Tremblay screams from the backseat. "No! I would never hurt her. You don't understand. I have a gun for protection. That's all."

Erick takes the outburst in stride. "And what do you need protection from, Miss Tremblay?"

Her soft French accent utters a phrase that shocks both Erick and me. "My father is Antoine Bergeron. If you know anything about the maple syrup mafia, you're familiar with the name. He sent me to the states for college, but by the time I finished, his notoriety was catching up with him. He didn't think it was safe for me to return to Canada, so he arranged for me to emigrate."

My eyes are wide as saucers. My psychic senses must've known about the connection, even though it hadn't bubbled to my consciousness. "So when I used that name—"

Her breath shudders. "Exactly. Edith didn't tell me your full name until you rushed off so suddenly, but, as soon as she did, I grabbed my pocketbook and ran. I had no way of knowing if it was a message from my father, or a threat. It certainly couldn't have been a coincidence. My first thought was to get to my father and find out what I was supposed to do. If someone was trying to kill me, I thought he would be my best protection."

Erick's hands grip the steering wheel, twisting forward and back as though he's working the throttle on a motorcycle. "What does any of this have to do with Carol Olsen? Did she find out you were having an affair with her father-in-law?"

Miss Tremblay lays her head back and gazes up at the ceiling of the cruiser. "I suppose it's all going to come out now. She and I kept each other's secrets for so long . . . I never thought it would come to this."

He squares his shoulders. "Well, it has come to this. Tell me the nature of the relationship between you and Mrs. Olsen, and tell me the truth about the last time you saw her."

Miss Tremblay wrings her hands, swipes the tears from her cheeks, and inhales a shaky breath. "Carol and I were involved. It's why she left Wayne."

Turning my head to the side, I glance at Erick and silently mouth, "What?"

He ignores my pantomime. "Please continue, Miss Tremblay."

"My father sent me enough money each month to get by, but Carol was always the dreamer. She wanted more. She wanted us to be ridiculously wealthy. So she refused to divorce Wayne, because she knew he would inherit the cranberry farm someday, and thought that would be our ticket. I had my doubts. Working alongside Niklas every day didn't give me much hope in the inheritance scheme. He was healthy as an ox, and none too fond of his wife. Most days he spent twelve hours at the farm. Occasionally he even slept in his office."

"Go on."

"I wanted to make Carol happy, and thought I could speed things up with a blackmail scheme. I befriended him, brought him coffee and lingered in his office, and occasionally ordered dinner for the two of us. Honestly, when I got to know him, I really disliked the blackmail idea. So I dragged my feet."

The whistle on my teakettle can only be silent for so long. "For ten years?"

"Yes. I know it sounds ridiculous, but I didn't want to sleep with him. He's not my type, you know?" Her voice cracks a little, and my heart hurts for her loss.

Erick gestures for her to continue.

"I kept coming up with excuses every time Carol pushed for blackmail photos. Besides, she kept working a variety of her own scams. But when she dove into the maple syrup trade, I was afraid. I knew how dangerous it could be, and I thought I'd pull the extortion trigger and save us both."

My arm is cramping and I have to adjust the angle I'm holding the recording device.

"It wasn't difficult to coax Niklas to a hotel. Carol hid in the closet and took some compromising photos. I didn't even actually have to sleep with him. I offered to give him a massage, and, during the rubdown, he fell asleep. The photos told a different story, and we were sure we could get him to pay."

Erick nods. "What happened when you gave him the photos?"

Carol Tremblay groans and hangs her head. "That was the day Norma visited the office."

Sheriff Harper presses her. "Did Norma Olsen come into the office often?"

"*Absolument pas.* I mean, absolutely not. In all the years I'd worked there, I'd only seen her three times. Including that day. Niklas was out inspecting one of the cranberry bogs for dewberry invasion, and she insisted on waiting in his office. I was sitting at my desk sweating profusely. The corner of the envelope was sticking out from under the blotter on his desk. As the minutes ticked away, Mrs. Olsen got antsy. She started poking around, and she found the pictures."

Once again, my pressure valve releases. "Did she confront you? Did you run?"

Miss Tremblay shrugs. "The angle of the photos never showed the face of the woman. Carol and I planned it that way. But once I saw her pull out the envelope, I wasn't going to stick around to find out. I grabbed my purse and ran to my car. I called Niklas to tell him his wife was waiting in his office and she looked angry. He hung up on me."

I turn toward the backseat. "Was he upset about the incident in the hotel room?"

My mouth is running, and Erick's stern gaze reminds me I'm supposed to be seen and not heard.

"Not likely. He just didn't like to be disturbed when he was in the bogs."

Sheriff Harper leaps back into the fray. "So what happened when Niklas talked to his wife?"

Carol Tremblay sighs and shakes her pretty blonde head. "She insisted he retire, effective immediately. He negotiated for two weeks' transition and leaned heavily on Wayne."

"So Wayne Olsen knew about the retirement for two weeks?" My face scrunches with concern.

She hems and haws. "Not exactly. Niklas didn't want anyone to know he was retiring. He was insistent that Wayne come in and learn more about the business, but it wasn't until last Friday night at the actual retirement party that Wayne discovered when he'd be taking everything over—when business reopens after the holiday break."

A relieved sigh escapes Erick's lips, and he stares off into the distance. I can't be sure whether he's collecting his thoughts, or if he's lost his train of thought. Luckily, I'm happy to jump in.

"Now for the part you keep avoiding. When was the last time you saw Carol Olsen—alive?" I move the recorder toward the metal divider.

She swallows hard, looks at the recorder, and briefly glances at me. "In the woods, behind that Twiggy woman's cabin."

Erick is back online. "And what were you doing in the woods behind Twiggy's cabin?"

"Once I admitted how the blackmail scheme

had failed, Carol wanted me to seduce her husband. I told her I couldn't do it. I told her I didn't want to do it. So she came up with the crazy notion of getting pictures of Wayne and Twiggy, and using them to blackmail Wayne into buying her out of Crimson Crest. Since they were technically still married, you know,"

"Solid plan."

Erick darts a scornful gaze in my direction. "Moon, let's keep it professional."

"Copy that."

"While we were sneaking around in the woods trying to decide the best vantage point to get photos, a shot rang out."

The sheriff's head drops forward. "Miss Tremblay, do you expect me to believe that you and the deceased randomly had an idea, known only to the two of you, and yet a killer managed to find you and kill Carol Olsen. Could you please explain to me why someone would want to kill Mrs. Olsen?"

Carol Tremblay seems to shrink in the backseat, and she hugs her arms tightly around her stomach as she hunches forward and whispers, "She was wearing my coat."

My eyes are brimming with unshed tears and I seek out Erick's. He nods toward the phone and I end the recording.

CHAPTER 17

AN UNEASY SILENCE stifles all conversation inside the cruiser. My extrasensory perception confirms Carol Tremblay is telling the truth, and clearly in mourning.

Erick's jaw is tight, and his hands grip the steering wheel even more fiercely. It doesn't take a psychic to figure out what he's thinking.

Carol Olsen wasn't the target. She was a victim of mistaken identity. Carol Tremblay was not the murderer, she was the intended victim. And last, but not least by any means, the murderer is still at large.

Time for me to focus. Put all my special gifts to use and come up with something that will close this case and save a woman's life. Miss Tremblay is heartbroken. She lost her life partner, but, even worse, the survivor's guilt is crushing her. I'm sure she can't help but wonder what would've happened if she'd worn her own coat that day.

Don't worry, I'm not going soft on Carol Olsen. She seemed like a real piece of work. She clearly put Wayne through the wringer more than once and was willing to do just about anything to make a buck. I'm not saying the world will be worse off without her, but my heart goes out to those she left behind.

Sinking into myself, I twist the mood ring on my left hand and work hard to clear my mind of distracting thoughts.

Feelings of anger and revenge tighten my chest as the word *vendetta* pops into my head. Simultaneously, my mood ring burns, and I glance down to see maple syrup spilling from a large steel drum. Looks like the kind of drums they transport crude oil in, but I'm no expert.

"Miss Tremblay?"

Her breath is ragged, but she replies. "Yes."

"I have a hunch they targeted you because your father double-crossed someone. Would he have any reason to dispose of perfectly good maple syrup?"

Carol gasps and presses a hand to her chest. "How could you—?"

Erick looks at me and arches one eyebrow.

"I think it has something to do with that. Do you know if he has any partners, or—"

"I don't know if he's done it lately—we've been out of touch for several years—but I remember one time he forced exporters to buy from him, by sabotaging their inventory. I don't know exactly what that meant, but he may have poured it out."

"How long ago was that?"

"At least five years ago. But my father has a lot of enemies. He's an unscrupulous businessman who won't take no for an answer. If he did it once, it's possible he did it again—more recently."

Erick looks at me and scrunches up his face in confusion.

With my hand below seat level, so Miss Tremblay can't see, I give him the gesture to simmer down. "Carol, you're going to be in danger until we catch the person who murdered Mrs. Olsen. It seems to me you were the intended target. Once word gets out that it wasn't you wearing that jacket, I'm sure the killer will try again. Would you be willing to help us catch him or her?"

She sniffles and asks for a tissue.

Erick retrieves a tissue box from under the driver's seat. I push one through the metal grating and wait while she blows her nose and wipes her tears. "If it means we can catch the person who murdered her, I'll do whatever you ask."

"Would you be willing to lie to your father?" I chew the inside of my cheek while I wait for her reply. I know it's a big ask, but if she's as estranged from her father as it sounds, I'm hoping her loyalty to Carol Olsen will win out.

"Maybe. What did you have in mind?"

"Let's assume that the assassin was either a rival, or was hired by a rival. I want to call your father with a ransom demand, and then I'll put you on the phone and you'll need to act terrified."

Her breathing comes in shallow gasps and she shakes her head. "I don't know. I don't know if I can do this."

"If he's recently double-crossed someone, he may say their name or give us some other clue that would lead us to the killer. I know it's a gamble, but if it pays off, it means— It means she didn't die in vain."

Carol Tremblay tucks her blonde hair behind her ears and presses a hand over her mouth as she considers my plan. "All right. I'll do it."

Erick looks at me and shakes his head.

"I'm not asking you to participate, Erick. But you know I'm right. If Antoine Bergeron gives us a clue to the killer's identity, we'll have a much better chance of protecting her."

He eases the squad car to the side of the road

and turns off the engine. "We're not doing this at the station."

"Copy that. Can you hand me her phone?"

Erick rifles through the box of bagged evidence and pulls out a clear plastic bag holding her phone. "Put on a pair of gloves."

Nodding my head, I pick up the gloves he's pointing to, put them on, and carefully remove the phone from the evidence bag.

After I join Carol Tremblay in the backseat, we go over the plan one more time.

"Pardon, but you left the door open. It's getting awfully cold in here. Can you close it?"

"It will be more realistic if you're shivering. I'm going to leave it open, all right?"

She nods, takes the phone, and places the call.

"Put it on speaker. And let me talk first."

A deep voice with a thick French accent pours from the speaker. "Chère fille? Is it you?"

I loosen my throat to lower my voice an octave and lean into my gruffer tones. "I'll ask the questions, Bergeron."

"Who is this? What have you done with my daughter? If you harm a hair on her head—"

"What will you do? Pour out some more of my Canadian gold?" I'm spitballing here, but hopefully I'm on the right track.

"Olsen? Are you working with the old man

now? It's not enough that you attempted to steal the contracts of my exporters, now you're in league with Leblanc?"

"You didn't think we'd let you get away with it, did you?"

"I poured out a few barrels to teach you a lesson. This isn't worth the life of my daughter! What do you want from me?"

I look at Carol and shrug. She mouths to me, "All the sugar makers."

"I want first crack at all the sugar makers, Bergeron. You get out of my way, or you'll never see your daughter alive again."

He moans, and there's a loud thumping on his end of the phone. Possibly his fist hitting the table. "How do I know you haven't already harmed her? Put her on the phone."

Glancing at Carol, I arch an eyebrow and lift my shoulders.

She nods and reaches for the phone.

My plan to leave the door open has worked marvelously. Her teeth are chattering in earnest. Her voice is broken and filled with fear as she speaks to her father. "Papa? Papa, they mean to kill me."

"Put Olsen back on the phone." His tone is all business now.

Interesting that he thinks I'm Carol Olsen. He

clearly hasn't heard about the murder that took place south of the Canadian border. However, that luck won't hold out long. We need to get some details to flush out Leblanc. "You're to meet Leblanc at the usual place with one million in US currency. You have twelve hours."

"What? One million? US?" He growls, and the sound of shattering glass tinkles down the line. "It will take me at least two days to get the money and fly out to Pin Cherry. Ask Leblanc for more time."

Erick waves a hand to get my attention and drags a finger across his neck. I end the call, and we all breathe a sigh of relief. "Is that enough?"

Erick shrugs. "Let's hope. Turn the phone off in case he tries to call back. You did a good job, Miss Tremblay. Hop up front, Mitzy. I've got to call Paulsen."

Before exiting the backseat, I can't stop myself from giving Carol Tremblay a comforting hug. I know what it's like to lose someone you care about. She squeezes my hand and thanks me.

Sheriff Harper eases the cruiser back onto the road as he calls dispatch.

"Dispatch, Sheriff Harper here. Send Paulsen and Johnson to pick up Niklas Olsen."

"Bring him to the station?"

"10-4. Hold him for questioning."

Even with my special gifts, I can't see where Erick's logic is headed. "Why are you bringing in Niklas? Shouldn't we be calling CC to ask him to pick up this Leblanc character?"

Erick shakes his head, and his eyes are stormy. "You heard what Bergeron said, 'Are you working with the old man now?' and when you mentioned the usual meeting place, he immediately assumed Pin Cherry. Also, Leblanc—"

"Means The White! The old man with the white hair is Niklas Olsen. But that means—"

Carol Tremblay sobs from the back. "That means he tried to kill me in retaliation for the blackmail, and he was secretly running illegal maple syrup behind everyone's back."

My wheels are spinning out of control now, and I'm certain there's actual smoke pouring from my ears. "He must've employed you to have leverage over your father. How do you think he knew you were Bergeron's daughter?"

"Maybe Carol mentioned that we were old school chums when she recommended me for the job. I'm certain I never mentioned it. I'm always quite careful."

My hand shoots across the car and I grip Erick's arm. "What if he meant to kill his daughter-in-law? A coat might confuse a hired gun, but Niklas would know the difference."

Erick nods thoughtfully. "But his illness . . . He can barely walk."

My mouth blurts before my brain engages. "I could grab his medical records if—"

"Absolutely not. We can subpoena records, Miss Moon."

"Of course. Whatever you say, Sheriff." Sufficiently scolded, I fold my hands in my lap and sit quietly for the rest of the ride.

ERICK LEAVES me to fend for myself as he escorts Carol Tremblay into the station. It's unclear whether she's here as an actual suspect, or if completing her interview is simply a matter of proper paperwork.

I stop at the front desk and clear my plan with Furious Monkeys. "Is it all right if I head back?"

She chuckles. "Isn't it always?"

Fair play to the gamer. Pushing through the swinging gate, I'm forced to stop in the bullpen when a scuffle in the hallway alerts me to Deputy Paulsen bringing Niklas Olsen toward Interrogation Room 1.

They picked him up quickly. I better grab a front-row seat in the observation room and see if this old fella has any tricks up his sleeve.

As soon as Paulsen leads him into the interrogation room, I rush down the hallway and dive into the room sandwiched between the two interrogation bays and flanked with wide one-way glass.

Erick is finishing up with Carol Tremblay in Interrogation Room 2. He has her recorded statement, but she's making some notes about dates and times, and her unsavory family connections. She signs the paper and pushes it across the table.

"Sheriff Harper, when may I collect Carol's body? I'd like to plan a proper memorial service, you know, before they move her into storage until the spring thaw." Miss Tremblay stumbles over her words, and fresh tears spring to the corners of her eyes.

Erick inhales sharply. "I'm sorry, Miss Tremblay, but Carol Olsen is technically still married to Wayne Olsen. He's the only person who can make arrangements for her remains."

Miss Tremblay's bottom lip quivers and she shakes her head. "That won't do. That just won't do."

He slides his chair back, gets to his feet, and places a comforting hand on her shoulder. "I'll talk to Wayne. He's a reasonable man."

The daughter of the northern hemisphere's most notorious maple syrup Mafioso gazes up at Erick as though he's personally promised to fly her to the pearly gates. "Would you? Oh, I'm so— Thank you. You have no idea what this means to me. Thank you." She clutches his hand with both of hers and squeezes tightly as tears trickle down her cheeks.

Sheriff Harper drags his hand away and exits the cubicle of uncomfortable emotions.

Clicking the room two speaker off, I rotate my attention toward room one and click the silver toggle.

Erick enters with a thick manila folder in his hands. He doesn't greet Niklas. Instead, he pulls out his chair, deliberately lowers himself into it, and drops the thick file onto the table with a thud. "Seems like you weren't completely honest with us the last time you were here, Mr. Olsen."

Niklas no longer appears the doddering, aged retiree. He lounges in the stiff steel chair as though born to it. His eyes glint with resistance, and he makes no response.

"Deputy Johnson has notified you of your Miranda rights, is that correct?"

Niklas nods once.

"Mr. Olsen, you'll have to reply verbally for the recording. Have you been advised of your Miranda rights?"

He offers an audible, "Yes." Followed by a silent sneer.

This is an absolute Dr. Jekyll and Mr. Hyde moment. The friendly, helpful gentlemen who suffered from a debilitating illness and retired at his wife's request has vanished. The man that sits across from the sheriff is cagey and defiant. I wouldn't trust him as far as I could throw him. And if you remember anything about my athletic ability, I can't even throw a ball decently.

"Mr. Olsen, is it true that you are involved in illegal maple syrup trade with several sugar makers in Québec?"

Niklas does not answer.

"Mr. Olsen, I have transcriptions of phone calls, copies of email messages, and copies of text messages between you and four of the most well-known maple rebels. You've been under surveillance by the Canadian Mounties for some time."

There's a distinct shift in Niklas Olsen's energy. He was confident he'd managed to stay under the radar of the authorities in the United States, but it clearly had not occurred to him that some of his contacts on the Canadian side of the border might be huge blips on the Mounties' radar.

"Do you know of any connection between your executive secretary Carol Tremblay and the Canadian businessman known as Antoine Bergeron?"

Niklas makes every effort to remain stoic, but my psychic senses pickup on a surge of fear and loathing. The name means something to him, and he absolutely knew about the connection.

Erick ignores the lack of response and moves on. "What did you do when your wife confronted you regarding the affair and the compromising photos taken of you and Miss Tremblay at a motel in Broken Rock?"

The crispy exterior of Mr. Olsen finally cracks. "There was no affair."

The sheriff removes several racy photos from the folder and pushes them across the table toward Mr. Olsen. "These photos tell a different story."

The muscles in the accused man's jaw clench twice. "That's what her father thought, too."

Pump the brakes! Plot twist. He used the blackmail photos that the Carols took of him to blackmail them? I shouldn't be rubbing my hands together so eagerly, but this turn of events fascinates me.

"So you were aware of Miss Tremblay's true identity and family connections."

"That's the only reason I hired her."

The phrase is so cold and calculating, my skin crawls like that of a shedding snake.

"So why would you attempt to blackmail Miss Tremblay?"

"I wasn't. I used the photos to manipulate her father to hand over some contracts. The cranberry business ain't what it used to be, Harper. Wayne doesn't want anything to do with it. Norma couldn't manage her way out of a paper sack. I could've sold the whole operation to one of those big conglomerates ten or fifteen years ago. But I thought my legacy meant something to my son. Boy, was I mistaken. Now that they've bought up all the mom-and-pop bogs, nobody is interested. I was out of options and I had to take care of my family. Had to provide for my retirement."

Erick shuffles papers and gazes directly at Mr. Olsen. "And by providing for your retirement, you mean illegally importing maple syrup, stockpiling it to drive up the price, and selling it at your convenience to the highest bidder?"

Niklas practically spits his reply. "That about sums it up."

Well, Erick definitely has him on the illegal importing, but I'm still not completely convinced this man murdered his daughter-in-law.

"Mr. Olsen, where were you Saturday evening between 8:00 p.m. and midnight?"

Niklas lifts his chin defiantly and crosses his arms. "You already seem to have all the answers, Harper. Why don't you tell me?"

"Very well. It is the belief of this department that you were trespassing on Susan Matthews' property—"

"Who's Susan Matthews?" Niklas tilts his head.

"You probably know her as Twiggy."

My jaw hits the floor faster than a drunk at happy hour. Twiggy's actual name isn't Twiggy? Did I know that? My entire world is turning upside down. Twiggy is Susan Matthews. I hope to never hear that name again. It doesn't fit.

Shoot, my existential crisis stole my attention from the interrogation. Erick is mid-sentence when I regain my focus.

". . . carrying a 308 hunting rifle with a silencer, and you shot your daughter-in-law, Carol Olsen. You did not seek medical assistance for her, but instead left her in the snow to die of her wound. That sounds like homicide in the first degree, Mr. Olsen. What do you have to say for yourself?"

The jutted chin drops, but his anger continues to rise. "She made a fool of my son—of my whole family. She was never interested in Wayne. Carol was not that kind of girl, if you know what I mean. She married him to try to get her hands on the family money. When she found out he didn't want to take over the Crimson Crest, she hightailed it out of their house and looked for another scam. She was always conning someone. I'm not convinced she even had feelings for this Carol Tremblay. I think it was just another one of her long cons." His hand smacks onto the table with enough force to make the whole surface tremble. "It may not have been right to take a life, but the world isn't going to be any worse off for the lack of Carol Olsen."

My extrasensory perception gets a jolt of anticipation emanating from Erick. However, on that side of the glass, he maintains his cool. "Mr. Olsen, are you saying you shot and killed Carol Olsen?"

The ire seems to have run its course, and his arms drop to his sides as his head dips. "I didn't mean to kill her. I wanted to scare them. She found out about my maple syrup deals and she was trying to worm her way into that. I was sick and tired of all her wheeling and dealing. Only meant to wing her, but my eyesight isn't what it used to be."

Erick's shoulders rise and fall as he takes a single calming breath. "Mr. Olsen, did you shoot Carol Olsen in the woods Saturday evening?"

The elderly man's eyelids rise and he meets Erick's gaze. "Yes. I shot Carol. But I didn't mean to kill her."

The hasty addition of his closing phrase seems more like a plan to mount his own defense than an accurate statement. If you ask me, he was tired of Carol Olsen messing around with his family, and he put an end to it the only way he knew how. And if it happened to hurt the secretary who tried to blackmail him in the process, seems like that was a bonus he didn't mind.

Erick removes handcuffs from his duty belt and

approaches Mr. Olsen. "Niklas Olsen, I am placing you under arrest on suspicion of the murder of Carol Olsen." He slips the handcuffs around the man's wrists and walks him out of Interrogation Room 1.

For the record, Mr. Olsen needed neither cane, walker, nor wheelchair for this journey. His medical condition seems as phony as his original alibi. When I place my hand on the doorknob, it twists on its own. Stepping back, I'm pleased to see Erick entering, and not deputy Paulsen.

"How did you get all those transcripts and stuff so quickly?"

He blushes. "It was ninety-five percent blank pages. I had some notes on the top, and a couple photos—"

My voice escapes me for a minute as I stare in awe. "You were bluffing?"

His voice is thick with emotion. "I learned from the best."

As I formulate my comeback—

He pushes the door closed behind him and pulls me into an unexpected embrace.

"To what do I owe this pleasure, Sheriff Harper?"

His hands slide down the curve of my back as tingles rise along my spine. "I just need to wrap my arms around something I can trust. I know my line of work shows me a window into the darker side of humanity, but some families are really messed up."

I snake my arms around his neck and gaze up into his beautiful blue eyes. "Lucky for us, we're totally normal."

My obvious joke does the trick, and he laughs softly as he presses his lips to mine. "So Christmas Eve supper at your dad's house tomorrow, right?"

"That's right, *boyfriend*. You're going to be front and center with all the Duncan-Moon—"

My conversation with Isadora floods into my head and interrupts my flow. The word family holds a different meaning for me now.

Erick brushes my snow-white hair back from my forehead. "What's wrong? I don't like that look. Is there something going on between you and your dad?"

Letting my arms fall away from his broad shoulders, I step back. "I have to take care of something. And I can't talk about it right now. Is it still all right if I come over to your place tonight, after I handle my business?"

Concern creates two lines between his eyebrows as he tilts his head. "You're not going to put yourself in any danger, are you?"

"Rude."

He lifts his hands in surrender and chuckles. "Come on, I have to ask."

"Fair enough. No. I will not be in any physical danger. It's more of an emotional minefield than anything else."

"Okay. I'll pick something up at the diner once I finish up my paperwork, and see you at my place, whenever you get there."

Pushing up on my tiptoes, I kiss his soft, full lips, squeeze my arms around him, and wish I never had to let go.

He's the first to extract himself this time. "Hey, save some of that initiative for later."

My cheeks flush pin-cherry red and he exits the room ahead of me.

Deputy Paulsen is dead center in the bullpen when I attempt to make my escape. "Hey, Moon."

Blerg. The last thing I need in my current fragile emotional state is a confrontation with Pauly Paulsen. "I was just leaving."

"You give Twiggy a message for me, eh?"

"I suppose. What's the message?" My arms are crossed, and my hip may be kicked out in a somewhat defiant pose.

Paulsen steps closer and lowers her voice. "You tell her I never thought she was guilty for a minute. Got that?"

The unexpected kind words from the bully-esque deputy, and the blind faith in my cantankerous employee, catch me off guard. Before I know what's happening, I throw my arms around Deputy Paulsen's shoulders and I'm hugging her tightly as she sputters. "Easy, Moon. Our entire department isn't up for grabs, you know."

I release her stout, stubborn form and chuckle as I sashay through the hanging wooden gate. I don't think I've ever seen her blush. Let's call that a win.

Outside the station, I plant my feet perpendicular to the street and my heart is torn in two directions. I could call Silas and drag this out, but I know what I have to do, and there's no point in chickening out or delaying the inevitable. Rather than head back to the bookshop, I steel my nerves and step into the diner.

Odell offers me the standard spatula salute through the red-Formica trimmed orders-up window.

The waterworks threaten to unleash. Swallowing hard, I inhale through my nose and exhale through my mouth—just as every yoga instructor in Sedona recommends—before marching into the kitchen.

"What's up, Mitzy? You here to eat or just chew the fat?"

"How would you feel about closing early today, Odell?"

He glances out the orders-up window at the

empty restaurant and shrugs. "I could be convinced. Whaddya got in mind?"

The tears are creeping to the edge of my eyelids now, and I think I only have room for one more sentence. "Can you just close, and come with me?"

The man has always been quick on the uptake. He looks at my face, removes his apron, and walks out to lock the front door.

He flips the sign from open to closed and leads the way to the back door. I slip my arm through his elbow, and we make our way down Main Street toward First Avenue and my bookshop.

I honestly wonder if I'm doing the right thing.

CHAPTER 19

THE BOOKSHOP and its secrets get closer with each step.

Odell must sense my unease. "What's goin' on, kid? You got something nasty clogging the pipes in your apartment?"

The leftfield query catches me off guard and laughter comes too soon and too loud. "Oh my gosh, it's nothing like that. But thanks for breaking the ice."

He runs a hand through his short grey buzz cut and shakes his head. "Breaking the ice? I thought I was practically family." His laughter is rough as a Brillo pad and comforting as a favorite shirt.

It's funny that he would mention family. He's more family than he knows. "I don't want to spoil the surprise."

"Well, I hope you didn't get me a present. Because I didn't get you one, and I don't plan on running out to the stores at this late date." He shoves a hand in the pocket of his dungarees.

Classic Odell. Practical, down-to-earth, honest. I hope those traits pull him through what I'm about to reveal.

We tramp across the street in the icy slush, and he pauses in typical Odell fashion. "Front door or side door?"

"Let's go in the front door. That feels right to me."

He shrugs his shoulders and waits while I fish out my key and unlock my beautiful door.

Stepping inside the darkened interior, our only guiding illumination is the light leaking through the windows from the streetlamp on the corner.

"Wait here." I race to the back room and flip the lights on. I remember the first time I walked into this place and hopelessly searched the walls by the front door for a switch. The indomitable Twiggy blew past me and solved my problem. Just another of the sweet memories I have of falling in love with this town and its people. I sure hope what I'm about to do doesn't ruin all that.

As I walk back, Odell meets me at the bottom of the circular staircase. I unhook the "No Admittance" chain and offer a warning. "Hurry. I gotta hook it back up in thirty seconds—or else."

He hustles up a few treads and waits for me. "No one wants to draw Twiggy's wrath, eh?"

The fresh incident of Twiggy landing on a suspect list, paired with Odell's comment, makes me giggle nervously. I hook up the chain and motion for him to continue.

He walks into the Rare Books Loft, pauses and turns a full three hundred and sixty degrees. "Boy, this place is gorgeous. Doesn't matter how many times I take a gander, each time is as sweet as the first. Did ya bring me up here to show me some books?"

I can sense his tension building, and I have to assume the last time he was in the apartment was when my grandmother was still alive. I smile, and push past him to pull the candle handle next to my copy of *Saducismus Triumphatus* and silently watch as the bookcase door slides open. "Come on in and have a seat. Like I said, I have a surprise for you."

He hesitates a moment, but walks forward like the brave soldier he is. Odell pauses next to the seating arrangement and chooses the settee. As he perches on the edge with obvious discomfort, Grams blasts out of the closet in mid-sentence.

"Finally! I have so many outfit—"

The sight of her makes me doubt my decision. Am I doing this? Yeah. All right, I'm doing this.

Isadora whizzes toward me at ludicrous speed. "Are you doing what? You better not be doing what I think you're doing, young lady!"

"Odell. I know this is going to sound crazy, and I won't blame you if you get up and run out of here, but Grams isn't as dearly departed as everyone thinks."

His brown eyes search my face for any hint of amusement. Finding none, he gets to his feet. "What are you saying, Mitzy?"

Here goes nothing, or maybe everything. "Silas and Grams figured out a way to tether her spirit to this bookshop. And I can see ghosts. So, I can see her and talk to her, and she has something very important to tell you."

He sinks back to the settee with an unreadable gaze.

I'm unsure if it's disbelief, shock, or dread. "Odell? Did you hear what I said?"

He grips his knees with weathered hands, and I can see his knuckles whiten as he struggles to steady himself. "I'm old, but my ears still work."

Uh oh. That sounds anger adjacent.

Isadora floats toward him like a cloud on a gentle breeze. "Of course he's angry, Mitzy. You should've talked to me about this. This is a terrible idea."

She's so busy scolding me, she doesn't realize how close she's come to Odell. But I immediately recognize the ghost-chill bumps rising on his arms.

His eyes widen and he looks at me. "Is it cold in here?"

"It's Isadora. She's here."

His face softens as hope fills the lines around his eyes. He braves a smile. "Myrtle, is that you?"

She swirls closer and another chill grips him.

"Well, if this is what you got me for Christmas, Mitzy, I know I can't top it."

Tears spill from the corners of my eyes, and I join him on the settee. "There's actually— I hate to be the one to— No. I take that back. I'm actually ecstatic to be the one to tell you this. And I'm sorry you're only finding out now. Although, speaking from experience, later is better than never."

His eyes are misty, and I feel like he's holding his breath.

"In a couple minutes, I'm going to leave. That stack of 3 x 5 cards on the coffee table is how she can communicate with you. She can write you messages or whatever. You can ask her anything you want. Make sense?"

He nods mutely.

"But before I go, I'm going to tell you this part

because, well, honestly, I don't entirely trust her to tell you herself."

Grams rests a bejeweled fist on her hip. "Well, I never!"

Without thinking, I toss back my usual response. "We all know that's not true, don't we, Myrtle Isadora Johnson Linder Duncan Willamet Rogers."

Odell chuckles. "You're startin' to make a believer out of me."

Swiping at a tear, I push onward. "Now, I hope you think this is wonderful news. I think it's wonderful news, and—"

He takes my hand and gently pats it. "Just say it, kid. The longer you wait, the harder it gets. Trust me, I learned that the hard way." His gaze drifts off, and I'm certain he's referring to keeping his true feelings about my grandmother hidden for so many decades.

"All right. You're my grandfather."

He smiles pleasantly, nods, and pats my hand again. "Of course. I'll always be your stand-in grandfather. What does that have to do with your news?"

"What I mean is, you can drop the stand-in. You're Jacob's father. You're my biological grandfather."

Isadora rockets toward the ceiling and her quiet sobs drift down like ghost rain.

Odell sits stock-still. Like a deer caught in the headlights or a jackrabbit listening to the approach of a predator from above.

"Please say something." I turn toward him, filled with worry and anticipation.

He chews the inside of his cheek, works his lips back and forth, and exhales.

My heart is thundering in my chest and I can't keep quiet. "I'm excited about this news. It's weird, and I don't know how my dad's gonna react, but I'm on board. I'm all for it. I want you to come to our Christmas Eve supper tomorrow night as my grandfather. Will you come?"

Odell's eyes darken and his voice is barely audible. "She's here, right?"

"That's right. She's up there, by the window. Do you want to ask her something?"

"Myrtle, we need to talk."

She flutters toward the 3 x 5 cards and picks up the pen.

His sharp intake of breath indicates any lingering doubts have vanished.

"All right. I'm gonna run next door and bring my dad up to speed. Unless you want to tell Jacob yourself?"

He shakes his head. "You do whatever you

think is best. I'm gonna need some time, kid. You just gave me a drink from a firehose."

Nodding, I get to my feet and put on my coat. "Grams, I expect you to be absolutely honest with Odell. There's nothing to hide. No more secrets. Promise?"

She clutches her pearls, and I can sense her struggling with her reply. "I'll do it, sweetie. I promise."

As I head toward the door to take my leave, Pyewacket crawls out from underneath the bed, saunters across the room, and curls up next to Odell on the settee.

"I leave you in good paws, Odell. I'm hanging out with Erick tonight, so stay as long as you like. Grams will show you how to set the main alarm when you leave. And, I hope we'll see you at supper tomorrow night."

He presses his lips together tightly, but offers no reply.

Pushing the twisted ivy medallion, I wait for the door to slide open and step into the Rare Books Loft with a wistful grin.

My dad keeps insisting we build a Frida Kahlo/Diego Rivera walkway between the third floors of our buildings, but I'm not sure I'm *that* comfortable with living next door to him. I mean, I already have to deal with the constant ghost-trusions of Grams. I don't need my mama-bear of a dad interrupting my alone time with my beau. However, Jacob and I exchanged keys not long after he remodeled the building across the alley from my bookshop. So, I let myself into the Restorative Justice Foundation and take the elevator up to the penthouse suite.

Three sets of eyes spin from the supper table when the bells pings and the doors slide open.

Amaryllis is the first to react. "Mitzy! You're just in time. I was testing out some recipes for Christmas Eve supper, and I have an absolute mountain of garlic-mashed potatoes. Can I fix you a plate?"

My brain says no, but my stomach growls loudly.

My smart aleck stepbrother apparently has the hearing of a canine. "That sounded like a yes from your belly."

Rolling my eyes, I approach the table and take the empty chair next to my dad.

The spread laid out smells wonderful, and my brain finally catches up with my stomach. I am extremely hungry. Amaryllis is an even better cook than she is a lawyer.

A moment later, she places a plate in front of me, piled high with mashed potatoes, roasted root vegetables, and a juicy slice of prime rib.

"This looks amazing! Are we having prime rib for Christmas dinner?"

She sits down, lays her napkin and across her lap, and winks. "No. But pretending we were, so I could make a *practice* recipe, was the only way to get your father to drive to Grand Falls and pick one up for me."

Jacob smiles and they share an adorable chuckle.

"So, I guess the honeymoon is still going strong over here, eh?"

Stellen guffaws and quickly covers his mouth with a napkin.

Amaryllis blushes. "Are we really that bad?"

Stellen takes a long pull of his sparkling apple cider and smiles. "You guys are adorable. I can only hope I have the chance to be as in love as you two. Although, I gotta say, I'm pleased to be away at college."

Warm laughter fills the room, and, if not for the potential dark cloud of my news, I would feel as happy as ever.

It's almost been a year since my father married this amazing woman, and they adopted Stellen. I want to believe these people are the kind who value choosing a family, and will welcome Odell with open arms, but who can predict—

Right, the psychic. Sure would be nice if my

mood ring would give me some indication of which way this news is going to land.

To be clear, the ring does nothing.

Tales of successful rehabilitants in the Restorative Justice program, hilarious college anecdotes, and even a couple Pyewacket stories occupy the rest of our supper conversation.

At the end of the meal, Stellen offers to help Amaryllis clear up, and I put a hand on my father's arm. "Can we talk? In private."

He leans close and whispers, "If Sheriff Harper knocked you up, I'll have more than a word with him."

The thought nearly chokes me, and I pound an open hand on my chest in an attempt to catch my breath. "Don't even joke about that, Dad. Do not."

His grey eyes twinkle with mischief, and a broad smile sweeps across his face. "I don't know. Would it be so bad?"

"Dad!" I punch him playfully on the shoulder.

He pushes his chair back and beckons me to follow. There's a small study between the kitchen and the hallway leading to the bedrooms. We step inside and he grips the edge of the door. "Door closed or open?"

"Closed, for now."

We share the cinnamon-brown leather sofa, and he offers me a throw blanket.

"I'm all right. Eating always warms me up."

"What's on your mind, sweetie?"

"Grams and I had a bit of a tiff, and I forced her to spill some secrets she'd hoped to take to the grave. At first I wasn't sure if I had a right to tell anyone, but I've learned the hard way that keeping secrets rarely pays off."

He nods. "Your grandmother passed away a few years ago. Are you sure this secret even needs to come out?"

"Yeah, I think it does. Because it affects people who are still alive."

His spine stiffens, and I sense that edge he earned in prison warning him of imminent danger.

"It's not bad. At least I don't think it's bad. It's just—"

"Just say it, sweetie. The longer you wait, the harder it gets."

The déjà vu of that phrase is uncanny. Here I go using that word uncanny again. "You're right. I'm just gonna rip off the bandage."

He takes my hand and looks at me with all a father's love. "I'm ready."

"Cal wasn't your biological father."

Jacob's large hand slackens its grip on mine and there's cold sweat in his palm. "What? But they were married. I was a month premature, but—"

His eyes widen as several pieces of his childhood mythos crumble before him.

"Grams didn't know she was pregnant when she married Cal. She found out right after their quickie nuptials and decided to bury the truth. From the minute she told him she was expecting, everyone believed the child was his."

Jacob sighs heavily. "So, my real— No, I don't want to say that. Cal was my real father. The biological father, or sperm donor, was someone she met in rehab?"

My dad is understandably angry, and I'm hoping the truth will be a welcome relief.

"It's Odell. Odell Johnson is your father."

He hunches forward and drops his face into his hands.

I place a comforting hand on his back and rub little circles. "I know it's a lot, Dad. But I'd be lying if I said I wasn't excited. My grandfather is alive. Your dad is alive." Images of the moment I discovered my own father was alive come rushing back, and I hope Jacob feels some fraction of that positive energy toward Odell.

When he lifts his head, tears are streaming down his cheeks. "I missed out on the first twenty-one years of your life, Mitzy. I thought no one could possibly know how that feels. But Odell has missed more than twice that many years of mine."

Throwing my arms around him, I hug him tight. "But he didn't, Dad. He was here the whole time. Odell was at your games, at community events, and he went to your high school graduation. He may have thought he was going because he was secretly still in love with Isadora, but, whatever the reason, he was there."

Jacob shakes with silent sobs, and I hold on to him and squeeze tighter. Several minutes pass before he disengages, wipes his face with his hands, and lets out a loud exhale. "Whew! We'll sure have something to talk about at that Christmas Eve supper!"

I bite my bottom lip and sit back.

"What? What did you do, Mitzy?"

"Oh, I invited Odell before I knew. And I re-invited him after I found out. But, I also told him about Grams."

"Oh boy, she's not going to be happy about that." Jacob snuffles and shakes his head. "Wow, honey. You've been a busy little elf."

"You mean, she *wasn't* happy about that. I told him, then I brought him up to the apartment, and I left them alone with a stack of 3 x 5 cards and a pen."

Relieved laughter shakes my father's barrel chest. "That's my girl. Well, I suppose we better break the news to the rest of the family."

Warmth spreads from my heart out to the tips of my fingers and toes. *The rest of the family.* I can't tell you how many times I sat in a social worker's office or a foster home, dreaming that there was a family out there somewhere that wanted me. My own family, that would love me and accept me, and maybe even buy me new clothes. Grams certainly has the clothing part covered!

My dad stands beside me, slowly waving a hand in front of my face. "Looks like I lost you. Are you coming with me for this dog-and-pony show or am I on my own?"

"Sorry, I was thinking about how lucky I am to have a family at all. And the fact that it's expanding . . . Bonus!"

He helps me up from the couch and swallows loudly. "I see it that way too, sweetie. If Cal was still alive, this might be more difficult to manage. But, as usual, your timing is exquisite."

I take a mock curtsy and follow him to the living room with a smile nearly splitting my face in two.

WHEN JACOB and I emerge from the study, Amaryllis meets us with freshly topped up champagne flutes. "You're just in time! I want to make a toast."

My dad slips an arm around my shoulders and winks.

Amaryllis tosses her red-brown locks and raises her crystal ware. "To the best family I could have ever hoped to be part of, and to my favorite season of the year. Merry Christmas to my favorite husband, my favorite daughter, and my favorite son!"

We all clink glasses and take a sip of our champagne. Before Amaryllis can retire to the sofa, my father picks up where she left off. "I'd like to add to that."

Flecks of gold and green brighten her brown eyes and her smile sparkles.

Jacob inhales deeply and lifts his glass. "I'd like to make a toast to finding an amazing woman, who I surely don't deserve. And I'd like to make an additional toast to my snoopy daughter uncovering a wonderful family secret."

He moves to clink his glass to ours, but Amaryllis pulls her champagne back and wags a finger at him. "Oh, no you don't, Snugglebear. No one's acknowledging that toast until you spill the secret."

And now his wink makes perfect sense. Not only has he picked the right moment, but also, he's actually forced his audience to beg for the reveal. Maybe I get some of my smarts from him as well as my brilliant mama.

Jacob lifts his glass again and continues. "Turns out, Odell Johnson is my biological father. So here's to dads of all shapes, sizes, and origins. I've been blessed to have not one, but two great ones."

Before we can clink glasses, Stellen raises his higher and adds, "Me too."

Well, there's not a dry eye in the house when our glasses clink a second time.

And when Erick calls to tell me he's sorry he had to work late and can't cook for me, and can't pick up dinner because the diner is closed, I cry so hard I can't make the words. I'm trying to explain that I'm the reason the diner is closed, but—

My kind father gently takes my phone and invites Erick over for leftovers and an explanation.

A few minutes later, Erick shows up, concerned and confused.

But after Amaryllis fills his belly with her glorious food, and I work my way through half a box of tissue replaying the evening's emotional scenes, Erick is satisfied, in all the ways that matter.

We say our goodbyes and head back to his mom-free house. I won't bore you with the long list of things I love about Erick, but I'm definitely going to point out one of the top three.

This man has a heart the size of Texas, and even though we hardly ever have time to ourselves, he chooses to light a fire in his fireplace, make me a cup of cocoa, and snuggle up next to me on the sofa while I watch old Christmas classics and cry my eyes out.

"It's official, Erick Harper, you've earned yourself the 'Boyfriend of the Year' award. Now, the competition may be stiffer next year, so you might want to step up your game. However, for this year, you're a lock."

He removes the box of tissue from my lap, wipes a thumb across my cheek to remove a straggling tear, and envelops me in his safe, warm arms.

I'd be lying if I said things didn't take a delightfully romantic turn, but there's no need to kiss and tell.

When the early morning sun breaks through his thin drapes, I have high hopes for a lazy breakfast and multiple cups of coffee.

Sheriff Harper has other plans. As he leans over to kiss me goodbye, already in his freshly pressed uniform, my heart sinks.

"Don't look so disappointed, Moon. There's sure to be a Christmas Eve encore." He winks.

My skin tingles underneath his old college sweatshirt. "Copy that."

His mouth may be saying he has to go to work, but his kiss is absolutely telling me he'd rather not.

"I'll see you for the big holiday supper tonight. Be careful out there, Sheriff."

Erick lunges at me, slips a hand under the covers, and tickles me mercilessly. "You be careful in here, Moon."

One last inhale of his citrus-woodsy scent and I collapse onto the pillow as he struts from the room and calls out a final warning. "No peeking at presents. And no *hunches*!"

"Cross my heart."

Everyone's working so hard to put our relationship on the fast track, but in moments like these, everything feels exactly as it should be.

Perfect.

Although, I can't believe he left me to my own devices for brekkie.

My skills in the kitchen produce one adequate pot of coffee and a measly bowl of cold cereal.

Myrtle's Diner is closed for the holiday. In fact, they shutter all eateries in town for at least the next two days.

Mmmmm. Cereal. Crunch. Crunch.

I wonder if—

Blerg. I gotta get out of this house or I can't be held responsible for what might happen to the prezzies under our no-tree.

The streets of Pin Cherry are oddly quiet, and grey clouds hang heavy over the great lake.

"Looks like snow." A phrase commonly heard around town. I'm fortunate to have a short commute to my holiday festivities this evening.

As I muse over my growing family, my heart goes out to Miss Tremblay, who will spend this Christmas alone. To be fair, Norma Olsen will probably spend the holiday alone too, since Niklas is sitting in a holding cell. However, I'm having trouble finding sympathy for that piece of the puzzle.

The bookshop looks inviting, despite the brewing storm, and I can't wait to put the finishing touches on Erick's present.

No sooner have I "put a bow on it" than—
BING. BONG. BING.

"Who could that be?"

Pye's uninterested grunt is my only reply.

Racing down the stairs, I open the door to a fabulous surprise. "What are you doing here?"

Erick dips his head in that way that insinuates he's doffing a cap and grins. "It's not that I don't trust you—"

"Hey, I'm not sure I like the way this is heading."

He scoops his arms around me, plants an eager smooch on my lips, and starts over. "What I meant to say is that I can't wait to give you your present. Plus, I think it makes more logistical sense to give it to you now, so you can tell everyone at supper."

My mood ring isn't offering any hints, but my tummy is tumbling like a load of laundry in a commercial dryer. I might panic. I'm not ready—

"Moon, are you going to invite me in, or do you want to open it in the middle of the alley?" His words are playful, but there seems to be some nervous concern lurking behind his eyes.

"Oh, right! Come in. I'll run up and grab yours. Be right back."

His mouth drops open, but I make my escape before he can protest.

My hair is still ninety-percent bedhead and I'm

wearing jeans and a tee. Is this the outfit I want to be wearing when it happens? If Grams— Get a hold of yourself, Moon.

Smacking myself firmly on the forehead, I pick up his brightly wrapped package, take a deep breath, and head out to the loft.

Erick is kneeling on the Persian rug, and I think my heart stopped beating!

"Wait! I'm not ready. I mean, I think it's what I want, but—"

He stands and scrunches up his face. "You're not ready for a present? How do you know if you want it? You don't know what it—"

I stop a couple paces from him and our eyes meet.

He looks at my face, glances back toward the floor, and points to the spot where he was kneeling. "Whoa! Did you think— Is that what you want?"

Rushing forward, I drop his gift on an oak reading table and wrap my arms around him. "Everyone keeps talking about next steps, and grandkids, and I kinda panicked."

He kisses the top of my head. "We're in charge of this relationship, Mitzy. We get to decide what next step feels right. I know surprise proposals are super romantic, but I'm not a gambling kind of guy. When—notice I'm not saying *if* —when we get there, we'll both know it's time."

I loosen my arms and tilt my head back.

His warm, blue eyes are brimming with love.

"Yeah. We're in charge. I like the sound of that."

Erick kisses me softly and whispers, "Do you want your present or not?"

Shoving the red-and-green package I just finished wrapping at him, I stall. "You first."

He tears the paper, opens the box, and laughs. "You got me a gun?"

Pointing at the weapon, I clarify. "I'm giving you my gun, or, rather, the gun I obtained. Pye and Grams insisted I get rid of it, and Silas said the Yule fire wasn't—"

His lips are on mine, and the rest of my speech evaporates. "Thanks, Moon. This is the nicest thing you could've possibly given me."

"Really? You like it?"

He chuckles. "It's no engagement ring, but it's a good next step."

"Touché."

His hand brushes mine and he passes me an envelope.

Schooling my features, I prepare to act like a gift card is a thoughtful gift. I paste on a smile, loosen the flap of the envelope, and slide out the card.

He's holding his breath as I read the inscription.

"Families and memories go hand in hand. Love

you, Erick." I take the folded paper gift certificate from the card and smooth it open. "Oh, Erick!" Cue the waterworks!

His strong arms are around me in a flash. "I didn't want to tempt fate, but I figured once the initial shock wore off, your dad would be okay with the Odell situation. I thought maybe you'd like to get a family picture with your whole family. You know . . ."

"Thank you! This is such a wonderful idea. Pictures mean so much to me, since I lost all those memories in the foster system. Now I have a new, and expanding, family, and I can't wait to get some foolish pictures in matching sweaters—or some such nonsense."

Erick smiles. "You're welcome. And, I gotta get back to work if I plan to finish in time to make this supper gig." His lips brush my cheek and he heads down the spiral staircase.

Leaning over the thick banister, I call after him. "I'm calling next year's race. Erick Harper, 'Best Boyfriend' two years running!"

He chuckles, and the alley door thunks closed behind him.

And to think, I used to loathe the holidays.

CHAPTER 21

I'M NOT certain what sort of magic Amaryllis is working in the kitchen next door, but I swear I can smell the delicious aromas wafting across the alley.

With no one to distract me, this day threatens to be the longest in history.

My morning started far too early because of Erick racing off to work to complete all the reports surrounding the Carol Olsen homicide. And, despite the brief shimmering moment of perfection when we exchanged gifts, the ticking of the metaphorical clock is driving me mad.

Now, I'm lounging around my apartment hoping Grams forgives me for sharing her ghostly existence with her first husband, or at least appears to offer me some company and conversation.

But it's almost noon, and there's no sign of her.

Christmas Eve supper is scheduled for 5:30 p.m. sharp.

"When all else fails, it's time for the impossible."

Pyewacket is unimpressed with my announcement and flops a paw over his head to block my needy pontifications.

I toss on skinny jeans and a T-shirt that pictures a stack of books and reads "Never judge a book by its movie," and head next door.

When the elevator pings and the doors slide open, my father and Stellen look at me with desperation widening their eyes, while Amaryllis is as cheery as ever. "Mitzy! Come on in. I can always use an extra pair of hands in the kitchen."

Quickly taking in the scene, I wink at the boys. "Do you think we can get rid of these two? I was hoping we could have a little girl time."

She stops in the middle of the kitchen and wells up with emotion. "Oh, Mitzy, that would be so wonderful." Picking up a dishtowel, she flicks it at my father's behind. "You get on out of here. I'm sure you and Stellen can find a car to work on or a gun to clean. Leave this meal preparation to the women."

I'm not entirely sure I agree with her gender stereotypes, but when I see the look of relief on my father's face and receive a thankful finger gun from my stepbrother, I'm happy to take one for the team.

"Do you need an apron?" She adjusts her red-brown curls and tightens her high-pony.

No one has ever asked me that question in the kitchen in my lifetime. "I don't think so. And I should probably offer you fair warning. I'm not great in the kitchen. I heat things up in a microwave, I make a decent cup of coffee, and that's pretty much where the list ends."

Slipping an arm around my shoulders, she hugs me conspiratorially. "Nonsense. You're smart as a whip. I'll have you ready for *The Great British Baking Show* in no time!"

Yeesh. This woman is going to suffer the disappointment of a lifetime today.

"I'll let you work on the mince pies. Just cut the butter into the flour, to form a crumbly meal, and then press it into a ball. We'll need to let that refrigerate while you work on the filling."

My feet remain firmly planted in the middle of the kitchen.

Amaryllis notices my lack of motion and tilts her head to the side. "Have you never made piecrust, dear?"

Scrunching up my face, I avoid the question. "I can pick a lock with my eyes closed, I can hot-wire a car, and I can lift a wallet without drawing attention nine times out of ten."

She rushes across the kitchen and envelops me in a motherly embrace. "I'm so sorry, Mitzy. How stupid of me. Here I was planning this whole British Christmas supper menu in honor of your mother, and it never occurred to me that she died before she had a chance to pass on her knowledge of cooking."

Far be it from me to break the news to Amaryllis that my mother was no chef. She was indeed British, and she kept my belly full, by hook or by crook, every day until she left this earth, but she was no Mary Berry. "Don't worry about it. I never had much use for cooking. The other skills have served me a lot better over the years, but I suppose I should figure out how to make dinner for Erick at least once."

Loosening her arms, she grips both of my hands tightly. "Oh, Mitzy. You two make the most adorable couple! I just want things to work out. Is it wrong of me to hope for an engagement? Of course, not right now. But maybe next year? He's just the most wonderful guy. And I see in his face how much he loves you."

Boy, this woman is not one to hide her emotions. If I tell her about the kerfuffle that just went down in the Rare Books Loft, she will faint.

"Things are really great between us. And I'm happy with the speed at which the relationship is moving. I'm not going to jinx anything by making wishes or promises."

She shakes my hands up and down before releasing them. "Good point. Good point. Never look a gift horse in the mouth, my mother used to say."

Amaryllis gestures sweepingly to her well-appointed kitchen. "Today is cooking 101. I'm going to teach you all the basics, and when we sit down to supper with the family, I hope you feel as good as I do about making a wonderful meal for people you love."

"I hope so too." Secretly, I'm not sure what I hope, but I know that I don't plan to spend an entire day in the kitchen and have people regret it. So it's time to put on my pay-attention hat and make my moves count.

This woman is so organized it's a little frightening.

"Here's the menu. We're having roast turkey and cranberry-glazed ham. I know I should have simply picked one, but the leftovers last forever, and who isn't going to like more options?"

Sensing this is a rhetorical question, I keep my thoughts to myself.

"Then we'll have oven-roasted red potatoes, and —I had a hard time deciding on the stuffing—but I think I'm going to go with rye bread croutons and my sage and onion recipe. That seems like it will go nicely with turkey or ham."

Again, I don't feel my input is necessary.

"We're definitely making pigs in blankets and Yorkshire pudding. I know those are super popular in Great Britain. I'm sure your mother made them for you."

I seem to remember some kind of swine in a coverlet, but, if memory serves, they were hot dogs wrapped in ready-made dough from a can. Based on the swanky level of ingredients I see displayed on the counter, I don't think that's where Amaryllis is going.

"Of course, there will be gravy, cranberry sauce, and Brussels sprouts roasted with bacon! I know people have very strong opinions about Brussels sprouts, but trust me, this preparation is fabulous."

Just like my mom taught me, I nod and smile.

"And for dessert, we'll have Christmas pudding and mince pies. I couldn't decide between a traditional Christmas pudding or a figgy pudding, but when I was at the grocery store looking for ingredients, they didn't have any figs that met my standards, so I went with the Christmas pudding. That's already finished and soaking in brandy. I'm going to light it on fire when I serve it!"

Dear Lord baby Jesus! I didn't realize I would need utensils and a fire extinguisher for this meal.

"And last but not least, the mince pies. Maybe I already said that? Anyway, I think we might serve that with vanilla ice cream for anyone who's interested. What do you think?"

The habit of not answering sort of took over, and I fail to respond.

"Mitzy? Did I overwhelm you? Let's just take it one step at a time. By the end of the day you'll be surprised how much you've accomplished and how easy it really is."

"Copy that." I suppose I only have her word to take for it.

After doing as much damage as Amaryllis could accommodate in her kitchen, I hustle back to my apartment to endure Ghost-ma's wardrobe selection.

"Grams? Grams?"

Pyewacket allows his large head to loll off the side of the bed and stares through disinterested, upside-down golden eyes.

"Where's Grams? I haven't seen her since she and Odell— Well, you know."

He squeezes his eyelids closed and offers a complacent, "Reow." Can confirm.

Once more, with feeling. "Grams, I know you're upset with me, and I'm sorry that I spilled your ghostly beans to Odell. But the man is my grandfather! He deserves to be a part of our family, and I know we can trust him with our secrets. I hope you'll embrace the spirit of the season and forgive me. But in the meantime it looks like I'll have to pick out my own holiday outfit."

If that sentiment doesn't bring her ghost blasting through a wall, then I'm all out of options.

No ghost. No blasting.

However, the upside is I won't be teetering across the icy alley in a five-inch pair of Manolo Blahniks!

No sooner have the words formed in my mind than Myrtle Isadora snaps to life right in front of me.

"Yikes! You haven't scared me like that in quite a while."

A smug look curves one side of her mouth. "You deserve more than a fright. You had no right!"

"Are we speaking in rhymes now? Am I to sing my plea somehow?"

She floats toward me and her semi-corporeal fingers brush my cheek. "I can never stay mad at you. I do wish you had talked to me before you dragged Odell into this, but I'm glad he knows about you—and Jacob."

Due to my extreme maturity, I stop myself from chanting "told you so." Of course, simply thinking it means that Ghost-ma already got the message.

"Don't be a sore winner, Mizithra."

"I love you, Grams. And I'm glad you trusted me with the information, and I promise to be less impulsive in the future."

She hoots and hollers like a guest star on *Hee Haw* and slaps her ring-adorned hand on her designer gown. "You should take that show on the road, dear." Regaining her composure, she circles the massive closet, tapping a finger on her lip. "Let's see. What goes with the six-inch Jimmy Choo platforms?"

"Isadora! If you have any hope of having great-grandchildren, you better keep me in a shoe that won't kill me when I try to walk across the alley."

She stops, turns, and clutches her pearls. "What did you say? Did he ask? Let me see the ring!"

"Down, ghost, down. Like I've said more times than I can count, to more people than I care to mention, Erick and I have a wonderful relationship that is moving at the perfect pace. Do not pressure me. However, if you would like to win some potential great-ghost-mother brownie points, find me a two-inch heel."

The mere mention of great-grandchildren has her bubbling with excitement. No fewer than ten different outfits are tossed upon the padded mahogany bench.

Considering the brisk weather, I negotiate for a tailored pair of lined, grey wool pants and a refined, understated holiday sweater. This is not the kind of sweater that's going to win any hilarious contests. This is an elegant celebration of the season.

Once I switch into the new outfit, Grams insists I freshen my makeup and do something about my hair.

"Well, you can't wear a sophisticated outfit like that when your hair looks like something the cat dragged in."

"Reeeee-ow." A warning.

My eyes widen, and I shake a finger at Grams. "You better be careful. Thou shalt not take thy royal feline's name in vain!"

She chuckles and drifts off to scratch her ethereal fingers between Pyewacket's black-tufted ears.

A twist here and there with my styling wand and a spritz or three of hairspray, and I'm presentable.

"I'm sorry you can't come to Christmas Eve supper, but at least you're not spending it in a jail cell like Niklas Olsen."

Grams floats toward the window and her silly mood turns somber. "Tell everyone I wished them a Happy Christmas."

"A Happy Christmas? Are you British now? Before you answer that, I must inform you that Amaryllis planned the entire menu around traditional British dishes because she was sure that's what my mother would've served me."

Isadora presses a hand to her ample bosom. "Oh, that woman is absolutely the sweetest thing. I hope you didn't tell her your mother wasn't a cook."

"I didn't. Believe it or not, I've learned a thing or two about etiquette from a certain uppity ghost."

Before she can complete her retort, I slip out of the apartment, race down the stairs—even risking a holiday hop over the chain at the bottom of the staircase.

St. Nick smiles upon me, and I land safely on the ground floor.

When the elevator delivers me to the penthouse suite, the festive table is set with my stepmother's exquisite flair, and pretty much everyone has arrived. Twiggy and Wayne took a rain check and hopped on a plane to Mexico. They'd had quite enough of the weather and the murder accusations.

Silas, clad in an uncharacteristic green-and-red sweater vest, is braving winter's chill on the back deck with Stellen. They're deep in conversation as they puff on their cigars. You don't have to be psychic to see that my stepbrother, despite giving it the old college try, is green around the gills.

Boisterous voices in the den alert me to Erick's arrival. He and my father seem to be having an animated discussion of some sports team's something or other. Before I report to the kitchen for whatever duties Amaryllis has planned, I poke my head in and pass on Isadora's message. "She said to wish you all a Happy Christmas."

Jacob tilts his head. "So she's British now?"

I shrug. "This is what I'm saying. I think she must have an afterlife sense of smell that somehow helped her decipher this 'all UK' menu. She wishes she could be here, and that's her way of butting in, I suppose."

Erick leans back, cups a hand over his mouth, and whispers to my father. "Must run in the family."

Instantly planting a fist on my hip, I narrow my gaze. "I heard that, *Ricky*. I'd step lightly if I were you. Your mother has told me a few juicy tidbits that I don't think you would like me to share at dinner."

The sound of his mother's pet name for him, and my thinly veiled threat, do the trick.

He sits up straighter and nods comically. "Whatever you say, Miss Moon."

Jacob chuckles. "That's a smart man."

Following my stepmother's orders like a ready-made Stepford wife, I deliver all the lovely dishes to the table, and round up the menfolk.

Lively conversation and cross talk abound as we pass the delicious dishes around the table.

When the elevator pings, almost no one notices. No one but me.

Odell Johnson steps into the penthouse with hesitant discomfort. His grey buzz cut glistens with a hint of some type of hair product, and replacing his well-worn denim shirt is a red-and-green plaid flannel button-up that looks brand-new.

Nearly spilling the roasted Brussels sprouts with bacon, I shove my chair back and get to my feet. "Odell!"

A hush falls over the room, and all heads turn.

He swallows, and his Adam's apple makes a visible struggle of it. "I brought a pie. Hope that's okay."

As I take a step toward the door, my father pushes his chair back and motions for me to sit down.

No one speaks. Platters of food seem to hover in midair.

Jacob approaches the man who simply used to hold the title of one of Isadora's ex-husbands and local diner owner, and nods toward the counter.

Odell places the pie on the granite surface and waits for further instruction.

My father's hands are shoved deep in his pockets. Their voices are low, and my normal sense of hearing can't pick up the details. At least I know enough to avoid invading their privacy with my extra senses.

Heads nod, shoulders shrug, and finally my father offers his hand to the man who gave him life.

Odell grips my father's hand and fights to keep his emotions buried behind his well-lined face.

Jacob lifts his other hand, pats Odell on the back, and gestures to the empty seat between Stellen and me.

I don't possess the subdued talents of my father or grandfather. When Odell gets near the table, I launch myself at him, wrap my arms around his neck and squeeze. "Let me know when you're ready for me to start calling you Gramps."

My silly comment does the trick, and a warm chuckle escapes as his shoulders relax.

He holds my chair for me and then takes a seat.

The platters resume their circuit, and everyone's plate is overflowing with holiday fare.

Silas and Amaryllis valiantly keep the conversation light and flowing until chairs are pushed back from the table and we rub our full bellies.

Seems like the perfect time for a break. I tap

Odell on the back and motion for him to follow me. We step toward the bank of windows that face my apartment across the alley. I've never tried to send Grams a message from this sort of distance, at least not with any success. But here goes. *Isadora, if you can hear me, please come to the window and wave a 3 x 5 card at us, so Odell knows you're there.*

To his credit, he waits patiently beside me without making a sound.

Just when I think my efforts are in vain, a small index card appears in the window, sliding back and forth, displaying a beautiful heart-shape drawn by my grandmother.

Odell sniffles and wipes a weathered thumb under each eye. "Like I said, best Christmas present ever."

He slips an arm around my shoulders and I lean my head toward him. "You're welcome, Gramps."

End of Book 16

~A NOTE FROM TRIXIE

Woot! Odell is finally in the inner circle—and another case solved! I'll keep writing them if you keep reading . . .

The best part of "living" in Pin Cherry Harbor continues to be feedback from my early readers. Thank you to my alpha readers/cheerleaders, Angel and Michael. HUGE thanks to my fantastic beta readers who continue to give me extremely useful and honest feedback: Veronica McIntyre and Nadine Peterse-Vrijhof. And big "small town" hugs to the world's best ARC Team – Trixie's Mystery ARC Detectives!

I always appreciate the insightful edits of my no-nonsense editor Philip Newey. I'd also like to give a heaping helping of gratitude to Brooke for her tireless proofreading! (Despite her busy schedule.) Any errors are my own.

I'm especially grateful for the helpful guns, silencers, and ammunition info provided by Morgan.

FUN FACT: I have had the pleasure of picking and cutting my own Yule tree more than ten times! Full disclosure, several of those trips involved lengthy snowball fights.

My favorite line from this case: "For the record, it's a cover story, not a secret identity. I'm a snoop, not a superhero." ~Mitzy

I'm currently writing book seventeen in the Mitzy Moon Mysteries series, and I think I may just live in Pin Cherry Harbor forever. Mitzy, Grams, and Pyewacket got into plenty of trouble in book one, *Fries and Alibis*. But I'd have to say that book three, *Wings and Broken Things*, is when most readers say the series becomes unputdownable.

I hope you'll continue to hang out with us.

Trixie Silvertale (November 2021)

PARANORMAL COZY MYSTERY

Dangers & Empty Mangers

TRIXIE SILVERTALE

Sittin' On A Goldmine
Productions L.L.C.

CHAPTER 1

I'M HAVING what some might call a unicorn moment. Now, that may sound magical and unique, but, honestly, it's just abnormal and a little irritating. The unicorn, on this day, is standing in a queue. I know it doesn't sound like much, but, trust me, it has never happened to me since my arrival in Pin Cherry Harbor.

Oh sure, back in Sedona, Arizona, I used to have to stand in lines for all sorts of reasons. I would find myself waiting in a line at the checkout lane in a grocery store while a hapless tourist prattled on about their amazing experience at the whatchamacallit vortex.

Or perhaps I'd wait in a queue to pay for my gas as an old-timey local counted out dimes from their leather satchel to pay for a lottery ticket.

And let's not forget the joy of standing in line at the post . . . Oh, wait! Now I'm just making things up. I've never seen the inside of a post office in my life!

Honestly, though, I've never had to wait in a line for anything since I rode inside a smelly bus for nearly two days to arrive in almost-Canada and claim my inheritance.

Which leads me to my reason for standing in this abnormal line. This morning my grandmother and I—and, to be clear, that would be the ghost of my grandmother, which is tethered to the bookshop she left me in her will—were having a discussion about how much my life has changed. I talked about how fantastic it's been getting to know the father I thought dead, and how much better it is to have money than be trapped in either a poorly run foster home, or a dead-end barista job.

The foster system wasn't all bad, but it was mostly bad. There were a few good families in the mix, though. Foster mom number four really taught me to embrace my differences and appreciate the legacy of tenacious independence my mother left when she was taken from me so tragically. It's hard to lose a mother at any age, but for an eleven-year-old only child, discovering you're an orphan feels like the world stops spinning and kicks you into outer space just for fun.

What was I talking about? Oh, right. Standing in line.

The morning's wardrobe-related discussion with Ghost-ma uncovered a piece of her precious couture she can't remember picking up from the dry cleaner before she died.

Her exact words were, "Mitzy! This is serious! That Vivienne Westwood Worlds End Black 'Witches' Trench Coat is like one of my children! You have to rush over to the cleaners this instant. No one is getting a wink of sleep until I know it's safe."

So here I am, standing in line at said dry cleaners. A line of three people, which I can assure you, is unheard of at this latitude.

Each time Tanya disappears into the back to retrieve items of clothing, she stirs the atmosphere and a fresh wave of chemically impregnated air wafts over me. Ew.

Finally reaching the front of the queue feels like winning a marathon. Or, rather, what I imagine it would feel like to win a marathon, as I've never run more than a block or two in my entire life.

"Good morning, Tanya. I'm looking for a very special Vivienne Westwood coat my grandmother thinks she left here." As soon as the words are out of my mouth, I realize my mistake. "I mean, her will mentioned she left here." Lame save, but at least I tried.

The woman peers over the top of her half-moon readers. "Isadora passed almost three years ago. You can't be serious?" Her straight grey locks barely move as she shakes her head and rolls her wide-set eyes.

My heart sinks. "It was really special to her. Can you check?" It's also worth a small fortune, but I don't want to mention that.

The proprietor returns pretty quickly, and shakes her head a second time. This one comes with a scoop of silent "I told you so."

"Thanks for checking." I smile, nod, and exit. Well, I better embellish the bejeezus out of that search when I tell Grams the story.

Outside Harbor Cleaners, the endless winter has our tiny town in its grip. Last night I had to snuggle my uncooperative caracal underneath two thick down comforters to keep from freezing to death.

Before I make the run to my Jeep, I tug my stocking hat down over my snow-white hair, turn up the collar of my puffy jacket, and shove my hands into thick woolen mittens.

Pushing open the door, I jog for the Jeep. I can't risk an out-and-out run, due to hidden patches of ice lurking beneath the poorly shoveled sidewalk. I'm not exactly what one would call *coordinated*.

Ecstatic that I've made it to the vehicle and still manage to reside on my feet, I yank open the door and hop inside.

It's not warmer; it's just not as windy. And windchill can be deadly.

Poking the key into the ignition results in a fat load of nothing. There's a strange whine and a click, but there's no vroom vroom.

Cars are not my thing.

My father is out of town with his new wife on an important business trip, securing much-needed donations for the Duncan Restorative Justice Foundation.

Hmmmm. Hopefully, this is one of those boyfriend-to-the-rescue scenarios. Shivering as I remove a glove and hit the speed dial for Sheriff Erick Harper, I opt for speaker and try to keep my teeth from chattering.

His deep voice warms me. "Hey, I was just about to text and see if you were interested in an early lunch at the diner."

"I'd give you my great minds speech, but I'm currently stranded outside the dry cleaners and my blasted Jeep won't start."

Sheriff Too-Hot-To-Handle launches into action. "I'll be there in ninety seconds. Don't do anything foolish."

The call ends before I have a chance to express how rude it is for him to assume that I would do something foolish. However, my reputation precedes.

While I wait for my knight in shining polyester to navigate the three blocks from the sheriff's station, I engage in a silent argument with my stomach.

"The patisserie is right around the corner. I could dash over to Bless Choux and grab coffee and a chocolate croissant." My tummy growls with encouragement. "But I'd likely freeze to death and poor Erick would find nothing but a broken down vehicle and a frozen human statue of his former girlfriend." A sharp pain stabs in my gut.

Before the internal battle can continue, the local sheriff arrives Code 3. For you civilians, that means lights flashing and sirens blaring! Yeesh. I'm sure he was concerned for the safety of his citizens, but now I feel like a real putz. Luckily, I'm about to be severely distracted.

Tall, blond, and ruggedly handsome Sheriff Harper hops out of his cruiser, tugs at the flaps of his deerstalker hat, and eases open my driver's side door. "At your service, Miss Moon. Would you like to take care of the abandoned vehicle first or head straight to the diner?" His smirk indicates he already knows the answer.

"I would prefer to go directly to the diner. In fact, I'm strongly considering abandoning the vehicle permanently."

He offers me a hand and I step out of the Jeep, gripping his arm with the claws of death as he guides me back to his car.

Not for the first time, I'm pleased to be getting in the front seat of a police vehicle.

"You know there's a fine for abandoned vehicles, Moon. I recommend you call a tow truck and have your vehicle properly processed at the junkyard."

You guessed it, properly processed gives me the giggles. "Ever since my car got hot-wired, it's been giving me nothing but trouble. The headlights go dark for no reason, the radio cuts out every time I go over a bump, and the windshield wipers only have one speed—psycho fast. There's no way I'm taking that thing home. I'll call a tow truck."

He dips his head in that way that insinuates he's doffing a cap, and jogs around the front of the vehicle. Even in a heavy winter coat, that man can melt my heart.

"What were you doing at the cleaners? Actually, what were you doing out and about so *early* in the first place?"

"Hilarious. I do plenty of stuff before 10:00 a.m."

"I'm sure you do. But you do realize it's almost 11:30, right?"

I actually had no idea it was that late in the morning, but I'm not going to give him the satisfaction of finding out. "Of course. That's why I'm so ready for lunch."

He chuckles, and his big blue eyes sparkle. "Oh, that's why, is it?"

"Hilarious, Sheriff Smarty-Pants."

His soft kiss on my lips prevents any further debate.

Should I tell him about the coat? He's not into designer fashion and he definitely won't understand Ghost-ma's obsession with a single piece. Plus he might tease me about running errands for apparitions, and he already has enough ammo.

"Moon? Moon, where'd you go?"

Whoops! That would be me getting all wrapped up in my mind movies and forgetting about reality. "Nowhere special. Definitely nowhere as great as Myrtle's Diner."

My favorite local haunt is a quaint diner named after my grandmother. Her original name, that is. She goes by Isadora now, but when she was married to her first husband Odell Johnson, they opened the diner together.

I recently discovered that Odell Johnson is my father's biological dad and my actual grandfather. So despite the fact that I spent over six years in the foster system in Arizona, believing I was an orphan, my family continues to grow by leaps and bounds the longer I hang out in Pin Cherry Harbor.

Erick parks in front of the sheriff's station and escorts me into the diner.

Warmth and welcome envelop us as we stamp off our winter footwear on the doormat and slide into our favorite booth.

Waitress extraordinaire, Tally, greets us with two steaming mugs of java. Her flame-red hair twists into a tight topknot, as usual, and her ready smile makes us feel like family.

I glance toward the orders-up window and my grandpa offers us his standard spatula salute through the red-Formica-trimmed opening.

Sheriff Harper removes his coat and places it on the red-vinyl bench seat. "So what were you doing at Harbor Cleaners?"

"Oh, right." Pasting on a smile, I take a deep breath and hope for the best. "Grams suddenly remembered a special couture coat she left there a few years ago."

Erick nods, walks his hand across the table, and turns his palm up. I slip my hand in his before I continue.

"Tanya was obviously annoyed with my 'years too late' request."

He smiles as he glides his thumb along the back of my hand. "Success?"

"Negatory, good buddy. The coat was long gone. Grams will be devastated. I'd say that I don't care, but she'll probably make me search the world for a replacement. Hooray. So, I care, but not about the coat." We share a chuckle at Myrtle Isadora's expense.

Odell Johnson approaches the table, and the luscious aromas of our breakfasts waft toward us. I love that he always knows what his customers want. It's nice to be somewhere that feels so comfortable.

He places my standard chorizo and scrambled eggs with a side of golden home fries in front of me, and Erick gets a lovely stack of blueberry pancakes.

I open my mouth to request—

Odell retrieves a bottle of Tabasco sauce from his back pocket and sets it down before I can even begin to ask.

"Thanks, Gramps. You're the best."

He runs a weathered hand through his utilitarian grey buzz cut and clears his throat to hide his emotions. "It may take me some time to get used to that."

"Don't worry, I'll say it as often as possible, Gramps. Maybe we can cut that time in half."

He chuckles and raps his knuckles twice on the silver-flecked Formica table.

Rather than returning to the grill, he grabs the local paper from the counter, heads back to our table, and tosses it in front of me. "I figured you'd get a kick out of the headline."

He saunters toward the kitchen with no further explanation.

I glance at the photo of the First Methodist Church's Nativity scene and notice a strange anomaly. That's when my eyes are drawn to the headline "Where is God?"

My mouth falls open and, as my mischievous grey eyes catch Erick's, we both point at the image of the empty manger beneath the clever header and laugh out loud.

"I'd have to say Quince Knudsen hasn't headed back to college yet. The patriarch of the Knudsen clan did not write that headline. Quince's father is far too verbose, and worried about his newspaper's reputation, to come up with a pithy header like that."

Erick nods in agreement. "It's such a minor theft, I hate to lose any manpower looking into it. Would you mind?"

For a moment, I feel like I'm in one of those movie scenes where the camera pulls back rapidly and the room around the main character shrinks into the distance. And, as a film school dropout, I know what I'm talking about. "Did I hear you correctly? Are you officially hiring me for a case?"

He grins and shoves a maple-syrup-dripping bite of blueberry pancakes into his mouth.

I wait impatiently while he politely chews before answering.

"Not official. It's more like a boyfriend asking a girlfriend for a favor."

"Oh, in that case, I'm definitely too busy."

His jaw drops and his eyes widen. "Seriously?"

"Gotcha. Of course I'll look into it. I would've looked into it whether or not you asked me. The photo alone is enough to get my attention. Quince has got skills."

CHAPTER 2

Since I'm doing a girlfriend favor by looking into the missing baby Jesus from the First Methodist Church's manger, Erick is doing a boyfriend thing by taking care of my abandoned vehicle.

I have to get a new winter vehicle, though. I absolutely can't drive my grandmother's 1957 Mercedes 300SL on salted roads in blizzard conditions. In the meantime, I'm sure my dad won't mind if I borrow his truck while he's away.

Once I get my wheels sorted, my first stop is the office of the *Pin Cherry Harbor Post*. If, as I suspect, Quince Knudsen is still in town, he's my best lead. Not that he'll give up the information for free, but once I toss a little cabbage his way, the info should flow.

As soon as I enter the old brick building, which

houses the local paper, I can smell the ink. It always reminds me of my bookshop, but in a raw, straight-to-the-source kind of way. I approach the birch-clad reception area and walk straight past the bell, which squats below a sign instructing me to ring it.

I do not.

Instead, I head into the room behind the desk and find my quarry.

Quince twists from side to side in a dilapidated office chair as his fingers tap furiously on an ancient keyboard.

"Hey, when do you head back to Columbia?"

"Two weeks."

Welcome to Conversational Skills 101 with Quincy "Quince" Knudsen. This kid is a flipping genius with a 35mm camera, but he can't be bothered to put more than three words together in casual conversation.

"Got it. Did you take the empty manger pic?"

"Yah."

Keeping my chuckles to myself, I press on. "Who reported the crime?"

Shockingly, my question causes him to cease his assault on the keyboard and swivel toward me. He flicks his sandy-brown hair out of his eyes as he asks, "Crime?"

"Yeah. You don't think the baby Jesus got up and walked away on his own, do you?"

Quince snickers before he replies. "Not 'til Easter."

"Touché." I admire his quick wit. "Anyway, I figure someone took it as a prank. Sheriff Harper asked me to look into it. Who called it in?"

The young man shrugs. "No one."

And so begins the figurative pulling of the teeth. "All right. If no one called it in, then how did you know to stop by and get the picture for the front page?"

"It's on my way."

Taking what I've learned from past conversations with the photojournalist, and adding a soupçon of psychic skills, I deduce that the First Methodist Church lies along Quince's route to work. "Were you driving by on—?" It takes me a minute to remember what day of the week it is, how many editions of the *Post* there are per week, and when those editions would be put to bed. "You were driving to work on Tuesday and noticed the empty manger, and grabbed some photos. Right?"

"Yah."

I'm gonna go ahead and call that a success. "Do you know anyone at the church that I can talk to?"

"Nope."

"Copy that. Have you heard of any other holiday decorations going missing?"

"A couple plastic reindeer."

"Thanks. If I need more information on that, I'll let you know. And if you hear anything, or anyone reports an abandoned baby Jesus, you'll text me?"

"What's it worth?"

And there it is. My succinct source has a price. "How 'bout I drop a couple bills now, and a couple more if you come up with anything useful?"

He nods. "Sweet."

Sweet indeed. This guy sits in a chair, offers me a handful of words, and makes forty bucks. Must be nice. I grab two twenties from my pocket and hand them over.

Lucky for him, I've lived in the town that tech forgot long enough to learn that cash is king. Other than the credit card slidey machine I once observed with wonder at the dry cleaner, I've been living on a strict cash-only diet in almost-Canada.

As I turn to leave, there's a mumbled, "Thanks, dude," tossed in my wake.

At my bookstore, the search for the ghost of grandmothers past is underway. First stop, the third floor of the printing museum, past the photo-engraving exhibit, where Isadora enjoys working on her memoirs.

She recently received some positive feedback from a publisher who indicated they were interested in seeing the first several chapters. However, she's been dragging her ethereal feet and has yet to submit the requested materials. If you ask me, she enjoys writing and the *idea* of publishing a fair bit more than the rigors of literally publishing.

Third floor: no joy.

The trip back down the stairs to the first floor takes me through the large equipment exhibit and past our authentic Gutenberg press. I pause to admire the ancient machine before walking through the Employees Only door, back to the main floor of the bookshop.

Quietly making a serpentine path through the stacks, I confirm we are patron free before I start shouting. "Grams! Grams! Where are you?"

As predicted, my outburst does not produce the desired response. Instead of a ghost materializing at my beck and call, the heavy stomp of biker boots echoes off the tin-plated ceiling. Is it my imagination or is the enormous chandelier actually shaking a little? Kind of like the water in the glass in *Jurassic Park?*

While I puzzle over the physics of my query, my volunteer employee Twiggy stops in front of me, crosses her arms, and shakes her severe grey pixie cut in my general direction. "I hope you at least scanned for customers before you started hollering."

"I did."

She nods once, but then shakes her head. "I'd ask if you were trying to wake the dead, but I suppose you are." Twiggy cackles mercilessly at my predicament.

I'm happy to oblige. The woman works for free and seems to sustain herself solely on my haphazard personal misfortunes. Nothing serious mind you, just the occasional tumble onto my well-padded backside; or, before things got serious with Erick, there were some massive lovelorn mistakes. "I hate to ask, but have you seen any sign of Isadora or even Pyewacket?"

She tilts her head and nods slowly. "I fed his royal furriness this morning. He gobbled it up and ran to scratch at the back door. When I pushed it open, he took one look at the snow in the alley, twitched his black-tufted ears and hustled his tan backside up to the loft. Last I saw, he was snuggled up on the shelf next to your copy of *Mastering Artisan Cheesemaking*."

"Copy that. I'll check the apartment for Grams. Thanks."

I head for the wrought-iron circular staircase, but Twiggy doesn't budge. As I grip the curvy banister and attempt to climb over the "No Admittance" chain—which she insists be hooked up 24/7 —I teeter for a moment, catch myself, and land with a clamor on the other side.

She scoffs, clearly sorry I didn't cause a greater spectacle, and trudges into the back room.

At the top of the staircase, I take a moment to appreciate what I have. Scanning the beautifully curved mezzanine and its massive collection of arcane tomes, I breathe in the possibility of endless worlds. The oak reading desks are perfectly aligned, as usual, and each of the green-glass lampshades stands ready for action. Striding across the thick Persian rug, I pull down the sconce that serves as the candle handle, activating my sliding bookcase door.

No ghost pops out to greet me.

"Grams? Pyewacket? Is there anyone here who can help me with this case?"

Isadora morphs through the wall from the closet I call *Sex and the City* meets *Confessions of a Shopaholic*, and stares at my empty hands. "Where's the coat?"

"About that—"

She shimmers and the air in the room seems charged with electricity. "If Tanya thinks she can get away with selling a dead woman's—"

"Grams! Don't assume the worst. It's been several years. Tanya promised to ask her daughter-in-law if she remembered the coat. We're still working on it."

She fades and drifts aimlessly in my general direction.

"Hey, what's wrong? This can't all be about an old coat."

Her aura dims. "I was hoping to see Odell."

Oh boy, this is definitely my fault. Once I discovered Odell was my biological grandfather and pulled him into the small inner circle of people who know Isadora's ghost haunts my bookstore, I immediately became a matchmaker for afterlife romance.

"It's not like that, Mitzy. We grew close before I passed away."

Which brings me to my next point. "Grams, I'm sure you're as tired of hearing me say it as I am of having to say it, but you're not allowed to drop in and read my thoughts anytime you please."

She opens her translucent mouth to give her standard speech about how things are all muddled up, but I head her off at the pass. "If these lips aren't moving, you're not allowed to comment. That's our agreement, and I would really appreciate it if you would abide by it even thirty percent of the time."

Her standard "Well, I never" retort is not offered. She really is in a mood.

"I'm—"

"Grams!"

"Sorry." She twists one of her large diamond

rings and gazes out the six-by-six windows over-looking the harbor.

"Beg your pardon, but that word is supposed to mean something. 'Sorry' is hardly worth saying if you simply plan on breaking the rules again ten seconds later."

She hovers above the settee and grumbles under her breath.

"What was that? I didn't exactly hear what you said."

Ghost-ma groans and presses a bejeweled hand to her forehead. "I said, if you loved me as much as you say you do you'd fetch Odell."

I flop onto the scalloped-back chair and inhale sharply through my teeth. "I have a tiny problem with that. Maybe two. I'm not a dog, and Odell has a business to run. There are people in this town who depend on him for his amazing food and life-giving coffee."

My gentle teasing does the trick, and a hint of a smile graces Ghost-ma's lips.

"If it will make you feel better, I'll stop by later today and make sure he's planning a visit tonight."

Her glowing eyes gaze down at me with love. "And that's why you're my favorite granddaughter!"

"Thanks, but I'm your only granddaughter. Aren't I? Apparently, you've been holding out on me with a few hidden limbs of the family tree, so it doesn't hurt to double-check."

"Oh, Mitzy, you're such a card."

"I am indeed. Before you get sidetracked with your afterlife love life, I have some investigative questions."

She squares her designer-gown clad shoulders, smooths her burgundy silk-and-tulle Marchesa burial gown, and adjusts one of her many strands of pearls. "Ask away. I'm here to help."

"Thanks. I know you ran in a lot of different social circles and greased a lot of palms in this town, but I wasn't certain of your religious affiliations."

"They came and went. Why do you ask?"

"Did you happen to have any at the First Methodist Church?"

Her glow increases and her smile widens. "As a matter of fact, my fourth husband, Joe Willamet, was a devout Methodist. And he left a significant gift to the church when he passed. If I hadn't already been—"

"Three times divorced and rolling in cash?"

"Listen here, young lady, that nest egg I built is serving you quite nicely."

"You're not wrong." I offer her a grateful smile. "Back to my thing. I need some information regarding a missing baby Jesus. Whom should I talk to?"

Grams coughs, snorts, and nearly chokes in surprise. "Oh, sweetie. You really have to take this show on the road."

Taking a mock bow, I humor her. "I'll think about it. Any contacts?"

"The minister is very tightlipped and a tad standoffish, but the church secretary is an absolute sweetheart. Although, do not let her catch wind that you're dating the sheriff. She's a hopeless gossip!"

I slowly get to my feet and place a fist firmly on my hip. "And in this scenario, are you the pot or the kettle?"

Her laughter tinkles like soft bells as she vanishes through the bookcase into the bookstore beyond.

CHAPTER 3

THE FIRST METHODIST CHURCH is on a side of town that I don't have much reason to visit. So, when I pull into the parking lot, the unfamiliar sights momentarily flabbergast me.

Ambling across the snow-crusted asphalt, I take my time admiring the simple but impressive structure. The main sanctuary's massive arched roof supports a single black steel cross protruding from the peak with a flame shape swirling up on the left. The grand entrance is all glass, allowing a near-perfect view through to the elaborate stained-glass wall behind the pulpit.

The front doors are open, so I let myself in and meander down the center aisle, temporarily mesmerized by the floor-to-ceiling glass mosaic.

The image depicts Jesus cradling a lamb, and

the bucolic landscape surrounding him is filled with incredibly colorful details.

I've never been to Europe, but I've seen pictures. To me, this beautiful colored-glass collage surely rivals that of Notre Dame. As the impact of the initial beauty dissipates, my thoughts turn to the cost of heating such a vast arched-ceiling space in the winter.

Before I can get down to any hard calculations or concerns, a crisp voice calls out from the shadows.

"May I help you?"

When I turn, the sight that greets me feels as though it has been snatched directly from the blooper reel of *Keeping Mum*. The minister's face is almost a caricature. The image that next pops to mind is *Mr. Magoo in Hi-Fi*. A strange vinyl record my mother had in her collection.

Sensing a tidal wave of emotion rising at the thought of my deceased mom, I stuff it down with the deft skill of a seasoned foster kid and paste on a big smile.

"You certainly can. I'm Mitzy Moon." I extend my right hand as I walk toward the pastor.

His bulbous nose twitches, but there isn't a smile strong enough to lift his sagging cheeks. "Welcome to the First Methodist Church, Mrs. Moon."

I pull my hand back from his too-soft, clammy

grip and struggle not to wipe it off on my jeans. "Oh, it's just Miss. You may have been acquainted with my grandmother, Isadora—" For a minute I can't remember the surname of her fourth husband. Thankfully, the minister comes to my rescue.

"Isadora Willamet? Oh, she and Joe were such devoted congregants. I had heard the Lord called her home, but she wasn't a member of my flock at the time. The funeral services were held elsewhere. I pray our Lord welcomed her with open arms."

Doesn't seem like the right time to tell him she never made it to the pearly gates, and that he could express his condolences in person if he so chose. I wisely let it lie. "Yes, she very much enjoyed her time here. This is a beautiful little chapel."

His spine stiffens. "Sanctuary."

"Indeed." I'm not the person to get into an argument over the semantics of church-related room designations. "I was sorry to hear that someone vandalized your Nativity scene. Is there a reason it's still displayed in January?"

His brow furrows, and my psychic senses tingle with the heat of his judgment. "The Nativity scene remains on display through Epiphany. As I'm sure your grandmother told you, the gifts of the magi are bestowed on Epiphany. It would hardly be right to remove the Nativity prior to that momentous occasion."

"Of course. You're right." Yeesh!

An awkward silence hangs between us, and the mood ring on my left hand burns with a message.

Pretending to admire the *sanctuary* further, I turn and risk a surreptitious glance at the misty black cabochon.

The image reveals the minister behind the pulpit, in full Sunday regalia. Thanks for nothing! I've already deduced he's the pastor.

The minister clears his throat. "Is there anything else, *Miss* Moon?"

If I didn't know better, I'd almost think he was disappointed in me for being unmarried. Maybe it's time to try another tack. "Sheriff Harper asked me to look into things. I've had some success in the past—"

The cartoon character's entire expression changes and interrupts my flow. His heavily lidded eyes widen, his nostrils flare, and his lips finally find the strength to curve upwards. "Oh! You're that Mitzy Moon."

Swallowing my snarky response regarding the quantity of Mitzy Moons he assumes reside in this town, I nod and smile.

He ushers me toward a pew, and I take a seat on the less-than-comfortable wooden bench. "I was wondering if you made mention of the Nativity scene, in a special or important way, from the pulpit?"

His chinless jaw falls open, and he gazes at me with something akin to rapture. "So, it's true. The angels speak to you."

Oh, wow. This is the first I'm hearing this particular rumor, and I'm not entirely sure how to keep the abject shock from my face. "Mmhmm."

"Then I know our infant Lord and Savior is in good hands. The Sunday after the Lord's birth, I gave a sermon specifically addressing Epiphany. I always encourage folks to look at the coming year with fresh eyes and fresh hopes. Forgiving the transgressions of the previous year and celebrating the coming resurrection of our Lord."

Too much to unpack. I'll skip ahead. "Do you possibly have a list of the congregants that may have been at that after-Christmas service?"

His momentary lightness fades. "We don't take attendance."

"Of course not. It was a silly idea. I'm thinking maybe your message pricked the conscience of a specific congregant." Not being super familiar with religious jargon, I won't get much farther just continuing to repeat his words.

"Ah." He raises a finger and taps the side of his nose. "Mrs. Coleman can help you. The woman who plays the organ, and also serves as the church secretary. She took it upon herself to make an unofficial list of members who attend each week. We choose one name from the list of those who were with us every Sunday for an entire year, and then she and I attend Easter dinner at their home the following year. Our members consider it quite an honor." His grin returns.

Nod and smile. That's all I've got left. "All right. Perhaps if I could speak to Mrs. Coleman, and get a copy of that list, it would help me narrow the pool of suspects." As soon as I say the word, I know it was a poor choice.

His bushy grey-white eyebrows arch. "Suspects? In my congregation? Oh, Miss Moon, I assure you no one from this church had anything to do with this Nativity prank."

Time to get back on his good side. "I'm sure you're correct, Reverend. Although, it would certainly help me to know who's not responsible. Pin Cherry Harbor isn't a vast metropolis, but if I can at least start by ruling some folks out, it makes my job much easier. I'm sure you understand."

He sucks his bottom lip in between his teeth, and his thick eyelids lower as he contemplates my request. Finally, the minister leans forward and whispers, "If it's what the angels recommend."

Smiling, I manage to mumble an "Mmhmm,"

and he leads me through a side exit to the adjacent church offices.

The hallway seems dark and cave-like compared to the vast vaulted space we exited. He opens a door bearing the nameplate "Secretary," and the woman behind the desk looks up with a broad smile as we enter.

Teeth.

No matter how I try to reinterpret her face, all I see are teeth. The kind of chompers that surely garnered her the wrong type of attention when she was a schoolgirl. My heart goes out to her.

Carrying my own abnormally white mantle of hair through my school years had been an unwelcome burden. I'd been called many names, including *Powder* after the critically acclaimed movie, but, more often than not, ghost girl. If those kids only knew how prescient their comments had been.

Blerg. I zoned out and missed the introduction portion.

Mrs. Coleman is leaning over her desk with an eagerly outstretched hand and a slowly fading smile.

Lurching forward, I shove my hand in hers. "Sorry! I was reflecting on the gorgeous sanctuary and got distracted. I'm Mitzy Moon. Nice to meet you, Mrs. Coleman." When I attempt a deep breath, the cloying aroma wafting from the plethora of potpourri dishes nearly makes me gag.

She grips my hand with surprising strength and pumps it vigorously. "Hello. Hello, and welcome to the First Methodist Church of Pin Cherry Harbor. Are you applying for membership?"

The underwhelmed pastor fills her in on the nature of my visit, and Mrs. Coleman sucks a sharp breath in through her protruding teeth. "Golly! That theft caught me off guard. We've had that Nativity scene for almost forty years. Can you believe it?"

This feels like a question that doesn't need answering, so I nod and smile, and take shallow breaths.

"Well, I said, the whole world is going to H-E-double-hockey-sticks in a handbasket. So, I suppose I shouldn't have been so surprised. But you know how kids are these days. Just last month, we had an incident with two of our teenagers smoking outside Bible study. They just snuck out through a side door and they were hiding under the eaves of this very church. So bold!"

Thankfully, the reverend puts an end to her report. "Mrs. Coleman, I am sure Miss Moon has a busy agenda. If you could simply provide her with your special list from the Sunday before the theft, she will be on her way and can begin her investigation."

Mrs. Coleman seems to have heard my name and the purpose of my visit for the first time.

"Oh, my goodness! You're Isadora Willamet's granddaughter! Why, the ladies at bingo—"

I shake a finger. "You know what they say about gossip, Mrs. Coleman."

Her eyes widen and her jaw hangs open, revealing the full extent of her impressive front teeth.

Insulting the woman who holds the potential key to my case was not my intention, but she doesn't get my sense of humor. Offering an over-the-top wink, I try to save the exchange. "Only the good parts are true!"

Her entire expression lights up, and she throws a hand over her mouth as she gasps. Then she proceeds to repeat the entire joke—out loud. "You know what they say about gossip, only the good parts are true! That's so funny. Oh, my goodness, wait till I tell the ladies what a hoot you are."

There seems to be a richly fed rumor mill running behind the scenes in my beloved new hometown. It doesn't hurt to scoop a little truth in every once in a while. Maybe it will even out.

"Honestly, aren't you the best? Could I get that list?" My lungs are screaming for un-perfumed air.

The minister seems to have reached his fill of

meaningless chatter. "I shall leave you two ladies. You're in good hands, Miss Moon. My condolences for your grandmother."

"Thank you. I'll tell her you said that."

His thick, weighted eyelids peel back and he mumbles what must be a protective passage of Scripture under his breath as he sneaks out of the room.

I'd love to smack myself on the forehead for that slip-up, but I'd rather not draw any additional attention to it. Thankfully, Mrs. Coleman is busy rifling through her desk drawers in search of the requested list and seems to have missed the potential gossip goldmine.

"That's the strangest thing."

"What is?"

She pushes the last drawer closed and looks at me with utter confusion. "I can't find that week's list."

My claircognizance seems to snatch a word from the ether, and my silly old mouth shouts it out without thinking. "Stolen?"

She gasps, and her teeth once again take center stage. "Stolen? Why, I don't think so. Someone had to come in— It's just not done."

"It's possible that the person who removed the baby Jesus from the manger knew you kept the lists in your top drawer. Maybe they took the doll and the list."

A deep crease forms between her eyebrows, and she shakes her head violently. "Doll! The replica of the baby Jesus in the manger is no *doll*. And no one in our congregation would stoop to thieving. From the church office, no less. Not on your life. I probably had one of my senior moments and put it in the wrong file. Just give me a couple of minutes."

"I didn't mean to offend, Mrs. Coleman. Would you mind if I step back into the sanctuary and take another look at that stained-glass mural?"

Her expression immediately softens, and I hope I'm back on the gossip girl's good side. "Of course, dear. I'm sure that list will turn up in a minute and I'll bring you a copy."

"Thank you."

Slipping out of the cloud of potpourri-tainted air perfuming her office, I let my fingers bounce from the back of one pew to the next as I walk to the rear of the sanctuary for the best view of the stained glass.

As my left hand drags across the last pew, a whisper tingles up my arm and tickles my eardrum.

"Child."

Child? If that pew and my ring are trying to tell me that a child removed the baby from the manger, that could be a lead. But a child would hardly be wily enough to swipe the attendance list.

Stepping toward the center, I gaze up at the magnificent work of art.

When I pull my eyes away and return to the side door, it opens unexpectedly.

Mrs. Coleman bustles through, a bundle of nerves. "I'm so sorry, Miss Moon, but I can't find that list anywhere. I hate to think that you're right, but what if someone did take it?"

"Let's hope not. Does the list change all that much from week to week?"

She taps her fingernails on her teeth, and I have to bite my tongue to keep from saying something. Her gaze travels up and bounces from left to right as she scans her memory. "Well, the Sunday before would've been the official Christmas service, and that's always very well attended. The following Sunday would've had a much smaller crowd."

"Do you have the list from the Christmas service?"

She smiles, and the effort squeezes her eyes to slits. "Yes. That one is in my top drawer with all the others."

I'd hate to point out that "all" is a tad incorrect. "Could you make me a copy of that list? Maybe you could go through it and cross off anyone you remember not attending the next week. At least it would give me something to start with."

She claps her hands together and gives a little hop. "I'll hop right to it. You're as smart as a whip." Mrs. Coleman opens the door to return to her office and glances back to see if I'm following.

"I'll wait here. I don't want to interrupt your concentration."

The secretary points her finger at me and winks. "You are plum full of great ideas."

I hate to break it to her that the great idea has more to do with her office being *plum full* of pot-pourri than my brain spilling over with genius plans. However, no harm, no foul.

Less than five minutes later, she returns with a photocopy of the Christmas service list. More than half the names have been crossed out.

"Wow! Attendance really drops off after the holidays."

She bends her head and presses the palms of her hands together in prayer pose. "Everyone finds the Lord in their own way. Pastor always says, 'deeds not creeds.' So I can only hope that these poor souls are spending the rest of their Sundays doing good deeds, and that our dear Lord will take note of their good works."

I shake the list once and press my lips together. "Copy that. Thanks for the list." Turning to exit the church through the sanctuary, Mrs. Coleman's voice stops me in my tracks.

"You don't have to go back through the sanctuary, dear. This hallway leads you to a side exit right into the parking lot."

Nodding my thanks, I head down the hallway when a sudden question comes to mind. "Is this door always unlocked?"

Her megawatt smile beams down the hallway. "The Lord's house is open to all."

"Understood."

I push open the door and step onto the sidewalk. It's impossible not to notice the looming Nativity scene, mere feet from my current location. It would only take a second to hop over and grab the baby Jesus. If he weren't already missing.

The empty manger gapes at me, refusing to offer any additional clues.

CHAPTER 4

EASING MY FATHER'S TRUCK back onto the main road, I'm grateful for Artie, the town snowplow operator. I'm not sure how she does it, but she keeps the roads beautifully clear despite this year's near-constant snowfall. My winter driving skills have definitely improved since my first frosty months in almost-Canada, but I still prefer a clear road to one covered by snow with possible dangerous ice lurking beneath.

On the seat next to me the phone rings, and when I catch sight of the name on caller ID, I nearly veer into a snowdrift! Quince Knudsen is *calling* me? As in, not a one-word text. I'm getting a phone call where he'll be required to use at least a handful of words!

Must be important. I hit the speaker icon. "Hey, Quince, what's up?"

"I need to talk."

The sharp edge of emotion in his voice cuts through the phone. "What's going on? Are you in danger? Where are you?"

"Bookshop."

To be fair, I did ask a lot of questions in rapid succession, and there was virtually no chance that he would answer all of them. He picked the most important one and got straight to the point. "Understood. I'm just leaving the First Methodist Church. Do you want to meet at the diner?"

"No. Private."

"Copy that. I'll be there shortly."

And he's gone. A little part of me expected a "bye" or possibly an affirmative grunt, but I get it. The communication was finished in his mind. He'll save his possible verbosity for when he sees me face-to-face.

Doubling down on the advantage of a plowed road, I push the boundaries of what would be considered a safe speed and hustle back to the bookstore.

There's no time for fancy parking or garage codes.

I swerve across the lane of oncoming traffic, which is empty, so don't worry, and park against the curb in front of the Bell, Book & Candle. Jumping out of the truck, I risk a brisk jog to the front door.

Big mistake.

Five seconds into my brave pseudo-sprint, I hit a patch of ice and go down like a pyramid of toilet paper in a grocery store that met its match in a speeding cart.

Unfortunately, I fall forward and crack my denim-clad knee pretty solidly against the icy sidewalk. Slowly getting back on my feet, I hobble toward my beautiful hand-carved front door, but don't have time to admire it.

Inside the high-ceilinged shop, the massive chandelier glitters warmly. The cantankerous mood ring on my left hand stabs an icy circle around my finger. Glancing down, I see the vast expanse of a frozen lake. Great clue, ring. There are only about a million of those in Birch County!

"Hey. I need your help." Quince is agitated, and his usual lackadaisical expression and drooped shoulders are all tense and pinched.

"What's going on?"

"It's my uncle."

This is the first I'm hearing of an uncle. "On your dad's side?"

"Yah. My uncle Quade was murdered."

Under intense pressure, I have two modes: dark humor or impulsive action. Thankfully, the "act without thinking" takes over and I throw my arms around the young man and squeeze tightly. "I'm so sorry. When did this happen? Are the police looking into it?"

Quince is extraordinarily uncomfortable with my show of affection. He wiggles out of my hug and shoves both of his hands in the pockets of his jeans. "This morning. They said it's an accident."

Wow. This puts me in an awkward position. I'm eager to help Quince find out what's actually happened to his uncle, but it sounds like I'll have to directly defy my boyfriend's authority. "Sheriff Harper doesn't think it was murder?"

"Yah."

The unspoken part of the response is that Quince clearly doesn't agree. "I understand. Why do you think there was foul play?"

"My uncle went fishing every morning after the first milking. He's meticulous, like OCD meticulous. Same pattern. Time. And he doesn't drink."

The length of the speech gives me pause, and I wonder if there's a way to question the young man without making him feel judged. "So, I'm totally going to help you. Let's just get that part out of the way. But if you want me to do my job properly, I'm gonna have to ask some tough questions. It may seem like I'm doubting your story, or siding with the cops, but I'm not. I just need to make sure I understand. All right?"

He nods and swipes at his nose with the back of his hand.

"You said your uncle was meticulous. And you said something about milking? Can you explain?"

His hands fidget in his pockets and his shoulders shrug almost imperceptibly.

Biting my tongue, I wait for what I hope is additional information.

"He's younger than my dad. Divorced. He just does things in a particular way."

"Got it. And what about the milking?"

"He's a cheesemaker."

And here goes my brain. The second he says cheesemaker, all I can think of is *Monty Python*. "Blessed are the cheesemakers." Don't worry, I don't say it out loud. "Got it. So he milks his cows, I'm assuming, and then he goes ice fishing? Every morning?"

"Yah. He calls it his thinking time."

"So, this morning he milked the cows, headed out to the fishing house, and when he didn't come back after his thinking time, who called it in?"

"My dad."

"How did your dad know he wasn't back?"

"Breakfast."

Sadly, Quince is slipping back toward monosyllabic territory, and I'm having to rely on my extra senses to pull details out of thin air. "So your dad and his brother have breakfast together every morning?"

"Yah."

"Got it. This morning your uncle didn't show up, and did your dad go out to the icehouse?"

The young man can't bring himself to speak. Emotion twists his face as he nods.

"Your dad discovered the body?" There's no need for him to answer. "I'm so sorry. Did he call the police?"

Quince pulls his hands from his pockets, crosses his arms, and squeezes himself as a response.

The only sound in the bookshop is the wind whipping up from the great lake nestled in our harbor and buffeting the brick exterior.

"I heard it on the scanner." His voice catches and he looks away.

"Oh, man. That sucks. Again, I'm so sorry." I'm starting to sound like a broken record, but my heart is breaking for this kid. "You mentioned murder. What makes you think that?"

"Sheriff said Quade passed out, the fire burned out, and he froze to death."

Sorry, Erick, but if I'd been at the crime scene, I would've said this to your face. "They wouldn't have the medical examiner's report already. That sounds like a pure guess."

Quince looks up with pleading hazel eyes. "I know, right?"

"I'll talk to Erick. I can get a copy of the ME's report. In the meantime, can you show me the way to the icehouse?"

"Yah."

The somber drive out to the lake where Quince's uncle's body was discovered is wrapped in a heavy blanket of silence.

My curious mind is churning over the few details I possess, and I can't seem to let go of one burning question. I brave a quick query. "Are you named after your uncle or something? I mean, Q names aren't that common."

He gazes out the window, and his finger traces abstract patterns in the frost forming on the inside of the glass. "It's a family thing. My dad's name is Quintin." He sighs. "I suppose, if I have kids—"

This particular tradition seems more of a burden than a gift, but I'm so happy to have a family after six plus years in foster care, I'd embrace practically anything. Quincy, or, as I call him, Quince, Quintin, and Quade. I'm wondering when this tradition started, what other odd "Q" names I would find hanging on the Knudsen family tree if I were to climb any higher. Maybe I'd have to shimmy down lower? I don't know. I'm not a genealogy expert.

Quince gestures to the left, and I turn down an access road that parallels the shoreline of a frozen body of water. A small wooden structure, barely five foot by five foot and painted sky-blue, comes into view.

"That's it." He points to the shack.

Several sets of tracks mark the snow cover near the edge of the lake. I pull in as far as I dare, and we jump out of the truck.

The heavy clouds of the morning have blown free, and an incongruent bright-blue sky and white-gold winter sun gleam above the sparkling powder-covered ice.

We walk toward the icehouse wrapped with yellow tape that proclaims. "CRIME SCENE KEEP OUT."

When we get closer, I notice a large piece of paper taped to the crime-scene tape. On the white sheet, written in thick black permanent marker, is the phrase, "This means you, Mitzy."

"Rude."

Quince shrugs. "He knows I know you."

It's hard not to notice that the kid avoids using the term friends. Clearly, that's far too familiar for this young man. "Yeah, and he also knows I'm a bit of a snoop."

Quince turns to head back toward the truck.

"Hey, where are you going?"

He looks over his shoulder and scrunches up his face in confusion. "It says keep out."

I laugh out loud and put a hand to my stomach to aid in containing the hilarity. "Look, kid, it's a cute sign and all, but it's not going to keep me from investigating this case."

For the first time since I found him moping in my bookshop, his face lights up. "Sweet."

"Also, before I forget. You said something about your uncle not being a drinker. Why did that come up?"

"My dad said they found an empty bourbon bottle next to his chair."

"Oh, that's why Erick said Quade 'passed out.' Are you sure about the drinking?"

"No alcohol with his meds. Hasn't had a drink in over ten years."

"Copy that."

I circle around the icehouse, feeling for clues. This is one time where Quince's silence comes in handy. I need the quiet to focus and reach out with my extra abilities.

No sign of forced entry, but as soon as I turn my

focus toward the door, my clairaudience grabs the word *screw* floating on the breeze.

Taking two careful steps closer to the door, I notice a small hole just above the lock mechanism. I turn to my cohort and attempt to confirm my other-worldly information. "If someone put a screw right here"—I point to the mark—"would that prevent the lock from opening from the inside?"

Quince leans forward, squeezes his eyes, and chews the inside of his cheek. "I think so."

Now it's time for me to use my moody mood ring as a divining rod. A little trick I learned on another snow-covered case.

Crouching down, I remove my glove, hold my hand over the snow, and focus on the screw.

At first, the results are dismal.

Taking another deep breath, I attempt to visualize the screw being knocked loose by an overeager deputy—I'm assuming Deputy Paulsen. I have to pull my focus back and not be distracted by my dislike for her overbearing tactics.

A sudden heat emanates from my ring and my hand pulls to the right. The heat lessens as I move it too far.

I ease my fingers left and the heat increases. Making minuscule adjustments, I find the position where the heat around my ring finger is most intense and then plunge my bare hand into the freezing snow.

To his credit, Quince has remained utterly silent the entire time.

My fingers sting and burn with cold. Only my determination to help my friend pushes my numb fingers deeper.

Eureka!

Clumsily pinching my frozen digits around the screw, I extract it from the icy crystals and smile triumphantly. "Um, you wouldn't happen to have an evidence bag, would you?"

He shakes his head. "Film can?"

"That'll work."

Quince digs in the pocket of his coat and extracts the empty film canister. He pops off the lid and I drop the screw in for safekeeping. He presses on the lid and hands the canister to me.

I shake my head and lift my hands in the air as though it's a holdup. "I'm not supposed to be here, remember?"

A half grin lifts one side of his mouth and he nods. "I'll go see Sheriff Harper. Won't mention you."

Chuckling, I shake my head. "It's all right. You can say whatever you need to. There's probably not any recoverable evidence on that thing, but the fact that someone put a screw into the fish house to purposely jam the lock mechanism should at least make them reconsider cause of death."

Tears well up in the corners of his eyes, and I'm afraid his eyelids could freeze shut.

"We should get back in the truck. Come on." My clairsentience picks up on a wave of relief. I know he's grateful. I don't need him to cry to prove that.

The drive back into town is as silent as the drive out to the lake, but this quiet feels different—it's protecting a fragile hope.

We found something. And this is the way every case unravels. One thing leads to the next thing, which leads to the next thing, and, eventually, if you find enough things, you find the bad guy (or gal) and you can put them away.

Stopping in front of the bookshop, I glance toward my passenger and grin. "You should probably walk down to the station on your own. If I pull up in front and let you out, you're going to be fresh out of plausible deniability."

His laughter warms my heart, and he thanks me as he slips out of the truck and trudges up Main Street.

Dutiful daughter that I am, I fill up my dad's gas tank and park his truck back in his garage. I also tuck the keys under the visor, where I found them.

Before this case takes off, I better see about getting a new vehicle to replace my "retired" Jeep.

After I let myself in through the heavy metal door leading from the alleyway between my building and my dad's, I stomp the snow off my boots and acknowledge the shocking realization that I have no idea how one buys a car.

Time for a spirited consultation.

Grams has been spending a lot of time on the third floor of the printing museum. Rather than risk calling out her name and drawing Twiggy's wrath, I sashay through the "Employees Only" door leading from the bookshop into the adjacent exhibitions and trudge up to the third floor.

Her pensive expression and frantic writing worry me, but when I see the mountain of loose sheets in the trash barrel, serious concern sets in.

"Grams, is everything all right?"

A luminous head swivels toward the disruption and, I kid you not, actual ghost flames are flickering from her eyes.

"Never mind. Never mind. I can figure out how to buy a car by myself."

The pen clatters to the floor, and she zooms toward me. A sparkling blur of apologies. "I'm so sorry, sweetie. I've had writer's block for days, and I finally solved my story problem. My emotions are running high and interfering with my ability to grip things. I keep dropping the pen. I can't write as fast as the thoughts are coming to me—"

"Easy, girl. Sounds like a lot of ghost problems."

Fortunately, my joke lands and she laughs with relief. "Thanks, I needed that."

"Can I ask which part of the story is giving you problems? I thought you were writing memoirs. Seems like there would only be one version of those." Crossing my arms, I tilt my head and scrunch up one corner of my mouth as I wait for her to defend her obvious creative license.

"Oh, it's not important, dear. You said something about buying a car. I left you the Jeep and the Mercedes. Do you really need a third car?"

"Thing is, ever since the Jeep got hot-wired—" I pause and wait for her to nod in acknowledgment. "—she's had a whole host of problems. And she left me stranded in front of the dry cleaners. Luckily, I have a resourceful boyfriend who rescued me and took care of the problem. But, as you know, I prefer to be an independent woman."

She presses a shimmering hand to her ample bosom and laughs so hard she ghost snorts. "Understatement of this century, my dear."

Grinning mischievously, I meet her on her own terms. "People tell me I take after my dearly departed grandmother."

She winks. "Touché, as you're always saying."

"So, back to my thing about needing to buy a car. I actually really liked the Jeep, and I'm not opposed to getting another one. I just don't know where to go or what questions to ask."

Grams nods her head and adjusts one of her strands of pearls. "Oh, I know just what you mean. People often take advantage of a woman shopping for big-ticket items on her own. I found Silas Willoughby to be an incredibly useful bit of arm candy."

Now it's my turn to laugh until tears leak from my eyes. "Silas! Arm candy!" I have to bend over and support myself by placing my hands on my knees. The imagery flashing through my head is enough to make me pass out from my attack of the giggles.

Grams places a fist on her Marchesa-clad hip. "Well, arm candy might not be the right phrase, exactly, but you know what I mean. Call Silas. He'll know what to do."

"Thank you for helping me with my problem. Is there anything I can do to help you with yours?"

If ghosts could look guilty . . .

"What? Oh, don't trouble yourself. I'll figure it out. All in a day's work, I suppose."

"If you say so, Isadora."

I hurry toward the stairs and attempt to distance myself from the apparition before the inevitable thought pops into my head. A day's work? Has Isadora ever done a day's work?

An offended retort echoes down the stairwell. "I heard that, young lady."

"Get out of my head, woman!" Our shared laughter warms my heart.

CHAPTER 5

I LEARNED a new expression when I arrived in Pin Cherry Harbor: stuck in my craw. I have no idea what it means, but, at this moment, it feels right. That's exactly where my grandmother's advice is wedged.

It's not that I doubt the powers of the mysterious attorney/alchemist Silas Willoughby, but he drives a 1908 Ford Model T! If that was the last time he was wheeling and dealing for a new vehicle, I'm not sure he's the right man for the job. However, I will not be the girl who has to have her boyfriend hold her hand for every major life decision. If I'm flipping a coin, it's coming up Silas. Traipsing across the thick carpets in my swanky apartment, I flop down on the bed to make the call.

A hiss and a tan streak shoot out from under the frame as it creaks.

"Pyewacket! Geez! You scared me half to death! But I suppose I frightened you too. I'm sorry, Mr. Cuddlekins. Please come back and let me apologize properly."

Pyewacket's broad head and sharply tufted black ears peer around the edge of the door to my enormous closet. His large golden eyes squint, and waves of suspicion roll off him.

"I swear, I didn't know you were under the bed. I would never launch an attack against such a powerful adversary."

"Reow." Can confirm. He struts toward me and his thick stubby tail flicks with irritation, or maybe it's tolerance. The hairs on the back of my neck tingle, and I'm certain tolerance is the correct word. He gracefully launches onto the thick down comforter, circles once, and flops down facing away from me.

"I accept my punishment, oh furry master. Now, I have to call Silas and convince him to help me buy a car. Any advice?"

Pye yawns widely and exposes his dangerous fangs. His large head hits the bed with a thud and lolls toward me. One golden eye meets my gaze. "Ree-ow." Soft but condescending.

"Thanks for nothing, buddy."

. . .

Cut to—

Silas riding shotgun in my father's truck as we drive toward Broken Rock. There is a dealership there that he's fond of visiting. However, no matter how I phrase the question, I'm unable to discern whether he's ever actually purchased a vehicle from this location.

When I pull into the parking lot, my eyes wander up and down the scant rows of vehicles. They don't look exactly new. "Silas, is this a used car lot? I mean, not to be this girl, but can't I afford a new car?"

He harrumphs and smooths his great bushy mustache with a thumb and forefinger. "I am certain the estate your grandmother left you could purchase many new cars. I find used vehicles to be more discreet for your—line of work—for lack of a better word."

"Line of work? It's not like I'm a lady of the night, to use your terminology. I'm an amateur snoop. What does it matter what kind of car I drive?"

He steeples his fingers and bounces his chin thoughtfully on the tips of his pointers.

Blerg. I've earned myself a lesson. He's not

giving me any instruction, so I best take some deep breaths and tune in to psychic radio.

Stilling my spinning mind, I reach out with all of my extrasensory perceptions. Why am I seeing the dive bar Final Destination? Clarity rockets in and I slap my hand on my thigh. "You're right. Some of my undercover missions wouldn't have gone as well as they did if I were driving a fancy new car. Sorry I doubted you. Although, let me be clear, I'm no mechanic. If something goes wrong with this not-quite-new car, I can't always be calling Erick to bail me out."

A satisfied grin widens beneath his grey lip warmer and he nods. "Once we've completed our transaction, remind me to introduce you to Clarence."

The name means absolutely nothing to me. "Do I know Clarence?"

The satisfied smile fades instantly, and my mentor shakes his head. "One would not be introduced to an individual with whom one was already acquainted."

"You're not wrong." Sparing myself any further humiliation, I open my door and exit the truck. On the drive over, I was instructed to act disinterested and only point out flaws. Apparently, this is an important part of the negotiation strategy.

Tromping down the first row of vehicles, a

lovely Jeep, very similar to my previous vehicle, catches my eye. "Cool! This is exactly what I want, Silas."

He glances toward me with furrowed brows and my claircognizance knows in an instant I've disappointed him greatly.

An eager salesman jogs our way. He smiles brightly at me, but when he catches sight of Silas, his entire persona shifts.

Maybe my old alchemist is the perfect shopping partner.

"Hi, Mr. Willoughby. Just looking?"

Silas smooths his mustache and lets the man simmer in a moment of silence. "One is always looking prior to a decision. Are they not?"

The frustrated salesman smiles weakly and changes his tactic. "What about you, Miss? You see anything you like?"

Still recovering from my recent scolding, I gesture toward the Jeep I truly desire and attempt to *neg.* A term I learned from my young stepbrother. "Those don't look like snow tires."

The salesman is clearly eager to move things along and get us inside the warm building to sign papers. "Good eye, Miss. That vehicle came to us late in the fall, and we weren't planning on putting snow tires on her unless she sold this winter. You

take her off the lot today, and I'll put on a brand-
new set of tires for a hundred bucks."

I smile and open my mouth, but the voice that
responds is not mine.

"Oh, come now, we both know you don't have a
set of brand-new snow tires on the lot. I'm certain
any tires you placed on this vehicle would have a
minimum of 10,000 miles on their belts."

On their belts, under their belts . . . Silas is
crafty.

The salesman shrugs. "You got me there, Mr.
Willoughby. We'll put snow tires on, no charge."

Color me impressed. This negotiating thing is
harder than it looks. "How many miles does she
have on her?" I've heard guys ask that question.

The salesman nods. "Let me check."

He moves to the vehicle, turns the key to the accessory position and glances at the odometer. "Just under
80,000. Which is mint condition for a vintage Jeep."

Nice. I like that he didn't use the word old. Vintage has much more panache.

Silas clears his throat and steps toward the vehicle. "How can we be sure that the odometer hasn't
rolled over? Do you have a list of previous owners?
If it's a single-owner vehicle, I'd be inclined to accept your supposition. However, if this is a multi-
owner vehicle, I feel it's likely 180,000, good sir."

The salesman's lips are turning blue, and my own teeth are beginning a subtle chatter.

"Let's head inside and take a look at the paperwork."

I eagerly fall in line behind him, but Silas grips my arm.

"We shall peruse the remaining rows and meet you inside. That should give you plenty of time to assemble the necessary documents."

The salesman nods and hustles indoors.

As soon as he's out of earshot, I pitch a tiny fit. "Silas! I want this Jeep. It's four-wheel drive. I like this shade of green, and 80,000 miles is not that many."

"Would you marry the first man who asked you?"

The question hits me out of nowhere. Instantly, I'm picturing the first proposal I ever received back in Arizona. It was after a particularly intense night of partying and I honestly only remember the guy's last name. I think it was Centers. That can't be right. That's not a name, is it? Blerg. I don't even remember his last name.

Silas and his smug grin annoy me.

"All right. You win. I wouldn't— I didn't. Let's see what else they have."

He leads me on a serpentine tour of the small

lot. In the end, he finds a slightly newer Jeep, a beautiful shade of blue, with lovely snow tires.

As I admire the car with sparkling eyes, Silas chuckles. "You see, vehicles in the front row are the ones they *need* to move. The hidden gems are tucked away. This car is in excellent condition and they surely paid too much for it. This will provide an invigorating negotiation, but I believe the car will serve you well. Would you not agree?"

There's that phrasing again. Yes, I would not agree? No, I would not agree? As I place my hand on the front fender, a feeling of warmth and belonging radiates up my arm. My eyes widen with surprise and I glance toward Silas.

His proud grin says it all.

My mentor seems to be a couple steps ahead of me, despite my special gifts. "You're right, as usual. Now can we go inside and get a hot cup of coffee?"

"Indeed."

When we trudge indoors, the salesman is still rifling through paperwork on his desk.

Silas approaches and drops silently into one of the two chairs. "We have chosen the 1997 Jeep Cherokee with snow tires in the back row. Our offer is 3500 even."

The salesman drops the papers on his desk and looks aghast. "That's less than we paid for it. I can't let it off the lot for less than 4500."

Silas chuckles and leans back in his chair.

My mood ring gives me nothing, but I swear I can feel the number 3000 in the air. The salesman is lying! They only paid 3000 for that vehicle, and Silas must know it. I cross my arms and lean back like my trainer—ready to wait this guy out.

His gaze bounces back and forth like a tennis ball at Wimbledon. "I got to talk to my manager."

Silas nods. "By all means."

The man rises from his chair and vanishes into a back room.

I've watched this scene in so many movies, and I never believed a second of it. Is this actually how business is done? What a racket. I suppose you can't judge an entire industry by one experience, but stereotypes exist for a reason.

The salesman returns with an older version of himself in tow.

Oh dear, this is a family-owned business, and daddy is not happy with his son's performance.

The older gentleman has a salt-and-pepper mustache which pales in comparison to the one Silas is rocking. Although, Sales Daddy's beer belly is significantly larger.

"I understand you're interested in the '97 Cherokee. That vehicle is in excellent condition and we definitely can't let her off the lot for less than 4200."

Hold on! The price came down by $300 in under two minutes. I'm starting to understand how this game works. Before Silas can reply, I double down on our offer. "I believe we offered 3500, all in."

I feel a little burst of pride from my mentor.

Sales Daddy shakes his head, leans toward his son and mumbles something he clearly hopes is inaudible.

Lucky for me, I have extra audible.

Junior takes the ball. "I'm sure you're on a tight budget, Miss. We're willing to go as low as $4000. And I'll include taxes and registration."

I wait for Silas to reply, but he seems to be interested in continuing the experiment with me at the helm.

Shaking my head, I cross my arms and lean away. "You hit the nail on the head. I can't go a penny over $3500. That's my final offer."

Sales Daddy jumps in. "We need to look at some paperwork. Give us a minute."

I lift my eyebrows as though I couldn't care less, and shrug.

The two men retreat into the back room, and I risk a glance at Silas. He smooths his mustache with thumb and forefinger and nods his approval. A soft phrase reaches my ears, even though I don't see his lips move. *Be ready to walk out.*

My jaw drops a little, but I nod.

The father-son team returns. Daddy takes the lead. "The best we can do is $3800. You're basically robbing us at that price. I won't even be able to pay his commission."

Pushing myself up from the chair, I smile pleasantly. "I would think you'd have your own son on a profit-sharing program in a family-run business, but who's to say. I'm sorry we weren't able to come to an agreement."

I walk toward the door, and Silas follows. If I didn't know better, I'd say he's gleeful.

My hand is on the push bar, and I'm a second from exiting.

Junior calls out. "Hold on. Hold on. I'll take the loss. You can have it for 3500, all in, like you said."

As I turn to respond, Silas offers me a surreptitious wink and I nearly squeal. "That sounds great. Let's draw up the papers." I'm not sure if draw up the papers is the right phrase, but who cares! I just bought my first car! And I got a heck of a deal.

CHAPTER 6

I WON'T BORE you with the endless contract
signing details . . . Sometime later, I'm the proud
new owner of a vintage Jeep. Silas offers to drive the
new purchase back to the bookshop, and I return
my father's truck to his garage. Now that I've handled practicalities, it seems like the perfect opportunity to meet my boyfriend for a casual dinner and
pump him for information on the Knudsen case.

Lying on the padded mahogany bench in my
home for vintage couture, I stare at the cedar-lined
ceiling in the closet. The phone is on speaker and
the call rings through.

The sheriff's confident, warm voice fills the
space. "Hey, did you already solve the case of the
missing baby Jesus?"

Whoopsie. Once I got my teeth into the murder, I forgot I was supposed to be working for Erick. "I've got some good leads. How about you? Any interesting cases?"

His deep chuckle makes my tummy flip. "I wasn't born yesterday, Moon. Meet me at the diner in five, and I'll give you an update on Quince's uncle."

"Am I really that transparent?"

"Not at all. But there is a certain predictability to your—shall we call it—snoopiness?"

"Wow, just wow. I think that comment is going to cost you a free dinner. Looks like you're buying now, Sheriff."

"Not a problem. See ya soon."

The call ends, and I lazily push myself to a sitting position. Silas forced me into a "decent blouse" for our sales excursion. Now I have a fashion conundrum. Part of me wants to slip on a snarky T-shirt, but a smaller part of me wants to impress Erick.

I unbutton an additional button on the blouse and wink at myself in the mirror.

"Finally!"

Nearly jumping out of my skin, I clutch at my heart. "Grams! What have I told you about scaring the bejeezus out of me? Slow. Sparkly. Re-entry. Only. Please!"

"There wasn't time. I was afraid you were going

to lose the fashion battle and slip into your old ways. I'm so proud to see that you're finally paying attention to all my lessons. That blouse is delightful on you, and a little cleavage never hurts."

I blush self-consciously, and my hand reaches toward the button I just loosed.

"Don't worry, sweetie. Your secret is safe with me."

My eyes roll of their own accord, and I attempt to keep my thoughts regarding her finely honed gossip skills to myself.

Epic fail.

"Listen, young lady. My connections and access to information have helped you several times. Don't look a gift horse in the mouth."

The old adage makes me chuckle. "I really don't think of you as a horse, Grams, but you definitely are a gift."

Shimmering ghost tears spring to the corners of her eyes. "Oh, Mitzy."

I quickly raise an admonishing finger. "Don't you dare cry! I'll be forced to go to the cemetery, exhume you, and shove a handkerchief in your coffin!"

Her expression turns to shock. "Do you think that would work? Gosh, I was able to pick the ghost age I wanted, but I can't change my clothes. Do you think you could put outfits in there?

Maybe I could have a summer dress, a pant suit . . ."

I slip out of the closet before she can force me to make good on my empty threat. It's only a half-baked theory I've been playing with. It's not like I ran it past Silas or anything. As the bookcase door slides open, she's still rambling on about possible afterlife fashion choices.

Erick is already tucked into the corner booth, but, as I approach, he hops up to help me off with my coat.

"Thank you. If you're trying to butter me up for additional details about the empty manger, I hate to disappoint. I'm pretty convinced someone from the congregation took it, but until I can come up with motive, I'm going to have a hard time narrowing down the suspect list."

He slides back into the booth, and I sit opposite. He walks his fingers across the table, turns his palm up, and I slide my hand into his. It feels like home. And I very much like *home.*

Tally sidles up and, for once, her hands are empty. Her tightly wound, flame-red bun tilts from side to side as she offers each of us a broad smile. "What can I getcha? Coffee? Iced tea? Maybe a hot cocoa with whipped cream?"

"I'll take the last one!"

Erick smiles. "Me too."

There's no need to order food. My grandfather, Odell, is already hard at work on the grill. It never made sense to me before, but maybe the reason he always knows exactly what his customers want is because he's a little psychic. Silas thinks I inherited my gifts from my grandmother, but she only has visions. Some people call it clairvoyance. I have all the psychic senses and maybe one or more of them came from Odell Johnson. Food for thought.

Erick's free hand is slowly waving back and forth in front of my face and I bite my lip and wipe my eyes. "What did I miss?"

"I was telling you all about the Knudsen case. You missed everything. Too bad. Looks like our food is on the way. I won't have time to repeat the story."

"Erick Harper!"

Odell sets a beautiful burger and fries in front of me, and meatloaf with mashed potatoes in front of Erick. "Everything okay here?"

Before my smart aleck boyfriend can defend himself, I jump in and throw him under the bus. "Not even. Erick is refusing to share information about a case, but I have my ways."

Odell snickers too quickly. "I'd say. So my favorite granddaughter is on another case, eh?"

It's so strange to hear him say it. *Granddaughter*. Of course, it's literally some of the best news I've gotten in a long time. Most family secrets are meant to stay buried, but this one is definitely thriving in the light of day.

"I'm looking into the missing baby Jesus—"

"And she's not so secretly working for Quincy Knudsen. So, she's also looking into Quade's murder."

I gasp softly. "So it was murder."

He nods solemnly. "I had my suspicions. I was honestly just trying to spare Quintin's feelings, you know?"

I did know. I do know. "I get that."

Odell raps his knuckles twice on the silver-flecked white-Formica table, winks at me, and returns to the kitchen.

Pulling up my shoulders in anticipation, I bait the hook. "I have exciting news. So I'm going to be magnanimous and let you eat while I tell you my story."

Erick's big blue eyes widen with mock shock. "Is the news that you're not well? Because I've never seen you resist a plate of french fries."

In order to teach him a lesson, I shove several fries in my mouth and arch an eyebrow.

"I give up, Moon. Tell me your news." He picks up a fork and digs into his juicy meatloaf.

I fill him in on my car buying adventures and my expert negotiating skills.

He calmly swallows his food, wipes his mouth, and smiles. "Sounds like Silas is an excellent teacher. I know the dealership you're talking about in Broken Rock, and that father-son duo is a tough act to beat. Good for you. Did Silas introduce you to Clarence?"

It shouldn't surprise me that Erick knows Clarence. Pin Cherry is a rather small town. "Don't tell me you know him too?"

"Oh, for sure. He's helped me out with the Nova many times. What he doesn't know about cars isn't worth knowing. And he's fair as the day is long. You're in good hands with him."

"Well, that's two ringing endorsements from a couple of the people I trust most."

Erick smiles. "Good to know."

"Oh, don't let it go to your head, Sheriff."

He chuckles, and the remainder of our meal falls into silence as we devour our delicious suppers.

"All right, that's my news, Sheriff. What do you have for me?"

His eyes twinkle, and my extra senses pick up on his inner battle.

"If you're toying with the idea of baiting me further, *Ricky*. I'd advise against it."

His ready laughter is exactly what I'm hoping

for when I use his mother's pet name. To be fair, some of his old high school chums also call him Ricky, but, in general, with the status he holds in the community, people call him Erick, Mr. Harper, or, mostly, Sheriff.

"Sorry, Moon. Sadly, there isn't much to report yet. Because of the frozen nature of the—"

"Say body, don't say the other word."

He nods and presses his lips together in grim acknowledgment of the corpse. "Because of the frozen nature of the body, and the unusual sixty-degree temperature drop last night, the medical examiner has to send specimens to the state crime lab for verification. Her initial findings estimate time of death between midnight and 3:00 a.m. However, Mr. Knudsen claims he received a text from his brother at 5:30 a.m., confirming that the first milking was complete and their breakfast appointment was on after fishing."

Scrunching up my face, I shrug my shoulders and wag my head back and forth. "I think we both know that a text can be faked. What time was the body discovered?"

"We got the call around 9:00 a.m."

"That doesn't make sense."

Erick tilts his head and leans forward. "What do you mean?"

"The temperature would've been on the rise

with the sun, I'm assuming. I mean, I'm no meteorologist, but it does warm up when the sun comes out, right?"

"True. If Quade was alive at 5:30, he'd have been hard-pressed to freeze in the space of three and a half hours, or less."

"This is what I'm saying." I nod and munch on my fries.

"I agree. Something doesn't add up. We're bringing his partner in for questioning."

"Partner? I thought he was divorced. Is he in a new relationship? A nontraditional one?"

Erick shakes his head. "No. No. Not that kind of partner. This is a business partner. Oscar Wiggins. They own the dairy together. They're both artisan cheesemakers."

The hairs on the back of my neck tingle. There's something familiar about the name. Without thinking, I close my eyes and sink into a quick psychic replay of the previous two days. "That's where I saw it!"

Erick spills a little of his cocoa and dabs a napkin on his uniform. "What the heck, Moon?"

"Sorry. The name seemed familiar. Oscar Wiggins attends First Methodist Church."

He dips the edge of his napkin into his water glass and attempts to remove the remainder of the hot chocolate stain from his shirt. "And your point?"

"I don't have one yet. But I knew I'd heard the name before."

He lifts his cup and winks at Tally. "Well, that was totally worth a stain on my uniform."

"I'm sorry, Harper."

Erick smiles and shakes his head. "It's no big deal. If I didn't get one on there by the end of my shift, I'd worry something was wrong in the universe. Something about me and clean shirts, you know? Usually it's coffee, though. That's my go to."

I smile mischievously and lean forward. "Maybe that's why you're so attracted to me? I was one heck of a barista."

He leans across the table, and the heat rolling from his eyes makes my tummy flutter.

Fortunately, Tally arrives with a fresh mug of cocoa and interrupts whatever salacious comment Erick was about to make.

The interruption resets the energy at the table, and we finish our meal without further discussion of murder.

"I gotta get back to the station. I'll let you know if I get any update from the ME, but I don't expect it until late tomorrow—maybe even the day after. If you think of any more fascinating information about Oscar Wiggins, let me know, okay?"

"Ha ha. With that attitude you'll be lucky if I share any of my updates."

He chuckles, slides out of the booth, and kisses me squarely on my unprepared mouth before exiting the diner.

I can't resist a little peek over my shoulder. Leaning out of the booth, I watch my favorite exit. That man can leave anytime he wants. As long as he comes back, of course.

As I turn to situate myself in the booth, I catch sight of Odell shaking his head and chuckling through the red-Formica-trimmed orders-up window. My cheeks flush and I quickly raise a hand to shield my face from further mockery.

It might be time for me to pay Quince Knudsen a visit. I need to find out a bit more about the deceased's ex-wife and the current cheese partner. Before I set up my murder wall, I want to make sure I have a better understanding of how things interconnect.

CHAPTER 7

FIRING OFF a quick text to Quince rewards me with information that the *Pin Cherry Harbor Post* is closed for the week. The elder Knudsen is attending to his brother's estate, and Quince would prefer to meet at the bookstore. We set up a time, and I bundle up appropriately before exiting Myrtle's Diner to brave the Arctic winds whipping across the ice-locked great lake.

My previous experiences with Quince revealed his discomfort around the opposite sex. This tidbit leads me to believe that meeting in the back room on the first floor is preferable to inviting him upstairs to my apartment.

While I wait for him to arrive, I brew up a couple of instant hot chocolates and drop in some mini marshmallows.

A tentative knock on the metal alleyway door announces the arrival of my visitor.

I've seen neither shimmer nor shake of Ghostma, but I fire off a quick telepathic message instructing her to keep her distance just in case she's hovering outside the visual plane.

"Come on in, Quince. I made some cocoa."

A beat-up Chevy truck with rusted-out wheel wells sits in the alley as though abandoned. He rubs his hands together, shivers, and scoots past me to the back room.

"Is that your truck?"

"Yah."

Oh goody, my favorite game. Coax the words from the man-child. "Hey, I'm really sorry about your Uncle Quade. Erick is cooperating, so I'll have more information to work with, and I'll be able to eavesdrop on some interviews tomorrow. For now, it would help to get a better understanding of your uncle's life. Details about the ex-wife, and if you know anything about the dairy and his partner—Oscar Wiggins—that would also be great."

He looks at me as though English isn't his first language, and I sense him struggling mightily to find the courage to share what he knows.

"Look, Quince, I know chatting isn't your thing, but think of it as an important journalistic story. If I don't know the what, why, where, and when, I'm never going to be able to figure out *who* murdered your uncle. So I'm gonna ask you to put on your big-boy pants, and tell me everything."

He nods, takes a swig of hot chocolate, and wipes his mouth with the back of his hand. "K."

I hope that isn't him at his most verbose.

"Like I told you. My uncle is real particular, you know?"

I nod.

"Like, it's kind of a disease. It's why his wife left, you know what I mean?"

Once again, I opt for a physical head nod, rather than risk interrupting his flow with my own verbal response.

"They had a kid. She made my uncle's problems sound pretty bad to the judge, so she got sole custody—no visitation. The whole reason my uncle works so hard at the dairy . . . He's trying to win the kid back over."

"How old is the child?" I couldn't resist. A kettle can only be kept from boiling for so long once the heat is on.

"Oh, he's like fifteen. My uncle was old. Like almost forty or something."

My eyes widen and I stifle a scoff. I remember when I used to think the late thirties were old. As I creep toward my mid-twenties, I'm starting to take a different view of my approaching thirties. "Got it."

"So he took on a partner, to, like, make the dairy more successful."

"Enter Oscar Wiggins. Are they equal partners?"

"My uncle had fifty-one percent share. My dad told him to do that."

"Interesting. Have you ever met your cousin?"

Quince shrugs. "Maybe once, before the divorce."

I completely understand family drama. When my mother discovered she was pregnant and chose to keep me—but not track down the potential father—her parents disowned her. In fact, they couldn't even be bothered to make their way across the pond for her funeral. It's something I haven't forgiven them for, and I'm not sure I ever will. I don't know if I would've enjoyed being raised in England, but I have to think it would've been better than spending over six years in a badly broken foster system.

"Thanks. I know it's not easy to dig through all that family stuff. I'll see if I can sit in on the Oscar Wiggins interview tomorrow. Maybe that will give me a better idea of what they had planned for the dairy, and if those plans created any enemies."

Quince swirls the marshmallows in his cup and replies softly. "Thanks, dude."

He's not pushing his chair back and running for the door, so I lean into my extrasensory perception.

My clairsentience detects a need to be around people. A surprising sensation to receive from Quince. He prides himself on being a lone wolf.

"Would you like to meet my cat?" Lame. I'm honestly not great in the entertaining department.

He looks up, shrugs, and nods. "Sure."

Leading the way to the wrought-iron circular staircase, I offer my standard thirty seconds warning, as I unhook the chain.

He hustles up to the top of the spiral, and I connect the hook behind me.

When I reach the top of the stairway, I call out to my furry overlord. "Oh, Pyewacket? Pye, there's someone I'd like you to meet."

Quince glances toward me as though I may be a tad crazy.

"Don't look at me like that. For a caracal, he seems to have a fairly decent understanding of human speech."

My guest shrugs and wanders down one of the great, curved arms of the mezzanine. His fingers trace the spines and he's entranced. Glancing back toward me, he asks, "May I?"

I'm not sure which title he's looking at, but I'm worried I could draw Twiggy's wrath if I let him touch a valuable tome with his bare hands. I grab a pair of white gloves from the nearest oak reading table and stride toward him. "I'm not sure, but I think you're supposed to wear these. And lay the book down on one of the tables. Don't hold it by the spine."

He slips on the gloves and gently removes the book from the shelf. "Understood."

While he takes the 1646 edition of *Ars Magna Lucis et Umbrae* to a table, I wander the loft in search of the tan terror. As I pass down the opposite arm of the mezzanine, a book rockets out of the shelves, narrowly missing my head.

"Robin Pyewacket Goodfellow! You could've killed me. Stop being a spoiled brat and get down here to meet my friend."

Quince is seated at one of the reading tables, and the green-glass shaded lamp illuminates his selection. It also casts light upon his smirk. Apparently, it amuses him greatly that I speak to my fur baby as though it's human.

Pye saunters toward the interloper, while I retrieve the book from the floor.

Sure enough, it's that same cheesemaking text he was curled up next to earlier. "You can stop hurling books at me, Pye. I've made a note of the title and I will officially log it into evidence."

This comment definitely catches Quince's attention. "So the cat is a snoop too?"

Sighing, I place a hand on my hip. "Rude. I

think the word you're searching for is *sleuth*. And yes, he occasionally helps me on cases."

"Reeeee-ow." A warning.

"Duly noted, master. To be fair, he helps on all my cases."

Quince gazes down at the proud feline. "Cool."

Without further provocation, Pyewacket strides forward and aggressively rubs himself against Quince's leg.

"It would appear that he approves of your praise."

A tender smile erases years from the young man's face. I can almost imagine him as a child, frolicking with a family pet.

He carefully stretches his hand toward Pyewacket. The unpredictable feline takes a hesitant whiff and then licks the outstretched hand with his rough tongue.

Quince chuckles, and risks scratching the beast between the ears.

I swear there's a sound very much like purring coming from the high and mighty Pye.

As I walk away from the recently shelved book, my mood ring burns with a vengeance. I gasp and glance down at the swirling mist inside the smoky black cabochon. The image feels like déjà vu. It's the cover of the book that nearly beaned me: *Mastering Artisan Cheesemaking.*

Throwing my hands in the air, I admit defeat, return to the shelf, and grab the book.

While Quince and Pyewacket are enjoying a mutual admiration society, I plunk into a chair at the nearest reading table and bone up on the art of cheesemaking. Not much of what I'm perusing makes sense, but I feel as though I'm cramming for an exam. Phrases like traditional rennet, direct acidification, and recombinant bacteria flow into my brain to possibly be forever ignored. However, one of those strange phrases could come in handy tomorrow when I drop into the sheriff's station to evaluate Oscar Wiggins.

Pye has taken up residence on the table next to Quince's right arm, and the young man is diligently studying the engravings amongst the ancient text while he absently strokes the feline.

Somehow the day has gotten the better of me and my eyelids seem to be made of lead. "Hey, I think I'm gonna crash out. You're welcome to come back tomorrow if you'd like to keep looking at that book. Just leave it on the table with the gloves and I'll leave a note for Twiggy. That way, if she has a problem with it, she can take it out on me."

He chuckles, sits back, and removes the gloves. "Cool."

I walk down to the back door with him, lock up, and set the alarm. As I march toward my swanky apartment, I call out to Grams and the entitled feline. "It sure would be nice if one of you would hand over a clue about the missing baby Jesus! In case you've forgotten, I have two cases to solve now. Three if we're counting that infernal coat!"

Pyewacket ignores me, and Grams remains cloaked from my otherworldly receptors.

CHAPTER 8

THE BLEAK WINTER sun barely has the strength to penetrate my slumped-glass windows, and offers no warmth or promise of spring. As a resident of the Southwest, I'd heard rumors about something called seasonal affective disorder. I could never imagine such a thing. Most folks in Arizona would give a week's pay for a break from the relentless desert sun. However, now that I reside in almost-Canada, I long for a day filled with azure skies, dense cotton-ball clouds, and heat that penetrates to the bone.

For now, I'll have to settle for the warmth of my reindeer onesie pajamas and a thick flannel-lined bathrobe.

Stumbling downstairs, I pry open one eye far enough to brew a passable cup of coffee and pour a glug of questionable half-and-half into my cup.

Still no sign of my ghostly grandmother.

Time to hike up to the third floor of the printing museum.

Pushing the bar on the door and scraping across the finished concrete floor activates some strange level of hyper-hearing, which I've never experienced. The hairs on the back of my neck stand on end and there are murmuring voices.

Plural.

Even though I'm only half awake, I spin and grab the door leading back to the bookshop before it can slam. I ride it home as silently as possible and creep toward the base of the staircase. The usual comfort I feel in this part of the building evaporates as something in my psychic toolkit strains to identify the sounds.

I wish I could say I've gone up and down the stairs enough times to remember every spot that creaks, but it's simply not true. Another movie trope shattered. Most of the time I'm either in a ridiculous rush, or I'm having some sort of argument with Ghost-ma.

This trip takes on a new and spine-tingling twist as I struggle for silence.

When I reach the landing on the second floor, I'm forced to stop and re-evaluate my plan.

Or should I say, my complete lack of a plan?

I'm wearing pajamas, a robe, and I'm holding a

hot cup of coffee. Not exactly what one would call "ninja gear."

What are they doing in this museum? Suddenly, it occurs to me that many of the artifacts are probably more valuable than I imagine, and it wouldn't be the first time someone has tried to steal something from my place of business.

Now my curiosity transforms into a cold sweat. I should probably call Erick. As I struggle to fish my phone from the pocket of my robe, recognition dawns.

Odell! The other voice is Odell! Grams must be talking as she writes out the messages for him to read.

Now that I've identified the voices as Grams and her first husband, I feel like a peeping Tom who's fallen into the beams of a police cruiser's headlights.

It's completely inappropriate for me to eavesdrop on their private conversation.

Turning to creep back down the stairs and possibly steal some of Pyewacket's Fruity Puffs, my foot catches on the hem of the robe—

Next thing you know, I'm lying at the bottom of a flight of stairs next to a broken coffee mug, and I'm covered in stains of the same.

Odell thunders down the stairs and I call out weakly, "It's me. It was only me. I didn't mean to—"

"Mitzy! What the heck? Are you okay?"

He's at my side in a minute and helps me to a seat on the bottom step.

"What happened, kid?"

He's always been fond of me, but, somehow, now that I know he's my actual grandfather, his concern is warming a whole new part of my heart. "Don't worry. I'm totally fine. I couldn't find Grams . . . There were voices . . . When I figured out it was you . . . My exit was supposed to be stealthy."

His raucous laughter joins my grandmother's near squeal, and I drop my head into my hands. "Thanks, guys. Real vote of confidence."

Odell shakes his head, stands, and offers me a hand. "Here, let me help you up."

I take his outstretched hand and, as I lean forward to get to my feet, a sharp pain shoots through my left ankle. "Ouch!"

He scoops an arm around my waist. "Which ankle?"

"Are you psychic?"

My question catches him completely off guard, and he chokes on his denial.

"No more secrets, remember? Now that we know the truth about my genealogy, it seems like there's a real good chance I didn't inherit all of my gifts from Grams."

Odell looks down and smiles warmly. "Heck, I never thought of it in those terms. I figured I was smarter than the average bear, that's all."

"Oh, come on. You can't kid a kidder, Gramps."

He shakes his head and runs his free hand through his buzz cut nervously. "Maybe there's somethin' to what you're saying. I never thought much about it."

Ghost-ma swirls closer and chill bumps rise on Odell's exposed forearms.

His initial shock from discovering the existence of Isadora's ghost has been replaced with soul-bonding comfort. He glances at his arms and smiles broadly. "Whaddya think, Myrtle? Maybe I got one or two gifts too, eh?"

Grams giggles like a schoolgirl. "Tell him I think he's got all the gifts, sweetie."

Rolling my eyes, I look up at Odell and grin. "I'm really not interested in being an afterlife love-letter interpreter, so I'll just say Grams thinks you're the bee's knees and we'll leave it at that."

He chuckles. "We can debate the finer points of the family tree later. I'm taking you to the hospital. If it ain't broke, it's definitely a bad sprain."

Moaning with the gusto of a spoiled child, I slip my arm around Odell's neck and hop up onto my right foot. "All right, but you have to let me change. I'm not going to the hospital in reindeer onesie PJs."

He smiles and winks. "Aw, don't worry. You look cute as a button."

Punching him playfully in the side, I continue my protest. "It's not the cute factor that concerns me. I've seen all the hospital dramas on television. As soon as I get in there, they're going to take a pair of surgical scissors and cut these adorable pajamas right off me. These PJs are one of the few things I brought from Arizona, and I don't want to see 'em destroyed by an overzealous intern."

Both my grandparents chuckle at my protest, and Odell consents to help me up to the apartment and wait outside while I clumsily get changed.

Luckily, Grams joins me in the apartment and attempts to offer as much assistance as her semi-corporeal form will allow.

At long last, I work my way into a pair of flair-legged yoga pants, and top them off with a T-shirt sporting a huge fake bloodstain on the right side and the simple phrase, "I'M FINE," across the chest.

Grams protests, but I insist the joke will absolutely land with the audience in Emergency.

Her eyes roll as she floats to the exit and summons enough physicality to push the twisted ivy medallion inside the apartment that activates the sliding bookcase door.

Odell stands just outside the entrance with his back turned. "Are you decent?"

"Depends who you ask?"

He spins around and chokes when he sees my shirt. "You are one-of-a-kind, Mitzy Moon. One-of-a-kind."

I clumsily take a hopping, one-legged bow, and he hurries to my side to escort me down to my somewhat new Jeep. En route to the hospital, I attempt to convince him to park and allow me to walk in, but he pulls the "grandpa card" and insists on driving up to the emergency entrance.

An orderly bustles out with a wheelchair, and I glare at Odell. "I promise you, I'm going to remember this, Mr. Johnson."

He laughs too easily. "I'll park this thing and meet you inside. And don't break your other foot while you're waiting."

"Rude."

After explaining it's an ankle sprain and not a gunshot wound, as the humor of my T-shirt implies, the orderly wheels me inside and the nurse behind the desk smiles with recognition when I give her my name. "Oh, I've read about you in the paper. Were you working on a case when you injured yourself, Miss Moon?"

I'm tempted to offer a simple white lie, but the true story of my injury will bring far more laughs when she retells it in the break room. "I wish. Sadly, I was simply walking down the stairs at the printing museum, and caught my foot on the hem of my robe." I shrug and shake my head. "Just your standard variety klutz."

She leans forward and winks. "Gotcha. Your secret's safe with me. I figure you're working on the case of the missing baby Jesus and don't want to tip off Mrs. Coleman."

I didn't see that coming. Clearly, my attempt to tell the truth and not exaggerate my exploits turned into a supposed conspiracy. Wow! I can't imagine how frustrating it must be for the actually famous. I assume people make up stories and take creative license with celebrities' stories all the time. Another reason to enjoy small-town living.

Hold on, did she say, "Tip off Mrs. Coleman"? That warrants a follow-up question. "To be honest, I'm looking into that, but Mrs. Coleman was quite helpful."

The woman rolls her eyes extravagantly and scoffs. "Oh, honey, don't fall for it. She caught one whiff of the proposed Nativity 'upgrade' and she did not turn the other cheek. Apparently, her great-great-something or other gifted that set to the church. Well, you didn't hear it from me, but I wouldn't put it past her to tuck that infant savior in her own trunk to throw a wrench in the plans." She widens her eyes, lifts her brows, and shakes her head as she "Mm-mm-ms" under her breath.

The silence hangs awkwardly between us, and it's my turn. I lean toward the glass partition and whisper through the hole, "Thanks for the tip." Winking as the orderly wheels me away, she rewards me with a matching conspiratorial smile.

After x-rays and a physical examination—which proves more painful than my actual fall—the doctor shares my diagnosis.

"Miss Moon, you're suffering from a Grade 1 anatomical sprain and a mild concussion. I recommend the RICE protocol: Rest, Ice, Compression, and Elevation. You'll have to wear a Velcro boot for one to two weeks, and use a single crutch to keep the weight off the ankle. Do you understand?"

"Yes, ma'am." I feel like a kid in the principal's office getting assigned detention. This doctor's bedside manner could do with a "warm up." For the record, she was not amused by my graphic tee. Guess I wildly misread the room on that one.

She clears her throat and pinches her lips together. "As for the concussion, it's likely a Grade 2. Mild but requiring rest. Avoid operating a motor vehicle for at least forty-eight hours."

"Yes, ma'am." If I didn't live within hobbling distance of everything that mattered to me, I might put up a fuss. However, I'll still be able to make it to the diner and the sheriff's station. Sure, it'll take me three times as long, but at least I won't miss any important suspect interviews.

The doctor exits without any pleasantries, and a nurse enters with paperwork.

After signing myself out and taking my aftercare instructions, Odell picks up my prescription painkillers and drives me back to the bookshop to make sure I tell Grams about the precautions I'm supposed to be taking.

"She may not be able to stop you, but, if I know Myrtle, she'll find a way to make you do as you were told."

Lifting my eyebrows, I nod in agreement. "Oh, you don't know the half of it."

After handing me a pain pill, and making sure I drink the entire glass of water, Odell sets the medication in my bathroom. "It's on the counter," he says as he situates me on the settee, elevates my injured leg, and places the hospital-issue ice pack on my left ankle. "If you need anything, just call the diner. I can be here in five minutes or less."

"Thanks, Gramps."

He shakes his head and chuckles as he leaves.

Pyewacket creeps across the thick carpet as though he's stalking prey. He circles the contraption on my foot and lifts his nose in the air to see if the smell is one that should concern him.

"Don't worry. It's only a little walking boot to

protect my sprained ankle. Not all of us are blessed with your reflexes, Pyewacket. Or your endless supply of lives!"

"Ree-ow." Soft but condescending.

Satisfied with my explanation, the spoiled caracal saunters off to find his own entertainment.

The trip to the hospital, the tests, exams, and endless waiting chewed up most of my day. I hope I didn't miss the dairy partner interrogation.

Only one way to find out . . .

Time for me to update my boyfriend.

Would it surprise you to hear that Erick is not shocked by my report? In fact, he honestly can't believe I wasn't more seriously injured. He offers to come and pick me up for the Oscar Wiggins interview, but I insist I'm a self-sufficient, independent woman and will make my own way to the station.

The psychic in me warns that I'll regret that assumption.

CHAPTER 9

You know what? Being a self-sufficient, independent woman isn't all it's cracked up to be. As I crutch my way down Main Street, I'm out of breath and my ankle is throbbing. Maybe I should've taken two pain pills. It seems far colder outside than I remember, and the patches of un-shoveled sidewalk make my hop more dangerous than I'd hoped.

While I struggle to coordinate door, crutch, walking boot, and not falling over—

"Moon! I can't believe you wouldn't let me help you." Erick takes my crutch, slips his arm around my waist, and practically carries me to the observation room.

I would never admit it out loud, but he really is my knight in shining armor. I can be a modern woman and still accept a gallant gesture from Sheriff Too-Hot-To-Handle. "Thank you, kind sir."

"Not a problem, m'lady."

"I'll wait here for you, Sheriff."

He grins, kisses the top of my head, and walks out of the observation room.

From my perch in the glass-encased spy nook, I glean what I can from the interview subject's demeanor before the sheriff enters.

Oscar Wiggins sits calmly in Interrogation Room 2. His shoulders are broad and his strong hands show the scars of manual labor, but his vibe is more metro-sexual hipster than redneck farmer. He removes a miniature comb from his plaid shirt pocket and grooms his meticulously trimmed mustache. He slips it back into the pocket and admires his reflection. Not a single dark-brown hair on his face, or head, dares to be out of place.

I'm not picking up anything disconcerting through the one-way glass. That's a good sign. Although not helpful as far as suspects go.

I brilliantly use the tip of my crutch to flip the silver toggle switch, and Erick's in-charge work voice flows through the speaker.

"Now that we've got the particulars out of the way, thank you for coming in today, Mr. Wiggins. I understand you and the deceased were partners in the dairy. How long had you and Mr. Knudsen been in business together?"

Good job, Erick. Start him out with a softball question and loosen his tongue.

"I'm happy to assist in the investigation, Sheriff. Quade wasn't just a business partner, he was a good friend. Me and the wife used to have him over for supper at least once a week. It was tough for him, you know? Being all alone and everything."

Erick nods. "And how long had you been in business together?"

"Oh, right. What happened was, I worked for a big dairy down south, and the commute was killing me. I offered to do some consulting for Quade, and we just hit it off, you know?" He strokes his close-clipped goatee and nods.

A woman doesn't need clairsentience to pick up on Erick's frustration with the unanswered question. Hopefully third time's a charm.

"And when did you start this consulting?"

"Well, let's see." Oscar presses his thumb against his lower lip. "Seems like that was almost six years ago. Boy, time flies."

Erick makes a couple of notes in his pad and continues. "And when did you sign the partnership agreement?"

Oscar angles away and places both of his thick hands on the edge of the table—rhythmically strumming his fingers as he ponders the question. "Gee, I think I did the consulting for about a year, then I came on full-time at Quade's dairy. That maybe only lasted six or eight months, and— Well, he was in a bit of financial trouble. He was going to take out a big loan, but I suggested the partnership as a way to keep things afloat and avoid more debt."

"So would you say the partnership agreement was signed roughly four years ago?"

Erick is quickly losing patience with this attention-deficient interviewee.

"What? Oh, yes. Four years. Mmhmm. Sounds right." Oscar seems distracted by his own image in the one-way glass.

"And were you able to turn the dairy around? Was it profitable?"

Mr. Wiggins nods several times, but then he shakes his head and shrugs. "It was doing all right. Not necessarily turning a profit. We had plans to change all that. We were going to hammer out an agreement to sub-produce for one of the big dairies down south. It was going to put us on the fast track to success, you know?"

Erick scribbles in his notepad, and silence hangs in the air. I can sense Oscar's discomfort, but most people are uneasy when being questioned by law enforcement.

The sheriff stops writing and tilts his head.

"This sub-producing contract was your idea, or Quade's?"

Oscar shrugs and shakes his head in confusion. "I can't be sure who thought of it. We had a lot of long conversations over bourbon, after those weekly dinners."

Bourbon? Maybe Quince doesn't know his uncle as well as he thinks.

"Anyone else know about these conversations?" Erick taps his pen once.

"Tammy might remember, but as far as I know it just came up."

"And Tammy is your wife?"

The man laughs uncomfortably. "She sure is. And won't let me forget it for a minute. You know how the old ball and chain can be."

I angle my body forward and reach out with all my psychic senses. I can't wait to see how Erick answers that question.

"Can't say that I do, Mr. Wiggins. But I've heard the sentiment before. I'll make a note to ask Tammy about that line item. Is this sub-producer contract moving forward?"

Oscar takes a deep breath and schools his features carefully. There's a hint of excitement beneath his somber, well-groomed exterior. "Yeah, it's a real shame Quade won't be around to reap the rewards. But I feel good knowing it was his dying wish."

In case you're wondering, I'm not the only one who isn't buying that performance.

Erick crosses his arms and inhales—real slow. "His dying wish? Are you saying that this conversation about the sub-producing was the last thing you and Quade spoke about?"

Oscar swallows and shakes his head. "Well, no. I didn't mean it like that. It was just a stupid expression. Sorry, I'm a little shook up by all of this. Poor choice of words, Sheriff. I don't remember the last thing we spoke about. Probably something mundane, like cleaning the milking equipment or ordering more feed."

Erick nods, but makes a lengthy note in his pad.

"That'll be all for now, Mr. Wiggins. I'll speak to your wife about the contract conversation, and we'll be in touch if we need any additional information from you."

Oscar nods and hesitantly gets to his feet. "Is it all right if I leave, Sheriff?"

"You're free to go. But don't leave town just yet."

Mr. Wiggins' spine stiffens, and he hustles out of the interrogation room.

Rather than rushing out of the observation room to sit innocently in Erick's office, I feel as though I have permission to sit comfortably and wait for him to check in. My grown-up patience pays off as he peeks into the room.

"Any hunches?" He tilts his head hopefully.

"Not at present. Although, I'm curious to see if Tammy can fill in some details on that sub-producing tidbit." I reach for my crutch, but my thoughtful boyfriend beats me to the punch.

"There's no crime in asking for help, Moon." His tone is scolding, but he offers me one hand and holds the crutch in his other.

I smile and accept his assistance. "Unless you're asking for help to commit murder."

The comment hits him square in the gut and he exhales sharply before laughing. "Nice way to put it in perspective." He places the crutch under my left arm and holds my right hand until I'm situated.

Smiling up at him, with what I hope are feminine wiles, I ask, "In the interest of accepting help, could I possibly get a police escort back to the bookshop?"

He nods and purposefully chews the inside of his cheek. "Of course. Let me see if Paulsen is available." Erick turns, and I let out a little squeak of protest. He spins back with a smug grin on his face. "Gotcha."

"Good one, Harper. You definitely got me."

Graciously assisting me into the hallway, he

grabs a winter jacket from his office. "Deputy Baird, I'm headed—out for the night. Call me if you need me."

She frowns knowingly. "10-4, Sheriff."

I purposely avoid making eye contact with the perceptive deputy. My quick-to-blush cheeks will certainly confirm any suspicions she might have about exactly where Erick is headed.

Walking back toward the bookshop, just the two of us, reminds me of the first time we held hands. The thrill that raced up my arm that day hasn't lessened a bit. In fact, each day I spend with him makes me more and more sure that this is the path I'm supposed to be on.

I don't want to tempt fate by making too many plans for the future. I'm just going to hobble through the snow with this wonderful man's arm around my waist, and be grateful for all the treasures I've uncovered in almost-Canada.

Erick insists on unhooking the chain at the bottom of the spiral staircase, despite my Twiggy-related protests. He's far too acquainted with acci-dent-prone Mitzy to back down. In the end, we make it past and get the chain re-secured within the thirty-second window.

Hopefully banishing Grams from the apart-ment for the evening will go as smoothly.

As if on cue—

"I'm happy to give you and Erick some privacy, dear. All you have to do is ask nicely. You'd be surprised how cooperative people can be. More flies with honey, I always say."

As Erick reaches up to pull the candle handle, I clear my throat and mumble, "I have to take care of a little family business, Erick."

He turns hesitantly and searches the air around me. "Isadora?"

"The one and only." Navigating a slow crutch-supported turn, I address the ghost. "Grams, Erick was kind enough to walk me home and we're probably going to order some food and hang out. Would you please give us some privacy?"

Ghost-ma twists one of her diamond rings and adjusts a strand of pearls. "Now, that wasn't so hard, was it?"

Not willing to let her get in the last word, I send her a brief telepathic message. *You better hightail it to the printing museum, Missy, or there's going to be some hot couture, and that's H-O-T!*

Her face is a glowing mask of horror as she vanishes through the wall into the museum.

Threatening to start her vintage fashion on fire is always a power move.

"Are we clear?" Erick searches the air a second time and his eyes grow wide.

"All clear."

He helps me to the over-stuffed settee, and once I'm safely in a seated position, gently pulls off my coat.

Taking advantage of his nearness, I secretly inhale his citrus-woodsy scent.

Laying the coat over the back of the sofa, he asks, "I heard some mention of ordering food. Were you serious?"

Rubbing my hands together in anticipation, I grin. "I'm hoping. Do you think Dante might be working at Angelo and Vinci's? I'm happy to pay a delivery charge if he's willing to run over."

Erick smiles. "Nice. Now you're thinking like a local, and an heiress."

"You're not wrong." Rather than be offended, I take it as a compliment. I honestly don't mind spreading a little goodwill. The Duncan-Moon coffers can certainly cover a couple generous portions of the world's best lasagna!

Once the important business of ordering sustenance has been handled, and Dante has been promised a hefty tip, Erick throws out a suggestion. "Do you want to play a board game?"

I choke on my reply, and it takes several seconds for me to regroup and respond. "A board game? Look, Harper, I'm not going to pretend to be a relationship expert, but I don't want to move to the board game phase for at least a few more months."

He blushes adorably. "Yeah, it sounded wrong as soon as it came out of my mouth. It's just that you're kinda injured and I don't want to make things worse."

Perhaps I shouldn't, but it's so much fun to make him uncomfortable. "Make things worse? How do you mean?" Oh, that color of red looks so good on his cheeks.

"Well, you know— I was thinking—"

"Let me put you out of your misery, Sheriff. Why don't we start with supper and see where the night takes us?"

He swallows audibly. "Yeah, your plan is better."

CHAPTER 10

WHEN HARSH WINTER light stabs its early morning fingers into my eyes, my first instinct is to scold myself. What an idiot! I can't believe I forgot to close the blackout blinds before I went to bed.

Thankfully, those thoughts are kept on the inside of my head, and they are quickly replaced by a wash of warm, tingly memories.

Oh, that's right. Last night, when yummy Erick Harper was kissing the side of my neck, the last thing on my mind was window shades or morning.

Carefully turning beneath the thick down comforter, I risk a peek at my sleepover guest.

Erick, who grew up in Pin Cherry, must be more accustomed to the frosty temperatures. Sometime during the night, he got too hot—no pun intended; I swear—and pushed the comforter down, exposing his lovely washboard abs for inspection. Plus, his tousled, soft blond hair is begging me to run my fingers through it.

Exercising all the self-control I don't possess, I keep my hands to myself and enjoy the view for a moment longer.

Before I finish soaking it all in, one sleepy eyelid cracks open and a mischievous bright-blue eye locks onto me like a laser-targeting system. "Whatever you're planning over there, Moon, it will have to wait."

Struggling to swallow, I jump to my defense. "Planning? I wasn't planning anything. I was—"

He rolls onto his side and props up his mussed head of hair on one rippling bicep. "Mmhmm, go on. I'm gonna go ahead and let you try to finish that sentence."

A blush of heat creeps up my cheeks and I've never been so thankful for a caracal interruption.

Pyewacket lands with a thud between us and offers a warning thwack to my left shoulder.

"Message received, my furry overlord." I twist and groan and drag myself out of the heavenly cocoon. "I gotta pour some Fruity Puffs for Pye, but I'll be back to discuss whatever it is you think you know."

He sits up, stretches his arms wide, and tries to

speak as he yawns. "No hurry. I can watch you walk away all day."

I tug down the bottom of my sleeping T-shirt and giggle. "Hey, that's my line."

His hoarse chuckle echoes down the stairs as I limp toward the back room to fix a heaping bowl of sugary children's cereal for my entitled feline.

"I gave you an extra-large portion, because you were such a good kitty last night. Thank you for respecting my privacy." I nearly make the mistake of ending my praise by scratching his head between his black-tufted ears, but that's a mistake you only make once. Never interrupt a caracal when he's eating.

No sign of Grams—which is excellent.

I hobble upstairs, trying my best to keep the weight off my left foot, even though I forgot my crutch somewhere in the apartment.

Shambling back into the cozy room with high hopes, I'm disappointed to discover my drowsy boyfriend is no longer lounging on my antique four-poster. He's dressed and ready for action. "You're leaving? Already?"

Erick strides across the room in a slightly crumpled tan uniform, scoops me into his arms, and kisses me deliciously. "Some of us have to work for a living."

"Oh brother! I have a job. I'm looking into the

disappearance of the miniature Messiah from a certain local Nativity set."

His easy grin disappears, and his sheriff's voice joins the party. "Look, Moon, I want you to take it easy on that ankle. Sprains can take longer to heal than breaks. Don't push your luck. And if I know you, you're always pushing your luck. So act like a real heiress for one day. Sit on your sofa, eat bonbons, and watch old movies. I'll check on you at lunchtime."

He offers my cheek one last gentle kiss and walks toward the spiral staircase.

Yes, I do watch him leave. However, I don't let him get away without a fight. "I have never eaten bonbons in my life, Sheriff Harper!"

He laughs all the way out the alley door.

With all the ankle spraining shenanigans and everyone insisting that I take it easy, I nearly forgot about the curious case of Mrs. Coleman. However, today I'm unsupervised and I think it's time to grab my keys and take a little convalescence drive.

As I pick up my dealership-issue keychain, I fully expect Grams to burst through the floor or the wall and admonish me, but the apartment is silent. Twenty-four hours is almost forty-eight, right?

It's my lucky day.

The yoga pants I previously eased over my injured foot can certainly pass for one more day, and the T-shirt I slept in is barely even wrinkled. Plus, the message will serve as my mantra for the day. "Curiosity killed the cat, but satisfaction brought him back!" There's an image of a smug feline perched next to the idiom.

Managing the crutch, the circular stairs, and the "No Admittance" chain proves a tall order for my inborn clumsiness. So I breathe a heavy sigh of relief when I make it safely to the first floor, and get the chain hooked back in place without setting off the alarm.

Things are going swimmingly.

"And where do you think you're going, young lady?"

Spoke too soon.

Grams rockets toward me in a mini ghost-rage. "Keys? Why on earth do you have keys? You're not supposed to drive for at least two days!"

"Simmer down, Isadora. It's my left foot that's injured. All the driving stuff happens with the right foot. It's not like I have a manual transmission. Who even knows what that is anymore?"

She crosses her arms and strums her perfectly manicured fingers on the burgundy silk-and-tulle. "I don't know, dear. The foot isn't the issue. According to Odell, it's the concussion we're supposed to worry about. Plus, it all seems too dangerous. I don't like the idea of you poking around, looking for a potential murderer in your condition."

My jaw falls open like Old Mother Hubbard's cupboard. "My condition! It's not like I'm pregnant. It's a little ankle sprain. It's nothing."

Salty tears build up in the corner of Ghost-ma's eyes. "Just the thought of a great grandbaby . . ."

"Do not start with me. We've had this discussion, and we are not having it again. And it's not like I'm looking around for a killer. I'm not insane."

"But you have to find out who killed Quince's uncle?"

"All in due time. Right now, I'm simply following up on a missing Messiah lead. There'll be time to sweep up potential murderers after I've put things right in the Nativity scene."

Grams reaches an ethereal hand toward me and pats my shoulder. "You're a good egg, Mitzy. I'd be proud of you even if you weren't my granddaughter."

Grabbing the handle on the alleyway door, I can't keep the thought from popping into my head: *But it doesn't hurt that I'm an egg from your farm.*

"Well, I never—"

As I let the door slam closed, I spout my favorite refrain. "Oh, we all know different, Myrtle Isadora Johnson Linder Duncan Willamet Rogers."

Not for the first time, I'm pleased that the ghost

of my dear grandmother is tethered to the bookshop and can't follow me down the alleyway to continue her defense.

The parking lot at the First Methodist Church is freshly plowed, and the man-made snowdrifts at the back of the lot tower above my Jeep. They're also an unattractive muddy brown with streaks of black. I can't wait for the weather to turn, and all of this snowdrift nonsense to melt away.

Despite the exposed pavement, I take it real slow as I approach the sanctuary. Once inside, I tug off my beanie and shove it in the pocket of my puffy coat.

Mrs. Coleman's door stands open as I approach. The noxious potpourri has leaked into the hallway. I grab one last breath of fresh-ish air and crutch on in.

"Good morning, Mrs. Coleman. Do you have a minute?"

She beams warmly, teeth and all, and gestures to a thinly padded seat in her spacious quarters.

I lower myself onto the ruffled gingham as my gaze clocks the plethora of porcelain cats perched on every flat surface. How did I miss that last time?

"Did you find our Lord and Savior?"

That opening line reminds me of a very different discussion I had with foster family number three. "I think I'm closing in on Him. I've gotten some good leads. Which is why I'm here. Rumor has it the Nativity scene was scheduled for a makeover."

Her baleful gasp interrupts my report. "Folks just don't appreciate history anymore."

"I couldn't agree more. Was there anyone specifically opposed to the refresh?"

Her beady eyes dart left and right, as though seeking the support of her feline army. "There were congregants on both sides of the argument."

That tells me what I need to know about her. Old guard—definitely. Now, to define the new guard. "So, who was pushing for the change?"

"There were three or four ladies who were particularly adamant. Just didn't appreciate the nostalgia of the set we have. I said I wasn't against some thoughtful restoration, but throwing the whole thing, and the gift it represents, out the door . . . I said it seemed unchristian."

Whew! That comment must've ruffled some feathers, but I'll keep that side note to myself. "What's the status of the project now that the baby Jesus has gone missing?"

She shuffles some papers on her desk, pulls her lips together over her chompers, and sniffles loudly. "They're pushing forward vigorously. They claim it wouldn't be right to replace part of the set and not the rest. Even said something about favoritism or design flaws . . . It's all a blur, really. I just find the thefts upsetting."

"Thefts? Are you talking about the list?"

Mrs. Coleman tilts her head in confusion, but a moment later her lips curl into a wan smile revealing "all she wants for Christmas." "Oh my goodness! I forgot to tell you. I placed that list in the file with the copy for this week's bulletin. When I pulled out the folder to start the copies, there was the attendance list. So, there was only the one theft. I'm not sure what I was thinking when I placed it in there. The list is safe. Just the kidnapping of our sweet baby from the manger." She dabs at a nonexistent tear.

"Has there been a ransom demand?"

Her close-set eyes widen, and her mouth slowly forms a perfect O, but no sound comes out.

"I didn't mean to upset you, Mrs. Coleman. I thought maybe if it was more than a prank, there might have been some monetary motivation."

She shakes her head vigorously. "There's been no such demand. And if the pastor had gotten such a call, I certainly would know about it. Why just this morning I was saying—"

Before she can tell me what she said, I jump in.

"Could you write down the names of the congregants pushing for the new Nativity?"

The woman nods absently, but her gaze remains fixed on a point in space.

"Mrs. Coleman?"

She looks at me as though I've appeared out of thin air. "Oh, yes dear. Forgive me."

I'd love to make a missing-baby-Jesus quip right now regarding her forgiveness, but taking a moment to read the room . . . this isn't the time or the place.

She scribbles four or five names on a piece of paper, double-checks it, and hands it to me. "I spoke to the reverend about this. I said, 'If someone from our own congregation is behind this . . . Well, how disappointing.'"

I smile and nod as I take the slip of paper from her outstretched hand. "I'll keep looking, Mrs. Coleman. Don't worry."

"Thank you, dear."

And with that, I shove the slip of paper in the pocket of my coat, hobble down the hallway and out the side door.

As I HEAD BACK toward Bell, Book & Candle, I unhappily check something off my list. The attendance list wasn't stolen, which makes it less likely that a congregant is responsible for the theft of the baby Jesus from the manger. Only someone inside the church system would've known about the attendance list, and the connection between that missing roll sheet and the statuette made sense to me, at the time.

Now my suspect pool went from the folks in attendance at the First Methodist Church on a particular Sunday to anyone in Pin Cherry Harbor or the surrounding area.

Grrr. Argh.

Before I can get the alleyway door open wide

enough to stumble through, Grams is already hitting me with a complaint.

However, once I'm safely inside the bookstore, I realize her issue isn't with me at all. For the first time I can remember, she's legitimately upset with Pyewacket.

"You have to do something, Mitzy. That monster is dragging a horrible rag all over the bookstore. He tried to take it up to the apartment, and it took every ounce of strength I had to scare him back down the stairs. Can you imagine if he'd gotten the nasty thing near my couture?!"

"*Your* couture. Hold on a minute, Grams. I distinctly remember the wording in your last will and testament. 'Everything inside the Bell, Book & Candle Bookshop and Printing Museum is to become the sole property of Mizithra Achelois Moon.'"

Her tantrum ends abruptly, and she squeezes her expertly drawn eyebrows together, creating a soft furrow above her nose. "Did you honestly remember that phrase verbatim or are you using your psychic recall?"

The question catches me off guard and I have to let it rattle around in my noggin for a minute or so. "Well, I'm honestly not sure. I think I used my psychic recall. No. I did. I saw the page— I was on the bus—"

She floats toward me and whispers in awe. "Sweetie, you're getting really good. I remember when you used to take several minutes to calm yourself and focus before you could access your gifts. You did that in the middle of an argument! In the blink of an eye!" She claps her hands together gleefully and swirls around me as though she's an entire circle of children playing Ring Around the Rosie.

"Did I? I mean, I actually did."

Pyewacket rises onto his hind legs and rubs the nasty rag against my day-old yoga pants.

Grams chuckles. "I'm not sure you're doing that math correctly, dear. Seems like it's been more than one day." She purses her lips and looks down her nose at my sorely lacking sense of fashion.

"Ignore her, Pyewacket. There must be something very important about this rag." I remove it from his mouth, and he rewards me with a response.

"Reow." Can confirm.

"I'll take it up to the murder wall and officially log it into evidence."

As I spin on my crutch to make my way upstairs, Pyewacket leaps in my way and offers a frightening warning. "Reeeee-ow."

"Easy, big guy. I'm on your side. Remember?" Dangling the filthy rag between my thumb and forefinger, I look at Grams and shrug. "Any ideas?"

She floats backward and shivers with disgust.

"All right, Pye. Help me out here. If you don't want me to take this upstairs, do you want me to give it to Erick?"

He plunks his tan behind down and seems to shake his head in a very human way.

"So that's a 'no' to Erick." Running through my short list of options, I choose my photojournalist friend next. "Is it something I should ask Quince about?"

"Reow." Can confirm.

That's one for team Mitzy. Before I can continue my Twenty Questions with the cat, the word icehouse hits my brain like an invisible mortar round. "Icehouse? Do you want me to go back out to check the icehouse for something?"

"RE-OW!" Game on!

Spinning the keys around my finger, I head toward the back door.

Grams summons all of her otherworldly strength, takes semi-corporeal form, and plants a fist on either hip—directly in my path. "I will haunt your apartment till the end of times! You and that sexy sheriff will never have another moment's peace."

"What's the deal? That's a little harsh."

"You call that Quince Knudsen and tell him to pick you up. I'm not against you continuing your investigation. You know how smart I think you are, dear. But you get the boy to drive you out there and watch your back. You're not at your best, physically. I'd never forgive myself if something happened, sweetie."

"Copy that."

A quick call to Quince confirms that he's as bored as I am, and happy to drive me out to his uncle Quade's ice-fishing house.

The drive out to one of the hundreds of lakes dotting the Birch County countryside seems longer than I remember. Perhaps it's the psychic itch begging to be scratched that makes the journey interminable.

"Did you ever go ice fishing with your uncle?"

Quince shrugs. "Couple times."

"Not your thing?"

He sighs and taps his thumb on the steering wheel. "He really likes to be alone. Like, for real."

I shrug and shiver. "Can you turn the heater up?"

Quince shakes his head and groans softly. "It's kinda busted."

Just the thought of no heater sends my body into a full spasm. "What? How busted is kinda?"

He snickers. "Pretty much totally. That's why

there's duct tape on the windows. Grab those hoodies behind the seat, if you want."

"Dude!" My panic has sent me headfirst into the young man's word pool. "We could freeze to death."

The smile disappears from his face in a flash, and he grips the steering wheel with both hands.

"Oh shoot. Quince, I'm so sorry. My brain just goes into the dark humor anytime I get uncomfortable. I honestly didn't mean to—"

His Adam's apple bobs as he struggles to swallow. "It's cool. No biggie."

It absolutely was a biggie. A monstrous faux pas. Even though it didn't cross my mind at the time, the callous reference to freezing to death clearly seems like an attempt to make light of his uncle's passing. Sadly, I've been in this situation a few too many times before, and I've learned the hard way that the more I talk, the worse I make it for myself. I shiver in silence and take winter's wrath as the penance I deserve.

The next turn sparks something in my memory and a sense of relief floods over me as we draw near the icehouse.

Quince parks and meets me at the edge of the frozen lake. "What are we looking for?"

"I'm not exactly sure, but I'll know it when I see it."

"Do we break the yellow tape?"

"Hold on a minute." Following the crime scene tape around the structure that's barely larger than a port-a-potty, I find the loose end tucked under and carefully pull it free. Unwrapping the "not" present, I instruct Quince to keep his gloves on as I open the door.

"I'll check the outside while you check the inside. There's not really room for both of us in there. If you don't find anything, we'll swap."

He blushes at the mere thought of having to be in such close quarters with me, and I begin my search of the exterior.

It's a simple wooden structure with a small window opposite the door. The roof is slightly pitched and the blue paint peels and curls from the effects of the harsh weather.

Other than the screw we recovered earlier, there are no unusual marks on the exterior of the tiny building. The window is closed tightly, and the snow has drifted halfway up the side of the windward face.

"Anything?"

He grumbles for a moment and manages an audible, "Nope."

"Me neither. Wanna swap?"

He steps out and nods as I complete my inspection of the circumference. Quince heads off in the direction I arrived from, and I step inside. Wow, what a difference. Just getting out of the wind warms me up several degrees.

Starting on my right, I perform a diligent visual scan. Nothing has been damaged. Fishing pole hangs from its hook, and the only item that seems disturbed is the chair, which previously held the body. I don't plan on touching that.

A voice penetrates the thin boards. "Find anything?"

As I'm about to call out "no joy," a strange pull tugs at my extra senses. Twisting the handle of the tiny wood-burning stove, I open the door and a heavy scent of smoke hits me. I'm not sure why this has my senses all atingle, but something isn't right.

"Hey, come here a second."

Quince's bright-red nose and wind-whipped watery eyes appear in the doorway. "What is it?"

"Not sure. I know this is going to sound weird, but something feels funny about the stove. It smells really smoky."

My young sidekick chuckles. "You know it burns wood, right?"

Standing and placing a hand on my hip, I shake my head. "Not helpful. Tell me how it works."

He rolls his eyes and looks at me as though I'm crazy. "You put the wood in, you throw in some birch bark or newspaper, light a match, and feed the fire. A lot of guys use pellets. My uncle was a purist."

The shock of the lengthy response catches me off guard.

He leans in the doorway. "Does that make sense?"

Nodding, I step closer to the stove. "This handle, on the straight piece of pipe, is that the flue?"

He nods. "Yeah. And you always crack a window to keep the airflow going. It's a small space—"

Our eyes meet, and our combined gaze shoots toward the secured window.

Quince is the first to voice our concern. "He wouldn't run the stove with the window closed."

"Is there a chance he was fishing without a fire going?"

He shakes his head vigorously. "You heard how cold it got that night. The sun woulda barely been peeking over the horizon when he got here after the first milking. There's no way he didn't start a fire."

"The rag!"

Quince tilts his head like a confused puppy. "The what?"

Pushing past him, I exit the icehouse and stumble toward the left side where the stovepipe exits the structure.

"Mitzy, what are you doing?" The photojournalist stares at me with concern. Rising to my tip-toes, I shove my arm, mitten and all, into the pipe. A second later, I yank it out and dangle the filthy rag. "Ta dah! Someone wanted to make sure smoke couldn't get out. I wonder if your uncle died of smoke inhalation, and the freezing came after?"

His entire demeanor changes. Quince steps back and rubs a gloved hand over his mouth as he shakes his head. "Carbon monoxide."

"What's that now?"

He continues to shake his head as he replies. "The closed window, the blocked stovepipe. Even a small fire would burn up the oxygen in there in no time." He sniffles, looks away, and his voice is barely a whisper. "At least I've heard carbon monoxide poisoning is painless."

Without thinking, I walk toward the boy and wrap my arms around him.

Him not pulling away is testament to the impact of our discovery.

"Should we take the evidence to Erick?"

Quince nods. "If we leave it here, someone could come back and take it. I'll get my camera and snap a few pics. The closed window is as important as that rag."

He retrieves his camera, which likely cost more than his entire hooptie. Which is what we call a beat-up, janky, piece-of-trash vehicle.

While he documents the scene, I attempt to gather additional information from the filthy fabric.

No such luck.

"I'm done. Let's hit it."

"Hold on, I have to put the crime-scene tape back." Using the cheat of a psychic replay, I re-wrap the icehouse exactly as we found it. "There. Now no one will be the wiser."

"Cool. Maybe the sheriff can pull fingerprints off that rag."

Far be it from me to burst Quince's balloon, but I don't think they can pull prints from cloth. Although, there may be some particulates that will lead them to the killer.

One thing is for sure. There's no denying it now. Quade Knudsen was absolutely murdered.

CHAPTER 12

THE DEPUTY whom I've nicknamed Furious Monkeys occupies the front desk with her usual flair.

"Good morning, Deputy Baird."

Her eyes remain locked on the screen of her phone as she battles her way through another level of her favorite game. "He's in his office."

"Thanks."

As I push through the crooked wooden gate separating the front waiting area from the bullpen, a surprising voice pulls my attention back.

"Hey, what level are you?" Quince rests his elbows on the counter and glances at the deputy's screen.

She grins. "Just crushed 328."

"Cool. I'm 330."

The shock that grips Baird's face is palpable. "You're Superbomb? The only one to crack 330?"

Quince makes a poor attempt at hiding his smirk. "Yeah. Mad respect though, GunandBadge."

She accepts the compliment, nods, and watches her virtual-opponent-come-to-life follow me toward Erick's office.

Deputy Gilbert taps away on a typewriter and barely looks up as we pass. It still shocks me to see someone typing at an actual typewriter! But it shouldn't. After all, this is the town that tech forgot. And things like old-fashioned paper passbooks at the bank and a majority of businesses that take cash only are par for the course around here.

Whispering over my shoulder, I can't resist gathering more gaming intel from Quince. "How long have you been playing that game?"

"Since the beginning, dude. I'm an OG."

I stop in my tracks and turn toward the photo-journalist, who continues to surprise me. "OG? You, my young friend, are about as far from an original gangster as one could get."

He scrunches up his face and shakes his head. "No, dude. It's true. No numbers after my handle. All the solid names are taken now. So the noobs have to steal good handles and add numbers to make a unique username."

I feign a curtsy. "Well, I beg your pardon, good Sir Superbomb."

He scoffs and flicks his wrist at me. "Let's get this over with."

We continue into Erick's office, and the second I walk through the door without my crutch, he's on his feet, shaking a finger in my direction. "Moon! You're not supposed to put any weight on it."

Lifting my hands in the air as though it's a stickup, I jump to my own defense. "Easy, officer. I'm unarmed. And I'm un-crutched."

He pounds his fist on a stack of papers on his desk and shakes his head. "What emergency caused you to take this risk with your own health?"

"It's not that big of a risk, Erick. This walking boot thingy is doing all the work. I'm keeping most of the weight off it." I quickly shift to my right leg to make good on my claim.

Before he can offer any further admonishment, Quince jumps in. "We found some evidence."

Erick chuckles coldly and presses a hand to his forehead. "Do I even want to know?"

"Don't worry, we didn't disturb anything inside. This rag was shoved in the open end of the stovepipe at Quade's icehouse."

I can almost hear the wheels turning behind Erick's intense blue eyes as he adds this clue to his list. "Hm, there would be no reason for them to check for carbon monoxide. Normally, the bright pinkish-red color of a corpse gives immediate visual indication. However, the freezing of the body would've canceled that out. Whoever set this up knew how to cover their tracks." He grabs an evidence bag from a box on the dented file cabinet behind his desk. "Drop that in here."

As I place the filthy piece of cloth in the evidence bag, I can't resist a little sass. "Sir, yes, sir."

"Sorry, Moon. I appreciate you bringing the evidence in, but I wish you'd stay away from my crime scenes."

I offer him a pouty frown. "But I help you."

"It's not that. I'd just love for you to take care of that foot like it matters."

Shrugging, I avoid his gaze. "I'm a fast healer."

He chuckles and rubs a hand across his mouth. I'm not sure what he's hoping to prevent himself from saying, but I suppose I'll take it as a gift. "You two run across anything else?"

"This and a tightly closed window, but that's all so far, Sheriff." I place a hand on my hip and flash him a smile with a bonus wink.

"Okay, then. Thanks again. I'll get in touch with the medical examiner, and if we can confirm elevated levels of carbon monoxide that could give us a new lead."

"What about the rag? Can you run it for particulates?"

He crosses his arms in that way that always distracts me from the matter at hand. "Don't worry, Moon. I still know how to run an investigation, despite the fact that I have amateurs clamoring to take over my department at every turn."

At least he laughs after he says it, and I add my forced chuckle to the mix.

"You'll let us know what the ME finds out, right?"

He drops the evidence bag on his desk, places both hands on the surface, and exhales with force. "I feel like that's a foregone conclusion."

"Good. Let me know if you want to meet up for coffee later."

Turning, I poke Quince a couple of times and nod my head toward the exit. I get it. He's young. He hasn't learned the art of how to quit while you're ahead. I happen to know that even a noncommittal promise of a peek at the medical examiner's report is the best I'm going to get on this visit. My plan is to hightail it out of the station before I say anything to kill my advantage.

Quince shuffles forward but grumbles over his shoulder. "Okay, okay, you don't have to go aggro."

I hardly think my gentle nudging is aggressive behavior, but I'll let the matter drop. Unfortunately, the mere discussion of coffee has got my stomach grumbling. "Want to grab some grub at the diner?"

"Nah. Gotta get back and help my dad."

"Copy that. I'll let you know what I hear from Erick."

"Sweet."

He dives into his rust-bucket truck, and I head toward french-fry heaven.

Seems like an off time of day to visit the diner and traffic is light. Instead of a booth, I choose a stool at the counter, so it will be easier to chat with my grandfather. Plus, my foot is throbbing like a . . . So I elevate it on the next stool. I should've taken some pain meds to go.

Odell grins through the orders-up window and offers me a spatula salute. The oil in the fryer sizzles as the basket of fries drops in.

The whole frozen cheesemaker thing has kinda put me off dairy. I open my mouth to mention I'd like to skip the cheese on my burger. But then a sneaky little part of me wants to test my theory about his possible psychic abilities, so I press my lips together and keep my cheesy secret to myself.

Tally's daughter Tatum is covering the afternoon shift today. She lazily wipes the counter in front of me and smiles. "Mom said you were helping Quince Knudsen. Are you two friends?"

"If you could call it that." On the surface, her

question seems innocent enough, but my extrasensory perception picks up on something beneath. "He's helped me on a case or two in the past. Quince has the inside track on what goes on around here—with all of his years working at the paper."

Relief loosens her shoulders, and she ceases the pretense of cleaning the counters. "Oh, cool. He's like super good at taking pictures, right?"

Well, now anyone with half a brain can see she's more than a fan of his photos. "Mmhmm. He was in here the other day, but I don't think your mom was working . . ." I leave the unspoken question hanging in the air and I'm rewarded with the gentle blush of her cheeks as she looks down and rearranges the salt, pepper, and ketchup.

"Oh, yeah. He comes in sometimes. You know, the paper is just up the street."

Odell interrupts our visit as he slides my plate of food onto the counter.

My mouth opens slowly and I point to my cheese-*less* burger. "How did you know?"

He grins mischievously, winks, and raps his knuckles twice on the counter before returning to the grill without a word.

That settles it. I don't need to run any more tests. That man may not know he has some kind of supernatural ability, but there's no way he can occupy a branch in my family tree without at least a trickle of something in his veins.

"I'm about to demolish this burger, Tatum. Why don't you tell me how long you've had a crush on Quince, and if there's anything I can do to move things forward, while I power through this deliciousness?"

Her eyes widen and she starts to shake her head, but as the hint of pink in her cheeks shifts to a darker red, she nods and giggles. "I should've known better than to talk about him in front of you. My mom says you're 'special.'"

My mouth is way too full of golden french fries to argue with her use of the word special. I attempt to pass off a confused shrug and gesture for her to continue.

She glances over her shoulder at Odell, who kindly pretends to be too busy to notice her not working, and fills me in on the particulars. "Like, I was a senior when he was a sophomore, so even though I thought he was super talented and, you know, hot, it wasn't cool to let anyone know. You know how high school is, right?"

I roll my eyes and nod.

Tatum shrugs. "So, you get it. Then I went away to college, and I was only home on breaks. It's not like I could go trolling around the high school. That would be super lame."

Swallowing quickly, I gulp down some soda and squeeze in a reply. "Yeah, I get it. I think you made the right call."

She nods confidently. "But once he graduated, I'd see him in the diner. I was on break . . . He was on break. You know?"

Boy, did I know. When I think back to how my relationship with Erick started with me being a suspect and turned into me being a practically respectable consultant . . . I completely understand. Take whatever opportunity the Fates hand you. "Does he talk to you? Because he can barely be bothered to put two words together when I ask him questions."

That information brightens her smile nearly a thousand watts. "Um, he totally talks to me. He was telling me all about his dark-room setup, and his camera, and, like, this thesis project he's working on for some self-directed program at Columbia."

My eyes twinkle and I smile as I lean forward. "Are you into cameras or dark rooms?"

Tatum giggles and shakes her head. "Not really, but I just like to hear him talk."

I smile and nod at her strategy. "That's not a bad plan. I went to a broomball game, tried cross-country skiing, and even attended the Renaissance Faire in an attempt to make some headway with the men in my life." We share a laugh. "What would you say is your best move?"

She takes one more nervous glance over her shoulder and leans extra close. "Sometimes I give him free milkshakes."

My whole face lights up as I imagine the joy that must bring my penny-pinching photo source. "That's a super good idea. Does he know you like him?"

She stands up and tucks a loose strand of hair behind her ear. "Well—you know—um—I'm sure he probably thinks I'm friendly. But, like, I *like* him, like him."

That's a lot to unpack. "I'll see what I can do."

She blanches, and the color drains from her face as her eyes widen. "Don't tell him I told you."

I tilt my head and smirk. "Hey, I'm special, remember. I got you."

She gasps and I can sense her heart racing. "Okay, but, like, be cool."

If you assume that my mind instantly goes to the John Travolta movie, you're right. *Get Shorty* may have been the vehicle that facilitated his comeback, but *Be Cool* solidified it.

"Did you hear what I said, Mitzy? You can, like, be cool about it, right?"

"Ice cold. No worries."

She giggles nervously and reaches out to bus my dishes.

"See ya 'round, Gramps."

Odell shakes his head and chuckles. "If you two hens are done clucking, I need a word, Mitzy."

Uh oh. I hope I'm not in trouble. I can't think of anything I've done to draw his wrath, but acting without thinking is one of my hidden talents.

When I step into the kitchen, Odell sets down his burger flipper and steps toward me. "Hey, you're looking into the murder of that Knudsen kid's uncle. I thought you should know, him and his neighbor have had a long-standing property feud. Quade seemed to be particular about everything in his life except fence repair. And that neighbor got awful tired of the cows ransacking his cornfield. I heard him complaining to beat the devil over his coffee more than once. I'm not saying the guy's mad enough to murder somebody, but it never hurts to have another suspect, right?"

I cross my arms and grin with satisfaction. "So, Grams was right."

"About what?"

"Snooping runs in the family."

I USUALLY BLAME my bad decisions on an empty stomach, or alcohol. But, I have to admit, I'm making this one sober and fully fed. Plus I slipped into the apartment and got some pain meds, so I feel invincible-adjacent.

My ankle pain has downgraded from throbbing to a dull ache. Most people would take that as a good sign, and continue to follow their doctor's orders. I, however, take it as a sign from the powers that be that I need to pursue this investigation with renewed vigor. This fresh lead about the neighbor must be handled.

Erick has his hands full with the recent evidence Quince and I provided, and the medical examiner is still waiting for confirmation of the time of death from that lab down south. Looks like it's time for me to hop in my vehicle and pay Quade's neighbor a visit.

At least I toss my crutch in the backseat, in case of emergency.

A quick text to Odell results in a surprisingly rapid response. Apparently, he likes to cluck as much as the hens. He sends me the neighbor's name and directions to the property, without a single warning or "take it easy."

I'm certainly not one to play favorites, but right now Gramps is at the top of my Most Awesome People list.

Sadly, the weather has no interest in "best of" lists and takes one of its notorious sudden turns for the worse. The sky that moments ago sported puffy white clouds is now thick with ominous grey warning.

Things definitely don't improve when I turn down the narrow county road which dead-ends at Herman Pettit's corn farm. It's a struggle to keep out of the snowbanks pressing in on either side of the single-track lane. On the plus side, the defrost on the new Jeep actually works, and I can see out the front window.

I'm not sure how much traffic uses this road, but I turn on my headlights just in case.

There can't possibly be any harvesting to handle or seeds to plant in the middle of winter, so

I'm hoping I'll find Herman tucked in his cozy abode.

After letting myself in through the screen door that accesses the three-season porch, I knock politely on the front door of the modest two-story farmhouse.

No answer.

A second, louder knock produces no response.

Thanks, universe. Why make it easy for the girl who's hopping along on one and three-quarter legs.

Glancing around the extensive property, I take note of several outbuildings, including a well-maintained barn.

Before I attempt the lengthy trek to where I hope to find the man I'm looking for, I grab my *emergency* crutch from the Jeep.

As I hobble along, the scent of burning wood hits me. About the same time I see the puffs rising from a small round pipe on the barn's roof.

In the movies, people always slide or pull open the giant doors at the end of the barn for a dramatic reveal. There's no way I'm going to try a stunt like that with a crutch and a somewhat bum foot. I opt for the smaller, human-sized door to the left.

It's unlocked. Will wonders never cease?

There's someone in the barn, busily wrenching away under something that could be a combine harvester, or a *Tyrannosaurus rex*, for all I know about farming equipment.

Rather than surprise him and take a chance on an unfriendly welcome, I call out politely. "Mr. Pettit? Mr. Pettit, it's Mitzy Moon from the Bell, Book & Candle. I hate to interrupt you—"

He rolls out from under the massive piece of equipment on one of those low-to-the-ground mechanic's creepers. I know the official name of the item because of a failed student film that attempted to re-create a dangerous scene from a *Charlie's Angels* movie. I mean, everyone lived, but barely.

Herman is a red-haired man with a carefully waxed mustache that smells of tobacco and leather, and he's far younger than I expected. Mid-thirties, stout, with strong hands and keen eyes. "Broken or sprained?" he asks.

If I had a nickel for every time I'd answered that question in the last few days, I'd be a— Oh wait, seems like I'm already as wealthy as anyone would need to be. Pasting on my best fake grin, I offer up a congenial response. "It's a bad sprain. Folks tell me I'd have been better off with a break. But I'm not sure I agree."

He wipes his hands on a red rag tucked in the pocket of his work pants and nods. "A sprain might hurt a little more in the beginning, but it will heal faster in the end. Don't listen to those fools. People are always so eager to repeat every nonsense old wives' tale they've ever been told. What can I do you for?"

I wish I could say that's the first time I've heard that folksy twist of the phrase since I came to Pin Cherry, but it's absolutely not. However, far be it from me to say anything to Herman Pettit that might indicate he's following the crowd. He obviously takes his hipster farming duties quite seriously. "Well, like I said, I'm Mitzy Moon. I help the local sheriff on a case-by-case basis. So you're under no obligation to cooperate with me or answer any questions, but I heard you're the man to talk to about what goes on in these parts, and I need a shortcut to some answers."

The respectful tone combined with some subtle flattery seems to do the trick. Herman glances around, takes the compliment in stride, and nods for me to continue.

"I understand you've had some trouble with cattle getting into your property and damaging crops. Is it all from the same herd, or are there multiple offenders?"

At first, his gaze is suspicious, but his burning need to be heard wins out. "Well, I tell you what, I filed more than one complaint with the sheriff, or whatever deputy he sends out to humor me. Nothing ever happens, though. The cows keep breaking through different parts of that fence and my crops keep payin' the price. I guess that's what passes for justice in this backwater town."

"I'm sorry to hear that, Mr. Pettit. Do you recall who repaired the fence, or fences?"

That does the trick.

"Oh, it was always the same flippin' fence! Pardon my French. I was the one who had to handle the repairs. Now, I'm not saying I'm an expert. I've only been working this land for five years, but what could I do? Prim and proper Quade sure wasn't gonna fix it. I did the best I could, but his cattle are strong and stubborn. Once they make it through, they just keep coming. Cost me thousands! Thousands of dollars that I don't have! Not one of those complaints I filed ever amounted to a hill of beans."

"That's a real shame. If you like, I'd be happy to look into those complaints and see if there's anything I can do."

The bait has officially been dangled. There's a strange shift in his energy, and my psychic senses can't decide if it's regret or relief.

"Well, I'm not sure what anyone can do about it now. I heard Quade Knudsen froze to death in his icehouse. I suppose that so-called partner of his will finally get to sell the whole operation."

My mood ring tingles and I glance down in time

to see a wheel of cheese. Not that the image does me much good, but there was something about the way Herman said "so-called partner" that could do with a follow-up. "Gosh, it's good to hear your tribulations will be over, Mr. Pettit. Thank you for your time today. I'll see myself out."

As I twist around my crutch and head for the small door, he calls out. "Hold on, Miss Moon."

I pause, and he rummages through a tall metal cabinet at the end of his workbench.

"It's only a sample size, but I sure appreciate you looking into things." He hands over a small plastic bag closed with a red twist tie at the top.

When I catch sight of the label, I have to chuckle. "Pop's Corn!" A huge red handlebar mustache cradles the name. "I love it. Thank you, Mr. Pettit, or should I say Pop? Looks like a storm's comin'. You take care."

As I trudge through the snow, back toward my vehicle, the only thing that stands out about that conversation is how I'm sounding more and more like a local each day. Look at me, talking about the weather and getting popcorn samples!

Time to get back to the bookshop before anyone figures out what I've been up to.

Whoever said "the best laid plans of mice and men" has absolutely met my grandmother. Before the alleyway door can even close behind me, she's already schooling me about taking additional risks driving with my concussed head.

"I understand your concern, Grams. But would it make things better if I told you I have another suspect to add to the murder board?"

She taps a finger on one of her strands of pearls and chews the inside of her cheek. "It might. What did you discover?"

"Your new boyfriend gave me a tip." The giggles grip me almost immediately. I'd hoped to hold a poker face for at least a few seconds, but no such luck.

"Are you talking about Odell? He's not my boyfriend, Mitzy. He's my ex-husband, and he's human!"

"So are you—sort of."

She pushes my suggestion away with a wave of her hand. "Psh. Tosh. I'm an earthbound spirit. A ghost. Not in the least human!"

"Sometimes, when you're not having a tantrum, you can take corporeal form. I'd say you're sort of more human-*light* than ghost."

This new concept clearly intrigues her. She floats up toward the Rare Books Loft and passes through the thick balustrade.

I negotiate the dangerous spiral staircase and chain, and meet her in the apartment.

"Human-light? That has a nice ring to it, dear.

However, my days of husbands and special friends are over. I'm grateful for Odell's company, but part of me is sad that he lacks genuine human companionship in his own life."

"His diner is full of people, Grams. Maybe he never remarried, but it's his own choice. I think he actually prefers solitude."

"Well, you're the psychic, sweetie." And with that, she grabs a pen off the coffee table and hovers above our stack of 3 x 5 cards.

"Make a card for Herman Pettit. He's a young popcorn farmer that shares a property line with the deceased."

"Oh, well, property disputes can be deadly. Has he taken possession of the disputed land now that Quade's out of the picture?"

"Um, it wasn't exactly that kind of property dispute. Quade's cows are always breaking through the fence and getting into the popcorn farmer's field."

Grams suffers an attack of the ghost giggles and distracts me from my careful explanation. "I'm sorry, dear. You have to stop saying popcorn farmer. All I can picture is some Wild West cartoon cowboy with a giant handlebar mustache riding through his fields attempting to lasso giant pieces of popped corn as they shoot into the air like Roman candles."

"You're half right, about the mustache at least, but what's a Roman candle?"

"Sweetie, I forget how young you are. Back in the days before unending frivolous lawsuits, a lot of things were unregulated. Roman candles were a powerful type of firework. Practically as impressive as the huge displays the municipalities used to put on. We would take one of those things, shove it in the ground, light the fuse, and colorful rockets would fire hundreds of feet into the air. It was fantastic."

"Sounds fabulous, but it's not something that would get a lot of support in a state that's primarily desert—and suffers from its own set of massive wild-fires almost every year. But I can picture it." Closing my eyes, I picture my grandmother's words, and, for a moment, I see a night sky exploding with color.

"It's magnificent, Grams."

She hums softly and sighs with memory. "Please continue your story, dear."

"All right, and I agree to stop using the term popcorn farmer. I'll stick with the farmer, or pos-sibly the corn farmer. Even though he has the most adorable name for his product." Reaching into the pocket of my puffy jacket, which is draped over the back of the settee, I extract the sample and turn the label toward Grams.

She squeals and covers her mouth with one hand. "Oh, that's clever. You should invest in his company straightaway. I'm telling you, that Mr. Pettit is going places."

"He might be, but I think I'll wait until we take him off the suspect list before I give him any money. Sound good?"

She taps her shimmering finger to the side of her head and smiles. "You're exactly as smart as you look."

"Thanks, Grams. Herman seems like an exceptionally calm man, and he answered my questions without any hassle, but something felt off. He said he's filed several complaints with the sheriff's department about the cow intrusions, but Erick never mentioned anything about a dispute with a neighbor."

"Maybe the man was lying. You know, sweetie, people will say anything when they're under suspicion."

"But I didn't accuse him of anything. I didn't even bring up Mr. Knudsen's death. He's the one who brought up the incident, and my psychic antenna didn't pick up on dishonesty."

"Maybe the pain meds are blocking your messages."

"Wait? How did you—?"

"You left them out on the counter in the bathroom. I noticed a few more were missing. You can hardly call it snooping when it's right out in the open."

"Accurate."

She shrugs and offers a semi-apologetic smile.

"I'll stop taking them and see if I can manage. I don't think there's been any side effects, but we should play it safe, right?"

"I agree, dear. We know what happens when you're cut off from your powers." She shudders with an unpleasant memory.

"I need to call Erick and let him know what I uncovered. Maybe he's had time to talk to Tammy."

"Who's Tammy? We don't have a card for her."

"We better make one. She's part of Oscar's alibi."

Grams, dutiful as ever, makes a card for Tammy and floats it toward me. Tacking it on the board, I run a connecting piece of green yarn from her to Oscar and a second one from her to Quade. If the weekly suppers were a reality and not a fabrication, she was definitely acquainted with the deceased.

Grams nods thoughtfully. "I absolutely agree."

Turning, I point a finger to my lips and shake my head. "Even though you shouldn't be agreeing, because I didn't say anything out loud."

"You were facing away, Mitzy! There was absolutely no way for me to make visual confirmation. I heard what you said, and I assumed the lips were moving."

With a heavy exhale, I hobble back to the settee. "I'll allow it."

"Thank you for your leniency, dear." She snickers and swirls toward me.

"Oh brother."

Retrieving my cell phone from my coat, I place a call to Erick on speakerphone. There's no point trying to have a private conversation with a ghost circling around me like a possessed carnival ride.

"Hey, Mitzy, do you need something?"

Mmm mm, that voice. My initial instinct is to tell him exactly what I need. The eavesdropping ghost of my dear grandmother prevents me.

She winks at me and grins wickedly.

"Nothing I can announce in front of present company. You're on speakerphone."

He chuckles. "10-4."

"I called to give you an update. Apparently, Quade had some serious disputes with the farmer who owns the adjacent property."

"Herman Pettit? Do you mean to tell me you drove out to his farm in your condition?"

"Why does everyone keep saying that? I sprained my ankle, I didn't fracture my spine!"

"Let's not tempt fate, Moon. What did you find out?"

"Herman claims he's filed a series of complaints with your office. He acted like he'd spoken to you directly about the problem of Quade's cows and had several subsequent discussions with your deputies. But you didn't mention he could be a suspect. Why?"

Erick pauses, draws a sharp breath in through his teeth, and continues. "I believe I spoke to him the first time. And I can't honestly say how many other reports he may have filed. Complaints like his are considered nuisance complaints. They're usually followed up by the deputy with the least seniority on the force at the time. They're seldom, if ever, given any sort of—"

"Oh, I get it. Some kook growing popcorn has an issue with cows, and the local sheriff doesn't take it seriously."

Grams hovers in front of me and wags a finger. "More flies with honey."

I wave her away and frown.

Erick exhales loudly. "It's not like that, Moon. Things have to be prioritized. His issues may not have gotten the attention they deserved, because of other more serious issues. I'll have Deputy Johnson pull the file and see if we missed something. I appreciate the tip."

"Anytime, Sheriff." I offer a break in the conver-

sation for him to reciprocate, but nothing is forthcoming. Not a problem. I'm happy to pry.

Ghostly chuckles from across the room offer no
argument.

"Did you question Tammy?"

"Not yet. I'm not sure if it's worth our time."

"What? It's absolutely worth your time. Oscar's
entire statement basically hinges on Tammy confirming his alibi."

"Not to pull the *sheriff* card, but this is my investigation, and I'm not sure what you mean, Moon.
We don't have time of death yet, so we're not confirming alibis."

"All right. You got me on a technicality, Sheriff.
But he said the plans to subcontract for some big dairy
down south were made by him and Quade. Seems
like you should confirm that with Tammy before he
has a chance— Never mind. I'm sure the first thing he
did when he got home was to tell her exactly what he
said. That watering hole's already been poisoned."

"If he told us the truth, she already knew about
the planned sale." Erick's tone takes on a defensive
edge, but I do like that he said "us."

"You might have a point."

"That's better, sweetie. Kill him with kindness."
Grams grins.

A moment of pensive silence hangs in the air.

"I'm gonna see if Quince will take me out to the dairy." Inhaling deeply, I prepare to end the call.

"Look, Moon, that might not be a crime scene, but I don't need you poking around—"

"What? You're breaking up. I'll try to call you later."

End.

"Mitzy, I'm surprised at you. Why would you take such a tone with Erick? He only has your best interests at heart." Grams crosses her arms over her ample bosom and arches one brow.

"I don't know. My ankle hurts and I need a solid lead." Struggling to my feet, I hobble toward the bathroom and my pain meds. Despite the warning from Grams, I take two to get ahead of the pain curve.

A quick text to Quince secures me a guided tour of the dairy.

UDDERLY BRILLIANT IS NOT what I expected! I pictured a couple of cows with big bells around their necks, a hand-hewn three-legged stool, and a stainless-steel milk pail. What I discovered is that this dairy is next level.

Quade may have insisted on keeping an artisan feel, but his morning milking did not involve hands-on contact with Bessie, or any of the other five hundred cows housed at *Udderly Brilliant*.

The barn, if you can call it that, is an industrial-grey building constructed entirely of metal beams and corrugated metal siding. Inside, five concrete platforms stretch the length of the barn and are divided into individual stalls with dedicated milking equipment for each. All the "milkers" feed into a massive collection tank. To be honest, it's a little *Matrix*-y.

"This place is huge."

Quince nods his head and follows that gesture with a lackluster shrug. "Not compared to the big-time players down south."

I'll take his word for it. After passing through the large harvesting area, he leads me into a much smaller back room with shelving units that reach above my head, and large stainless steel sinks.

"What's this area for?"

"Uncle Quade never used any growth hormones, but his cows were on a vitamin regimen and some got special additives to their food specifically for the flavors that would be passed on to the cheese."

Wow! His verbosity is throwing me for a loop. Either he's really into making cheese, or he's taking this investigation more seriously than I thought possible. "But how do you keep it straight, with that octopus milking monstrosity?"

He grins knowingly. "The Classy Gals, as my uncle nicknamed them, were milked separately."

Ah ha, now I'm going to see my three-legged stool and movie-trope milk pail. "Before you show me that room, is this some kind of cleanup station?"

"Pretty much. Any sterilizing of equipment or individual feed troughs would be done here." He points to a sturdy shelf above the sink and opens his mouth to speak. No words come out. Consternation squeezes his eyes to slits, and he shakes his head in disagreement with whatever's going on in his mind.

"What is it?"

"Quade would never leave the chlorine bleach and the phosphoric acid open at the same time. He was very careful with his chemicals. Mixing those two together could create chlorine gas."

"That sounds deadly."

"In the right quantity, yah." Quince nods and moves to put the caps back on the containers.

"Don't touch anything. I'm calling Erick right now. I know it doesn't seem like much, but it's not how your uncle would've left things, and we have precious little to go on right now. It could be a clue."

Quince nods and passes his carefully trained photographer's eye over every inch of the space. He snaps a couple pictures on his phone while I inform Erick of our find.

The sheriff is asking a series of questions, which I have no intention of answering, so I cover the phone with one hand and whisper sharply to Quince. "What are you doing? You don't take digital pics."

He glances at me and frowns. "These aren't for the paper."

"Copy that."

"What? No, I was talking to Quince, not you. I was distracted. You really should come and take a look at this. We'll keep poking around. See ya soon."

I end the call before he can instruct me to get back into my vehicle. Approaching the sink area, I take a focusing breath and reach out with my psychic gifts.

Nada. Bupkus.

"Mitzy, what are you doing?"

"Oh, um. Just looking around. You know, to see if anything catches my eye."

He shrugs. "I'll show you the Classy Gals' suite."

We step into the adjacent mini-sized milking room, which contains two stalls and what appears to be its own collection tank. The room is sterile, but cozy.

"Was this your uncle's personal project? Would anyone else have milked the cows?"

Quince scrunches up his face and shakes his head. "Very particular, remember?"

"Got it. So anyone who knew your uncle's routine would know that this would be the last stop on his daily schedule."

"Yah."

I may be an amateur sleuth, but I'm not even close to an amateur cheesemaker. Nothing seems out of order, and my moody mood ring is no help.

My tour guide steps closer than he's ever dared and points to the collection tank. "That should be empty."

"Why?"

"The milk should be in the Processing Room. Uncle Quade would never leave it in a collection tank."

"Seems like we have two things for the sheriff to look at when he gets here." I nod my head with more confidence than I feel.

Quince glances around the room and bites his lower lip. "The deputies were already here. But if they weren't familiar with the process, they wouldn't have noticed stuff like the chemicals, or this milk."

While we wait for Erick or one of his deputies to show up, Oscar Wiggins tromps into the room with the sinks, and, when he sees us returning from the Classy Gals' suite, his jaw falls slack.

Quince offers a halfhearted wave. "Hey, Mr. Wiggins."

"Oh, hello. You're the nephew, right?"

Quince nods, and I hop forward to introduce myself. "I'm Mitzy Moon. We haven't met." Technically, I know who he is, because I eavesdropped on his interview at the sheriff's station, but he doesn't know that. There's a hint of tobacco about his person, and I lean in with my outstretched hand to get a better whiff. Something familiar, but I can't place it.

He smiles but doesn't offer to shake my hand. "You'll have to excuse me, I need to wash my hands." He steps toward the sink and the open chemical containers, and Quince and I exchange a worried glance.

Once Oscar finishes with the soap and water, he grabs a paper towel and turns toward us with a shrug. "Was there something I can help you with? I don't think your uncle kept any of his personal effects out here."

It almost sounds defensive, but no hairs are tingling on the back of my neck, and I'm not getting any hits to my super senses. "Oh, we're waiting for Sheriff Harper."

He crinkles the paper towel in his hands with unnecessary force and the muscles in his jaw flex. "He's headed out here?"

My eyes dart toward Quince and he shakes his head almost imperceptibly.

Time to play dumb and see how far that gets me. "Yeah, actually I'm a consultant with the department and I'm looking into a local theft." I have no idea where I'm going with this.

Oscar lifts his chin and carefully strokes his goatee. "Theft? What brings you to the dairy?"

He has asked an excellent question and I have

absolutely no answer. Think. Think. Think. My mind is a total blank. What the heck is wrong with me?

Quince steps forward. "She's not looking into the theft here. She just bummed a ride off me." He gestures to my leg. "I needed some pictures for the paper before I drop her off." Lifting his cell phone, he wiggles it back and forth.

Oscar nods. "Oh, that's okay. Just keep it tasteful. We don't want any negative publicity to ruin the sale."

My mouth opens before my brain has time to engage. "Sale? I thought it was a sub-producing contract?"

The dairy owner's gaze narrows, and he steps toward me. "Where did you hear that?"

Great, another excellent question I can't answer.

Quince saves me once again. "She works with the sheriff. You know how it is in a small town."

The explanation seems to appease Oscar. He still looks a shade suspicious, but I'm not getting any kind of weird vibe. "Well, you two had better see yourselves out. I've got to attend to that gosh darn fence before hot-headed Herman Pettit starts waving his shotgun around again."

My mouth starts to open, but a firm hand grips my arm. Quince is actually willing to touch me, of his own free will. It must be important. I take the hint and keep my mouth shut.

Oscar strides back into the vast milking operation and disappears out the far door.

Quince lowers his voice. "He didn't even notice the chemicals were open."

"Yeah, and he thinks you take pictures with your phone. He's clearly not real observant. Plus, if he'd been up to no good, his conscience would've caused him to at least glance toward the shelf."

Quince pulls away and scrapes a hand through his long bangs. "You okay on your own for a minute?"

I shrug. "Probably. Where are you going?"

"Need to check on something. I'll be back in, like, two minutes." He grabs a stool from the small milking room and helps me lower myself onto it.

"Thanks."

He nods and jogs off in the opposite direction from Oscar.

Meanwhile, as luck would have it, Deputy Paulsen shows up and waddles into the barn.

I offer a friendly wave from my three-legged seat and she returns my gesture with a scowl and a firmer grip on the handle of her holstered gun.

As she approaches, the sound of polyester rubbing against itself grows louder. "What kind of trouble have you gotten yourself into now, Moon?"

"No trouble. I came out here with Quince, so he could pay his respects to his dearly departed uncle. Apparently, Quade was very particular about the way he did things. The same routine, always the same sequence of events. You get the idea."

She nods with irritation. "This little story got a point?"

Using the tip of my crutch, I gesture to the two open chemical containers on the shelf. "That's chlorine bleach and that one's phosphoric acid. Both used in cleaning and maintenance of various systems around the dairy, but they should never be mixed together, because—"

"Yeah, chlorine gas. We all took high school chemistry."

"All right. My point is, you found an empty bourbon bottle at the crime scene, but Quade didn't drink. Alcohol would've reacted with his medication. Everyone assumed he passed out and froze to death. What if someone used some other method to knock him out and planted him in the icehouse with that decoy bottle to make it look like an accident?"

She runs her tongue over her top teeth and makes an impatient squeaking noise. "I thought your theory was carbon monoxide poisoning? Now you think somebody knocked him out with chlorine gas, got him liquored up, locked him in a fish house, sabotaged it so he would get carbon monoxide poisoning, and he froze to death on top of it? You really do have an active imagination, Moon."

This woman knows exactly how to push my buttons every single time she interacts with me. "Look, Paulsen, I'm trying to find a murderer. I think it's a little early in the investigation to be turning our back on any potential lead."

She opens her mouth to offer what I'm sure she thinks is a snappy retort, but a breathless Quince interrupts her delivery.

"She's dead!"

Without a moment's hesitation, Paulsen draws her weapon. "Show me."

Quince turns to lead the way, and I struggle to rise from the tiny stool. After two false starts, I finally get a low enough grip on the cross member of the crutch to create the right leverage point and pull my largesse from my tuffet.

Luckily, Deputy Paulsen and her short-legged stride are an easy target. With some expert crutching, I catch up in no time.

Quince leads us to the back of the barn and lifts a large black tarpaulin.

Paulsen groans and shakes her head.

I opt for a gasp and scream.

Oscar Wiggins comes barreling around the

corner of the barn and screeches to a halt when he sees Deputy Paulsen. "What's going on here?"

Paulsen holsters her gun, steps forward, and crosses her arms. "I'll be asking the questions, Wiggins. What happened to the heifer?"

"She didn't make it back to the barn, and when we had that terrible cold snap the other night—"

Quince is agitated, and he's not about to accept Wiggins' halfhearted explanation. "This is one of the Classy Gals, Wiggins. My uncle would never leave her out of the barn."

Wiggins' eyes dart to the bright pink X sprayed on the cow's right rear haunch, but he attempts to play dumb. "I don't know what you're talking about, kid. It's a cow. We have five hundred of them, you know. Sometimes they die. Cycle of life."

Quince turns to Deputy Paulsen. "I bet toxicology tests would show she died of chlorine gas poisoning."

Deputy Paulsen shakes her head and waves him off. "We don't do postmortems on bovines, kid."

I wait for my mood ring or one of my amazing psychic abilities to confirm Quince's idea, but nothing happens. Super. Well, my basic senses know a good idea when I hear one. If someone released chlorine gas in that small space in hopes of sedating or even killing Quade, the cow might've been a second, accidental victim. My fingers are already dialing the sheriff's station. Turning away, I give a brief but muffled explanation to Erick, and a moment later Deputy Paulsen's radio springs to life.

"Paulsen, Sheriff Harper here." She depresses the button on the side of the mic clipped to her shoulder. "Go for Paulsen."

"Tape off the area and get Johnson to pick up Doc Ledo's rig. Take the cow to his place and ask him to run toxicology."

Her shocked expression quickly turns to malice as she realizes I pulled rank. She scowls at me as she replies. "10-4."

Oscar puts up a fuss, but Paulsen threatens to throw him in handcuffs if he tries to interfere.

He wisely raises his hands, backs away, and disappears.

If I weren't on crutches, I would definitely give chase.

"You should wait inside, Mitzy. Do you need help?" Quince nods in my direction.

"No, I can manage. I'll go watch over the—"

Quince joins me in shouting, "The chemicals!"

CHAPTER 15

IN PURSUIT of the vanishing Oscar Wiggins, Quince easily outpaces me and my barely functioning tripod gait.

As I round the corner, raised voices echo through the vast barn.

"Don't touch that, Wiggins! I know you murdered my uncle!" A stool tips over and tools crash to the floor as a struggle ensues.

"Look, kid, I didn't kill anyone! Your uncle and I were partners. Get off me!"

I reach the back room just in time to witness Wiggins fling the wiry Quince across the room.

The young man's head crashes into a shelf.

He hits the ground and doesn't move.

Every ounce of film-school dropout inside of me begs for this one movie trope to be true. No matter how many times people get hit, or shot, or bang into things, they don't die. The hero always gets back up and keeps fighting.

Unfortunately, disappointment is the flavor du jour. Quince doesn't move. Oscar's eyes are wild, but before he can blurt his series of excuses, my fingers are already dialing.

Wiggins moves toward me with an angry growl. Lifting my crutch to create a physical barrier, I shake my head as I speak into the phone. "Sheriff Harper, Oscar Wiggins just attacked Quince Knudsen. Quince is unconscious in the barn at the *Udderly Brilliant* dairy. Please send an ambulance and more deputies."

Erick barely has time to announce that he's on his way before he ends the call, and less than twenty seconds later Paulsen enters the clean-up room with her weapon drawn. He must've radioed her as he ran to his patrol car.

"Hands where I can see 'em, Wiggins." She aims her gun dead center on the man's chest and tilts her head toward me. "Check the kid for a pulse, Moon."

My mouth hangs open and I'm left speechless. The idea that the impact killed Quince never entered my mind. Flinging my crutch to the side, I hobble-run toward his limp form. The two fingers on my left hand slide along his neck and thankfully find a pulse. "He's alive." My voice catches in my throat. I didn't realize how much I'd grown to care for this shutterbug.

Paulsen adjusts her aim and exhales loudly. "So it looks like just one murder charge for you, Wiggins."

He opens his mouth to protest, but she shakes her head and steadies the gun with threatening clarity. "Save it for the interrogation."

He swallows, shakes his head in disbelief, and keeps his hands in the air. She shifts her weapon to her right hand and retrieves the handcuffs from her duty belt. For a pudgy schoolyard bully, she moves with surprising speed. Oscar Wiggins is securely handcuffed and being led out of the building in under thirty seconds.

She glances over her shoulder. "I'm going to lock the accused in the back of the cruiser. Keep an eye on the kid. I hear the sirens. The ambulance will be here any minute." She shoves her quarry forward with more force than necessary, and I breathe a sigh of relief.

Although, I don't hear any sirens. Attempting to access my extrasensory hearing proves fruitless.

Instead, I focus on the unfortunate victim. "Hey, Quince. Can you hear me?" Brushing his sandy-brown bangs back from his face, I shake him gently.

No response.

I've seen enough crime drama to know that moving a victim is never a good idea for an amateur like me. I'll just wait helplessly until the paramedics arrive.

As if on cue, the wail of sirens pierces the winter air.

Erick makes it through the door before the emergency crew. "Moon, are you okay?"

"I'm fine. I mean, other than the sprained ankle and whatever from before. It's Quince. He's nonresponsive."

The sheriff drops to his knees next to the awkwardly sprawled young man and immediately checks for breathing and pulse. Before he can examine any further, the paramedics burst in and take over.

He offers me his hand, helps me to my feet, and retrieves my abandoned crutch.

Big, wet tears are welling up in my eyes. "I'll never forgive myself if—"

Erick slips an arm around my waist and kisses the top of my head. "Sounds like you're starting to understand how I feel every time you dive into one of these dangerous investigations."

I stifle a sob and gasp for air. "Don't lecture me, Sheriff."

He gives me a comforting squeeze. "It's not a

lecture, Moon. It's a reality check. Quince is young, and I'm sure he'll be fine. But if Oscar Wiggins is our murderer, things could've ended much worse."

The paramedics coordinate their lift of the stretcher and head for the ambulance.

Sheriff Harper salutes them and calls out, "I'll get in touch with his dad."

The young woman carrying the rear of the board nods in his direction and disappears into the main barn.

"Do you think he's gonna be all right? Wiggins tossed him pretty hard."

Erick scrunches up his face and shrugs. "I'm hoping he'll be fine. I need you to come in and make a statement, since you witnessed the assault."

"Sure, of course. Whatever you need. That man is clearly dangerous."

My boyfriend isn't as quick to agree as I'd hoped. Instead, he continues in sheriff-mode. "What brought on the physical altercation?"

"They were arguing. See those open chemicals on the shelf?"

Erick walks toward the shelf and takes in the potential meaning in a flash. "And?"

"Well, Quince and I were thinking that Oscar didn't know anything about the possible chlorine gas stuff, because when he came in to wash his hands, he didn't notice the open chemicals or even look at the shelves."

"Seems more likely that he purposely avoided looking at them to hide his possible guilt."

What Erick's saying does seem pretty logical. Why didn't my psychic senses give me a tipoff? The image of me throwing two pain pills down the hatch with half a glass of water comes to mind. What if Grams is right about the meds interfering with my gifts?

Erick is standing directly in front of me and leaning forward in concern. "Moon, are you having some concussion related issues?"

"No, just reviewing things in my mind. You know how I get."

He smiles. "That I do. Now what about this dead cow?"

I proceed to show him the Classy Gals' suite and crutch my way to the back of the barn so he can have a peek under the tarpaulin.

"We'll pick up the cow and see if Doc Ledo can determine cause of death. Meanwhile, we finally got confirmation on time of death from the big lab down south. Quade Knudsen died of carbon monoxide poisoning between 11:30 p.m. and 12:30 a.m. He subsequently froze before his body was discovered."

Leaning on my crutch, I lift my right finger, but

Erick waves away my question and continues. "They also found traces of chlorine in the lung tissue. Whoever tried to kill him was determined not to fail. They chose a hat trick of weapons."

My head spins with all this new information, and my empty stomach is swirling with the aftereffects of taking medication without food.

Since my ride headed into town in the back of an ambulance, Erick agrees to give me a lift back to the bookshop.

I wish I had the energy to convince him to grab some food for my upset stomach—which is quickly turning into nausea and a headache, but I'm fading fast. The best thing for me is a glass of water and some shuteye.

Grams is none too happy when I share the story of the mishap at the milk farm.

"Mizithra! You could've been killed." Tears spring to her eyes and she clutches her pearls as she sobs dramatically.

"Well, I wasn't. But Quince was definitely injured, and it was all my fault. I'm gonna take a quick nap and then I'll head over to the hospital to see how he's doing."

She opens her mouth to protest, but I wave my finger threateningly. "An innocent bystander almost died because of me. Me and my stupid twisted ankle. If I'd been able to drive myself out there, nothing would've happened to poor Quince. No more protests. I'm taking a nap, and then I'm going to the hospital, and I don't want to hear another word about it."

Ghost-ma pantomimes locking her lips with an invisible key and tucking it into her cleavage.

I don't have time for banter. After popping a couple pain pills, I drop my crutch on the thick Persian rug and collapse onto my bed.

Cut to —

Blackness. The kind of heavy darkness that envelops you in a damp, windless cave.

The throbbing in my ankle must have been the cause of my waking.

However, this nap started during the day, and it's clearly the middle of the moonless night. Not sure exactly what happened, but visiting hours are obviously over at the hospital. Probably best if I pop a few more pain pills and crash out until morning.

Using the post at the foot of the bed to pull myself to my feet, I stumble into the bathroom and reach for the pills beside the sink.

No pills. Using both my hands to feel all around the vanity in the darkened bathroom, I come up empty-handed.

A quick limp to the light switch illuminates the scene. My pain meds are nowhere to be found.

Checking the floor in case I accidentally knocked them off, I discover an empty amber canister in the trash. Shaking my head with befuddlement, I rub my eyes and do a double-take of the scene. I know I took a few pain pills, but I certainly didn't blow through an entire bottle.

And whether it's extrasensory perception or historical data, I know beyond a shadow of a doubt that my grandmother is to blame.

"Myrtle Isadora Johnson Linder Duncan Willamet Rogers. Show yourself this instant."

Of all the times for her to choose the slow, sparkly reentry—

"You've got to be kidding me."

"I'm not sure what you mean, dear. This is the reentry you told me you preferred."

"You're not wrong. Thing is, I have a bit of a situation on my hands and I'd like to address it as quickly as possible."

She paints her features as the portrait of innocence, and, once again, I know exactly where I got my acting skills.

"Now, Mitzy—"

"Save it, Isadora. What did you do with my pain medication?"

"Mitzy, you have a problem." She crosses her arms and avoids my question.

"Here we go again. Grams, I respect your struggle with alcohol, and I'm glad you found AA and turned your life around, but I'm not an alcoholic. And the actual problem I have is a badly sprained ankle. I need the pain medication because I'm in pain."

Walking faster than recommended for my healing ankle, I blast through her spectral form and flop onto the bed.

She swooshes after me and continues her lecture. "I hear what you're saying, sweetie, but I have more experience in this area than you do. You might not be an alcoholic, but you're a little too dependent on the pills." Her chin lifts defiantly.

"Grams, it's only been a few days. I wouldn't call that dependency."

"I'm sure you wouldn't, which is why I had to intervene. You were taking more than the prescribed dose, and sometimes you were taking them at shorter intervals than recommended as well. You absolutely know the medicine is interfering with your psychic abilities, and if you're honest with yourself, I don't think you're in that much pain."

My hands ball into fists at my side and I take several deep breaths to avoid saying something I'll regret. "To be clear, I'm an adult. I don't need a nursemaid. Now it's the middle of the night, my ankle is killing me, and I have no way to get back to sleep!"

The image of Ghost-ma flickers. "Is it killing you, really?"

Her tinge of remorse forces me to examine my situation more carefully. If I'm honest with myself, the pain isn't unbearable, but it's uncomfortable and inconvenient.

She hovers next to the bedside table and clicks her tongue. "Inconvenience doesn't require heavy-duty opioids, sweetie. The fact that you don't think you can get to sleep without the aid of your medication should be of more concern to you than it is."

I want to shout at her to get out of my head, but, in my mostly lucid state, some of what she's saying makes sense. The pills were an easy fix. When I numbed the pain, I could continue sleuthing my way around town on an ankle that should've been elevated with ice and rest, or whatever that crabby doctor said.

Grams arches an ethereal eyebrow and offers soft confirmation. "Mmhmm."

"Hey, let's not gloat. You may be right about me using the pills too freely, but that doesn't give you the right to judge the crap out of me in the middle of the night."

She bows gracefully. "Understood. Maybe you

could make yourself some hot chocolate and see if that will help you fall back to sleep. You and your foot could do with some additional rest. There'll be plenty of time to visit sweet young Quince tomorrow."

Exhaling with unnecessary force, I carefully swing my feet to the floor.

Crutch: check.

Hobble: check.

Ghost gloat: double check.

CHAPTER 16

AFTER THE HOT chocolate eases my transition to dreamland, I'm rewarded with several luscious dreamtime episodes starring Sheriff Too-Hot-To-Handle.

Morning comes too soon.

In an effort to prove my grandmother wrong, I choose to skip refilling my painkiller prescription. Instead, I wiggle into a fresh pair of yoga pants, a pullover hoodie sporting a picture of a naked cupcake with the tagline, "Sprinkles are for winners," and a beanie to cover my white haystack of hair. Adding a layer of the appropriate winter garments, I grab my crutch and hobble on down to breakfast-town—medication free.

I barely make it through the front door of Myrtle's Diner when Tatum accosts me. "Oh my gosh!

What happened to Quince?" Her eyes are wide, and my drug-free psychic senses get a blast of young-love panic.

Lifting one hand in a gesture that begs reprieve, I offer a compromise. "I tell you what, if you let me have a seat, and bring me a cup of coffee, I will absolutely tell you anything you want to know."

She bobs her head like the appropriately named dashboard doll and dives behind the counter.

Stretched out in a red-vinyl booth with my leg elevated on the seat next to me, I smile warmly as Tatum approaches with my cup of liquid alert. Her hand is shaking and a little go-go juice spills from the cup.

"Why don't you sit down?"

She slides into the booth and leans across the table eagerly.

I glance toward my grandfather behind the grill, and he subtly nods his approval.

Sneaking a quick sip, I launch into my tale. "Let me start by saying everything that happened was my fault, and I honestly wish I could trade places with Quince."

Tatum swallows audibly and sniffles. "Is he going to be okay?"

"I'm headed over to the hospital as soon as I finish breakfast. Erick assures me that Quince is young and invincible, if that counts for anything."

She nods, bites her lip, and blinks back tears. "I heard he was unconscious."

"Yeah, he got into a struggle with the suspected killer, and the guy shoved him into some shelving. Quince definitely hit his head. But I honestly don't think it's serious. I promise I'll update you as soon as I leave the hospital."

She draws a quick breath and bites her lip again. "Thanks. Here's my phone."

I type in my phone number and hand the cell back to her.

She immediately sends me a text. "That's me. You can text me, like, from the hospital if you want."

"Copy that."

A flash of relief relaxes her tense shoulders. "So he was fighting the guy?"

It's no skin off my nose to make the kid sound like a hero. "Totally. We had put a few pieces of the puzzle together and it was really starting to look like the guy was the murderer, and Quince ran back to make sure he didn't tamper with evidence. By the time I got there, your boy Quince was all over him!"

Her cheeks flush, and she smiles proudly. "He's, like, the best, you know?"

Taking a big sip of coffee and letting her savor the moment, I nod my agreement. "He really is."

Odell approaches with my breakfast, and

Tatum scoots out of the booth and casts her guilty eyes toward the floor.

"So, is your secret crush gonna live to tell the tale?"

Tatum looks up with eyes as wide as saucers. "Huh?"

Odell's gruff chuckle warms my heart, and I answer for her. "Quince is gonna be great. I just wish there was someone to run a story about him in the paper. The hometown hero, you know what I mean?"

He slides my scrambled eggs with chorizo onto the table and follows it with a bottle of Tabasco. "I know exactly what you mean." Odell winks at me and returns to the kitchen.

Tatum busies herself wiping down tables and refilling sugar shakers.

Once I finish my scrumptious meal, I balance on my crutch and scoop up my dishes. It's a little precarious and I'm wondering if I'm going to make it safely to the dish bin when a familiar voice interrupts my progress.

"Let me help you with that, Moon." Sheriff Harper snags the dishes from my hand and deposits them in the bus bin behind the counter. "Can I offer you a ride to the hospital?"

My mouth hangs open like a broken shutter on a haunted house, and, before I can regain my composure, I witness a sly wink exchanged between my boyfriend and my grandfather.

I don't know how Odell managed to cook and send a text, but I do not like it when these two work together. I do not like it one bit. "Yes, I graciously accept your offer, Sheriff." Glancing over my shoulder at Odell, I narrow my gaze and shake my head.

He pretends to ignore my nonverbal warning and scrapes away at his grill.

Erick helps me out to the patrol car parked at the curb and heads toward the Birch County Regional Medical Facility.

"Have you heard anything? He's going to be all right, isn't he?"

"They put a couple of stitches in the cut on his head, but nothing was fractured, and there's no serious internal bleeding. They're going to release him later today, and the doctor told me there shouldn't be any complications."

"Thank goodness! I still feel terrible—"

"Don't beat yourself up, Moon. The kid's quick thinking protected the evidence. I wish he hadn't gotten hurt, but I'm grateful Oscar wasn't able to cover his tracks."

"Yeah, about that. Have you questioned him?"

Erick nods. "Yeah, we got a few answers out of him before he demanded a lawyer."

"Bummer. Anything useful?"

He shrugs. "Honestly? I don't think so. He tried to put the blame on Herman Pettit. Makes no sense to me."

I ponder the tactic. "Yeah, that's a little odd. I mean, Herman didn't exactly like Quade, but he didn't know his routine. He couldn't have known that Quade would—"

"Well, we're bringing Herman in for questioning. So, we'll find out exactly what he knows."

My eyes light up and I offer the sheriff my best sexy smile. "Any chance I might get front row seats to that?"

He grins wickedly, walks two fingers across the seat and turns up his palm as he says, "I'm not sure you can afford tickets."

My skin tingles all over, and I know there's a blush creeping up my cheeks. "You underestimate the value of my estate, Sheriff. I'm willing to pay whatever it takes."

Direct hit!

Erick's tender blue eyes widen, and he leans toward his door with a sharp intake of breath. "Whoa. I forgot who I was dealing with."

I slide my hand into his and wink. "See that it doesn't happen again."

We park near the entrance to the large hospital, and he instructs me to sit tight and wait for assistance. Even though I have some personal issues with the phrase "sit tight," I do as I'm told.

He comes around to my side of the vehicle and gallantly helps me extract myself and my crutch from the cruiser.

As we pass through the sliding doors at the main entrance, he tips his head in that way that insinuates he's doffing a cap, and the stern woman at the reception desk startles and smiles broadly. Traveling with a sheriff's escort seems to be just the ticket.

The elder Knudsen, or, as I've recently learned, Quintin, is posted up next to his son's bed. His features are pinched, and the second we walk into the room, I feel his nerves flare. His brother was recently murdered, and now his son attacked . . . I can hardly blame the man for being a little jumpy.

Quince sees me and beams. "Did you get the evidence?"

I grin and tilt my head toward Erick. "The sheriff said you done good."

The young man's smile widens, nearly splitting his face in two, and he nods. "Sweet."

"Unfortunately, as Deputy Paulsen would say, he lawyered up, as the guilty always do."

Quince's smile fades, but before he can comment, his father jumps in with an unrequested explanation. "It's an unfortunate side effect of the legal system that criminals are often offered more protection than their victims. Seems to me that this Oscar Wiggins was caught red-handed. I am sure the founding fathers didn't imagine protecting murderers when they carefully crafted our country's constitution. However, the climate in the 1700s was vastly different from where we find ourselves—"

Sheriff Harper to the rescue. "Don't worry, Quintin. We'll file the necessary paperwork and get the information we need. Your son did the department a huge favor by locating that evidence and protecting the crime scene. Of course, we'll need him to come down to make a full statement when he's feeling better."

Quintin smiles, and his massive frog-like eyes blink several times behind his thick glasses.

A sudden flash of heat around my ring finger makes my heart jump. *Please don't be bad news*, I silently hope as I glance at the misty black dome.

The ring shows me an adorable picture of Tatum holding a milkshake. Aha! Now's my chance. "Hey, did I mention Tatum was totally worried about you? I'll let her know you're all right."

The normally monosyllabic Quince smiles eagerly. "She was? Sweet. Yeah, tell her I'm, like, gonna be fine. I'll come down to the diner to tell all about the fight and stuff."

Arching one of my eyebrows, I smile and nod. "Sure, I'll tell her that."

The intensity of my gaze brings a slight flush to his cheeks, and he looks away self-consciously.

"You should take her ice-skating to celebrate. I heard something about the hockey arena being open for free skate on Sunday afternoons."

His Adam's apple bobs ferociously, and my extra senses pick up on his nervous anticipation.

"In case you were wondering, Quince, she'll say yes."

He smiles adorably and jerks his head to flick his bangs back without thinking. "Ahhh! Dude. My head."

"Yeah, you might want to take it easy on the head flicks for a few days."

Chuckles ripple through the crowd, and Quince shrugs. "I'll try, dude."

"Glad you're okay, *dude*. Me and the sheriff better head out and wrap up this case."

I offer a single nod to the elder Knudsen and crutch on out.

Erick suffers from a severe case of good manners and gets involved in a rather lengthy verbal exchange before he catches up to me.

"I can't believe you let yourself get sucked into a conversation with Quintin! That man is a walking Wikipedia rabbit hole."

The sheriff lifts one shoulder and smiles. "Hey, a voter is a voter. I have to win votes wherever I can."

The smile fades from my face as the harsh taste of reality hits me full force. "Oh, right? I totally forgot you're an elected official."

He opens my door for me and grins. "Yeah, that tracks. Maybe now that you've had a little reminder, you can keep your eavesdropping shenanigans on the down low."

"Absolutely, Sheriff. Whatever I can do to support your campaign."

His shoulders shake with laughter as he circles around the front of the vehicle to the driver's door.

Back at the quaint little sheriff's station that I still think of as a cross between Sheriff Valenti's office in *Roswell* and good old-fashioned Sheriff Andy Taylor's digs in *Mayberry*, Erick escorts me into his office.

Deputy Gilbert pokes his head in. "Pettit is in two, Sheriff."

"10-4."

Erick stands and rifles through some files on his desk. Eventually, he settles on a thin manila folder and adds a few stray photographs to the file. "Enjoy the ambience of my *office*, Moon."

"10-4."

He shakes his head and crosses the hallway into Interrogation Room 2.

As soon as the latch clicks, I get my one-gal, three-legged race into motion and crutch it into the observation room. When I ease open the door, shock barely begins to describe the emotion that hits me.

"What do you think you're doing in here, Moon?" Deputy Paulsen occupies the one and only chair, and she has a large piece of what I can only assume is wild game-based jerky in her hand. This assumption rests solely on smell—which ain't great.

"Oh, I thought this was the bathroom."

She scoffs openly. "This room is for official sheriff's personnel only. You can wait in his office."

I toy with the idea of bandying my confidential informant status about, but I'm fairly certain that won't get me anywhere with Paulsen. "Sure, I'll do that."

Clumsily rotating my operation, I exit the observation room.

Dagnabbit! I need to hear that interview.

If at first you don't succeed, try, try again.

Taking a deep breath, I grab the handle on the door of the occupied interrogation room and stumble my way in.

Erick looks up in frustration. "Can we help you, Miss Moon?"

I smile and shrug. "I was hoping I could help you. Deputy Gilbert mentioned that Mr. Pettit was in this room. Since I'd promised him I would look into those cow incidents . . . I thought maybe this thing was about that."

The sheriff exhales through his teeth and gestures toward a chair. "It hasn't come up yet, but it might."

As I take my seat beside Herman Pettit, the smell of mustache wax and tobacco pricks a memory I can't quite grasp. "Do you smoke, Mr. Pettit?"

Erick opens his mouth to protest my interference, but Herman Pettit shakes his head and moves to answer. "No, no. Why do you ask?"

"I smell tobacco. Isn't that weird?"

He grips the edge of the table with his thick hands and chuckles. "Actually, it's not that strange." He gently strokes his tightly curved red handlebar mustache, and adds, "The mustache wax I use is tobacco and leather scented. It's nice, don't you think?"

"It is. Where do you get something like that?"

The seemingly innocent question brings a strange response from Herman. He swallows audibly and crosses his arms.

Odd.

He shifts in his chair and mumbles, "Oh, it was a gift."

"Wow. How nice." I smile and nod for Erick to continue his interview.

He sighs and attempts to maintain his professionalism. "Mr. Pettit, have you—"

"Ah ha!" I jolt to my feet and my crutch hits the ground with a clang.

"Miss Moon, please control yourself." Erick leans back and gazes at me with concern.

As I slip from my mind movie back into reality, I attempt to cover my outburst with a weak chuckle and a weaker lie. "Sorry, I just remembered I have an appointment." Stooping, I collect my crutch and head for the door. "If you'll excuse me."

Both men are left in my wake with their eyes wide and their jaws flapping in the breeze.

My knowledge of Deputy Paulsen's whereabouts now seems beyond serendipitous. I approach the innocent and impressionable Deputy Gilbert. "Hey, I need to ask Mr. Wiggins a quick question. Is it all right if I head back to the cells?"

He looks around the bullpen for a superior officer, and finding none makes the executive decision to help me out. "Sure, I guess. You're not planning on staying in there long, are you?"

I widen my eyes and smile. "Oh, of course not. I never push my luck."

Regardless of the fact that this answer is one hundred percent falsehood, it offers the deputy the reassurance he requires.

"Follow me."

He grabs a set of keys from a hook on the wall

inside Erick's office, and I grow concerned that he may have misunderstood. "Oh, I don't need to go in the cell. I just need to ask a question."

"Yeah, I got that. We installed a new security door. Sheriff Harper is putting in some security upgrades prior to the city council's inspection."

Security upgrades? City council inspections? I can't even! Just when I'd fooled myself into thinking that I knew everything there was to know about Erick's life. "Gosh, that sounds like a lot of bureaucratic nonsense."

Deputy Gilbert smirks and leans toward me as he whispers. "The old salts on the force say this kinda stuff happens every four years, but, between you and me, I'd call it polishing a turd."

The phrase accurately describes pretty much my exact thoughts about the station's interior design, and I laugh too easily. "Right? I'd sooner see a little money go toward a computer or two, before I worried about a security door protecting a few cells that are usually standing empty."

He smiles, but shifts to a more serious tone. "Don't let the small town fool you. The cells have occupants more often than most of our residents realize."

"Point taken. I appreciate you escorting me back."

He nods as he unlocks the new security door.

"Yeah, I'll have to stay. Procedure, you know?"

"Oh, sure. No problem."

Deputy Gilbert double-checks that the heavily riveted metal security door closes behind us and motions for me to continue to the cell while he remains by the hatch.

He's a thoughtful guy. I honestly hope he doesn't get into trouble for letting me back here.

As I approach Oscar Wiggins' cell, he jumps to his feet. "Are you gonna let me outta here? I didn't kill anybody. I swear."

"Hi, Mr. Wiggins." I wiggle my fingers in a halfhearted greeting.

He takes one look at my hair and my crutch and shakes his head. "You? I got nothing to say to you."

"Look, I'm not here to make any accusations. I hope you're as innocent as you say. I only have one question."

He crosses his arms and stares at me with beady, uncooperative eyes.

I need him to walk just a little closer. Whispering nonsense under my breath, I glance toward him for a response.

"What?" He shakes his head and scoffs.

I whisper additional nonsense, but enunciate the words *freedom* and *innocence*. That one draws him in.

He takes two steps closer to the bars. "I can't

hear you. If you came back here to ask me something, you might as well speak up."

Leaning forward, I inhale deeply and smile. I knew I'd smelled it somewhere before! "Where do you get your mustache wax, Mr. Wiggins?"

He steps back and smooths his sharply trimmed dark mustache with the side of one finger. "My mustache wax? I don't get it anywhere. My wife makes it."

All sorts of psychic bells and whistles are going off in my head.

Mr. Pettit and Mr. Wiggins, who are technically sworn enemies, just happen to use the same mustache wax? I think not. "Your wife, Tammy, makes mustache wax?"

For some reason, this topic pierces his veil of sworn silence. "Sure. Sure. She makes all kinds of grooming products for men. She said my scruffy beard and unruly mustache were her inspiration." He lifts his chin proudly and smiles.

"Well, it looks great. Whatever she puts in that stuff is magic."

His genuine smile crinkles the corners of his eyes. "She's really talented. The house is a disaster area, though. She's like a mad scientist, but I think things are finally gonna turn around for us."

"Turn around? Have you been having relationship troubles?"

His jaw tenses, and his goatee seems to flinch. "I think I'm done talking to you."

"Understood." I nod politely and hobble back toward the waiting deputy.

Deputy Gilbert unlocks the security door and holds it for me. "Did you get the answer you needed?"

"I sure did. Thanks for your help."

Lucky for both of us, I make it back to Erick's office, and Gilbert replaces the key, before the sheriff exits the interrogation room.

When Erick returns to his office, I'm grinning like the cat that swallowed the canary.

"That look concerns me, Moon."

He leans back in his chair, and part of me feels that he's crossed his arms in a purposeful attempt to distract me.

"I may have found the break in the case you've been waiting for, Sheriff."

Erick stretches his arms up and laces his fingers together behind his head. My eyes dart down and his deep, throaty chuckle makes my skin tingle. "Save your rewards for later. What have you got?"

I'd love to say I have a case of heart palpitations and possibly mild heat stroke, but I'm not about to let him get the upper hand. "Did you know that Tammy Wiggins makes men's grooming products?"

"I think you mean Tammy Smythe-Wiggins."

His smug grin is the last straw.

"Whatever her name is, she makes a tobacco-and-leather-scented mustache wax."

His arms fall to his sides, and he leans forward. "The product used by Herman Pettit?"

"The very one. It's also used by her husband. Which would indicate she has a personal fondness for the scent. I can only think of one reason why Herman Pettit would be using the same scented mustache wax as her husband."

Erick takes a deep breath and shouts. "Deputy Gilbert, get in here."

Gilbert darkens the door with a face full of regret. "Well, she's your girlfriend, sir."

Erick's expression shifts to concerned confusion. He glances at me and shakes his head. "I don't even want to know. Bring in Tammy Smythe-Wiggins. Code 3."

"10-4." Deputy Gilbert wastes no time in sprinting toward his vehicle.

The sheriff gestures at the departing deputy and frowns. "I'd appreciate it if you'd resist using your feminine wiles on my staff."

The unintentional double entendre makes me giggle and blush. Words escape, but I manage to choke out an "Mmhmm."

He blushes but maintains his stern visage.

"Um, I need to get back to the bookshop. Call

me when Tammy gets here?"

He stands, saunters across his office, and threads an arm between my crutch and my body as he squeezes my waist. "Just making sure I have your vote in the upcoming election, Miss Moon."

Erick's nearness and serious tone send me into another giggle fit. "You kidding? I'm not even registered to vote in Birch County."

He pulls away and crosses his arms. "Democracy is the cornerstone of civilization. I'm not sure I can date a girl who doesn't vote."

The matter-of-fact statement catches me off guard. I stumble backward in shock.

My chivalrous boyfriend can simultaneously save me and stand for his principles. As he catches my elbow and pulls me close, he whispers, "The election isn't until November. You've got plenty of time to get registered."

"Copy that."

He kisses me softly on the lips, and I shamble back to the bookstore in a fog, shouldering a combination of bliss and consternation.

As soon as I make it through the intricately carved front door, I shout, "Grams! Grams, I need to talk to you!"

The distinct sound of biker boots stomps from the back room, and Twiggy gestures down the historical fiction aisle where an actual customer must be browsing. "I've told you a thousand times, call me Twiggy. 'Grams' makes me feel old."

My skin flushes with embarrassment as I realize Twiggy's generous effort to cover my faux pas. "Sorry, Twiggy. That's the last time. I promise."

She crosses her arms and rolls her eyes, indicating she's not falling for my pseudo-promises for one minute.

However, she actually takes pity on me and unhooks the chain so I can stumble up the wrought-iron circular staircase with one less obstacle.

"Thanks."

"Don't get used to it, doll."

Classic Twiggy. I grab the candle handle next to my copy of *Saducismus Triumphatus* and wait impatiently for the bookcase door to slide open. Once inside, the intense throbbing of my ankle reminds me of my desire to prove my grandmother wrong. I flop onto the overstuffed settee and elevate my aching leg.

Grams floats absently from the closet and startles into a freeze-frame when she sees me. "I didn't hear you come in."

"Wow. You must've been planning quite an outfit. Dare I ask?"

A strange melancholy seeps from her flickering aura, and she drifts toward me without purpose.

"Grams, what's wrong?"

"What, dear?"

"You seem like you're a million miles away. What's on your mind?"

"I was wondering if the last time I wore the Vivienne Westwood trench was with Odell?"

"The missing coat? The one the cleaners lost? Did you remember something?"

Her head tilts oddly, and she runs her tongue across her shimmering teeth. "Didn't I tell you?"

"Um, no. That would be why I don't know, and why I'm asking."

"Of course, dear. I understand."

I lift my hands in the air and nod encouragingly.

She smiles wistfully and hovers above the scalloped-back chair. "I thought maybe Odell might remember something, so I mentioned it to him the last time we were chatting."

"And?"

"Well, he said all coats look the same to him, but I told him to donate a few things to the library's charity auction before I passed away. That obviously sounds like something I'd do, right?"

"Yes, it does. So now we solved the mystery. The matter is closed?"

"Not exactly."

"Dear Lord baby Jesus, Isadora. If I'm going to have to drag everything out of you as though you were Quince Knudsen, I'll lose my mind. Just tell me the whole story. All at once. No stops." Whew! The lack of pain medication is definitely getting to me.

She crosses her arms and taps her coral lip with a perfectly manicured finger. "You don't say."

I narrow my gaze and glower in her general direction.

"Fine, fine. I'll get on with it. Dear, sweet, Odell said when we first met—"

"Yeesh! I don't need that much backstory!"

"Let me finish, young lady."

Taking a pantomime from her repertoire, I grab an invisible key from the air, lock my lips, and stuff it down my shirt.

"You're such a hoot. Anyway, Odell said he would call the library to see if they had a record of the items I donated."

"Great googly moogly! What does that have to do with 'when you first met'?" I'm beginning to think this coat is her "Rosebud." Classic *Citizen Kane* callback. The clever idea brings a smile to my lips.

"It's not that clever, sweetie."

I point my fingers at my lips and shake my head.

"Let it go, dear. The point of the story is Odell's generosity."

All of my resistance melts away like an ice cube

left on the counter. "You're right, Grams! That's absolutely the sweetest thing. It's nice to know I'm not the only one who's here for you."

She zooms down to eye level, and her ghostly irises are sparkling. "Isn't it just?"

"Seems like you're positively giddy. What are you really up to?"

Grams presses a hand to her bosom and widens her eyes. "I'm not up to anything. Odell mentioned how he'll visit me every day after you and Erick get married—"

"All of you need to stop this nonsense. I am not getting married." Once the words pass through my lips, a strange sensation washes over me. Erick and Odell are quite close. It's entirely possible that Odell knows something I don't, despite my psychic gifts.

"That's exactly what I was thinking, sweetie."

I point my fingers at my lips and shake my head.

"Oh Mitzy, let it go. Odell said once you and Erick are married, you'll want a place for yourselves. Erick lives with his mother, you live with your ghost mother, and having a clean slate to build whatever you want, seems like the perfect plan."

"*IF* I get married, I'll cross that bridge when I come to it." I lift my left hand and wiggle my fingers. "The only thing missing from this perfect arrangement . . ."

She glances at the antique mood ring and frowns. "Well, you'll just have to switch that to your right hand."

"I don't think I can."

"What do you mean? Is it stuck?" She reaches a glimmering hand toward my ring finger.

"Not physically. But psychically, I think that's where it has to be."

"You've never tried it on your right hand, dear. How would you know?"

Crossing my arms, I tilt my head and arch an eyebrow. "Between the two of us, which one is a living psychic?"

She opens her mouth to protest, but instead sighs dramatically. "That's not fair. I have the occasional vision."

"I accept that. And I'm not trying to brag, but even by Silas's standards, I have exceptional gifts. If I say the moody mood ring stays on the left hand, then that's where it stays. Deal?"

Ghost-ma throws her glowing limbs in the air. "Fine. I'll tell th—" She slaps a ring-ensconced hand over her mouth.

"You'll tell who, what?" My heart races, and I can't be sure if it's panic or excitement.

Grams pulls the old disappearing ghost trick, and my opportunity to interrogate her further vanishes.

CHAPTER 18

I MAY HAVE STORMED out of the apartment in a huff after Grams ducked out on our conversation, but as soon as I reach the top of the spiral staircase, my mood ring flashes an image of the chain.

Twiggy!

Heading to the back room, I run through possible scenarios to entice my stubborn employee to take my side.

"Hey, do you have a minute?"

Twiggy slowly rotates her dilapidated office chair toward me as though she's the captain of a starship, and I've interrupted her daily log. Her expression makes it clear that I have seconds, not minutes, to make my case.

"Look, I'll be quick. Grams was asking me a lot of weird, ring-related questions and then she almost let something slip about telling 'them.' Somebody better tell me what's going on!"

Twiggy lifts her foot and places one biker boot on the opposite knee of her dungarees. "Or what, kid?"

"Or . . ." She has a point. My threat is beyond empty. "I don't know. I got nothin'. The point is, I hate surprises. It's a long story that starts with my mother's unfortunate death, and, despite all the fantastic things that have happened to me in the last few years, I'm still not a fan. No matter what, I can't stand being surprised. I'm a passable actress, though. So if you give me some idea what's going on, I promise I'll act surprised."

Twiggy rewards me with a knee slapping. "I told those fools it was pointless to try to surprise the psychic!" She continues to laugh uproariously at my expense.

"So there is a surprise. Dish."

She tilts her head and savors the moment. I'm utterly at her mercy, and she's enjoying it way too much. "Tell you what. I'll give you the broad strokes, and then you keep your snoopy little nose to yourself. Not all surprises are bad."

It sounds like the best, and probably only, deal I'm likely to receive. "You have my word."

The response seems to satisfy her, and she nods her head as she begins the tale. "I'd say your grandmother is the instigator, but she ropes more folks into her production with each passing day."

"My grandmother? She was super focused on something about a ring. I hope Erick's not trying to set up a secret proposal at my birthday party."

Twiggy lifts both hands in the air and stares me down. "Would that really be so bad?"

"That's not the point. I don't want to get into it. Just tell me more stuff about Grams and her production."

"Well, I suppose Isadora had a bit of a guilty conscience. Those first few months you were here, she didn't know when your birthday was. The second year she was trapped in that cursed piece of jewelry. So, this year she's bound and determined to make your twenty-fourth birthday one for the record books."

Even though the thought of a massive gala terrifies me, a whisper of relief spreads throughout my body. "Is that all? She just wants to plan some ridiculously elaborate birthday party?"

Twiggy rotates her chair, opens the drawer under the built-in desk, and pulls out a thick stack of pages. "It started with once a week, but now I find a new to-do list, scratched out in creepy ghost handwriting, on my desk every day. Decorations, catering, musicians, guest lists, valets . . . Isadora seems hell-bent on breaking the bank."

Leaning on my crutch, I chuckle and catch my breath. "I'm sure I'll hate every minute of it, but it makes me happy to make her happy. I let go of special days and big parties a long time ago, but my dad and Amaryllis had a pretty fantastic wedding here, so I suppose having a comically over-the-top birthday party at the bookstore will at least be a fraction of fun."

She slaps her hand on her thigh. "That's the spirit, doll. Whoever said your birthday party should be about you is dead wrong."

We share a snicker at Grams' expense.

"So who's involved in this crazy plotting and planning? I don't want to put anyone on the spot unnecessarily. I know Grams has probably threatened to haunt anyone who breaks the rules."

Twiggy's dark eyes widen. "Did she say that? If you somehow got me cursed, you'll never hear the end of it, kid."

"Don't worry, she's not around."

Twiggy checks her arms for ghost chills, leans forward, and continues in a whisper. "All the usual suspects. Odell, your dad, Amaryllis, Stellen, Erick, me—"

"Erick? How did Erick get into the inner circle?"

"Well, I had to tell him what the permits were for."

I nearly drop my crutch. "Permits? This party is gonna be so big there are permits?"

Twiggy enjoys one more cackle. "She wants to close off the cul-de-sac for the band, and she's got a bonfire planned as well, weather permitting."

Shock grips me. "Weather permitting indeed! If this coming March is anything like the last one, the cul-de-sac will be under six feet of snow!"

Twiggy sighs and rubs her hand across her mouth wistfully. "I learned a long time ago not to argue with your grandmother. What Isadora wants, Isadora gets. If she could figure out a way to hold a wedding reception outside in December, she'll manage to have a birthday party anywhere she wants any time of the year."

I have to laugh. "You're not wrong."

She drops both feet to the floor and exhales. "Well, let's see your surprised face, doll."

I grip my crutch with one hand, open my eyes as wide as saucers, and press one hand to my chest as I gasp. "Oh, my gosh!"

Twiggy gives me a slow clap as she turns back toward our antique computer.

As I head out into the stacks, I shout a "thanks" over my shoulder.

Hmmm, I can't believe I haven't heard from Erick. Deputy Gilbert should absolutely be back with Tammy by now.

Grabbing my cell, I fire off a quick text.

PING.

"He came back empty-handed."

My first instinct is to run upstairs and grab the map, and the pendulum, and scry for her location—but luckily my restored extrasensory perceptions reward me with a clairaudient message before I have to struggle with the stairs.

Herman Pettit.

I want to hear the happiness in Erick's voice when I give him the news, so this time I choose to place a call. As soon as he answers, I blurt, "She went straight to Herman Pettit's. I'll bet you anything they're packing their bags and getting ready to make a run for it."

At least he thanks me before he abruptly hangs up.

Now we wait.

I don't remember Twiggy mentioning Silas on the list of Isadora's birthday accomplices. I need to call him and see if he has any ideas for pain management. It's come to my attention that my grandmother was absolutely right about the way the pain medication was affecting me. I can't take a chance on refilling that prescription and potentially taking the easy way out too often or too many times.

For some reason, the children's section beckons

me. I teeter as I lower myself onto a large bright-green beanbag chair without incident.

Placing a call on speaker, I reach out to Silas. He answers on the second ring.

"Good afternoon, Mizithra. How are you re-covering?"

And he keeps trying to convince me he's not psychic. "Interesting you should mention my recov-ery. I'm having some difficulties."

Ignoring my failure to follow the proper greeting protocol, he continues. "That seems bur-densome. How may I assist you?"

"I was wondering if you knew some type of spell, I mean, transmutation, to reduce pain?"

"Did the doctor not prescribe some type of medication to assist in pain management?"

"Um, yeah, she did. The problem is, I had a little trouble monitoring my dosages."

"Addiction?"

"No, Grams intervened before it could get too serious, but, I have to admit, the substance was in-terfering with my powers. The problem is, she flushed all my pills down the toilet, and now my ankle hurts like a—"

"Language, Mizithra."

"What? I was going to say like a tight pair of pants on Thanksgiving."

The hearty sound of his laughter is reward enough.

"So, have you got anything up your sleeve, or in that magical tweed coat of yours?"

The depth of his concern is clear in that he doesn't take the time to correct my use of the word magical. "There are two transmutations that may assist. I should have time for a short tutorial en route to the airport."

"What now? Did you say airport?"

"Indeed. Earlier today, I received some unfortunate news. My brother Jedediah has been unwell, as you know. However, his nurse reached out this morning and informed me he has taken a dark turn. They do not expect him to recover. I chose to fly rather than waste precious time on a train. End-of-life predictions are notoriously unreliable. I may have a few days with my brother, or perhaps a few months. Either way, I put my affairs in order and have arranged to stay with him till he crosses over."

The discussion of a close relative passing threatens to loosen the manhole cover keeping all of my feelings about my mother's death at bay. "I'm so sorry, Silas. I know you and your brother are close, and I'm sure this must be difficult for you."

"When one reaches my age, or that of my older sibling, certain facts of life are inevitable. Jedediah has lived a full life. He will be missed, but neither he nor I have regrets."

"I wish I had that kind of clarity about death."

"One day, it will find you. Meanwhile, live each day to its fullest." His voice catches, and he covers it with a brusque harrumph.

"I'll try. We will miss you in Pin Cherry, but I completely understand. I promise to stay out of trouble while you're away."

And, for the second time during this phone call, I receive surprising guffaws for my outstanding remarks.

"Rude. I can stay out of trouble, most of the time."

His wise voice says otherwise. "I have come to understand that you would not be yourself without your penchant for mischief. Acceptance is one of the greatest gifts one can give oneself. I am pleased with the progress you have made with your gifts and your alchemical studies. I shall not beat my brow against the mountain in a fruitless attempt to change your nature."

"Thanks, I think."

"You are welcome. It was indeed meant as a compliment. I shall be on my way shortly and should see you before the hour."

Before I have a chance to express my gratitude,

Pyewacket darts out of the shadows and scrapes his deadly claws along the side of the beanbag chair.

"Pyewacket! You spilled the beans everywhere!"

A concerned voice echoes from the speaker on my mobile phone. "Mitzy? Are you injured?"

"No, I'll live. It's just that I was actually sort of comfortable, in this huge beanbag chair in the children's book section, and Pyewacket came out of nowhere and ripped the side open with his razor claws!"

Silas harrumphs into the phone, and I can easily picture him smoothing his mustache with thumb and forefinger. "Interesting. Perhaps there is a deeper meaning."

"The only thing deep about it is my rear end sinking deep into the middle of this stupid chair! There's absolutely no way I'm going to be able to get out of here on my own."

Silas attempts to stifle a chuckle. "Fear not. Elevate your leg, see if you can pry any additional details from Robin Pyewacket Goodfellow, and I shall see you posthaste."

DESPITE THE ENCOURAGEMENT from my mentor, Pyewacket offers no additional explanation for his actions. Instead, he lies atop the low two-shelf bookcase filled with colorful early reader books and squeezes his eyes to slits. Meanwhile, the beans continue to ooze from the wound he caused. I've never been trapped in quicksand, although I've seen many a movie that featured that classic scene, but I assume there's a similar sinking sensation with a potentially more terrifying outcome.

In my case, each passing minute sinks me further into a compromising position. Not compromising in a tawdry way, compromising in the sense that no amount of compromise will ever again get me on my feet. I could call for Twiggy, but the thought of her discovering me in this predicament brings me no pleasure. Plus, I'm sure she would cackle herself near to death before she offered me any assistance.

As my backside sinks lower, my foot ends up somewhat elevated. Last night's lack of sleep officially catches up with me, and my heavy eyelids fall like the curtains at the end of a Broadway show.

"Mizithra, it seems you have already uncovered the secret of relaxation."

Blinking in confusion, I swipe at the drool trickling from the corner of my mouth and yawn loudly.

Silas covers his mouth politely as he yawns in response.

Looking up at the wizened alchemist, I chuckle. "Good news, Silas, you're not a psychopath."

He tugs at his bowtie and harrumphs. "I should think not. What on earth is the catalyst for such a declaration?"

"Ah, forget about it. It's just a stupid movie trope about how psychopaths, or maybe it's sociopaths, won't yawn in response if they see someone else yawn. It's something to do with their lack of empathy or— I don't know. I'm babbling. Can you help me out of this thing?"

"All in due time. Did you deduce Pyewacket's message?"

"Deduce his message? What I deduced is that

he's a spoiled brat, and he thought it would be hilarious to trap me in this chair. Was there more?"

Silas smooths his mustache with more agitation than I've previously witnessed. "I fear it is worse than your grandmother believed."

"What's worse?"

"This misplaced anger results from your rapid development of a dependence on the pain medication. But we'll get to that in a moment. On the phone, you made an exclamation about spilling the beans. What is it that you feel Pyewacket revealed?"

I have to bite my tongue. I'd love to make an incredibly snarky response and gesture to the pile of *revealed* beans on the floor, but one stern lecture from Mr. Willoughby is enough on this day. "I don't think there was a message, Silas. It was when I was about to call you . . . I felt drawn toward the children's section, and I sat in the beanbag chair. The next thing you know"—I gesture to the rip and pile of stuffing innards—"this happened."

He tugs on the lapels of his fusty tweed coat and ponders my report. "Drawn to the children's section, you say?"

"That's what I said."

He steeples his fingers and begins to bounce his chin on the tip of his pointers.

Oh boy. The lesson has begun, and I'm

coming up empty. "Children. Beans. I don't know. Spilling the beans on children?" I lift my hands in an "I give up" gesture, and, with a resounding mental "click," the pieces fall into place like the tiles in a master's game of Tetris. "Somebody spilled the beans about a child! This isn't the first 'child' clue either. When I was at the church, I touched one of the pews and the word 'child' popped into my head. Is there a secret about a kid, Pyewacket?"

"Reow." Can confirm.

Silas grins with an almost fatherly pride. "Well done, Mizithra. Now let us address your pain management." He reaches for a small chair and struggles to sit comfortably on the minuscule seat.

As comical as it is to watch him adjust his round belly and his large coat, I dare not chuckle.

Finally, he gets situated. "The thing about pain is that it exists most acutely in the mind."

"That doesn't sound totally true. When I sprained my ankle, it actually hurt. I didn't imagine it hurt."

"Certainly. Your point is valid. However, my point is that pain is relative."

I cross my arms and grumble. "I'm *relatively* sure I'm in pain."

He ignores my response. "Give me your hand."

"Finally." I reach out my hand, thinking that

he's going to hoist me out of my bright-green prison, but I'm completely wrong.

Silas pinches the skin on the back of my hand, and I yank it back with a yelp. "Ouch. That stings."

"Did it hurt more or less than your ankle?"

"Well, I'm not sure. I wasn't thinking about my ankle. I was thinking about how much my hand hurt."

He nods as though he's made an amazing point. "Exactly."

"What do you mean? You can't just say *exactly* and think that's a—" Oh, wait! He can. Because before I even finish my sentence, I understand exactly what he means. "I get it. When I sit and focus on the pain in my ankle, and give it all of my attention, it hurts quite a lot. However, when I'm distracted by sleuthing or hand pinching, it doesn't hurt nearly as much."

Silas nods. "Excellent. Now the key is to discover the thing that will consume your attention, distract you completely from your pain."

Without even trying, the first thing that pops into my mind is Erick. "I think I've got something."

He chuckles knowingly. "I assume you do. When the pain is getting the better of you, you must quiet your mind. Visualize a bubble of white light—"

"Like the Good Witch from Oz?"

Silas stares at me with utter disappointment. "I don't follow."

"Glinda, the Good Witch, travels in a— Never mind. Not what you meant. I'm listening. Please continue."

He harrumphs, but moves on. "Visualize the pain leaving your body and entering the bubble. Release the ball of light holding the pain and allow your mind to drift toward this alternate thing that holds your rapt attention. If your focus falters, gently pull it back. When combined properly, the bubble of light and the shift of focus will release you from the prison of pain. The more you practice, the more adept you will become."

"Can I use the bubble for other things? Could I offer to put someone else's pain in the bubble?"

His eyes shimmer with emotion. "It is so like you to think of others in this way. When we first met, I never imagined your heart housed such generosity. To answer your question, I have witnessed a man so fully relieve the pain of a patient that the surgeon was able to perform an operation in the field without anesthesia."

My inner sense of knowing hardly needs to ask the question, but my outer snoop must. "Was the man who removed the pain you?"

He casts his eyes downward. "One has no need to seek acclaim for one's actions. A selfless gesture is far more effective when the giver expects no reward."

"Understood. I hope you can take away some of your brother's pain. I know that's why you're going."

A ready tear trickles over his round cheek and down his droopy jowl. "Indeed. If it is within my power to ease my brother's passing, I will offer my assistance without hesitation."

Grabbing my crutch, I awkwardly shove myself towards Silas. He reaches out and catches me as I struggle to embrace him. "I'll never understand what Fates conspired to bring you and me together, Mr. Willoughby, but I'm grateful, and my life will never be the same."

"Nor will mine, Mizithra Achelois Moon."

"Ree-oow." A rarely heard intonation from our feline overlord, but it seems to indicate conspiratorial agreement.

My phone pings with a text notification as I'm escorting Silas to the front door. It's easy to guess that the message is likely from Sheriff Harper, but after the tender moment Mr. Willoughby and I exchanged, I don't dare check my phone in front of him and break etiquette.

He turns, smooths his mustache with thumb and forefinger, and smiles warmly. "May I drop you at the sheriff's station?"

Despite my newfound pain management transmutation, the thought of poking my way through
the snow and ice for a couple blocks does little to
entice me. "That would be—"

"Divine?" Silas winks.

"Exactly. Let me grab my coat."

At the curb, Silas protests as I offer him one last
overzealous hug before exiting his ancient au-
tomobile.

He putters away, and I enter the sheriff's station
filled with hope and brimming with secrets.

Erick instantly walks out of his office as though
a hidden production assistant cued him from
offscreen.

I wave like a complete dork, and he smiles with
all the love and acceptance I've come to appreciate.
"Great tip, Moon. They were loading suitcases into
Herman's truck when the deputies arrived."

He strides through the bullpen and holds the
rickety wooden gate open for me.

"What about the kid?"

Erick's facial expression changes from satisfied
to shocked in the blink of an eye. "What did you
just say?"

Time for a quick subject change. "It's not important. So, Gilbert caught up with Tammy and
Herman before they hit the road?"

He releases the wooden gate, and it smacks me

on the backside. My eyes open wide, and if it wasn't for the suspicious look on Erick's face, I might think he meant it in a playful way.

"You look unhappy with me, Sheriff. Did I do something?"

He drags a thumb along the side of his stubbled jaw, bites his bottom lip for a second, and shakes his head. "You and your hunches. I sent Paulsen out to the Pettit place. Gilbert's a good deputy, and he can handle riding shotgun on something like that, but I didn't think he was ready to play lone wolf."

My face nods in agreement on the outside, but my brain is spinning wildly. I know the other shoe is going to drop, and I don't want to be an ant on the sidewalk when it does. "Good call. So, she got 'em?"

He nods and gestures for me to lead the way to his office. Once inside, he lowers his voice and narrows his gaze. "When Paulsen was loading Mrs. Smythe-Wiggins into the backseat, Herman shouted something about being careful with the pregnant lady. I'm going to see what additional information I can gather during the interview, but it sounds like you already knew about the child. Mind telling me how?"

My dry throat squeaks audibly as I struggle to come up with a plausible answer.

Erick exhales and places his hand on the doorjamb. "Never mind. I'm not in the mood for a song and dance."

He steps across the hall, and my voice is barely a whisper as I call out, "Wait. Erick, I—"

"Relationships are built on trust, Mitzy." He grips the handle of the door to the interrogation room and glances back at me with more than hurt in his eyes. "You trusted me enough to tell me about your grandmother. Why are you still holding back?"

Without giving me a chance to respond, he opens the door and steps inside.

A good girlfriend would burst into the interrogation room and shout her secret to the world, but I'm just an orphan who tripped and fell into a series of fortunate events. The idea of my psychic secret being "out there" makes my chest constrict. Memories of schoolyard taunts and crying myself to sleep still have a powerful effect on my "trust" gene. Maybe I'm not a good girlfriend. Maybe someone like me is better off alone.

Shoving the emotions down where I hide all of my deepest feelings, I step into the observation room and flick the silver toggle. It doesn't take clairvoyance to see that Erick won't be taking any guff during this interview.

Tammy is nothing like I pictured her. Her sleek black hair is shinier than a raven's feather, and her eyebrows are on fleek, if that's still a thing. She's definitely watched more than one Kardashian contouring video, and if her lips are naturally that plump, I'll eat my beanie.

Erick finishes verifying names and addresses, and before he can ask any questions, Tammy launches into her performance. Don't get me wrong, it's very good, but I have certain extrasensory advantages.

She wrings her hands and weeps openly. "Sheriff Harper, you have to believe me. Oscar is a monster. He's been planning to murder Quade ever since they signed that contract. Oscar used to be a lawyer in the big city. He's cutthroat. When he had his existential crisis and quit his job, we were basically ruined financially."

Erick crosses his arms and leans back. He's clearly not going to interrupt her with any of his prepared questions. There could be some value in this one-woman show.

Herman pats her gently on the back, and she allows herself an aching sob before she continues. "When he told me he wanted to make cheese, I thought, okay, I can do it. Seeing all these online influencers making their farmstead goods, I thought I could contribute some side income with, you know, products that would support him while he figured out his business." She snuffles and draws a ragged breath. "Since we moved up here, he lost his mind. He had all these big plans for the dairy, but Quade wasn't on board. Nothing was going his way, and he started taking it out on me." She pats her chest and gasps for air.

Erick allows himself a brief question. "And that's when the abuse started?"

She nods and shudders. "Well, my men's grooming products were flying off the shelves. I had thousands of likes for my store and over 300,000 social media followers on three different platforms. I was pretty much an influencer. And he hated me for it."

Hashtag humblebrag. This Tammy is a piece of work.

Herman twists the curve of his mustache and mumbles something encouraging.

She sniffles and continues. "So, I ran into Herman at a local craft fair." She looks at him and gushes about his stache. "When I saw that mustache, it was a disaster! I just knew my special wax could help him. He started out as a customer. It was totally innocent."

My mind immediately flashes to Jessica Rabbit: "I'm not bad, I'm just drawn that way." Oh, Tammy, never responsible for your own actions, eh?

Once again, Erick speaks as little as possible. "And then the affair started?"

She looks down, in what I'm calling feigned

shame. "Yes. I'm not proud of it, Sheriff. I was in a terrible situation. Herman understood. He comforted me."

The statement catches me off guard and I snort a little as an audible response rockets from my mouth. "Is that what the kids are calling it?"

She digs through her bag for a tissue, and Erick seizes the moment. "And how long after the affair started did you ask Herman to kill your husband?"

Tammy gasps and nearly drops her tissue.

Herman leans back and shakes his head repeatedly. "Kill her husband? We never talked about killing her husband."

Erick leans toward Herman and a chill wraps itself around his next sentence. "So, who did you discuss killing?"

Tammy attempts to hide her face behind the tissue, but her eyes give her away. Something in Erick's question touched a nerve.

She dabs at her eyes, even though her airbrushed makeup hasn't budged. "Sheriff, if you're trying to figure out who murdered Quade Knudsen, you may as well know it was my husband. He had motive, means, and opportunity."

This little social media influencer has streamed one too many episodes of *NCIS*.

"That will be for the department to decide. Where were you between 11:30 p.m. and 12:30

a.m. on the night Quade Knudsen was murdered?"

She opens her mouth and gasps. "Me? What makes you think I had anything to do with it?"

For those of you at home, please note she didn't answer the question.

Erick exhales and taps his hand on the table. "Please answer the question."

"I was at home. Probably asleep. I've been having terrible nausea."

Nice one. Play the sympathy card for the poor little pregnant woman.

"Can anyone confirm that?"

She shakes her head. "Of course not, Sheriff. My husband wasn't home. He's the one that needs an alibi, not me."

"I'll let Mr. Wiggins speak for himself. How about you, Mr. Pettit? Where were you on the night in question?"

Herman pulls out his phone and scrolls through what I'm assuming is some sort of appointment app. "That was the day I had a meeting with the grocery store rep in Chicago. I took a late flight home. I was probably on the plane. Maybe I was driving home. I didn't know I would need an alibi, Sheriff. I didn't take notes on my own whereabouts."

Erick makes several of his own notes in his pad before responding. "No problem, Mr. Pettit. We can easily verify the meeting, the flight, etcetera. I'll need the name of the man you were meeting with."

Mr. Pettit twists one handlebar of his red mustache. "Of course. Hold on." He swipes and scrolls on his phone and provides the sheriff with the information.

Erick returns to questioning Tammy. "What gives you the idea that your husband killed Mr. Knudsen? Did he ever discuss plans to do so?"

Tammy shakes her head. "Not in so many words. After all, Oscar was a lawyer. He knows better than to say something like that out loud. But he always talked about how much he hated Quade, and what he would do if he owned the dairy by himself."

"If your husband had such knowledge of the law, what did he plan to do with his 49% of ownership after taking Mr. Knudsen out of the picture? Quade's will specifically listed his son as the beneficiary of his 51% share in *Udderly Brilliant*."

The moment of complete mortification that flashes across Tammy's face is definitely viral-video-worthy. She quickly schools her features and attempts to recover. "I have no idea, Sheriff. I'm sure he had some plan to outsmart the minor and move forward with whatever bigger and better plans he kept talking about. You'll have to ask him."

Erick stands, snaps his notebook closed, and

opens the door. "I intend to. We'll have additional questions for both of you after I speak to Mr. Wiggins. Deputy Paulsen will hold your passports, and we'd appreciate it if neither of you attempt to leave town while this investigation is ongoing."

A flare of anger shoots from Tammy's eyes as Herman gently pats her on the back and presses her toward the door. "I'll see that she gets home safely, Sheriff. We— We, um— We weren't planning on leaving town. She was upset. I was going to take her to the doctor."

Oh brother. Does he really think anyone's buying that? Erick doesn't even bother to reward the flimsy excuse with acknowledgment. "I'm sure we'll be chatting again real soon."

SITTING IN THE OBSERVATION ROOM after the interview with Tammy and Herman ends, I stare at the door handle, hoping to force Erick's entrance with my mind power.

No joy.

He's upset with me, and clearly he'd rather avoid me than have an argument. I get it. There are plenty of conversations I enjoy avoiding.

Normally I'd run to Grams for advice, but something tells me this is a job for Odell.

Zipping my coat up to protect my neck and pulling my winter stocking cap down over my ears, I exit the observation room and hobble past Erick's closed office door.

I can't be sure whether the temperature has actually dropped, or if it's the chilly ache in my heart that's causing me to shiver uncontrollably as I head to the diner. Whatever the cause, I'm pleased to be greeted by the warmth inside Myrtle's.

There are a couple of regulars in a booth, and an elderly gentleman I don't recognize skimming through the paper at one of the four-tops by the front window. I grab a stool at the counter and raise my bum leg onto the seat next to me.

Odell offers a spatula salute through the orders-up window, but stops in mid-motion. He takes a second look at my face, drops his metal burger flipper with a clatter, and strides out of his kitchen. "Did you and your grandmother have a tiff over wardrobe?" He chuckles and smiles tenderly.

"I wish. I have a pretty good track record of making up with Grams. She gets upset with me, but she never stays angry for long. This one seems more serious."

"What did you do to Erick now?"

"Rude!"

He tilts his head and waits.

"All right." I lean toward him and lower my voice to a breathy whisper. "I had some information about his investigation that was absolutely not public knowledge. He wasn't really buying the hunch thing and wanted details. I wouldn't give any."

Odell straightens, rakes a hand through his

close-cropped grey buzz cut, and exhales loudly. "Honesty. You can't go wrong with honesty."

My eyes roll dangerously. "I can't do it. You know what Erick's like. He's too honest for his own good. Next time someone asks him where he got his lead, he'll blurt something out about Mitzy and her —" I point to my head and shrug. "You know. And then everyone will know!"

"I don't think you give the sheriff enough credit, kid. He's more discerning than you might think."

The keeping of the gigantic birthday-party secret springs to mind, and I allow one corner of my mouth to lift in a halfhearted smile. "You might be right, Gramps. The problem is that this is like a dangerous video game. I only get one life, and if sharing my secret with Erick crashes and burns, there's no respawn button. You know?"

He squeezes his eyes partially shut and deep wrinkles form around the corners. "Respawn?"

"Yeah, it's a video-game thing. It's like a reset button where you get a chance to play a section of the game over again. But now you kinda know how it works and where the enemies are, or whatever. It's like a do-over. Got it?"

Odell sniffs once and nods. "Yeah, it's too bad we don't get one or two of those in our lifetime."

I sense his thoughts shifting to my grandmother and what might've been. Now that I know he's my biological grandfather, I have less justification for my grandmother giving up on their relationship and marrying Cal. I always used to say that if she hadn't married Cal and had my father, I wouldn't be here. However, I've since learned that Odell Johnson is actually Jacob's father, and I'd be here whether or not she married Cal. But I still believe that everything happens for a reason. If my father hadn't been raised by a multi-millionaire railroad tycoon, he never would've rebelled. Which means he probably wouldn't have been involved in the largest armed robbery in almost-Canada. And—taking this little mental gymnastics exercise further—he wouldn't have learned the lessons he learned in Clearwater and he wouldn't have started the restorative justice program. And now my mind movies are turning into TED talks for one! "I mean, in the final analysis, everything happens for a reason, right, Gramps? The issue I'm struggling with is whether I want those things to happen right now—or not."

Odell sighs and places his weathered hand on top of my tapping fingers. "Everyone will try to tell you what to do, Mitzy. At the end of the day, you're the only one who can make the decision. You're the one who has to live with the consequences. What I think of Erick Harper doesn't matter."

Blinking back tears, I nod in agreement. "Yeah, it's the consequences that are tripping me up. Despite my—abilities—I can't seem to get a single message about those sneaky consequences."

My loving grandfather squeezes my hand. "Life isn't about knowing every outcome. Sometimes you have to take a risk. You seem like the type of girl who's more than willing to leap before she looks. What's really holding you back?" He raps his knuckles twice on the Formica countertop and returns to the grill without a backward glance.

That's an excellent question. One I don't have an answer to. For now, I'll shove it all to the back of my brain and focus on this case.

Tammy seemed hell-bent on incriminating Oscar. If she is carrying Herman Pettit's child, the desire to get rid of her current husband makes some weird kind of sense. However, a lone pregnant woman couldn't move an unconscious body from the dairy all the way out to that icehouse by herself. If Herman Pettit is the man who helped her, why was Oscar trying to hide the evidence of the dead cow at the dairy?

My stomach sours, and I shockingly exit the diner without eating anything. The more clues I uncover, the more suspects I have.

And questions! Nothing but questions.

I need to get back out to that dairy. Maybe I can figure out how the noxious gas got into the Classy

Gals' suite. There has to be something that will help narrow down the list of suspects.

I could call Quince to drive me out to the dairy, but I haven't taken any pain medication in roughly twenty-four hours, Oscar Wiggins is still in a holding cell at the sheriff's station, and I may need to get super psychic to dig up some new information.

It's probably best for everyone if I go alone.

On the drive out to *Udderly Brilliant*, I struggle with the ever-shifting facts of this case.

Quade lost consciousness because of exposure to chlorine gas, then someone moved his unconscious body out to the icehouse where they took the time to build a fire to keep him warm, but then stuffed a rag down the stovepipe to allow carbon monoxide to build up inside this tiny structure.

According to the medical examiner, he died of carbon monoxide poisoning and his body was subsequently frozen.

Did the killer predict the unseasonal temperature drop? Was it a complete shock to everyone? If so, the freezing of the corpse was never part of the plan.

But as soon as I take that off the table, I have to address the empty bourbon bottle.

I never met the victim, and I have no way of knowing whether or not he avoided alcohol due to his medication. However, Quince has a sharp eye for details and a nose for news. If he says his uncle didn't drink, I'm inclined to believe him. Which means someone poured some bourbon down an unconscious man's throat, and took an empty bottle along with the body out to the icehouse.

Why? Why would they care whether—?

Now we're straight back to the weather. If they knew about the unusual plummeting subzero temperatures, the bottle of bourbon would certainly have sent law enforcement down the wrong path.

Erick said the freeze covered any visual evidence of the carbon monoxide poisoning, and if Quince and I hadn't discovered that screw, it seems pretty likely that Quade's death would've been permanently written off as an accident.

Somebody tried to cover something up, but then they also murdered a man. Granted, they nearly got away with it, but the move to the icehouse was more than a hasty cover-up. It was an active homicide.

As I pull into the dairy, I'm shocked to see several people working in the vast barn. Truth be told, it never occurred to me that Quade and Oscar would need employees. But let's be honest, if you have five hundred cows, it's pretty unlikely that you'll be able to milk them twice a day all by yourself.

Hopefully, these employees won't give me any trouble.

Hopping out of the Jeep, I grab my crutch from the backseat and attempt a nonchalant shamble to the small milking room behind the cleanup area.

No one pays me any mind.

If I'm honest with myself, back in the days when I was working as a barista, I wouldn't have given two hoots if some stranger wandered into our stockroom. "Above my pay grade" was my standard refrain.

A quick scan of the back room reveals the open chemicals have been resealed and everything is in shipshape on this side of the suite.

Passing through the door, I take a moment to focus my energy and unleash all of my special abilities. Nothing is out of place. The collection tank stands empty, and the smell of bleach and other chemicals is thick in the air. So, it's also been cleaned.

The thing is, the cows don't come in this way—through the chemical storage area. So there has to be another exit.

Stepping around the small milking stalls, I hop a railing, pull my crutch between the bars, and walk down the ramp to a rear exit. It's a tight turn and a small ramp. All in all, the total space isn't much bigger than an average bedroom.

The rear exit has a large vented panel in the door, but someone has taped it over with plastic and duct tape. Could be a winterizing measure, or it could be a "let the chlorine gas build up inside here" measure.

Balancing myself on the crutch, I kneel to get a closer look at the plastic covering. There's a slit in the thick-mil sheet that could allow access to a tube. If someone had mixed the chemicals in a container and pushed a hose through this opening, they could have left the premises and let the gas do its work. Assuming their intent was to kill. Although, if their intent was to disable, they only needed to wait until Quade hit the floor, then they could have disposed of the apparatus, retrieved the body, and taken it to—

Shoot! His snowmobile was parked beside the icehouse. I'm certain they didn't move an unconscious body on a sled. But loading a snowmobile and a body into a truck means it has to be Oscar.

As I climb into the Jeep, I continue to twist my brain into a pretzel.

I'm overthinking this. Oscar disabled Quade, took him to the icehouse, and attempted to cover his tracks by planting the bourbon bottle. Then he tampered with the stove to create the perfect environment for carbon monoxide poisoning. The temperature drop was just a lucky break.

If that's what really happened, why do I feel so—

Before I can complete that sentence in my head, my fingers are already speed dialing the sheriff.

I place the call on speaker and start the engine to get a hint of heat going.

"Hey, I know you're upset with me, and trust me when I tell you I'm even more upset with myself. Let's call a truce until we solve this murder. All right?"

Whether his grunt is one of acknowledgment or agreement, I don't clarify. I push onward.

"Did you impound Herman Pettit's car?"

"Paulsen didn't feel the need. She loaded them into the cruiser, and Gilbert examined the vehicle for any additional evidence."

"What was in the trunk?"

"Why? Do you think they transported Quade's body in that vehicle?"

"No, but I don't want to say what I think."

He grumbles. "But you expect me to share my information."

"Erick, I promise I'm going to tell you exactly what I'm thinking. Just ask Deputy Gilbert what was in that trunk."

"Hold on." He places me on hold and comes back on the line less than two minutes later. "Two suitcases—which definitely blows a hole in the story about taking her to the doctor—a gas can and tube for siphoning gas. I suppose they didn't have time to fill up. Maybe they didn't have enough cash, and they thought they might need to steal gas as part of their getaway plan. I don't know."

"Erick, you've got to get your hands on that gas can. I'm almost one hundred percent certain that it never contained gas. I think that was part of the delivery system for the chlorine gas."

There's a long silence on the other end of the phone. "Hunch?"

"Not even close. This was straight up investigative work. I went back to the dairy and found a thick sheet of plastic taped over the vents on the back door of the Classy Gals' suite. There was a narrow slit that would've allowed a tube to be slipped through to deliver the chlorine."

He exhales. "Nice work, Moon. We'll take care of it."

CHAPTER 21

BACK AT AMATEUR SLEUTHING HEADQUARTERS, there's a sheriff's cruiser parked in the alley, blocking the entrance to my garage.

Uh oh.

The good news is, the lights aren't flashing, so it's safe to assume I'm not going to be accused of murder—for like the third time!

Turning off my engine, I hop—and that's literally on one leg—out of my Jeep, and grab my crutch from the backseat.

By the time I've organized myself and all my accoutrements, Erick is approaching with an uncertain but hopeful look on his face.

My eyes dart nervously. "Hey."

He offers a weak smile. "Hey."

Taking a step back, I slam the rear door and tilt

my head toward the bookshop. "Can we talk inside?"

He nods, hesitantly takes my keys, and opens the heavy metal alleyway door.

I crutch my way inside while he eases the door closed behind us.

My volunteer employee, who either purposely ignores our entrance or is so engrossed in entering the weekly order that she doesn't hear us, occupies the back room.

Shrugging, I continue toward the spiral staircase.

Erick silently rushes ahead and unhooks the chain for me.

The thirty-second timer counts down in my head, and I hurry to the best of my clumsy abilities. He secures the chain behind us.

This silent march toward the apartment is unnerving, but I can't think of anything to say. Apologizing without details seems hollow.

He pulls the candle handle, and we both stare straight ahead, like strangers in an elevator, while the bookcase door slides open.

Inside the apartment, I lean my crutch against the back of the sofa, remove my winter gear, and ease onto the seat. Before I have a chance to handle it myself, Erick scoops up my injured leg and elevates it onto the settee.

"Thanks."

He nods and lowers himself onto the scalloped-back chair.

An awkward quiet thickens the air between us, and there's a great deal of fidgeting and swallowing. Neither of us has a chance to break the silence.

"Oh, Mitzy! I'm so glad you're back." Grams bursts through the wall from the bookshop and surges toward me. She sees Erick and stops short. "Oh dear, did I interrupt?"

In an attempt to handle otherworldly protocol properly, I inform Erick first. "Grams is here."

His eyes track back and forth across the room and he shrugs. "Can she give us a minute?"

Grams presses a hand to her lips and arches one perfectly drawn eyebrow. "This looks serious, dear. Is everything all right?"

"We need some privacy, Grams. Understood?"

Her eyes widen and shimmer simultaneously. "I'll make myself scarce. But I'll expect a complete update later."

Before I give her my verbal response, I send her a brief telepathic message. *This is personal and private. Don't expect any details.* Then I offer the verbal response for all souls in the room. "Thanks. Bye for now."

Ghost-ma crosses her arms and vanishes in a huff.

Erick sighs. "All clear?"

"All clear."

He offers the first olive branch. "I got a judge to sign a warrant pretty fast. Paulsen and Johnson headed out to the Pettit farm to see if that gas can is still in the trunk. If not, the warrant allows us to search the property and impound the car if necessary."

He's volunteering information and using his business voice. Not good.

Erick leans back, folds his hands in his lap, and looks at me with irresistible puppy-dog eyes.

As irresistible as he is, I'm not ready. I thought about everything Odell said, and I thought about my life here in Pin Cherry, and I absolutely thought about how much I care for Erick. And at the end of all that thinking, I landed on not revealing my deepest secret. Odell got me thinking about what was really holding me back, and it's stupid and selfish.

To his credit, Erick sits in patient silence, while my brain continues to spin in circles.

I lost my mother at eleven, I ping-ponged through mostly hellish foster care for over six years, and then I landed in Pin Cherry Harbor.

I'm happy here. I'm special. I'm useful. One slip up, and all of that goes away. I know how it sounds, but I can't go back to the way things were before. Maybe my outlook is too doomsday, maybe it will change, but, right now, I know I'm not ready. So, I'm going to tell a little white lie, and you're going to have to trust me when I say it will all work out.

Sheriff Harper scrapes his hand across his polyester pant leg and exhales. "I don't want there to be any secrets between us, Mitzy. I may not be able to see ghosts, but I can see you're hiding something."

Before he throws down an ultimatum or a *Sophie's Choice*, I float my falsehood-filled balloon. "It's the pain meds. I was taking too many. I don't know whether it made me hallucinate or just made me super crabby, but it wasn't good. Grams actually flushed my pills down the toilet! So I'm clean and sober." I lift my hands as though it's a holdup. "Clean and sober, and ready to apologize."

His need to believe me supersedes his years of training. In a flash, he's kneeling next to the sofa, slipping his arm around me and gently touching my face. "I knew something was off. You know how much you mean to me, right?"

Emotion constricts my throat, and I simply nod.

Erick kisses me softly and smooths the hair back from my face. "Mitzy, I love you. I've never felt this way about anyone. I want—"

My lips are on his, and I have to stop him from saying whatever he's going to say next.

When I come up for air, I struggle to take control of the conversation. "Erick, I love you. I've never said that to any living soul besides my mother —and look what happened to her." I'm powerless to hold back the tears.

He scoops his arms around me and whispers into my neck. "What happened to your mother was terrible. I can't begin to imagine what you went through in foster care, but that part of your life is over. You deserve good things. Trust is a risk, but I promise it'll be worth it."

Between my sniffles and sobs, I manage to whisper, "I'm scared."

He kisses my cheek. "We're all scared. Let's be scared together. It's so much better than being scared alone."

"All right."

I'm not sure what I've agreed to, or what he actually offered, but something shifts. Whether it's in the real world or in my psychic fantasy, I can't be sure. Wherever it's occurring, it's wonderful, and my heart feels as though it can't fit inside my rib cage.

Without asking, he scoops me from the settee and carries me to my four-poster bed.

My tingly tummy gets the wrong idea.

Matters are quickly clarified as he places me on the down comforter. "You told me your mother used to read to you, and after she passed away you avoided books. Then the universe dumped a bookshop in your lap. I think the underlying message is clear."

I swipe at the tears on my cheeks. "Oh, is that so? And what do you think the underlying message is, Sheriff?"

He bends and kisses my forehead. "You're surrounded by books. Clearly, I should read to you." He grabs a pillow, gently lifts my injured leg, and elevates it. "What's the title of your choosing, Miss Moon?"

Without warning a deeply buried memory rockets to the surface like a torpedo. "*The 18th Emergency*?"

He scrunches up his face. "Are you asking me or telling me?"

"*The 18th Emergency*. That's the book my mother was reading to me . . . Well, you know what I mean."

Erick nods. "You never finished the book?"

"Never. Until this moment, upon pain of death, I couldn't have remembered the title. I buried it. I mean, like, super deep."

He smiles. "Stay put." Without waiting for a response, he exits the apartment.

I'm assuming he's headed downstairs to consult with Twiggy. The odds of such an old, random title being in my actual bookstore seem about the same as the odds of being hit by a meteor.

When he returns less than five minutes later with a book in his hands, I have to wonder if it's time to check the skies.

"You can't be serious? Is that it? Was it in my shop this whole time?"

He smiles, but there's a strange look in his eye. "It wasn't. Twiggy said this book arrived two days ago in an unmarked package."

The hairs on the back of my neck tingle, and I swear I can feel my mother in the room. "No way."

He turns the book toward me and shows me the cover. "Way."

The sight of the unmistakable red-and-white cover unlocks a series of memories. An emotional montage explodes inside my head.

My backpack.

Our little apartment.

My mother's loving gaze.

Her soft British voice reading me to sleep.

An aching whisper escapes my lips. "Mama, I miss you."

Erick lays the book on the nightstand and scoops me into his arms. "I wish I could've met Coraline. I know from the picture we found that you have her eyes. But if the eyes are the windows to the soul, I feel as though I kind of did meet her."

I cry it out in his arms. Eventually, the tidal wave of emotion subsides.

He releases me and grabs a box of tissues from the bathroom. When he hands them to me, I mop the years of shuttered pain from my face.

Without another word, Erick retrieves the book from the nightstand, drags the scalloped-back chair to the bedside, and sits. "Shall I start from the beginning?"

If I open my mouth, I'll start sobbing again, so I nod and grab another tissue.

"The pigeons flew out of the alley in one long swoop . . ."

The gentle cadence of his voice soothes my spirit and eases my pain. Without realizing it, I drift into a dreamland filled with happy memories of my mother.

MORNING TOUCHES my heart with a flash of sadness as the Technicolor memories of my mother fade to black. I twist toward the pillow beside me, seeking comfort. Instead of a handsome sheriff, I find it cradles a single sheet of paper.

As I reach for the note, Grams slowly sparkles into existence beside the bed. A tear is trickling down her cheek as she clutches a strand of pearls. "I'm telling you right now, sweetie. If you don't marry that man, I will burn all your snarky T-shirts!"

"Easy, Beetlejuice. I'm barely awake. And it seems like you're reading my mail now, as well as my thoughts."

"It was out in the open—"

"Save the excuse-planations, Grams. Let me

read what I'm guessing is a lovely note from my boyfriend, before you threaten me or my precious tees any further."

She sniffles and floats backward a few inches.

Gripping the note in one hand, I roll onto my back and read these lovely words:

Dear Mitzy,

I know I can never fill the hole left when your mother passed, but thank you for letting me read you to sleep. Happy to do it any time. I said relationships are built on trust, and I have to admit it's a two-way street. I love you enough to spend the rest of my days earning yours. After you grab some breakfast at Myrtle's Diner, head into the station to observe my follow-up interview with Oscar Wiggins.

Yours for as long as you'll have me, Erick.

Of course, silent tears are streaming down my cheeks by the time I finish reading the note. I don't know what I did to deserve the world's best boyfriend, but I'm going to do everything in my power not to screw it up. When Silas gets back to town, I plan to bribe him into teaching me some type of transmutation for building trust. I'm sure it exists somewhere inside of me, but it's buried under so much trauma I can't seem to get a solid grip on it.

Grams has had all she can take. She swirls forward and wraps her ethereal arms around me. "He's got to be the best man on the planet, dear. And he's lucky to have you, too. I know you have to process some things, but don't take too long. A gentleman like that isn't one-in-a-million—he's once-in-a-lifetime."

I snuggle into the warm energy of acceptance that envelops me, and offer the only response I can find. "And how would you know?"

She swishes back and looks at me in shock. My poker face melts into loving laughter, and Grams shakes her head. "Oh, dear! You're referring to Odell, aren't you?"

"I am. I would have to say that he's your once-in-a-lifetime, right?"

She gazes out the six-by-six windows overlooking the still frozen great lake, presses a hand to her heart, and sighs with emotion. "He is. I only wish I'd realized it while I was still living that lifetime."

"Don't beat yourself up. We all have regrets. The wonderful news is that you and Gramps are finally getting a second chance. It's a super weird second chance, with all sorts of afterlife abnormalities, but still—"

Ghost-ma swirls toward me and attempts to grip my hand in hers. Her emotions are causing her to flicker, and it feels as though the heat of a candle flame is moving closer and farther away.

"You better go and get your breakfast, dear. Don't keep that sweet man waiting."

"Copy that." Lifting my slacker leg out of the bed, I teeter to a standing position. "Hey, my ankle feels a lot better."

Grams rockets to the crutch, pushes it toward me, and plants a fist on her silk-and-tulle-covered hip. "Don't spoil it by taking chances."

"Yes, mistress." Gingerly stepping forward to take the crutch, I slip it under my left arm and stumble into the bathroom to prepare myself for the day.

All the while, she's attempting to talk me into something with a plunging neckline, but I have to insist on my standard skinny jeans and a T-shirt. However, I play a little fast and loose with the top half of my outfit. The tee features a small stand of black-and-white birch trees and the tagline "Basic Birch."

When I reach for my puffy coat, she snatches it and floats toward the ceiling. "At least wear the red Olivia wool wrap coat. Please, dear. In honor of my missing trench." Her ghost eyes are wide and pleading.

"Seems like I don't have a choice, since you coat-napped my usual option!" I storm into the closet, grab the Olivia coat, and slip it on as I march out of the bookshop.

Once I'm clear of her thought-dropping, I admit the coat is fabulous.

Breakfast is quick and uneventful. Odell chuckles at my T-shirt and wishes me luck with the case.

When I arrive at the sheriff's station, I'm shocked to discover Furious Monkeys not on duty.

"Hey, Deputy Johnson, where's Furi— I mean, Deputy Baird?"

He smiles and shrugs. "Everybody gets a little time off once a week."

"Good policy." I point to the sheriff's office. "Is it all right if I head back?"

He grins too easily. "I'm not going to be the one to say no to the sheriff's girlfriend."

I roll my eyes entirely for his benefit and head back to Erick's office. As I approach the doorway, he's bent over some paperwork on his desk, which has him so engrossed, he doesn't hear me.

My extra senses float the word *party* to my brain, and I attempt to shuffle backward before I publicly spoil the surprise that I already secretly know about.

Depending on how well you know me, you may have figured out what happens next. I catch the walking boot encasing my sprained left ankle on the tip of the crutch and fall backward.

The commotion brings the sheriff running out of his office. He takes one look at me and shakes his head. "I'm not even going to ask what happened. I'm simply going to help you back on your feet, Moon."

"Thank you kindly, Sheriff Harper."

He chuckles, grabs my crutch in one hand, and lifts me to my feet with the other. "Are you okay? You didn't break or sprain anything else, did you?"

A silly grin curves up the corners of my mouth, and I give my backside a little slap. "Right as rain. It's almost like the powers that be knew I needed some extra padding back here."

He kisses my cheek softly and whispers for my ears only, "Did you sleep all right?"

My tummy flip flops and my skin tingles where his breath brushed across it. "I did. When I woke up, I found a deliciously sweet note in my bed from an amazing man."

Erick leans back, and his eyes widen. "Some man left a note in your bed? Is it a stalker? Should I send deputies over to dust the scene for prints?" He chuckles before he can finish the ruse.

"Ha ha. You're welcome to send deputies over anytime you want. The only prints they're going to find are yours!" I flash my eyebrows and whisper, "And they're everywhere!"

Now it's his turn to blush with embarrassment. He quickly changes the subject. "Let me get you set up in the observation room, and then I'll grab Wiggins from the cells."

As he turns to lead the way, I grip his hand and mumble, "Thanks for trusting me. I'm sorry I need more time."

He squeezes my fingers. "Take all the time you need. I'm not going anywhere. Are you?"

Too many emotions are bubbling too close to the surface. Time to use a little of my so-called humor to reset the vibe. "Absolutely. I'm *going* into this observation room. Sound good?"

His shoulders shake with laughter as he leads the way, and fetches an extra chair to elevate my leg.

I may not be a bonbon-eating heiress, but I can't say I mind being tended to by the world's sweetest man.

ERICK LEAVES me to my own devices, and a few moments later he leads Oscar Wiggins into Interrogation Room 2.

Wiggins is much the worse for wear. His super-groomed facial hair is wild. Stubble covers the entire lower half of his face, and I'd swear his beard is growing faster than a werewolf's hair in the full moon. Just guessing.

The sheriff presses the record button, reminds Oscar of his Miranda rights, confirms he wants to proceed without counsel, and launches directly into the tough questions.

"Mr. Wiggins, additional evidence has come to light that puts you squarely in the crosshairs of a homicide charge. Right now, the district attorney is looking at murder one. Too many components of this crime were premeditated, as evidence will support. Your wife already shot a hole in your alibi. She claims you were not home on the night in question, and she indicates you had motive, means, and opportunity."

Now I know Erick is bluffing. He would never say something like that to a suspect. But he only has disconnected bits of evidence, and he needs a confession to seal the deal.

Reaching out with all of my senses, the regulars and the extras, I wait for Oscar Wiggins to reply.

"What? I'm not the one who killed him! I found him collapsed in the small milking room and I dragged him out of there around 10:00 p.m."

Erick nods. "If that's true, why didn't you call for medical assistance?"

"Well, there was a half-empty bottle of bourbon right inside the door, and I knew Quade wasn't supposed to mix alcohol with his medication. He always had soda water when he came to our house for supper. I figured something awful must've happened. Bad news, you know? Something about the ex-wife and the son . . . I had no idea. But I knew that negotiations with the big dairy down south were tenuous at best. I couldn't afford for him to wake up in that state and take it as a bad omen."

Erick folds a few pages over in his notebook,

taps his pen on a specific page, and continues. "So you claim you found the body, and then what?"

There's a sensation that Oscar is struggling with the next part, but I'm not able to get a clear read on why.

"I moved the body."

Sheriff Harper writes something in his notepad. "So you're the one who moved Quade's unconscious body to the icehouse where he froze to death?"

Why would Erick say that? The ME's report stated carbon monoxide poisoning as the cause of death.

Oscar leans forward and wrings his hands. "Look, I'm a lawyer, Sheriff. You're trying to get me to confess because you don't have a solid case. I'm here to tell you I didn't kill him. I loaded his sled in the back of my truck, put him in the front, and grabbed the bourbon bottle for set dressing. Then I took him to his icehouse, poured a little bourbon on his shirt, and left the empty bottle next to his chair." Oscar lifts his hands in a plea for understanding.

"Unfortunately, Mr. Knudsen's lifeless body was discovered in that very icehouse. You've admitted you placed the body. Why should I believe you aren't responsible for his death?"

Oscar shakes his head in disbelief. "Because I built a huge fire in his stove. I put in birch bark, some of the newspaper he had there, and several logs. Figured he'd sleep it off, wake up and not really remember what happened. I thought if he woke up in the icehouse, that would remove any suspicion about the dairy deal."

"Why would he be suspicious about things at the dairy?"

In Oscar's haste to clear his name, he may have said too much.

"Okay. Okay. To be perfectly honest, Quade wasn't entirely on board with the deal with the big dairy."

Clapping my hands together with satisfaction, I mumble, "I knew it."

"Tammy was sick and tired of being a farmer's wife. I was coming home every day smelling of cow manure and Lord knows what. She'd had enough. The deal wasn't to be sub-producers for the dairy down south. I wanted to sell the whole operation. Quade wasn't entirely convinced."

Something about Oscar's posture and the nearly imperceptible beads of sweat at his hairline tell me he's holding something back. Just as I'm about to tap on the one-way glass with the tip of my crutch, Erick swoops in. "Oscar, when you say he wasn't 'entirely' convinced, what does that really mean?"

Oscar drops his face into both of his hands,

moans, and rubs fiercely at his stubble. "I'm trying to be a good husband, Sheriff. Tammy said if I didn't close the sale, she was going to take matters into her own hands."

My eyes widen. Whoa! Here I was thinking Tammy was a behind-the-scenes Siren whispering into the ears of Oscar or Herman. Turns out she might've been the mastermind!

Erick handles his surprise with more finesse. "Mr. Wiggins, is it your statement that your wife killed Quade Knudsen?"

"No— Well, I don't know. It was such a strange coincidence. We had that big fight in the morning, and then—"

"Who had a fight? You and Quade, or you and your wife?"

"Me and the old ball and chain."

The sheriff lets all this new information simmer as he pages through his notepad. I've known him long enough and seen him conduct enough interviews to know that the notepad is a prop. The man's mind is like a steel trap.

And suddenly, Erick takes a page from my book and tosses a question from left field. "What do you know about the gas can and rubber tubing, Mr. Wiggins?"

Oscar's messy goatee drops and his mouth hangs open like an abandoned mine shaft.

"Mr. Wiggins?"

There's a strange glint in Oscar's eye. "Was this tubing clear?"

Erick leans back and crosses his arms. "It was. How would you know that?"

Mr. Wiggins leans forward, and the expression on his face reeks of desperation. "Did you hear what I told your partner about Tammy's business? About her mad scientist stuff?"

"Are you referring to our consultant, Miss Moon?"

"Yeah, that's the one."

"Does that information have a bearing on this case?"

Oscar slams his meaty fist on the table. "Absolutely. Tammy has a pile of tubing like that. She extracts essences. I don't know. I'm just telling you, I've seen the tubing at our house. She uses that stuff all the time."

Erick uncrosses his arms, and I wish I could see his expression. His energy is tinged with anticipation. "Mr. Wiggins, you're admitting that part of the apparatus used in Quade's attempted murder comes from your house. How do you think that's going to look to the district attorney?"

"I know exactly how it's going to look, Sheriff. And you have to ask yourself if a seasoned attorney would hand you a piece of information like that—knowing full well it puts another nail in his coffin."

My head nods of its own accord. Oscar is right. If he were as talented an attorney as his wife claims, he would never be careless enough to hand the prosecution evidence.

Wiggins is nodding. "Plus, I told you, I built a fire to keep Quade warm. I didn't have anything to do with him passing out and freezing to death."

Erick leans forward and taps a finger slowly on the table as he enlightens Mr. Wiggins. "Quade Knudsen died of carbon monoxide poisoning—before his body was frozen—and with no alcohol in his bloodstream."

Oscar's eyes widen, and he leans back as this new piece of information slaps him across the face. "I opened the window."

The sheriff shakes his head. "The window was closed and locked when we discovered the body. It's your word against crime-scene evidence. Mr. Wiggins, I'm placing you under arrest—"

"Wait. Sheriff, it doesn't make sense. Even if the window was closed, the stovepipe is four inches in diameter, there's no way—"

Before Oscar Wiggins can finish that sentence, I'm rapping my crutch madly on the window.

Erick's shoulders pinch with frustration, and he suspends the interrogation.

The door to the observation room opens, and he leans in. "Yes, concerned citizen."

My eyes must be sparkling, and my heart is pounding with excitement. "The rag! I don't know why I didn't think of it before. I don't know exactly how it happened, and I think Oscar Wiggins is telling the truth. It's all about that rag."

Erick's spine straightens, and he narrows his gaze. "Hunch?"

"Not exactly. When I went out to Herman Pettit's farm and talked to him about the fence-breaking incidents, he was working on one of his machines. He stood up and wiped his hands on a rag that was tucked into his pocket. A *red* rag."

Erick's expression brightens. "If we can link one of the substances on the red rag you pulled from the stovepipe to something at that popcorn farm—"

My sudden guffaw interrupts Erick's train of thought.

"What's so funny, Moon?"

"Sorry. It was something Grams said about popcorn farmers lassoing the kernels as they popped off the cob . . . I'm sorry. It's just a hilarious visual. You know how I get."

My eyes slide to his biceps as he crosses his arms. "Oh, I definitely do, Moon. I'm going to go ahead and place Oscar under arrest, in case this rag theory doesn't pan out. If I don't charge him with something, I have to let him go. And whether he's guilty or innocent, I don't think him being free is a good idea right now."

Erick returns to the interrogation room and, as he's placing Wiggins in handcuffs, the cheese-maker looks directly at the large pane of one-way glass and shouts. "Tammy stole the baby Jesus! Ask one of her gal pals on that church committee!"

Getting to my feet, I pat myself on the back and smile. "And that's what we call a *twofer*. Two crimes solved *fer* the price of one."

Erick dispatches Paulsen to bring Herman and Tammy back to the station. Excitement is high, and I have a slip of paper in my other coat with a suddenly pertinent list of names.

As I rush back to the bookshop—as fast as crutchingly possible—A quick call to Silas confirms he landed safely and will be at his brother's bedside, but reachable by phone in case of emergency. I'd love to tell him not to worry about me, but I think we all know that would be futile.

Grams dropped my puffy coat on the settee when she abandoned the apartment. I can't believe I forgot about the list. Pulling the slip of paper from the pocket, I scan the scrawled list of names. I actually know one of these ladies. Tilly Sikanen, Tally's sister, who works at the bank.

Tilly answers on the first ring. "First Bank of Pin Cherry, how can I invest in your day?"

"Hi, Tilly. It's Mitzy Moon. I'm in a hurry so I'll get right to it. Tammy Smythe-Wiggins stole the baby Jesus and I'm trying to figure out where she put it."

"Oh, my goodness! I supported a fix up of the set, but not vandalism. Good gracious! Was anyone injured?"

I don't have time for folksy banter. "We'll discuss it later. Any idea where she might've stashed the Messiah?"

Silence. Well, not complete silence. There's a soft humming.

"Any clue would help."

"You know, I think I saw her at Second Chance Finery a few days ago. They have the cutest—"

"Thanks, I'll check it out." I hate to be rude to any of the Sikanens. They are one of the nicest families in all of Pin Cherry . . . But the clock is ticking.

Second Chance Finery is a historic home converted into a functional storefront for the First Methodist Church's fundraising and outreach ministry. The thrift shop spans the first and second floors, and the basement houses a soup kitchen. If that statue of the infant Savior is here—it definitely qualifies as irony.

The elderly ladies organizing donations and

pricing items are too absorbed in their gossip to take notice of me.

Perfect.

Reaching out with my extra senses, I feel for the Nativity statue.

A gentle warmth creeps up my left side. As I turn toward the sensation and walk along the racks, the heat increases.

At the end of the aisle, the temperature reaches unbearable levels and I'm forced to unzip my coat.

My whole body vibrates like a bed in a cheap motel. Not that I have first-hand knowledge, but I've seen the movies.

My left hand moves as though a rope is pulling it.

My fingers grip a coat on the rack.

I expect to slide the coat to the side and reveal the hidden baby—

Nope.

The COAT!

I may not have found the child of God, but I found Isadora's baby!

The Vivienne Westwood Worlds End Black "Witches" Trench Coat is in my grasp.

There's no baby Jesus at this thrift store, but the lead paid off. I overpay for the coat and drive straight back to the bookshop—at a reasonable speed on the icy winter roads.

Abandoning my crutch at the bottom of the wrought-iron spiral staircase, I hobble-step to the apartment, shouting shamelessly all the way. "Grams! Grams! I found it!"

Her face pops through the sliding bookcase like a creepy attraction at an amusement park haunted house, and the shock nearly knocks me off balance.

"You found what? The missing Nativity statue?"

Lifting the coat toward her as though it were a sacred offering, I take a clumsy bow. "The coat!"

Her image flickers, and a moment later, oodles of ghost tears spill from her eyes. "Oh, Mitzy!" She attempts to take the jacket from my arms, but her emotions are running high and sapping her energy.

I head into the apartment, and carefully arrange the precious garment on the settee for her viewing. "Now, I expect the full story. I can't explain what forces conspired to bring me and this blasted coat together, but I deserve to know why it's so important."

She floats toward the coat and reaches through the fabric. "It's still here."

Kicking out my hip, I attempt to steady myself on my good leg. "Are you trying to tell me you left something in a coat pocket forty years ago and it's still there?"

Her ethereal fingers wrap around my hand and

pull it toward the left lapel. Pressing my fingers into the coat, I feel the object in my heart before I feel it in my hand. "It's a ring."

She nods, blubbers for a few more seconds, and then smiles as though the sun rises only for her. "It's the wedding ring Odell gave me. I told Cal I'd gotten rid of it, but I couldn't. I sewed it inside the lining of my favorite coat—right above my heart."

Now we're both crying.

"I brought your father home from the hospital in this coat. I can't tell you how much it means to have it back, dear."

"I understand, Grams. I can't believe you dressed in designer duds to bring home a baby, but I'm sorry I gave you a hard time about the coat. It all makes sense now."

Her glimmering arms encircle me, and my whole body hums with love.

"Do you want me to get the ring out of there?"

She explodes like a firework and her joyful voice echoes through the room. "Yes, please! I'd love to see it again."

Grabbing my emergency-haircut scissors from the bathroom, I approach the coat with purpose. Grams coalesces into a nearly solid wall in front of me. "Don't you dare cut a hole in that priceless coat!"

"I'm only going to snip a few stitches. I promise

I'll be careful, and if I'm not able to fix it, I'll personally take it to the tailor in Broken Rock and see that it's done properly."

She flutters with relief and allows me to complete the task.

"Here it is." I cradle the ring in my palm and hold it up for her to view.

"It's the simplest and cheapest of all my wedding rings, but it holds the most valuable place in my heart." She surges with emotions.

I examine the plain circle of gold, with barely a flake of a diamond in the setting, and smile when I see the inscription. "To Myrtle: My forever."

She glows with love.

"Grams, I'm going to put this in your jewelry box. I'll leave the lid open so you can admire it, but I have to get back to the station. We are about to break this case wide open!"

She silently follows me to the jewelry box and floats in a bubble of happiness as I slip out of the apartment.

One day, I hope someone feels that way about me. Maybe *someone* already does. I need to put my big-girl pants on and take that leap Odell mentioned. Seems like Gramps knows more about romance than I ever will.

CHAPTER 24

PAULSEN DRAGS Herman Pettit into Interrogation Room 1, while Deputy Johnson deposits Tammy in Interrogation Room 2.

Gazing through the one-way glass at Tammy, I'm eager to watch Erick pry the truth from her lying, over-plumped lips. However, my head whip pans to the other side when he enters Room 1 first and sits down to question Herman.

"Mr. Pettit, I'm sure you understand how things work in a situation like this. When there's more than one person involved in the conspiracy to commit murder, the person who cooperates always gets a better deal."

Herman Pettit twists manically at his red handlebar mustache. The gesture would be hilarious if the situation weren't so grim.

Erick waits patiently, allowing the information to sink in and hopefully motivate Mr. Pettit.

Nothing is happening, and I skipped the line for patience. The delay is driving me nuts. Maybe I should tap on the window and offer to come and tell Herman about the rag I saw tucked in his pocket. Before I make my move, Erick bluffs with the confidence of a seasoned poker player.

He places an evidence bag containing the soiled red rag pulled from the stovepipe on the table and lets it sit like a grenade between them.

The panicked waves of fear rolling off Herman Pettit tell me everything I need to know. Each time I see Erick in action, my respect for his instincts grows. I have the benefit of my psychic abilities to predict that Herman is about to crack, while the sheriff is simply using his years of experience and going with his gut.

Herman twists his mustache so viciously, it tugs at the corner of his mouth.

Erick takes a deep breath and pulls the proverbial pin from the evidence grenade. "You are aware that we obtained a warrant to search your property, Mr. Pettit. Would it surprise you to know that we discovered several rags exactly like this one?"

Herman shakes visibly, leans back in his chair, and the hand that was twisting the mustache slowly creeps across his mouth as though he's keeping a terrible secret. Which, to be fair, he is.

The sheriff moves in for the kill. "This evidence bag holds the rag we pulled from the stovepipe at Quade Knudsen's icehouse. The medical examiner's report confirms that he died of carbon monoxide poisoning. Whoever put this rag into that stovepipe is looking at a first-degree murder charge. That's life in prison, Mr. Pettit. Is there anything you'd like to tell me before I go and offer Tammy the same deal?"

And the tower of Jenga blocks falls!

"Listen, Sheriff, you gotta understand. She was in a horrible situation. She's carrying my child. I had to do something."

"She can file for divorce. Things could've been handled in court. The thing that doesn't check out, Mr. Pettit, is why would you go to the trouble of creating a dangerous substance like chlorine gas and then—"

Herman doesn't allow the sheriff to finish the hypothetical. He's eager to spill the beans. Pyewacket's omniscience is irrefutable.

"It wasn't my idea, Sheriff. I was cleaning up her mess."

Erick's shoulders relax, and a confession is imminent. "Cleaning up whose mess?"

Herman gives his mustache a final tug before he grips the edge of the table and tells all.

Tammy came up with the idea to kill Quade. She devised the device to deliver the gas, and she placed the apparatus at the dairy. According to Herman, Tammy wanted to kill Quade at the dairy in order to frame Oscar. Two birds with one stone or some such logic.

When Oscar discovered his unconscious partner and moved the body out to the icehouse, Tammy had to come up with a new plan. She couldn't risk Quade regaining consciousness.

Doing his mistress's bidding, Herman drove his snowmobile across the frozen lake, closed and locked the window, stoked the fire, shoved the rag into the stovepipe, and jammed the lock with a screw to be safe.

The cold snap was a bonus they hadn't predicted, but Herman was sure the empty bottle of booze would explain how Quade passed out and let the carbon monoxide get the best of him.

"Let me make sure I understand what you're saying, Mr. Pettit. It's your statement that Tammy Smythe-Wiggins planned to murder Quade Knudsen at the dairy and frame her husband for the murder. Is that correct?"

"Yes, Sheriff. That's exactly what happened. She even figured out how to clone Quade's phone so she could text the brother. I wouldn't have even gotten involved, but—"

Erick leans forward. "But you had to clean up her mess."

He nods. "Yes. Yes. Like I said, it wasn't my idea."

"Unfortunately, Mr. Pettit, Quade Knudsen died of acute carbon monoxide poisoning, not exposure to chlorine gas, and the elements froze him postmortem. The only person who committed murder was you."

Herman's shoulders and his mustache seem to sag simultaneously. Erick doesn't deal the final blow and place him under arrest. Instead, he lets Herman Pettit stew in his own mustache wax, and steps into the hallway.

With the case wrapped up, there's only one thing left.

I may know she stole the baby Jesus from the Nativity scene, but I won't truly feel satisfied until I return the infant to the First Methodist Church.

A while ago Silas taught me a neat little trick—I mean, transmutation—for snatching an answer from someone's mind whether or not they speak it out loud. It's something to do with how people instinctively answer truthfully in their mind before they choose how to respond verbally.

I haven't been practicing this one, so I'm not

sure how it will turn out, but it can't hurt to try. Poking my head into the hallway, I see no sign of Erick.

As quick as I'm able, I pop into Interrogation Room 2 and smile as Tammy and Deputy Johnson both turn my way. "Hi, Tammy. I was hoping you could tell me where you put the baby Jesus?"

Taking a deep breath, I reach out with everything I've got in the "extra" tank. Wait for it . . . Bingo! There's the location I need! "Did you really think you could force the church into replacing the historical gifted Nativity, by stealing part of it?"

Tammy presses her lips together to stifle her reply, but she can't stop her head from nodding in agreement.

Yeesh! This woman suffers from a severe lack of imagination.

With a Cheshire-cat grin pasted across my face, I close the door and hobble into Erick's office. "I know where the baby Jesus is!"

He looks at me, scrunches up his face, and chuckles. "Would you like to share?"

"Hiding in Herman's hayloft!"

Laughter spills from the sheriff's perfect mouth. "Sounds like a tongue twister. Is it a hunch it's hiding in Herman's hayloft?"

"I deserve that." I let him have his moment, before waving it away with a flick of my wrist. "Can somebody take me out there to recover it?"

He smiles, gets to his feet, and gently pulls Deputy Johnson into the hallway. "I need you to take Miss Moon out to the Pettit farm. Our existing warrant covers the barn."

Deputy Johnson looks from Erick to me, and back again. "10-4, Sheriff."

On the drive out, Johnson twists his hand back-and-forth around the steering wheel as though he's trying to peel an onion layer by layer.

"What's on your mind, Johnson?"

"Um, Tammy didn't answer you. I was in the room and she didn't say anything. So, how do you know it's at the farm?"

Oops. Plot hole. When in doubt, lie it out. "I don't know anything for certain. It's sort of a hunch."

A strange smile creeps across his face as he nods. "My dad says the angels talk to you. Is that true?"

I'd only heard one person in town spouting this crazy theory. "You're the preacher's kid?"

Deputy Johnson laughs so hard tears leak from the corners of his eyes. "10-4. I haven't heard that since high school."

"Hmmm. The pastor of the First Methodist Church is your dad. Are you a typical preacher's kid? Did you get into law enforcement to make up for your misspent youth?"

Johnson's face turns serious, and he tilts his head toward me. "Wow. He was right about you. You really do know stuff."

I hate to burst Deputy Johnson's bubble and tell him that tropes about preacher's kids exist because they're often true, and that there was no angelic chorus whispering in my ear. However, I prefer to stay focused on the mission at hand before we get sidetracked. "Honestly, let's not give me too much credit. I'd rather focus on getting that Nativity scene back together."

He nods. "10-4."

At the Pettit farm, Deputy Johnson scrambles up the ladder into the hayloft and dust rises as he tosses bales, and sifts through loose hay. "I found Him!"

From the ground floor, I can't resist. "Are you saying you found Jesus, Deputy Johnson?"

He hurries to the edge of the hayloft and holds the infant Savior aloft as though he's reenacting a scene from *The Lion King*. "I found—"

My laughter floats up, and he shakes his head. "Oh, I hear it now."

"I figured you would, Deputy. Bring Him on down. I'll let you be the one to call your father and give him the good news."

Johnson tucks the baby Jesus under one arm like an oversized football and climbs down the ladder. "My dad's not too worried about it. I'm going to call Mrs. Coleman. She said she hasn't slept a wink since the theft corrupted the historical scene."

"You're a good egg, Johnson. Pin Cherry Harbor is lucky to have you."

His phone is in one hand as he waits for Mrs. Coleman to answer. He looks at me and smiles wistfully. "Nah. I'm not taking any credit for this. It's you that we're lucky to have."

And while he breaks the good news to Mrs. Coleman, his words sink into my heart. Maybe the town is lucky. Maybe I'm lucky.

Either way, if home is where the heart is, Pin Cherry Harbor is home.

End of Book 17

~A NOTE FROM TRIXIE

Say *cheese*! Pyewacket continues to be my hero! I'll keep writing them if you keep reading . . .

The best part of "living" in Pin Cherry Harbor continues to be feedback from my early readers. Thank you to my alpha readers/cheerleaders, Angel and Michael. HUGE thanks to my fantastic beta readers who continue to give me extremely useful and honest feedback: Veronica McIntyre and Nadine Peterse-Vrijhof. And big "small town" hugs to the world's best ARC Team – Trixie's Mystery ARC Detectives!

My fantastic editor Philip Newey definitely saved my bacon on this one. Thanks to him, I satisfyingly filled a major plot hole. I'd also like to give a heaping helping of gratitude to Brooke for her tireless proofreading! (Despite her holiday schedule.) Any remaining errors are my own.

I'm especially grateful for the helpful chemistry info provided by Michael. Thanks to Josh and Morgan for the mustache inspiration!

FUN FACT: When I was in the eighth grade, I had a massive crush on the son of a local dairy farmer. Cheers to what *curd* have been, Leonard.

My favorite line from this case: "Are you saying you found Jesus, Deputy Johnson?" ~Mitzy

I'm currently writing book eighteen in the Mitzy Moon Mysteries series, and I'm planning a big surprise. Mitzy, Grams, and Pyewacket got into plenty of trouble in book one, *Fries and Alibis*. But I'd have to say that book three, *Wings and Broken Things*, is when most readers say the series becomes unputdownable.

I hope you'll continue to hang out with us.

Trixie Silvertale (January 2022)

PARANORMAL COZY MYSTERY

Heists & Poltergeists

TRIXIE SILVERTALE

Sittin' On A Goldmine
Productions L.L.C.

HAVE YOU EVER HAD THE FEELING something is about to be very wrong? I'm not talking about a passing thought that slips through your brain and disappears. I'm referring to that undeniable shiver deep in your gut.

Well, I'm having one right now. I'm standing in line at the bank, staring at the wig on the lady in front of me—and boom.

Tummy shivers and hairs stand on end on the back of my neck.

It's nothing against the wig. I have a drawer full of them back in the apartment I share with the ghost of my deceased grandmother.

As I'm about to dismiss the thought as a potentially misguided psychic hit triggered by the woman's elaborate garb, the antique mood ring on my left hand encircles my finger in an icy chill. Glancing at the swirly black mist inside the smoky cabochon, an image struggles to appear. But then . . .

BANG!

"This is a robbery!"

Everything seems to slow down, and I feel as though my ears are stuffed with cotton. I don't remember crouching, but I suppose that was an instinctual reaction to the gunshot.

Turning toward the sound, I'm surprised to see the White Rabbit standing on top of Tilly's desk, waving a handgun. Before I can marvel at the cartoon-like mask and fuzzy white ears, the Queen of Hearts, in all her Wonderland glory, hops over the counter and begins tearing cash out of drawers as a terrified bank teller attempts to keep her hands in the air, and simultaneously open said drawers.

Guarding the exit is none other than a shotgun-toting Mad Hatter, with a wild wig and a crooked top hat covering his real hair.

Could this day *get* any weirder?

Just when I'm about to be disappointed that the guest of honor is missing . . . Alice, of Wonderland fame, sporting her signature blonde locks, and the Cheshire Cat come in through a hallway that must originate at a rear entrance from the alley behind the bank.

I may be in the middle of a dangerous armed robbery, but the film-school dropout inside me experiences a moment of intense satisfaction that the Wonderland tea party is complete.

Of course, the entire time I'm swirling around in my mind movies, the White Rabbit has been informing the handful of patrons and employees what to do to avoid being shot.

Oops. That was probably kinda useful information, but I'm getting ahead of myself.

Let's start at the beginning . . .

CHAPTER 1

WHOEVER INVENTED THE BIRTHDAY MANTRA "my day, my way" has never met Grams. I mean, who would've thought the ghost of my dearly departed grandmother could wreak so much havoc in my life?

Not me.

You live—then you live with a bossy ghost—and you learn.

I've learned a lot of wonderful things since a malodorous bus dropped me farther north than I'd ever traveled in my life. My grandmother's dying wish, to find her missing granddaughter and leave her a mountain of cash and an amazing bookshop brimming with ancient magic-filled tomes, has afforded me a lifestyle I never could've imagined.

Back when I was slinging coffee and living

without hot water in my sketchy studio apartment in Sedona, not even the most skilled pseudo-shamans in the Southwest could've manifested the idea of a place like Pin Cherry Harbor.

Not to get sidetracked, but I'm sure there were some legit shamans in Vortex-ville. I just never happened to serve coffee to any of them.

Back to the dilemma *du jour*. It will be my twenty-fourth birthday in three short days. Ever since a terrible accident took my mother shortly after my eleventh birthday, the day of my arrival into this world stopped being something to celebrate. As I bounced my way through a series of unimpressive foster homes, I learned to scale my hopes way back. There were no cakes, there were no presents, and there certainly were no parties.

So, when I arrived in almost-Canada and had the bejeezus scared out of me by the ghost of Myrtle Isadora, and the bonus discovery of a living father, it never occurred to me to mention my birth-date to either of them. Which, for the record, is March 21st, the first day of spring.

Please don't explain to me how the position of the sun dictates the vernal equinox, and how the date shifts based on astronomical variables. If we're going to be friends, and I hope we are, you need to get on board with this thing I have about my birthday. March 21st. First day of spring. My birthday. End of story.

Due to my error of omission, my first birthday here passed without a trace, and the second birthday extravaganza had to be abandoned due to my grandmother's spirit suffering temporary cursed imprisonment in a pendant—as the result of a decades-long feud with a local gypsy. But that's a different story.

Welcome to this year! Grams' spirit is once again free to roam the bookshop at will, she's able to summon the strength to hold a pen for great lengths of time, and she spends each and every day making to-do lists for the people in her inner circle of surprise party planners.

Spoiler alert: I'm a psychic. Trying to surprise a psychic is a plan doomed to fail.

However, because of my deep and abiding affection for Ghost-ma, I've pretended for several months to be unaware of their surreptitious activities.

Now the massive celebration is looming, and I'm not sure I'm prepared to step into the megawatt spotlight she's certainly rented.

I need to calm my nerves and indulge in some comfort food, and there's no better place to do that than the diner owned by my grandmother's first husband, Odell Johnson.

"I'm heading off to the diner, Grams."

No response. At least I can breathe a sigh of relief that she wasn't close enough to be thought-dropping.

"Last chance to be disappointed in my outfit—"

"Ree-ow." Soft but condescending.

"Hey, Pyewacket. Are you filling in for Grams?" I bend to scratch his broad tan head between his black-tufted ears.

"Reow." Can confirm. His short, thick tail flicks left and right.

"Well, you're doing her proud, son."

He silently leads the way to the back room and swats his empty bowl at me with one large, needle-clawed paw.

"I wouldn't dream of leaving without feeding you." Grabbing a box of his favorite sugary children's cereal from the cupboard, I heap his bowl and step back. I learned quickly that this half-wild caracal does not tolerate affection at mealtime.

As I place a hand on the alley door—

"Mizithra! Were you going to leave without saying goodbye?" The shimmering spirit places a bejeweled hand on one hip and straightens her burgundy silk-and-tulle Marchesa gown with the other.

"No need for formal names, Grams. I called out a farewell, and got nothing but radio silence. I figured you were hard at work on your memoirs."

"Oh, that makes sense, dear. I was busy with—" Her ghostly eyes widen and her perfectly drawn brows lift.

"With what?" Purposely holding a blank space in my head—a recently perfected skill—I wait.

"I'm not sure I like this new 'skill,' sweetie." Ghost-ma purses her lips and shakes her head.

"Of course you don't. You normally spend half your time snooping around in my private thoughts. I may not know how to keep you out, but I can make sure the shelves are bare when you're poking around. Maybe you'll be able to finish your memoirs with all this extra time."

"Well, I never!" She clutches at one of her many strands of pearls.

Opening the door, I step into the slushy alley and toss a familiar refrain over my shoulder. "I think we both know that's not true, don't we, Myrtle Isadora Johnson Linder Duncan Willamet Rogers!"

As the door bangs, I hear one last ethereal request. "Say hello to Odell for me."

That would be the "Johnson" in the long list of former husbands' surnames.

THE MARCH WEATHER is still draped in icicles and stirred by frosty breezes swirling across the great lake nestled in our harbor. Despite the short walk from my bookshop to Myrtle's Diner, the gust of warm air that greets me as I step inside the hallowed eatery is eagerly welcomed.

Slipping off my mittens, I wave to my grandfather and inhale the scent of potato products and java. He gives me the standard spatula salute through the red-Formica-trimmed orders-up window.

That's my cue to slide into a booth and accept the steaming mug of go-go juice that is almost instantly delivered by the world's most amazing waitress, Tally.

"How's your week shaping up, Mitzy?"

This would be her thinly veiled attempt to see if I have any knowledge of the pending surprise party. I've fielded a number of these questions in the last couple of weeks. "No big plans. Just going to stay indoors and keep warm. I hear there's a storm on the way."

She smiles, satisfied that I'm still in the dark about the big doings. "Well, good for you." Her flame-red bun bobs up and down as she hustles from booth to table, refilling coffee cups and chewing the fat.

Having a favorite restaurant and enjoying a cup of coffee I didn't have to make myself—with yesterday's grounds—are luxuries I still appreciate every day. A long sip of the diner's delicious black gold warms me from the inside out.

The only thing that could improve on this perfect moment—

A whoosh of cold air delivers a shiver and a tingle, as Sheriff Too-Hot-To-Handle strides through the diner's door and into my scene.

My inner film director is over the moon with this perfect timing. Since the two of us are well acquainted, I can't actually call this our "meet cute," but dagnabbit if that man isn't adorable.

His cheeks flush with color when he catches me sizing him up like a chocolate croissant, and he stomps the snow off his work boots before joining me in the booth.

"Morning, Mitzy. I'm surprised to find you here."

My jaw sags and my eyes widen, but then I catch sight of his teasing grin. "Ha ha, Sheriff. If you're trying to make me feel bad about eating at my grandfather's restaurant four or five days out of seven, it's not going to work. My whole thing is 'family first.'"

Erick chuckles as he removes his shearling-lined uniform jacket and tucks it onto the seat. "I think you meant to say, french fries first."

"Rude."

He smooths down his long, slicked-back blond bangs, walks his fingers across the table, and turns his palm upward. It's a move he stole from my repertoire, but I hold no grudge. I slide my hand into his and we both smile stupidly as he squeezes my fingers.

In a weak attempt to deflect the fry comment, I mention, "For your information, it's well before noon and—"

Odell approaches the table and slides my usual scrambled eggs with chorizo and a bottle of Tabasco sauce in front of me. "Your pancakes will be out in a minute, Sheriff."

Erick nods.

Regulars like Erick Harper and I have no need to order. The owner has a very special knack for knowing exactly what his patrons need. Odell raps his knuckles twice on the silver-flecked white Formica table and returns to the grill.

"Did you hear about the storm?" I wink at Erick and squeeze his hand. There's nothing locals enjoy more than discussing the weather—or so I've learned.

He rubs his thumb along my fingers and smiles. "There's no storm coming. What makes you say that?"

"Wishful thinking, I suppose."

"Last I checked, you weren't a fan of cold

weather. What on earth would make you wish for a storm that would prolong your suffering?"

"First of all, winter is growing on me. I may not be a fan of freezing, but I've learned to enjoy several snow-based activities."

Before I can get to my second point, he jumps in. "Is one of those activities discovering corpses?"

What can I say? The man has a point. "You're not wrong. However, I was referring to things like cross-country skiing, snowmobiling, cutting my own Christmas tree . . . You get the idea."

He shrugs. "If memory serves, you discovered a dead body during each of those endeavors." Laughter shakes his shoulders and I'm forced to hang my head in mute agreement.

"Listen, I don't go looking for trouble. Somehow, it seems to find me."

Erick leans back, yawns, and stretches his muscular arms as he nods in agreement. "You don't have to convince me, Moon. There's something about you, and one day I'm going to figure out what it is."

The friendly banter ends. The crux of our current dilemma rears its ugly head before his pancakes have a chance to arrive. Secrets.

I endured more than my share of teasing during childhood. My strange, bone-white hair and almost colorless grey eyes led to an enormous amount of taunting. Of course, my orphan backstory offered plenty of ammunition as well. Once I escaped the foster system and struggled to make it on my own, I had one mission: fit in. If people wanted to party, I partied the hardest. If the dare was to climb on the statue of a horse and take a selfie, I was first in line. The role of ringleader was always preferable to outsider.

Now I have this crazy set of psychic gifts that truly do make me a form of freakish—not to mention my budding skills as an alchemist—and I'm terrified to let the truth out. Erick is no dummy. He knows there's more to my hunches than I'm letting on, and it's causing some serious friction in our relationship.

Suddenly I'm aware of long, sexy fingers wiggling in front of my face and a soft voice whispering, "Mitzy. Oh, Mitzy Moon. Are you in there?"

Oh brother. In addition to my psychic situation, I have a terrible habit of retreating to a world housed solely within my mind. I found a great deal of comfort there as a child, but the habit is a bit off-putting to most adults. "I was sort of running through my to-do list for the day." Lame. He's never going to buy that.

He sits back, grabs a forkful of his syrupy blueberry pancakes, which must've arrived while I was catatonic, and shoves it in his mouth.

I can't believe he didn't have a snappy comeback. Fine. Two can play this game. I shove golden-brown home fries in my mouth and stare back at him with a serious "game on" vibe.

Erick takes a swig of his coffee and smiles. "I'd love to get a peek at that to-do list. Let me see how close I can get. Item 1: eat breakfast at my grandfather's restaurant. Item 2: walk back to my bookshop. Item 3: . . ." He gazes up at the ceiling and comically taps his chin, as though he's deep in thought. "Boy, I'm having trouble coming up with number three."

I'd love to tell him I plan to spend the rest of the day avoiding my grandmother and her thinly veiled party plans, but I know he's a member of the surprise team and I don't want to spoil their fun. "Actually, Sheriff, my little stepbrother, Stellen, and I have some 'get in a car and drive' plans."

He wipes the drip of syrup off his lickable lips and smiles. "Oh, I forgot he was home on spring break. How's he doing?"

"In school? He's crushing it. But emotionally he's struggling. He wants to go to the cemetery and visit his parents' graves, so that part is a bit of a downer."

Erick nods. "Yeah, the kid's had it pretty tough. I'm sure glad your dad and Amaryllis adopted him. He deserves some good things in his life, you know?"

"Copy that. Plus, I can visit Isadora's headstone and leave some flowers or something."

We share a confused look.

I shrug. "Is that weird?" Leaning forward, I whisper, "I never think of visiting her grave because I see her every day. But normal people put flowers on graves, right?"

His dreamy, blue eyes spark with a dare. "Yes, *normal* people do."

CHAPTER 2

IN SITUATIONS WHERE my back is against the wall
and I'm out of options, I tend to rely on dark humor
or my barely passable acting skills. Here goes
nothing . . . and, ACTION! "Shoot! I'm gonna have
to take this food to go. I'm supposed to meet
Stellen." Before Erick can react, I slide out of the
booth and grab a to-go box from behind the counter.

Returning to the table, I pack up my half-eaten
breakfast, as he shoves pancakes into his mouth
with unnecessary force.

"See you later. I'll try not to stumble across any
corpses." The false cheeriness of my tone is sur-
passed only by the imitation brightness of my smile.
As I lean down to place a quick kiss on his rugged
jaw, I catch his mumbled come back.

"Sounds like a tall order if you're headed to the cemetery."

I turn up the wattage on my smile, wave to my grandfather, and rush out of the diner without a backward glance.

Yes, I feel bad about bailing on that conversation for the umpteenth time, but I've seen all the movies, I've watched all the television shows. When the girlfriend reveals her strange powers, it never ends well.

Maybe I'm a chicken. But also, maybe I'm a genius. If I can avoid the topic and act normal, there's a chance this whole suspicion thing will blow over. I don't have to get *hunches*. I don't have to solve crimes. I came to Pin Cherry on a whim and stayed because of relationships, not sleuthing.

When I told Erick that family was the most important thing to me, I wasn't making that up. So, starting today, I'm going to turn over a new leaf. I'm going to mind my own business, and keep my extrasensory perceptions to myself. Like he always says, the sheriff's department was solving crimes before I came to town. Seems like there's no reason they can't keep solving them without my help.

The tension in my shoulders vanishes, and, despite the icy wind, a sensation of warmth spreads through my body. I have a brilliant plan, and I get to spend the day with my brother. He could use the support, and I can absolutely use the distraction.

Instead of heading into the bookshop, I turn left on First Avenue, walk straight past the Bell, Book & Candle Bookshop, and continue to the alley that separates my store from my father's restorative justice offices and penthouse living quarters.

I have a key, because that's how my family rolls, so I let myself in and take the elevator to the top floor.

PING.

Two sets of eyes turn toward the sliding doors, but Amaryllis is the first to grin broadly and rush toward me. "Mitzy!"

Next thing I know, she's hugging me tightly, patting me on the back, and offering me a cup of coffee—which I politely decline—all at the same time. If this woman is anywhere near as good a lawyer as she is a hostess—opposition beware.

Stellen takes the calmer approach to my arrival and offers me a cool-guy fist bump, one-armed hug combo. "Hey, Mitzy."

"Hey, yourself. Are you ready to head out?"

He glances at Amaryllis, looks down at the ground, and shoves his hands deep inside the pockets of his jeans.

I hardly need my special abilities to sense

there's a problem. "What's up? Did you change your mind?"

Amaryllis squeezes her hands together, tilts her head to the side, and exhales loudly. "He's having second thoughts. He forgot it was your birthday week, and now he thinks it's in poor taste to drag you out to a cemetery."

My face scrunches up in confusion as I shake my head. "Birthday *week*? Are you nuts? This isn't about me. You're hardly ever in town, and Dad already told me you're planning on doing some kind of summer-school program . . . This is important to you. I'm your sister. Granted, I'm pretty new at the job, but I think this is one of the things I'm supposed to do. It's, like, Big Sister 101, right?"

His hair has grown inches since I last saw him and long black curls hang across most of his face. He tucks them behind one ear and his bright-green eyes gaze up at me with hope. "You sure? I could go by myself."

"Look, bro, I haven't celebrated a birthday DAY, let alone a week, since I was eleven, so I kind of forget it's even a thing. Hanging out with you is what's important to me. I know how much moms matter. Your mother's death may have been expected, because of her illness, but that doesn't mean it's been any easier to deal with. This coping business is something we share, all right?"

He nods. "Let me get my stuff."

Stellen disappears down the hallway toward his room, and I catch Amaryllis wiping a tear from the corner of her eye. "It's really sweet of you, honey. I know it can't be easy for you."

"Hey, when his father was killed and you and dad stepped up, I knew I had to do the same. He's such a great kid. It makes it easy."

Now there's a tear leaking from the corner of my eye, and Amaryllis wraps me in another one of her signature bear hugs. For a petite woman, she has the strength of a championship wrestler.

Stellen emerges from his room with a piece of paper in one hand, and a small stuffed squirrel holding an acorn.

"Did you—"

He lifts the squirrel and turns it back and forth. "He died of natural causes on the campus. You know my dad was always disappointed I didn't take up the family taxidermy business. I figured he'd appreciate the gesture."

"You really are the best kid, buddy. What's the slip of paper?"

His eyes glisten with unshed tears. "My report card."

And, in that moment, I feel as though we share one soul. Back in elementary school, when I still cared about grades, I would've given anything for my mother to see my report card and tell me how smart I was. Something unspoken passes between us, and he rubs his eyes furiously.

He places the items on the counter, slips into his jacket, and presses the button for the elevator.

Amaryllis reaches out and squeezes my arm as I step into the elevator with Stellen and his offerings.

"There'll be hot cocoa and fresh snickerdoodles waiting for you."

As the doors slide closed, I appreciate her not saying "have fun." Visiting gravesites isn't that sort of activity. The little squirrel in Stellen's hand looks at me knowingly. I can almost swear I see his nose twitch.

We load into my Jeep and drive in silence to the cemetery.

The groundskeeper is busy plowing snow from the walkways with his compact ride-on mower fitted with a snowplow attachment.

We wait patiently for him to notice us and turn off the engine.

He hops from the small vehicle and offers us that flat smile and head nod I remember seeing a thousand times. Death is an uncomfortable subject. Even for a man who literally makes his living caring for the deceased, the topic is one he still approaches carefully.

Smiling, I step forward. "Hello. We're looking for Stan and Crystal Jablonski?"

A dark shadow passes over his face and he tilts his head toward Stellen.

It's a small town. Everyone knows the sad story of his mother's losing battle with cancer, and his father's senseless murder. He turns and points to a small stand of leafless birch near the base of a hill. "Head straight toward those trees, take a left, and their plots are about halfway down, right after the black granite bench."

"Thank you."

Stellen follows me silently.

As we approach the black granite bench, the name Lindy McElroy gleams up from its surface. "Beloved mother and wife."

What will my headstone say? The moment I'm about to disappear into one of my mind movies, a sharp stab of sorrow shoots off Stellen like static electricity in the dark. Right, better get back to my big-sister duties. "Hey, I'm going to walk up the hill and visit Isadora's headstone and give you some privacy. Sound good?"

He's working so hard to hold back his emotions, he can barely nod his head.

Slipping away, I follow my detailed psychic memory back up the hill to the beautiful headstone for Myrtle Isadora Johnson Linder Duncan Willamet Rogers.

The delicate cardinal I purchased from the statuary in Broken Rock perches atop the headstone with the grace of a living creature. If not for the sprinkling of snow on his back and its dark granite color, I could almost make myself believe he's about to take flight.

Sadly, the bouquet of flowers in the small vase next to the massive slab of granite holds nothing more than shriveled floral remains.

It would appear Odell has abandoned his frequent cemetery visits now that he's in the ghost club.

Part of me is inexplicably sad about this development. There was something so touching about his steadfast care for my grandmother's plot. Although, I'm hardly one to talk. I've lived in Pin Cherry for over three years, and I've only been here once—twice counting today. It's awfully difficult to remember that someone is dead, and worry about a piece of stone and some grass, when you see them and feel their love every day. Of all the things that I discovered when I came to Pin Cherry, I think the existence of Ghost-ma is the most precious to me.

Reaching out, I brush snow from the little cardinal's back and kneel in front of the headstone. My finger traces the letters etched into the polished surface. I whisper each name quietly when I finish. If I'd hoped for some otherworldly experience, it does not arrive.

As I stare at the headstone and the decaying flora, my mind wanders into an Ebenezer Scrooge ghost of Christmas future scenario.

Who will visit my grave? Have I left an impression on this world? Are my philanthropic foundation and my monetary gifts to the community enough?

A soft tapping on my shoulder sends me leaping into the air like a cat who saw a cucumber—or is it a zucchini?

"Sorry, Mitzy, I didn't mean to scare you."

"It's all right. I was—"

Stellen presses his lips together, and my gaze takes in his red eyes and ragged breathing.

"Yeah, we don't have to talk about it. Let's go get some of that hot chocolate Amaryllis promised us."

He struggles to swallow and nods. I put my arm around his shoulders and try to absorb some of his pain as we make our way back to the Jeep.

His relationship with his father may have been rocky at best, but I know firsthand the pain of missing a loving mother who didn't get enough time on this planet.

CHAPTER 3

AFTER POWERING THROUGH two steaming mugs of cocoa and more snickerdoodles than anyone should count, I head back to the bookstore. My volunteer employee, and Isadora's best friend in life, is scanning over today's to-do list when I approach the back room.

"Hey, Twiggy. Anything I can do to help?"

She gets to her feet, tromps across the floor in her unmistakable biker boots, and stares at me without a word. Silently, she turns the punch list toward me. Twiggy is the only one who "knows I know."

My eyes widen in mock horror. It's the longest one yet. Grams is going straight-up ghost crazy planning this birthday extravaganza.

Before I can react, Pyewacket head butts me

and drops a stuffed rabbit from the children's section at my feet. His tail flicks impatiently as I bend to retrieve the item.

"Hey, buddy. I don't have time to play. Isadora is mad with power, and I need to help out." I leave the plush bunny on the floor.

"Reeeee-ow." A warning.

"Easy, Mr. Cuddlekins. We're friends. Remember?" Crouching, I pick up the rabbit and sigh. "If it's that important to you, I'll make a note of it."

This response seems to please him. He stalks out of the room without a backward glance.

Twiggy blows a raspberry. "Perfect. I've got this ridiculous list, and a crabby kitten. This day is really lookin' up, kid."

Shrugging helplessly, I offer the only help I can. "How about I walk over to the bank and get the drawer money for you?"

Getting the cash for the daily register operations in the bookstore has always been Twiggy's job. In fact, it was the hot topic of debate one of the first times she put me in my place. I was acting quite superior, and throwing around my heiress status, when she bluntly reminded me I know next to nothing about running a bookstore. Ever since, I've learned to respect the severe grey pixie cut and the wealth of information that comes along with it.

"That'd be great, doll. As you can see, I'm full up."

"Copy that."

As I turn to leave the back room, I trip over my own foot. Stumbling forward, I catch myself on the doorjamb and bang my head lightly. When I stand up, groaning and pressing a hand to my forehead, an all-too-familiar cackle resounds behind me.

"Thanks, kid. I needed that today."

And that, ladies and gentlemen, is why she works for free. She just wants to have front row seats to Mitzy's Believe It or Not Klutz Show.

Rather than head up to my swanky apartment and get pulled into an inevitable wardrobe debate with Grams, I skip out the side door and head down Main Street to the bank. I appreciate all the couture she collected for me, but I'll take my skinny jeans and a tee any day of the week.

The same number of boarded-up windows and long-vanished businesses exist as the first day I set foot in this town. However, now that I know the residents and call this place home, those little eyesores disappear into the background. The bustling diner, Rex's drugstore, and, of course, the sheriff's station take center stage.

Main Street looks lively, and well-kept. In fact, someone painted the windows of the bank with elaborate spring and Easter decorations. It must be a hobby of Tilly's—Tally's sister—because their brother's veterinary clinic and Myrtle's Diner sport similarly themed decor.

Quick backstory on the Sikanen family: Tally works at the diner. Tilly works at the bank. They're sisters. Their parents named each of their children after the town where he or she was conceived. The oldest sister in Tillamook, Wisconsin—Tilly; the youngest, in Tallahassee, Florida—Tally; and the middle child, the veterinarian brother, in Toledo, Ohio—Doc Ledo.

There are more employees in the bank than I would've expected, but the mood is cheery, and Tilly offers me a friendly wave as I enter.

The only hint of similarity between her and her sister is the welcoming smile. Where Tally sports a flame-red dye job and a tight bun, Tilly has let herself go mostly grey, or grey-blonde. She keeps her hair short, heavily backcombed and hair sprayed within an inch of its life.

Tally hustles around the diner in comfortable grease-resistant-soled shoes, slinging coffee and french fries with remarkable expertise.

Tilly walks with the grace of a finishing school graduate, and I've never seen her in anything besides kitten heels.

There's only one customer in line.

Hopping in line behind the other customer, I'm

mesmerized by the blue-black sheen of her hair. Thanks to some handy tips from the ghost of the fashion diva who lives in my bookstore, I can tell this perfectly bobbed hair is of the synthetic variety. The elaborately dressed woman in front of me is wearing a wig. No judgment. I rely on them heavily in my undercover work.

My mind wanders back to previous cases and, without warning—

BANG!

What the—

"Everyone on the ground. This is a robbery. My friends and I are only here for the money. You cooperate, you don't get hurt."

It surprises me to discover that I'm already on the ground. I don't remember how I got there, but the sudden shock of a shotgun blast to the ceiling probably had something to do with it. Ballsy move by the masked gunmen! The bank is across the street from the sheriff's station and barely half a block down. Even the distracted Deputy Furious Monkeys might hear a gunshot.

"Follow those rules! Nobody gets hurt."

Blerg. The entire time the guy in the rabbit mask was talking, I got lost in the world inside my head. Now that I've regained an awareness of the outside world, it's time to admire the clever disguises worn by the bank robbers. The rabbit-masked guy, Wonderland timekeeper the White Rabbit, complete with large ears, stands on top of Tilly's desk. I can't see her, but I hope she's safely on the floor somewhere behind him. And yes, somehow Pye knew there would be a rabbit in my day. I'll be sure to give him credit when I get out of here.

The tall, unkempt, and crazy Mad Hatter guards the front entrance with the shotgun that surely put the hole in the ceiling. And the woman who used to be standing in front of me turns out to be a Queen of Hearts look-alike, and is hard at work stuffing cash from the teller drawers into a knockoff Gucci backpack.

They can't be very good bank robbers if they can't even afford a real Gucci. Am I right, Grams? Unfortunately, my paranormal sidekick is tethered to the bookshop and will be of no use in my current situation. However, just when I thought things couldn't get any more interesting, I'm rewarded with the blockbuster movie-trailer entrance of Alice and the Cheshire Cat! Her standard blue dress and white apron are paired with opera-length white gloves, harlequin tights, and black Doc Martens, while the Cat's wardrobe combines a plushy head with tight black jeans and a black-and-purple striped leather coat. Fantastic. The gang's all here!

Now, to get down to the business of figuring a way out of this mess. Think. Think. Think.

"I said down on the ground!"

Oops. During my intense brainstorming sesh, I seem to have stood up. Before I can hustle myself back down to the chilly granite floor, some helpful bank employee calls out, "You can't threaten her. She's the sheriff's girlfriend."

It doesn't take a psychic to figure out how that information is going to be used.

The White Rabbit hops from the desk—no pun intended—and stalks toward me. If not for the cartoonish mask covering his face, I'm sure I'd be treated to an annoying sneer.

"Well, well, well. Did you hear that, friends? We've got ourselves a top-notch hostage. This here is the sheriff's best girl."

The Mad Hatter snickers as he drops the blinds on the front windows and peers between the slats.

"How's the take lookin', Queenie?" the White Rabbit calls.

The individual in the Queen of Hearts disguise sports a high Victorian collar and red-and-gold corset. From this distance, I can't be sure if it's a woman or a — Hold on! What's the point of psychic powers if I can't use them to clarify some information? Reaching out with my special abilities, I confirm that the person in the Queen of Hearts regalia is a tall, slender man. But the Alice character is definitely a woman.

The Queen of Hearts holds up her imitation designer backpack and shakes her head. "Not enough to pay for the tea party, Ears."

Oh brother. I love a good cover story as much as the next guy, but let's not beat a dead horse.

The White Rabbit hooks an arm around me and brandishes his pistol as he shouts, "Who runs this joint?"

A man whom I have to assume is the bank manager, because I've never met him, gets to his feet and waves a hand as though he's back in high school homeroom and the teacher is taking roll.

The White Rabbit lifts his chin in recognition. "You're gonna have to open the vault, pal."

The comfortably round, balding man inches forward. In the movie version of this scene, the director would've already established that the man is days from retirement. I allow the classic trope to infiltrate this real-world disaster.

"Um, you'll have to excuse me—Mr.—um, Rabbit. Our vault . . . no money. Um, only safe deposit boxes." The poor man is shaking and stuttering like a teenager giving a reproductive-cycle presentation in health class.

"What's that, old man? You trying to tell me you got no money in your vault?"

The Mad Hatter calls from the window, "Ears,

we gotta hit it. There's some action over at the pig farm."

Despite the gun waving near my person, I nod in acknowledgment of the clever reference to the Pin Cherry sheriff's station. My action does not go unnoticed.

"You think your boyfriend is gonna come and save you? I got news for you, doll face. You're our ticket out of this one-horse town."

They say fortune favors the bold. "Well, if you were planning on using that ticket, I'd say the bus left thirty seconds ago."

The White Rabbit shoves the gun under my chin and growls into my ear. "I might look like a cuddly storybook character, but I can assure you I'm not joking. You cooperate, or you die."

Looks like I'm officially down the rabbit hole now! "Understood." I mumble my response carefully, to avoid irritating the criminal or activating his itchy trigger finger. My cooperation is rewarded with the removal of the firearm from my jawline.

He aims the gun at the bank manager and offers him a fresh threat. "Either you open that vault, or I shoot you. Seems like a pretty simple choice."

I'd have to agree with that heist logic.

The bank manager struggles to swallow, presses a hand to his chest, and staggers toward the vault.

The Queen of Hearts has finished raiding the

drawers, and vaults back over the counter. As the man in glam attire approaches, the teller calls out a warning from behind the counter. "Mr. Curb has a bad heart. Please don't hurt him."

The White Rabbit turns to offer her some two-bit threat, but Hatter interrupts his flow. "They're on the move, Ears. It's now or never."

The furry criminal presses the gun into the middle of Mr. Curb's back, and the bank manager shuffles forward in fear.

When he reaches the massive steel door, he removes a heavy key ring from his coat pocket, and his hand shakes violently as he attempts to open the door.

"Mr. Curb? I'm Mitzy Moon. Would you like me to open the door for you?"

The terrified man turns to look at me while Mr. Rabbit struggles to pick a target for his weapon. "Hey, doll face, I call the shots."

"Absolutely. It just seems like you're in a bit of a hurry, and I think I can operate that key a little faster than Mr. Curb. But it's up to you." My bravado is as false as false can be. Inside, I'm scared for the safety of all the hostages. If the movies have taught me anything, the money's insured. It's the loss of life that's irreplaceable.

"Hand her the keys, Curb."

Mr. Curb's tremulous hand nearly drops the

keys before I get hold of them. The White Rabbit shoves me toward the door, and I slip the key into the lock.

The terrified bank manager sweats profusely as he offers me a tip. "You have to turn it several times, dear."

That reminds me of the hefty brass key that opens my bookshop. Its unique triangle barrel must be turned three times to activate the tumblers hidden within the intricately carved wooden door.

There's an audible click within this thick metal door, and Mr. Rabbit pushes me out of the way. He grips the large circular handle and twists it counter-clockwise.

Interesting. He knows his way around a vault, which means this probably isn't his first robbery. Plus, he's taking quite a chance sticking around after his lookout warned him of law enforcement on the move. Maybe he doesn't rob banks for the money. Maybe he robs them for the thrill of the chase.

The massive steel door creaks open and reveals a single wooden table in a well-lit interior. The table is empty. Three visible walls are nothing more than row upon row of safe deposit boxes.

The White Rabbit turns to face Mr. Curb and I imagine his whiskers twitch as he raises his gun. "Where's the cash?"

"Well, like I said, this is only—"

The White Rabbit lunges forward and presses the gun to Mr. Curb's chest. "Don't waste your breath. Where's the cash?"

The color drains from the bank manager's face, and it looks as though he could drop any minute. Mr. Curb points down, as though he's indicating Satan's domain, and whispers in a frightened tone. "In the old vault."

The White Rabbit shouts over our heads. "Alice, Smiley, you're with me. Queenie, watch the back door."

The Queen of Hearts hustles toward the back door, but calls out, "What's going on?"

"There's another vault in the basement."

An update from Mr. Rabbit's front-window lookout. "Hope that hostage is worth it, Ears. It's not looking good out there."

"Calm down, Hatter. We've got a free ride on the Reading."

If I get his reference correctly, he thinks I'm his ticket to take a lap around the Monopoly board, penalty free. I've got some news for this poor misplaced storybook character: Sheriff Erick Harper doesn't play favorites. He won't let criminals walk free, just to save my hide.

The White Rabbit keeps his gun trained on me

while Alice and the Cheshire Cat lead the way downstairs.

The vault in the basement is . . . older. Darker. And, dare I say, sinister?

"You got the keys, doll face. Open it up."

He releases his hold on me, but keeps the gun trained squarely at my back as I move toward the locking mechanism. The antique mood ring on my left hand sizzles to life, and at the same moment my clairaudience reveals whispers within the walls.

Yeesh. This is how every horror movie I've ever seen starts. Some hapless coed ignores the warning signs and—

"Hustle up, doll face. The fuzz is breathing down our necks."

I want to focus. I need to focus, but when he talks about law enforcement breathing down his neck—you guessed it—images of Erick Harper's hot, inviting breath on my neck distract me.

"Now!"

Right. I fumble with the key ring and grab the only other key that looks old enough to belong to this vault. As I insert it into the lock. *Twist. Twist. Clunk.* And is that a hiss? The whispering grows louder.

The White Rabbit grabs my shoulder and pulls me back as the Cheshire Cat and Alice open the vault.

I wish I could report that my psychic senses were glitching. But when the ghostly form of a ski-mask-covered face oozes out of the barely open vault, the White Rabbit and his gun suddenly become the least of my worries.

CHAPTER 4
ERICK

"PAULSEN, I want you to get a sniper on the roof of
Rex's, and send two deputies down the alley behind
the bank." The flaps on my ridiculous deerstalker
hat are interfering with my peripheral. Time to sac-
rifice warmth for visibility. I yank the cap off my
head and throw it into the vehicle.

"That's a 10-4 on the deputies in the alley,
Sheriff. But we don't have a sniper. You're the best
shot on the force."

Not to toot my own horn, but Deputy Paulsen
is correct. "What's the ETA on the reinforcements
from Broken Rock?"

"They're five minutes out."

"10-4. When Boomer gets here, send him up.
He's a better shot than me any day of the week."

Paulsen's grim expression seems to show disagreement, but she always keeps it professional. She widens her stance and nods her head. "10-4."

"Johnson, take a position east. Stay sharp." He's one of my youngest guys. I can't risk putting him too close to the action. I don't plan on losing anyone today.

Johnson jogs in the direction I pointed, tightening the strap on his Kevlar vest as he goes. I don't know what we're dealing with, but Deputy Baird said she heard a gunshot, and somebody at that bank triggered the silent alarm. Reaching into my strategically parked cruiser, I grab the bullhorn, stand behind the door, and make first contact. "This is Sheriff Harper. We have the bank surrounded. We're interested in negotiating the safe release of the hostages. Who do I have the pleasure of negotiating with?"

No response.

There's a quick bend in one of the slats of the blinds behind an Easter basket filled with brightly painted eggs. I wish Mitzy could see this scene. I know how much she enjoys great imagery. Something tells me she'd get a kick out of a bank robbery decorated for spring. Pressing the microphone clipped to my shoulder, I check in with my deputies and make sure everyone's in position.

Paulsen and I have secured Main Street, and sent all the looky-loos indoors. Gilbert has the west and Johnson has the east. Baird and the new guy headed down the alley. I'd feel better if we had that sniper in place, but it'll be a couple more minutes before that concern is addressed.

"Sheriff, we found the vehicle."

"You sure, Baird?"

"10-4. Ran the plates. Came up registered to a vehicle reported stolen down south two days ago."

"Get Clarence on the horn."

"10-4."

Now they'll have to negotiate with me whether they like it or not. In less than five minutes, their cleverly hidden getaway vehicle will be dangling from Clarence's big steel hook. "Dispatch. Patch me into the bank."

There are a series of clicks and a long pause, but eventually there's ringing.

And more ringing. A frustrating amount of ringing. Doesn't sound like anyone's going to answer. "Try another extension."

"10-4." Dispatch works her way through the roster at the bank. Finally, I'm rewarded with a soft whisper. "Pin Cherry Harbor Bank & Trust, how can I invest in your day?"

You have to hand it to Tilly. Even in the middle of a terrifying situation, she puts her best foot forward. "Tilly, it's Sheriff Harper."

"Oh, geez, Sheriff. It's awful. There are five of

them. With big guns. They've taken Mitzy hostage!"

The blood in my veins turns to ice, and I feel a sickening plunge in my gut. After two tours overseas, I figured a bank robbery is hardly something to get excited about. That changed the instant Tilly spoke *her* name. Knowing that the woman I love is messed up in this, and might have a gun pressed to her back, just raised the limit at the table. I hate to say, I'm not much of a gambler.

"Sheriff? Sheriff, what should we do?"

"Everyone needs to remain calm. We've got the situation under control out here. Once I get them on the phone, I'll find out what they want. You better hang up now, Tilly. I don't want you putting yourself in any danger."

"I don't know about danger, Sheriff. They all went down to the basement, to the old vault. Anyway, there's only the one boy up here at the front window, and a sweet young girl at the back door."

Classic small-town gossip. Bless her heart for giving me every single piece of information I could've wanted. Before I can thank her properly, there's a terrified squeak, and an angry voice shouting something about killing hostages.

The phone hits something with a thud, but we aren't disconnected.

"Look, lady, I said everybody on the floor. Get over there in front of the counter with the others."

An uncomfortable silence.

"Nobody moves. Got it?"

My teeth feel like they could crack as I clench my jaw and listen intently. I heard at least four voices offer their agreement.

"Everybody drop your cell phones in here. Now!"

Thud. Clack. Clack. Clack.

Four phones drop into something, maybe a trashcan.

Lights and sirens rip onto the end of Main Street, and Johnson signals the cars to halt.

Boomer leaps out of his vehicle, helmet in one hand, long-range sniper rifle in the other. His dark brown eyes glint with excitement as he crouches low and jogs up the sidewalk.

"Harper."

"Good to see you, Boomer. I need you on the roof. ASAP."

"10-4. How many unfriendlies?"

"Five. Unconfirmed."

"Hostages?"

"Four in the main room. At least one more in the basement vault. Also unconfirmed."

"Do I have the green light?"

"Negative. On my order only."

"Come on, Harper. You're takin' all the fun out of it."

Doesn't seem like the most professional thing to tell him, but Boomer and I go way back. "Nothing fun about it. My girlfriend is in there. So, on my order, and that's final."

"Understood, bro. I'll let you know when I'm in position."

The cool wind has nearly disappeared. This morning Boomer would've had to factor in twenty-eight to thirty mile-per-hour crosswinds. Now—I lick my finger and hold it up—it's dropped to under three.

I need to get someone talking. The key to any good negotiation is establishing rapport with the leader. The putz who threatened Tilly and left the phone off the hook can't possibly be the mastermind behind this heist.

Paulsen paces beside her cruiser like a tank on maneuvers. Her mother is a teller at the bank, but if that's causing her any worry, she's keeping it on lockdown.

The thing I can't figure out is what led them to the vault in the basement. That was abandoned fifty years ago after a security guard and a masked gunman killed each other in a robbery gone wrong.

I wasn't around back then—I wasn't even a twinkle in my mother's eye—but when you work law-enforcement in a small town, there are certain stories folks never forget. Point being, there's no money in that vault. As far as I know, they house the weekly cash delivery in a relatively compact safe hidden behind a false wall in the manager's office. I wish I knew what took them to the basement.

"I'm in position, Sheriff."

"10-4, Boomer. Anything to report?"

"Yeah, it's colder than a witch's—"

"Not on this frequency. Let's keep it professional out there."

Deputy Johnson and the new guy both offer confirmation of message received. As for the rest of the deputies, it's easy to imagine them snickering into their gloves.

The last car of reinforcements arrives from Broken Rock. Paulsen sends them into the sheriff's station to man the phones and stay warm. There's no telling how long this standoff will last, and we'll need reinforcements with unfrozen trigger fingers if we hope to keep our advantage.

CHAPTER 5

INSIDE MY LITTLE PSYCHIC HEAD, there are at least five emotions swirling around, struggling to get the upper hand. The ghost of a former bank robber slipped out of the basement vault. Based on reactions, I'm pretty confident in saying I'm the only one who can see the thing. However, I have no interest in letting this sketchy ghost find out that he's been seen. I cough and let my gaze dart to the floor.

"You see the cash, Smiley?"

The Cheshire Cat and Alice peer into the dark cavern, pop a light on from one of their phones, and grumble loudly. "Nothing, Ears. That guy sent us on a wild-goose chase!" The two co-conspirators complete their search of the ten-foot by fifteen-foot space, and exit in a huff.

My furry white captor loosens his hold on me

and turns all of his attention toward the fragile, fumbling bank manager. The only thing is, when I focus on Mr. Curb, I'm not getting any fear. I'm picking up on some subtle self-satisfied vibes and a hint of anticipation. Did he know about the haunted vault?

As if on cue, the lights in the hallway flicker, and an icy blast of air fills the space.

The three heist buddies exchange nervous glances. Alice says what they're all thinking, "Hey, like, what's up with the lights? And am I trippin' or did it get, like, mega cold?"

Both men nod, and the White Rabbit aims his handgun at Mr. Curb. "What's the big idea? There's no money in there. Why'd you bring us down to this Halloween freak show? Did you think we'd be scared?"

Mr. Curb returns to his fumbling and stuttering, but I'm picking up the truth beneath the bunny's words. The White Rabbit is scared, and so are his friends.

It doesn't seem like Mr. Curb can see the ghost, but it would appear that he's a firm believer in the paranormal. Perhaps he's heard stories, or had previous run-ins with the otherworldly resident of his bank. Now that I know his fragility is an act, I plan to help him use it to our advantage.

He stutters out a confused response, and the bank robbers are getting restless.

Time for some "more flies with honey," as Grams always says. "Hey, Ears. Can I call you Ears?"

He spins on his blue canvas high-tops and turns the gun sideways like every gangster in every movie you've ever seen. "You got something to say, blondie?"

"I appreciate all the effort you're putting into nicknames. Believe me, I do. My name isn't Blondie, or Doll Face. It's Mitzy. And the longer you guys hang out in this bank, the more time you're giving law enforcement to put their snipers in place."

Definite spike in the fear vibe coming from Alice. Perfect.

"You already know the sheriff and I are involved. Why not use that to your advantage, now, before things get out of hand or one of your partners gets nervous and takes this simple armed robbery to a whole new level?" I hope he picks up on what I'm implying, which is the danger of a restless crew and a room full of frightened hostages.

He's smarter than his cuddly mask looks. "We got a van out back. I don't need your help."

They say timing is everything . . .

The Queen of Hearts appears at the top of the

stairs with some bad news. "Ears, they're towing the van!"

It's tough to keep the grin from my lips. "You were saying?"

He grips the back of my neck and presses the gun hard into my chest. "How did you know?"

The truth is, I didn't know, but if I can somehow get him to believe that I'm able to predict — "You know how it is. When you've been dating someone for a while, you kinda get how their mind works."

Despite my elevated heart rate and shallow breathing, my bluff seems to float.

"Get back to the door, Queenie. Keep me posted. Blondie here—"

"Mitzy."

"Yeah, whatever. This one's got some ideas."

Mr. Curb breathes a sigh of relief, and the White Rabbit insists the manager lead us all back to the main room.

Trying to gather as much information as possible on my return trip, I let my eyes scan every inch of the bank as it flows past. Something might come in useful for psychic replay later. The first thing I notice in the main room is that all the hostages have been grouped together by the counter, and Tilly has a decidedly smug expression on her face. When I catch her eye, she winks and nods subtly towards her desk.

Fortunately, my extra abilities snatch the word *phone* from the air, and when I scan the desktop, I note the missing receiver. Someone's listening. Hopefully, it's someone who matters.

The White Rabbit drags me toward the front windows and peeks out. "What the heck, Hatter? You didn't tell me they set up blockades."

"I told you they were on the move."

The White Rabbit shakes his head, and I sense his anger rising. "On the move is a little different than in position." He pushes me into a seat and lazily aims his gun. "So what's the sheriff's next move?"

I need to test this relationship. I wait to see if he'll offer my name.

His mask bobs left and right. "Mitzy. What's his next move?"

Success. At some point, I may try to reach out with my psychic senses, but for now, I need to get one of these people out of here. "He's going to want to know your demands. If you want to get the upper hand, release a hostage before he asks for one. Then you'll have more negotiating power."

The White Rabbit's ears shake back and forth, and I can tell he's struggling with my recommendation. As he should be. My recommendation makes absolutely no sense. But my goal isn't to give him the upper hand, my goal is to get these hostages out one at a time.

He glances toward the row of hostages and back to the bank manager currently held at gunpoint by the one he calls Smiley.

"Bank manager or the old lady?"

Leaning forward, I lower my voice to a whisper. "Between you and me, the sheriff is a bit of a mama's boy. I think the old lady will get you more juice."

I'll apologize to Erick later for the slander on his person, but I really want to get Tilly out of this bank.

"You, in the pink."

Tilly presses a hand to her chest and looks from me to the ringleader. "Me? My name's Tilly Sikanen."

"Tilly, get over here."

"Oh, right away." She struggles to maintain her modesty and get to her feet in a skirt suit, but eventually manages the task. As she approaches, I can feel the air thicken with her fear. "How can I help you, sir?"

He points to the door, and that's the moment I realize I'm still holding the ring of keys.

"Hatter, cut the zip tie. Mitzy has the keys. We'll lock it proper after we let this one out."

Surprisingly, Hatter does as he's told without protest. He's absolutely *not* the brains of the operation.

"You're letting me out? Why thank you, son. My sciatica was bothering me something terrible on the cold floor, but I didn't want to complain."

The White Rabbit puts his hand on the door, and I step forward. He turns and aims the gun at me. "Don't get any bright ideas. She's the only one going out."

"Understood. But we haven't communicated that we're letting out a hostage. If you open that door, they might start firing. Is it all right if I call the sheriff?" Pulling my cell from my back pocket, I offer it up innocently.

Mr. Rabbit turns on his cohort. "You didn't take their phones?"

Hatter waves his gun dangerously toward the row of hostages. "I did. I did, mostly. She was with you. You should've taken it."

I'm not against internal strife. I just want it to kick in after Tilly is safely outside. "Look, guys. It's nothing to fight about. I didn't make any calls. And I'm asking permission to place a call that will help you out. You don't want anybody on your team to get shot, do ya Ears?" I'll try using the more familiar form of his name bandied about by his fellow robbers.

It catches him off guard, and he nods toward the phone. "Make it quick. Just tell him I'm releasing a hostage; don't try to give him any coded information."

"Copy that."

The Mad Hatter's head turns toward me when I speak the phrase. Perhaps he's had some experience on a movie set. Perhaps it's coincidence. A random clue that may or may not prove useful. I'll worry about that once they've released Tilly.

I hit speed dial and the call rings.

"Put it on speakerphone."

I tap the icon and comply, as a tense but familiar voice comes through. "This is Sheriff Harper. Who am I speaking with?"

Seems like Erick and I are more of a similar mind than I guessed. "Hey, Erick. It's Mitzy. We just wanted to call and let you know that they're going to release one of the hostages. So don't shoot, all right?"

Part of me hears him breathe a sigh of relief and part of me feels the rush of concern that floats through his body. Seems like I won't have to work as hard as I thought to hook up the psychic link. "We're sending out Tilly. The Mad Hatter's gonna open the door, and the White Rabbit has a gun trained on me. So definitely tell your men to stand down."

"10-4. Are you pulling my leg with these names, Moon?"

"No, sir. The Wonderland gang's all here."

The White Rabbit waves the gun at me. "That's enough."

The door opens, and I gently propel Tilly forward. She covers her eyes against the sharp light of the midday sun.

A series of commands echo through the phone as they flow over the radio, and rapid footfalls approach the door.

Ears shouts, "Shut the damn door, Hatter!"

Erick confirms. "We've got her."

I'm about to respond, but Mr. Rabbit grabs my phone and ends the call. "Lock the door, *Mitzy*."

CHAPTER 6

ONE DOWN, FOUR TO GO. Five if I count myself, but I honestly don't see that in the cards. At least Tilly is safe. I'll have to use everything Silas ever taught me to get inside the heads of these robbers. As I twist the key in the lock, my temporary connection with Erick vanishes. Maybe it was never there. It was probably wishful thinking. Regardless, I need to step up my game and figure out how to get the next hostage out.

"I'll be taking those." The leader of the gang offers his gloved palm, and I drop the key ring onto it. He tosses it in the pocket of his fancy orange waistcoat. And not for the first time, I have to admire the detail and authenticity of the wardrobe. Whoever chose the disguises and took on costume design has a flare. Was it the Queen of Hearts? Possibly. The man in glam definitely has the most style.

"I know you didn't ask, Mr. Rabbit, but you need to come up with your list of demands. If you wait until the sheriff asks for it, you'll look like an amateur. Don't make a long list. Don't make it a bunch of insane things. Figure out what you need to get out of here safely, ask for it, and offer a hostage in exchange for each line item."

The fuzzy-ear-topped mask tilts. "Seems like you might've done this before. You weren't planning on robbing this place today, were you?"

Time to reveal something and hopefully build trust. "Funny you should mention it. I guess it runs in my blood. My dad did fifteen in the state pen for armed robbery. Personally, I'm not much more than a petty thief, but I know what it looks like getting caught." No need to tell him I didn't know my father was even alive when he committed that robbery and did his stint in Clearwater.

"Whoa. Your dad's hard core. Smiley got popped for boosting a car when he was a minor, but his dad greased a few palms and got him off with some community service."

My plan is working. "Nice. I dated a guy who paid his way through school boosting cars. I know a thing or two about hot wiring. Which brings me back to your list. You need a getaway vehicle. And you need it soon."

The Mad Hatter pipes up behind us. "Hey, looks like shift change."

The White Rabbit leans toward the window to peek out, and I join him. He doesn't yell at me, which is progress.

One by one, Erick is calling in officers and sending out replacements. The new team is wearing a different uniform, probably from Broken Rock. They have far more officers on staff and generally back us up during large community events or situations like this.

Mr. Rabbit looks at the Mad Hatter and shakes his head. "Those guys look like SWAT."

No need for me to soothe his nerves. Let them think it's SWAT. It will motivate them to get moving on this negotiation.

"Maybe we'll just ask 'em to give us our van back." He moves away from the window and reaches under his mask to scratch his face.

"Possibly, but that van isn't gonna carry enough velocity to break through barricades. You need a bus. With a full tank of gas and curtains over all the windows."

The White Rabbit's masked face nods in appreciation. "Solid plan, blondie."

I let the comment lie and gesture toward a desk on the opposite side of the room from Tilly's.

If there's any chance that someone is still listening on that open line, I don't want to draw any attention to it. "I'll start making a list. They'll need some time to get the bus kitted out. Let's ask for food in exchange for a hostage to get the ball rolling."

The White Rabbit follows me to the desk, flops onto a rolly office chair and kicks his feet up as though he hasn't a care in the world. "Yeah, put that all down."

As I'm codifying the requests, the mood ring on my left hand turns to ice, and the hairs on the back of my neck stand on end.

Without warning, a stack of deposit slips flies off the center island and flutters to the floor like feathers in the wind.

The previously calm leader is on his feet in a second, aiming his gun into empty air. The masked ghost of yesteryear is enjoying a hearty laugh. I force my gaze to wander around the room as though I don't see him, but his wild polyester button down with its enormous collar and the high-waisted bell-bottom pants reveal a clue about his origin. Whoever this man is, it would appear he attempted to rob the bank in the 1970s. The shiny shirt is unbuttoned nearly to his ethereal naval, and there's a gaudy gold chain dangling from his otherworldly neck.

"Right on, sister. You like what you see?" He leers in my general direction.

Oops, I may have stared at a specific location for a tick too long. Better cover up fast. "What was that? Is there a door open?"

Mr. Rabbit jogs to the hallway and calls out. "Queenie, did you open the back door?"

"No. But I think I heard footsteps on the roof."

The inexplicable localized tornado is immediately forgotten. The White Rabbit extends the phone. "Call your sweetheart and tell him to pull back, or I shoot a hostage."

Taking the phone, I nod furiously. "Understood. And if he pulls back, let's send out the security guard in exchange."

Mr. Rabbit looks toward the lineup of hostages and leans back. "Security guard? The whole reason we targeted this joint is because they don't have a security guard. You feeling all right, doll face?"

My throat tightens and my stomach clinches with fear. The security guard seated at the end of the row of hostages isn't human.

There's a second ghost! And if he or his masked counterpart overheard, I may have tipped my hand. Time to lean into every blonde joke I've ever heard. "Whoops, I guess my roots are showing. It's a bank.

I just assumed there was a security guard. I thought that'd be the person you'd want to get rid of, you know? Never mind! When the cops pull back, we can send out the teller. She looks like she's about to faint. The last thing you need is a medical emergency on your hands. Then you'd have to let a doctor in, and who knows how that would turn out." I'm rambling and spitballing simultaneously. Never one of my best strategies. I'm eager to put as much dialogue distance as possible between my slip of the tongue and the next decision.

"Yeah, call your guy."

Putting the phone on speaker without being asked will hopefully gain me some additional brownie points.

"Sheriff Harper here."

"Hey, Sheriff. They're working on their list of demands. In the meantime, if you're willing to send some food over, they'll release another hostage."

"10-4. Myrtle's Diner?"

"That would be great. We've got five hostages, including me, and five *others*."

The White Rabbit smacks the phone from my hand and raises his gun. "I said no tricks. Remember? Don't be giving away information."

"Sorry! I was only thinking about a headcount for food. Honestly, I didn't mean anything by it." Now seems like the wrong time to tell him how they would already have that information from the hostage debrief with Tilly.

He sniffs sharply and rubs his free hand against his throat.

I hear opportunity knocking. "Are you guys thirsty? Should I have them send over some drinks?"

While he ponders that question, I retrieve the phone and discover the call didn't get dropped when the cell hit the floor. "Are you still there, Sheriff?"

"10-4."

His response is curt and to the point, but every one of my special abilities picks up on the tension, fear, and helplessness bubbling beneath the surface.

"Can you send over a few sodas and a few ice teas too?" I glance toward the hostages and shrug. Two of them nod their heads.

"Give us twenty, okay? We'll send someone in with the food."

Mr. Rabbit steps toward me, shaking his head and pointing his gun toward the roof.

"That's no good, Sheriff. We need you to pull your men off the roof immediately. Show us some good faith. When the food is ready, just have some-body drop it outside the door, and I'll pick it up—" I glance at the White Rabbit and tilt my head back and forth in a nonverbal request to proceed.

He nods.

"Yeah, I'll grab the food and we'll release a hostage. Deal?"

Erick's tone lightens, and I sense he's pleased with the way I'm running the negotiation. "We'll get the order placed, Moon. You be sure to—"

The White Rabbit grabs the phone, ends the call, and shoves my mobile into the pocket of his coat.

I hope that ring of keys in there doesn't scratch the screen. It's a weird thing to think about in a time of crisis, but I've never owned a legit new phone until now. I was really trying to take good care of it.

A typewriter crashes to the floor behind us, and the Mad Hatter fires his shotgun.

Less than a second later, a voice booms over the bullhorn. "You have ten seconds to let me know everyone's all right in there. If I don't hear from Mitzy, we're coming in!"

Shockingly, Mr. Rabbit seems to be frozen.

No time to waste. "Mr. Rabbit, I'm going to take my phone out of your pocket. I gotta call the sheriff or they'll come busting in with concussion grenades and who knows what else." I have no idea what the procedure is, but I need to use a word that sounds scary. I put my left hand in the air as I reach into his jacket pocket with my right. His gaze is locked onto the broken typewriter on the floor.

The call barely rings once. "Mitzy?"

Gone are the professional voice and the "Sheriff Harper" introduction. Erick is worried, and it shows.

"I'm here. Everyone's fine. A typewriter fell off one of the desks and the Mad Hatter overreacted. No one's hurt. You get your guys to back off and send the food. We're all right."

The White Rabbit snaps out of his daze, but the gun in his left hand hangs as limp as a wilting flower. "Just keep the phone, doll face."

I slip it into the pocket of my jeans and breathe a sigh of relief.

He shakes the gun toward the recent ruckus. "What's going on here? There's nobody over there. What made that typewriter—?"

When in doubt, lie it out. "You know how these old buildings are. The foundations are always shifting. Plus, they're drafty and unstable. A small town like this can't really afford to update their infrastructure. You saw how many buildings are boarded up on Main Street. I wouldn't worry about it. No one was hurt, that's the important thing."

While I soothe the ringleader's frayed nerves, the Mad Hatter approaches with his comically large head hanging. "I'm out, Ears."

"What?"

Hatter lowers his voice and leans toward the

leader. "I'm outta ammo. Normally, I fire one into the ceiling. Queenie grabs the cash and we go. I never had to fire a second shot or a third."

Mr. Rabbit reaches out and smacks the Mad Hatter upside the head. "You knucklehead! Don't let the hostages know. I'll see if Smiley has a backup."

The White Rabbit wanders off to check the Cheshire Cat's ammunition situation, and I stroll casually toward the hostages. I crouch at the end of the row, directly in front of the ghost of security guards past, and address the three remaining employees. "Is it true that you don't have a security guard?"

The ghost at the end of the row crosses his arms and sticks out his lower lip like a child being sent to timeout.

The teller answers. "Oh, you betcha. I know the whole story. There was a terrible robbery here when I was seven. Seems like a century ago, you know."

A century? I can't believe this woman's job involves math.

She tugs at her mousy brown bob and swallows audibly. "It was the talk of the town for decades, dontcha know. Folks were still jawing about it when my little Pauly was born."

This can't be happening. But there can't be that

many Paulys in Pin Cherry. Before my mouth can formulate the question, my special abilities deliver the answer. The teller is Deputy Pauly Paulsen's mother. Great, now I have guilt and I missed part of the story.

"Oh, there were a bunch of gunmen and a shootout, for sure. Some of our good citizens were murdered—our neighbor, Lindy McElroy among them. God rest her. Well, those robbers shot the security guard, and I think he even shot one of them. Anyway, that's when they stopped using the vault in the basement, and put the—"

I raise a hasty finger to my lips. Who knows exactly what she was going to say, but I could definitely sense she was about to give away a key piece of information about the missing cash. We definitely need to get her out of here. "Thanks for filling me in. When they deliver the food, we're going to send you out. All right?"

She gazes at me with grateful brown eyes that look nothing like her bully of a daughter's. "Honestly, dear? I'm getting out of here?"

The middle-aged man next to her stiffens. "I have a family. I should be the next one released."

My eyes seethe with contempt. "I suppose you would've been one of those men on the Titanic that shoved a pregnant woman aside to get into a lifeboat." I point firmly at the teller. "She leaves next. Any questions?"

He presses his lips into a thin line and shakes his head.

The ghostly guard looks up with a flicker of hope in his eyes.

At that moment, I take the risk—stare directly at him, and wink.

His shimmering mouth makes a perfect O and his eyes widen with a shade of hope they haven't seen in decades.

CHAPTER 7
ERICK

THE SOUND OF A GUNSHOT inside the bank really threw me off my game. Being on the outside, with Mitzy trapped on the inside, is wreaking havoc on my concentration. Squeezing the button on the side of my mic, I ask the relief team from Broken Rock to report. As the calls come in over the radio, I roll through the facts and my options.

My guys are safe inside the station, warming up and getting food.

Odell's packaging up the delivery for the bank. Paulsen wants to be the one to take it to the door. There's a gunman with an itchy trigger finger inside, and that means a simple food delivery is high risk. Seems like Paulsen has nerves of steel, though. And I'd rather accept a volunteer for the task than appoint a deputy to risk their life.

Thanks to the information we collected from Tilly and Mitzy's not-so-subtle hints, I know there are four hostages left. Wait, Mitzy said there were five hostages including her. I only heard four phones drop into the bin before Tilly came out. Maybe one of the remaining hostages is from an older generation and doesn't carry a cell phone.

Although, it could mean there's a child involved. My worst nightmare. I hate seeing kids in danger.

If I know Miss Moon, and I may know her too well, she's working every angle she can think of to keep the hostages safe and trick the bad guys into making a mistake.

The problem with Mitzy is that she's too willing to put herself in danger to accomplish her goals.

"Sheriff Harper, food is ready to go."

Odell's prior military training shows in every calculated movement. He's gotta be worried about his granddaughter, Mitzy, stuck in a bank with a bunch of armed robbers, but it doesn't show on his experienced face.

As he carries out a red milk crate filled with to-go bags and beverages, the sun shines on his silver buzz cut and he nods competently in my direction.

"Paulsen, you ready?"

"10-4, Sheriff. I take the delivery to the bank, place it two feet to the right of the hinge, so they have to open the door wide and let Mitzy walk out in full view. Boomer's in position and he'll be ready to take a shot at your command."

"Okay, Paulsen. It's go time. No heroics. Deliver the food and get back to safety."

Despite her current campaign for sheriff in the election later this year, Paulsen is a loyal deputy and always puts the assignment first. She may be occasionally hotheaded and generally suspect the worst, but she's reliable and, in the end, fair.

Paulsen takes the crate from Odell, and he saunters toward me.

"How's Mitzy holdin' up?"

"She has things under control. She's my point of contact on the inside and she's making a list of their demands."

His ready chuckle lightens my burden. "If I didn't know better, Sheriff, I'd say she's the mastermind behind the heist."

It feels good to laugh, even if it's only for a minute. "I was thinking the same thing."

Odell leans in close and whispers for my ears only. "Anybody updated Myrtle Isadora?"

The mention of the ghost of Mitzy's grandmother always blows my mind. When Mitzy told me she could see ghosts, and the ghost of her grandmother was sort of alive and well in the bookshop, I had serious doubts about her sanity. However, once I witnessed Myrtle Isadora moving things around the bookstore and felt the chill envelop my body as she passed by, they made a believer out of me. "Wasn't anybody I could tell. Would you mind doing the honors?"

Odell nods once and heads down the street in his shirtsleeves. I'm not sure whether it's the discipline he learned in the Army or just how hard-core the man is, but he makes winter in Pin Cherry look like summer in the Caribbean. Hopefully, it will actually warm up around here for the party.

The party! I need to stay focused on the crisis at hand, but there must be a hundred things to do for this grandiose birthday that Mitzy's grandmother, and her team, is planning. I have a special role to play, but if I can't wrap up this robbery and throw these idiots in jail, there's definitely going to be a last-minute change of plans.

Paulsen sets the food delivery down as instructed, but she doesn't retreat. Instead, she jogs out of sight of the bank windows, drops to the icy sidewalk and low-crawls back toward the delivery. I press my mic and hiss. "That's not what we discussed, Paulsen."

She doesn't respond, and I can't push my luck. If she makes a sound, one of the gunmen could overhear. My plans for a peaceful exchange will go straight out the window.

Paulsen turns her head toward me and gives me a non-verbal go sign. Shaking my head, I pick up the bullhorn. "The food has been delivered. Send out the hostage."

The door opens. The face that pops into the opening is a welcome sight.

My eyes drink in the sight of Mitzy in her curve-hugging skinny jeans and one of her classic T-shirts. There's a picture of a kitten tangled in yarn. Beside the image, the text reads, "Wildly Unprepared For The Day Ahead."

I want to smile and wave like a silly schoolboy, but I stuff my emotions down and keep it professional. Raising the bullhorn to my lips, I attempt a nonchalant tone. "Keep your hands where we can see them, Miss Moon."

She immediately stops and puts a fist on her hip. "Rude!"

That one gesture tells me all I need to know. She has everything under control inside the bank. My heartbeat returns to almost normal and, for the first time today, I dare to hope for a positive outcome.

She crouches near the full milk crate, and I watch as she leans toward Deputy Paulsen. Based on body language, there seems to be a hushed exchange.

A pair of white ears peeps into the open door-way, and I hear the voice of one of the gunmen. "Hurry up! Or we shoot one of the hostages."

Boomer's calm voice comes over the radio. "Green light, Sheriff? I've got the shot."

"Negative. Do not take the shot." I can't risk getting Mitzy caught in the crossfire.

Mitzy picks up the crate, turns toward me, and flashes *five* with her left hand. She adjusts the crate and flashes *four* with her right.

We know the armed gang consists of five members, so the four must indicate the remaining hostages.

She takes one step, pretends to stumble, or possibly she actually stumbles—she is adorably clumsy—and flashes *two* with her left hand.

Five gunmen, four hostages, and two? Two what?

She adjusts the crate, makes a weird wiggly motion with her left hand and ducks back inside.

Are there two more hostages? That doesn't make sense. If they were hostages, she would've included it in the count on the right hand.

What am I saying? I have no idea what she was trying to communicate with all the finger gestures.

The hostage exchange proceeds. A woman stumbles forward. It's Cheryl, Deputy Paulsen's mother. She honestly doesn't look as terrified as I would've assumed. When she steps into the harsh sunlight, she immediately wraps her arms around herself and shivers.

Paulsen lies stock still, and the door remains open.

"Boomer, report." I hold my breath.

"No shot. I repeat, no shot."

Well, at least I know my eyes aren't deceiving me. Once Cheryl reaches our side of the street, I motion her to come toward me and send her into the sheriff's station to be debriefed. All the while keeping my eyes locked on that door, as Mitzy swings it closed.

Tabling the cryptic message, I move on to what we need to do to get another hostage released. A couple of minutes pass, and I place a call to her phone.

"Hey, Sheriff. Thanks for the fries."

"You're welcome, Moon. Did you miscount the hostages? Or were those extra fries for you? By the way, you're on an open line being recorded by dispatch."

"Thanks for the warning." Her easy laughter fills my heart with relief.

"Do they have that list of demands together?"

"It's short and simple. They want a bus with a full tank of gas and curtains on all the windows. When it's ready, they want it pulled down the alley, and they'll leave the remaining two hostages in the bank when they board the bus."

There goes my blood pressure. "But there are three hostages remaining, Miss Moon."

"You're not wrong, C— C— sweetie. But I'm their ticket out of town. Once they're across the border, they'll set me—"

The call ends abruptly, and my head is spinning. Across the border? They can't possibly be headed for Mexico. I might not open fire on them for the sake of my girlfriend, but if they're headed for Mexico, there are a multitude of states between here and there where the authorities won't take so kindly to fugitive armed robbers.

Wait . . . C-C-sweetie? She wasn't stuttering. CC! My buddy in the Canadian Mounties! They want to head for Canada. That tells me two things. They're listening to Mitzy more than anyone should, and they don't have a solid grasp of international law. Canada and the US have an extradition treaty. But what they don't know won't hurt my gal.

"Dispatch, get on the horn with the bus service

to secure a vehicle, and tap Clarence to find out how long it'll take him to kit out the set of wheels."

Now my only job is to keep the heat low on this pressure cooker of a situation and make sure the remaining hostages are left alive in the bank when the gunmen board their getaway vehicle—with Mitzy.

CHAPTER 8

DEEP DOWN, I've always believed that french fries can fix anything. Munching on these pieces of golden potato perfection in the middle of an armed bank robbery proves my hypothesis. Everyone, including the criminals, is blissed out on Odell's delicious food. I hadn't even considered the possibility of a food coma solving all of our problems, but as I take in the satisfied expressions throughout the room and imagine the ones beneath the masks, I'm considering believing in miracles.

I hope Erick figures out my crappy sign language. I'm not sure how it will help him to know that there are a couple of ghosts running loose inside the bank, but I always hear people say things like forearmed is forewarned—or maybe it's the opposite. As my full belly releases some happiness endorphins, I can almost hear Gene Wilder's Willy Wonka say, "Scratch that, reverse it."

The White Rabbit interrupts my mental gymnastics. "How long do you think it'll take your boyfriend to get our ride?"

For a moment I hesitate, then I remember that talking with my mouth full is hardly going to be the worst crime committed today. "There's not a bus station in town. Which means the closest one is probably in Broken Rock. That's about a half hour away. Then we need to factor in the time to fill the tank, put up some kind of coverings over the windows, and get it parked in the alley . . . I think we're looking at anywhere from an hour to an hour and a half. Why?"

"You think they're on the level?"

Slurping down some soda, I wipe my mouth with the back of my hand. "What do you mean?"

"Will they get the bus? Are they just dragging their feet until we let our guard down, or do you think they'll let us drive away?"

Wow, either these guys have never seen a single heist movie, or they've had an unusually good run of luck and assumed they'd never get caught. "Sheriff Harper is a straight shooter."

Five comical masks turn toward me in unison.

Waving my hands to fend off their overreaction, I have another go at my response. "That came out wrong. I meant it like, he's honest. If he says he's getting you a bus, he's getting you a bus."

As the rabbit maneuvers another handful of fries beneath his mask, I catch a glimpse of his blond mustache. I'll lock that tidbit away for later.

"What about you guys? Are you really gonna let me go when you get into Canada?"

For the first time, the Cheshire Cat speaks to me directly. "I dunno, Mitzy. You seem to have a knack for this sort of thing. Are you sure you don't wanna stick with the gang?"

I wish this had been the first time I'd been offered a chance to join an armed crew, and I hope this operation turns out better than that one. Loss of life, no matter whose, never sits well with me. "I appreciate the offer, Smiley. Honestly, I do. But I've got a lot going on here, you know."

Alice lifts her mask to take a bite of her burger and, unfortunately, reveals most of her face. I'm not exactly saying I could pick her out of a lineup, but her youthful face and the distinct mole on her left cheek are definitely emblazoned in my mind. "Like, what do you do around here?" she asks as she munches on her cheeseburger.

Rather than make myself sound too well off, I try to keep my story blue-collar. "I work at a bookshop."

Unfortunately, the middle-aged bank employee

who I offended earlier is either seeking revenge, or he's simply dense. "Don't sell yourself short, Miss Moon. She owns the bookstore and runs a generous philanthropic organization."

Blerg.

The White Rabbit sets down his soda and picks up his gun. "Things just got interesting. Not only do we have the perfect ticket out of town, but once we're safely on the other side of the border, we can ransom you for some additional dough."

Murmurs of agreement grumble through the gang.

If looks could kill, the glare I'm shooting Mr. Blabbermouth should drop him dead on the spot. His wide eyes and pale complexion, coupled with my special abilities, confirm his *blurt* was accidental.

"You're in charge, Mr. Rabbit. Although, the more you complicate things, the more opportunity you give law enforcement to catch up with you. Sheriff Harper is playing it cool, because he's interested in making sure all the hostages, including me, make it out safely. However, he's not a pushover. If you test him, you'll regret it."

The energy in the room shifts instantaneously, and I realize my mistake too late. Befriending the group was one thing, but publicly opposing their leader—not a good plan.

Me and my big mouth.

"Hatter, you got another one of those zip ties. Seems like doll face is getting a little too big for her britches."

As usual, my tendency to laugh in the face of danger takes over, and a chuckle escapes my lips before I have a chance to stifle it.

"You think that's funny, blondie?" Once again, he tucks the gun under my chin and presses it threateningly.

I offer my response through clenched teeth. "It wasn't funny. I have a real problem with authority. Plus, *big for my britches*, you know." I risk a pat toward my backside and, thankfully, Alice gets the joke.

"Ease up, Ears. She didn't mean anything by it. She, like, helped us out, you know. Just pump the brakes."

For once, I know when to keep my mouth shut.

Mr. Rabbit backs away and withdraws the gun from my chin, but doesn't return to his meal.

The initial survival instinct and the burning desire to fight back are hard to resist. But I think there's more to gain by cooperating. The Mad Hatter hands him a zip tie, and Mr. Rabbit secures it around my wrists. He leads me into the bank manager's office, shoves me roughly into a chair, and closes the door behind him when he leaves.

It's a good news-bad news situation. Good news: I have my phone in my back pocket and the blinds on the manager's office window are already lowered. Bad news: I have my phone in my back pocket, and my hands are secured behind my back.

Now, my attorney/alchemist Silas Willoughby taught me a transmutation for getting myself out of metal handcuffs ages ago, but I'm not sure if the same properties would apply to plastic zip ties.

RING.

No time to wonder.

RING.

I have to get that phone out of my pocket and answer that call before it rings again. Erick isn't going to take kindly to being ignored in this tense situation.

Fortunately, I'm good with my hands. Don't worry, a "that's what she said" floated through my brain too.

Sliding the phone from my pocket, I tap what I'm hoping is the right part of the screen, twist my head over my shoulder, and offer my greeting. "Hey, Sheriff. Sorry for the delay. I'm a little tied up."

The voice that sounds from my phone is not the one I expected. "Mizithra? Is this one of your attempts at comedy or are you sincerely in peril?"

"Silas! I'm so glad it's you. I'm being held

hostage by the White Rabbit, and there are two ghosts loose in the bank. Honestly, I don't know what to do."

"Oh, heavens. I fear you may have inhaled the smoke from one of those funny cigarettes I've heard about."

Classic Silas. I should've known better than to spout off a series of pop culture references without the proper etiquette. "It's not a drug-induced hallucination. There's literally an armed robbery at Pin Cherry Harbor Bank & Trust. There are five armed robbers all dressed like characters from Alice in Wonderland, three hostages including myself, and two ghosts!"

He harrumphs, and I can easily picture him smoothing his bushy grey mustache with a thumb and forefinger. However, the image of his jowls jiggling as he chuckles at my predicament is totally unexpected.

"Silas, this is no laughing matter. Right now my hands are zip-tied behind my back in the manager's office. They're threatening to kill a hostage if Erick doesn't meet their demands."

"It continues to be a surprising pleasure to speak with you, Mitzy. You may use the transmutation I taught you to remove the binding from your wrists. It may require more intense focus, but your abilities have expanded and I have faith in your success."

"All right. That's one problem solved. What about the ghosts? One of them is one of the original bank robbers. He might've killed more than one person back then."

A low grumbling spills from the phone and my clairsentience tingles with my mentor's concern. "This would be the infamous robbery gone wrong. The one that resulted in the death of Fred Clements."

"Is that the robber or the security guard?"

"Fred was the security guard and an old backgammon companion. The two of us wiled away dozens of Sunday afternoons over snifters of brandy and the backgammon board." A melancholy sigh escapes. "In fact, he knew Jedediah. They shared a love for the sport of golf."

There's no time for me to point out that an activity that involves standing on grass and riding in a cart doesn't sound like a sport. However, the mention of Silas's older brother does spark a psychic flutter. "Silas, you said 'knew Jedediah.' Was the past tense in reference to Fred, or did your brother cross over?"

"Indeed. My brother's transition was peaceful and our last days together were filled with fond reminiscing. There was an intimate service with his closest friends. He left most of his estate to his favorite animal rescue and a scholarly research grant at his alma mater. My call was meant to inform you of my return to Pin Cherry tomorrow. Although, I will make a future trip to his home to collect the treasured tomes he left me."

"I honestly want to hear the entire story, Silas, but I don't know how much time I have until they come back in. I think I can handle the gang, but what do I do about the ghosts?"

"Mizithra, I hate to sound like an impaired Victrola vinyl, but you must do what you always do. Discover their unfinished business and help them cross over."

"But—"

THE HANDLE ON THE DOOR to the bank manager's office slowly twists. I end the call and struggle to shove the phone back into my pocket.

When the door opens, I'm surprised to see the cheery mask of Alice rather than the rabbit's ears. "Mitzy? That's your name, right?"

"Yeah, that's my name. Come on in, Alice."

"No. Can't. I don't want Ears to see me. But, um, I just need to say that the guys are, like, getting antsy. And there's more super extra stuff happening. You know, with the lights and the temperature dropping. You were totally keeping them calm."

Now's my chance. "Alice, I know how weird this is going to sound, but do you believe in ghosts?"

For a moment, it appears her plastic mask has gained the ability to change its expression. She nods fervently. "Totally. Ever since my Nan passed, there's been— Things have happened. But is that what you think this is? For reals?"

"I'm no expert." Far be it from me to share my actual paranormal experience with my captors. "But what other explanation is there? I mean, I said the stuff about the building shifting, or whatever, because I didn't want the Mad Hatter shooting anyone. Honestly, though, I think it's ghosts."

Alice places a hand over the mouth on her mask. "Unfinished business. My Nan talked about that all the time before she died. She was, like, obsessed with finishing all her business. She didn't want to be trapped, you know?"

"I think you're right. You need to get me back out there. Maybe the two of us can figure out what their unfinished business is and get them out of here."

Alice nods her blonde plastic locks. "I'll talk to Ears. Sometimes he actually listens to me."

"Good luck."

She steps out of the room, and I'm tempted to try my hand at the transmutation Silas mentioned. However, I have no idea what will actually happen to the plastic band, and if it melts or something, I'd have a hard time explaining that. I'll hold off and see if Alice can work some magic on that darn bunny.

Hopefully Erick sent someone to update Twiggy, and maybe Grams will overhear. Yeesh, what am I worried about! News travels faster than light in this town. If Ghost-ma wasn't tethered to that bookshop, she'd already be here—cracking skulls.

This time, the door opens with forceful confidence. "Alice said she needs your help. You believe this nonsense?"

Not having the benefit of knowing which nonsense he's referring to, I keep my mouth shut and nod my head.

He stomps over, grabs a pair of scissors from the pen cup on the desk, and cuts the zip tie from my wrists.

"Thank you." Wow! I can't believe I didn't see the scissors. Here I was gearing up for some grand alchemical working, when there was a pair of scissors literally within reach.

"No funny business. No calls unless I say so."

It takes every ounce of self-control I don't possess to keep from giggling at a giant rabbit telling me "no funny business." Yet, somehow, I manage. "Copy that."

He storms out of the office and I follow in what I hope is a timid fashion. Alice is waiting outside. She grabs my hand and pulls me toward the hallway. "It started downstairs. I think we should creep back to the vault."

I glance over my shoulder and clock the security guard still sitting with the two remaining hostages and nod my head toward the basement. However, the masked disco delinquent is nowhere to be seen. "Sounds good. Do I lead or follow?"

She shrugs. "There's room to walk side by side."

Falling in step beside her, she presses her shoulder close as we head down to the old vault.

My mood ring is lifeless. There's no tingling on the back of my neck. I don't think the ghost guy is down here.

Stepping into the vault, Alice aims the light on her phone all around the corners. Nothing happens, so she assumes no ghosts.

However, when the beam scans the far corner, I see the ghost of the gunman, unmasked, wiping tears from his eyes.

"Total waste. There's nothing here, Mitzy. Let's head back upstairs."

"You go ahead. I'll hang out for another minute and see if anything happens."

She shivers visibly and steps back. "Cool. Sounds good. I'll hang at the back door with Queenie."

"All right. I'll come and find you in a few."

She backs out of the tomb-like vault and footsteps race to the upper floor. Complete darkness envelops me, and my heart races as I take a seat on the floor. "Hey, I know you're in here. I can help you. I don't have a lot of time to explain and I can't let anyone else know that I can see you, but I can help."

A soft glow emanates from the corner, and the formerly masked gunman floats expectantly toward me. "Hey, pretty lady. You sure you're not trippin'?"

"I'm not trippin'. I can see you."

"Groovy."

His vocabulary seems out of sync with his wardrobe. Although, if he grew up in the '60s, it kind of makes sense. Still, the wardrobe screams *Saturday Night Fever.* I can almost picture the gold cross dangling from a chain around his neck.

"Hey, seems like you have some regrets about what happened. Is that your unfinished business?"

"Regrets? Sure, I guess. I been chillin' in this bank with the guy I killed for over fifty years. It kinda had an effect on me. I just wanna keep on truckin', but —"

"Fate had other plans?"

"Right on, sister."

"Well, have you told Mr. Clements how you feel?"

"You know it. I apologized and everything. So,

why am I still here? It's a bummer, man. I don't get it."

"I've heard bits and pieces of the story. Sounds like more than one person was killed. Is it possible that you're responsible for more than one murder?"

His glowing eyes turn black. The frightening image of a hovering ghost with two soulless black holes for eyes causes my chest to tighten and my stomach to pitch.

"I never shot that lady. You hear? It wasn't me."

I raise both of my hands in surrender. "Hey, I'm not saying it was. I'm here to help. Remember?"

"Yeah, I don't blame the youngbloods. I would've done the same. We all said as much at breakfast that morning, you know?"

"Said what?" My head tilts with interest.

"If somebody goes down, we dump all the heavy stuff on them. Nobody dies in vain. No questions."

"All right. So you died, and they said you were the mastermind behind the whole robbery and that you shot all the people. Wouldn't ballistics have proven that the bullet didn't come from your gun?"

The blackness in his eyes is replaced by flickering flames. "You the fuzz? You pigs trying to trick me into a confession?"

"Hey, you're dead. Confession or not, you already paid the ultimate price." Taking a deep breath, I try a different approach. "What's your name?"

"Donnie. What's yours, foxy mama?"

"It's Mitzy." I choose to ignore the inappropriate comment. "Look, Donnie, I want to help you. I'm not a cop. Full disclosure, though, I am dating the current sheriff. But he doesn't know anything about this. All right?"

Donnie adjusts his snug polyester bellbottoms and tugs at the large points of his shirt's collar. "We're cool."

"So, tell me how you got blamed for murdering the woman."

"The lady was crying about her kid at home and made a run for the door. Tiny Tim threatened her and the security guard pulled out a back-up piece."

"This woman, was it Lindy McElroy?"

"S'pose it was. I heard plenty a talk—after I died." Donnie shrugs and continues. "I thought the rent-a-cop was gonna light up my buddy." He wipes a hand across his mouth. "I shot him and he got one off before he hit the dirt."

"Did the guard mean to shoot you, or was he still aiming at Tiny Tim?"

"Who knows? Tiny Tim shot that lady, but I shot the guard."

Hugging my knees to my chest, I lean toward the disco ghost. "Then what happened?"

"Tiny Tim tried to save me. We were tight. But the guard musta nicked an artery when he lit me up. I was bleedin' out fast. One minute I was sound as a pound and next I'm slipping away. Tiny Tim wanted to get me to my feet, but the whole room was spinning. I told him to peace out, and I asked him to take care of Shelly for me."

My insufferable snoopiness interjects. "Was Shelly your old lady?"

"Yeah. She was the best." He wipes an ethereal tear from the corner of his eye and continues. "Things got foggy real fast, but I think Tiny Tim put his gun in my other hand."

"So you died in the bank with a gun in each hand. As far as the cops knew, you killed everybody."

"Yeah. They threw it all on me. Just like we planned." His harsh empty laughter says he's no longer a fan of the plan that seemed flawless when he was alive.

"Donnie, I promise if you help me protect these hostages. I'll clear your name once this robbery is over."

"Whaddya take me for? You might be a stone fox, but I know you're only trying to save your own neck."

"Look, I don't like to brag, buddy, but I've solved a bunch of murders and other cases since I came to this town. And I happen to specialize in helping earthbound spirits cross over."

"Oh yeah? Like who?"

"I can't break my confidentiality. Part of my service is keeping the secrets I'm asked to keep." Not that any of that is true, but thankfully Donnie the disco burglar can't read my thoughts like Grams.

He nods, and his expression is dead serious. "I respect that. I'll help you—on one condition."

We all saw this coming, right? "What's your condition?"

"If I smell a rat, your little friend Tilly is—" He draws a finger across his neck in the internationally understood sign for murder.

"Understood. I double-cross you, Tilly pays the price. No problem. I always keep my word."

"What now, broad?" Donnie drifts absently around the dank, musty vault.

"I need to make sure you've changed your ways. You hustle up to the lobby and send Fred down, so I can brief him. I can't be seen talking to ghosts up there." I point toward the main floor.

Let it not be said that Donnie lost his sense of humor over the years. He takes my command seriously and launches into a spotless rendition of the Hustle. Mind you, my only reference is John Travolta's version, but Donnie does him proud as he dances his way out of the bank tomb.

The silence presses against my eardrums, and Erick's face fills my mind. Note to self: I may have uncovered the number one reason I'm avoiding having an honest discussion with Erick. If I promise to tell him the truth, I'll have to *keep* my promise.

CHAPTER 10
ERICK

I SHOULD'VE HEARD from Mitzy by now. Something's gone wrong. I know it. "Paulsen."

The small but tough deputy strides over and avoids eye contact. "Yes, Sheriff."

"We'll discuss your breach of protocol during the food delivery later. I'm gonna head inside and debrief Cheryl. I need you to take point on this operation."

"10-4." She swallows hard and looks up. "I know it wasn't protocol, Sheriff. I just wanted to find out if my mom was—"

I can't say I've ever seen weakness of any kind from Deputy Paulsen. But the emotion that tightens her throat and steals her words is palpable. Leaning forward, I lower my voice. "Hey, Pauly. Don't worry about it. You run things out here, and I'll make sure

she's taken care of. We got her out safe. That's all
that matters."

Deputy Paulsen's eyes speak volumes, but now
isn't the time to push. Her right hand grips the
handle of her gun and she nods sternly.

We both ignore the tears welling in her eyes.

"Sheriff, do I have the authority to give Boomer
the green light?"

"Negative. If they shoot first, all bets are off.
Otherwise, nobody takes a shot till I get back."

"10-4."

Leaving my capable deputy in charge, I head
indoors for a hot cup of coffee and hopefully some
insight.

Paulsen's mother sits in the bullpen with a wool
blanket tucked around her shoulders and a
steaming cup of joe in her hands.

"Cheryl, I sure was glad to see you walk out of
that bank."

"You and me both, Ricky."

The nickname brings a self-conscious flush to
my face. I forget how much time she and my mother
spend together. Somehow, when my mom calls me
Ricky, I can let it slide like water off a duck's back,
but I can't have my deputies picking up on that handle. "It's Sheriff Harper when we're in the station,
ma'am."

Her mouth opens in genuine shock and she nods. "Oh, you betcha. You betcha, Sheriff."

"You look pretty comfortable where you're at, Cheryl. Is it okay if I debrief you, here, in the bullpen?"

"Of course, Ri— Sheriff. I've got no secrets from you and my Pauly."

Taking out my trusty pen and pad, I pull up a chair. "We already have some of this information. But I want to go through the basics and make sure we didn't miss anything. How many armed robbers?"

"Well, now. I suppose there's five. But I'm not sure if that sweet little Alice is packing any heat. I can't say as I saw a gun. But there's definitely five in the crew."

"Okay. How many hostages?"

"Gosh! There was Tilly, and me, and Mr. Curb, and that blabbermouth Jeff, and, of course, your sweet Mitzy. My goodness, she's awful calm under pressure. I can see why the two of you are such a good match."

It's going to be harder to keep her on topic than I thought. "So, five hostages in total. Tilly's been released. Of course, you're here. That leaves Mitzy, Jeff, and Mr. Curb inside. Is that correct?"

"Oh, Sheriff, you don't have to take that formal tone with me. I'm not a suspect, am I?"

"Of course not, Cheryl. I just wanted to make sure I heard you correctly. Seems like Mitzy indicated there could be some additional hostages. She was trying to signal me when she picked up the food, but I've clearly misunderstood."

Cheryl tugs the blanket tight around her shoulders and leans forward. Her eyes widen and her voice is barely audible. "Well now, she might have been referring to the poltergeist."

You could knock me over with a feather. "A poltergeist?"

Mrs. Paulsen nods in complete seriousness. "Every once in a while, strange things happen at the bank. Mr. Curb always tries to brush it off, but I can see the truth in his eyes. He knows they aren't just accidents. Like today! A whole stack of those deposit slips flew up in the air. Now, he'd have to think I fell off the turnip truck yesterday to believe a wind came through the bank all willy-nilly."

Mrs. Paulsen's wild tale sheds a whole new light on Mitzy's signal. Two. The two and the wiggling hand: two ghosts. I'm not sure I would've figured it out without Cheryl's tipoff, but the wiggly hand gesture from *Wayne's World* might've sunk through my thick skull at some point. "So there's a poltergeist in the bank. Interesting."

"Now, don't look at me like that, Ricky. Sorry,

Sheriff. I'm not pulling your leg. You remember when that gunshot went off, don't you?"

I attempt to keep the worry from my face as I nod.

"Dontcha know, one of the typewriters flew right off a desk. There wasn't a soul around it. Well, no *living* soul! I'm telling you, the poltergeist knocked that typewriter off. And if the silly Mad Hatter hadn't been such a bad shot . . . Gosh, someone could've been seriously injured."

"So the Mad Hatter is the one watching the front door?"

"That's right. And I'll tell you something else. I think he's out of ammunition. I've got real good hearing. Ask Pauly. After he fired that second shot, I saw him slink over to the White Rabbit and they thought they were whispering, but ol' Cheryl picked up a thing or two." She taps her left ear with a finger and continues. "He was out of ammunition. I know they looked around for some spare, but I don't think they found any."

"Well, thank you for telling me that." Her tip isn't enough to have me risk storming the place, but it's something to think about. "You said there were five. Alice, the White Rabbit, the Mad Hatter, and who else?"

"Let's see . . . One young man is dressed up as the Queen of Hearts. And then there's a boy in a

Cheshire Cat mask. He's the one they said got arrested for boosting a car. Is that the right term, Sheriff? Boosting?"

"It's one of them, Cheryl. Can you tell me anything about their voices, or did you see any of their hands?"

"No hands. Whoever put those getups together thought of everything. They all have gloves. And their voices sound regular. You know, like they're from around here. Not nearby, 'course. More like city folk. But not far. You know what else I thought of, Sheriff?"

Cheryl Paulsen is an unstoppable force, so I best let my informant roll on. "What's that?"

"I don't think it's any accident that they've robbed the Pin Cherry Harbor Bank & Trust. Round here about everyone knows we don't have a security guard." She waves that tidbit away and chuckles. "But guess what else? It's not a chain. Well, not a national chain. Because, you know, if they were knocking off those big-name branches, the Feds would have been here in a heartbeat."

"That's an excellent point, Cheryl. I sure do appreciate all your helpful observations. Let me update the team, and see if I can find someone to drive you home."

"Oh pshaw! I'm not going to waste your manpower on giving me a ride home, Sheriff. I'm happy as a lark right here. In fact, why don't I pop into the diner and get you some food? I'm sure the lot of you must be half starved. You can't survive on donuts alone."

When my cell phone rings, I answer immediately. "Sheriff Harper."

"Hey, Erick. Did you miss me?"

No matter what my heart screams, I have to maintain a professional attitude. "Let's remember you're on a recorded line, Miss Moon."

"Copy that. I've only got a couple of seconds before they check on me. I'm downstairs by the old vault."

"Okay. Are the hostages all okay?"

"They were when I left. Did you get my hand signals?"

Whew! Somehow I have to let her know I figured out the part about the ghosts, without announcing to everyone listening that the local sheriff believes in poltergeists. "I did. After I talked to Cheryl and heard more about the typewriter and the deposit slips, I figured it all out." Mitzy is pretty sharp, she'll know what I mean.

"Cracked the code, eh, Sheriff?"

Despite the tension, she pulls a small chuckle from me. "Anything to report?"

"Someone's coming. I gotta go. Just wanted to hear your voice."

The call ends and my heart sinks.

My coffee is cold, the donuts are stale, and I have a bad feeling about this bus option.

Maybe I should call her back and see if we can come up with some kind of excuse to release another hostage. I hit the number and the call rings several times.

"Oh hello, Sheriff. Been a while since we talked."

"Yes. I'm calling to give you an update on the bus. It's proving difficult to find window coverings. It could delay delivery of the vehicle for another hour."

"Hold on, Sheriff." Mitzy must've turned away or put her hand over the phone.

Muffled voices, raised voices, Mitzy's calm tone, and she's back. "The White Rabbit said if you can get the bus here in thirty minutes he'll release another hostage."

"Any chance that hostage will be you?"

"Not unless Hades has suddenly frozen over, Sheriff. Can you do it?"

"I can get it here in thirty minutes with no curtains. Do we have a deal?"

A bit more mumbling filters through the phone before Mitzy returns. "That's affirmative, Sheriff. No curtains. Thirty minutes. You get a hostage."

The line goes dead.

Throwing my jacket on as I head outside, I offer an update to Deputy Paulsen. "So, I'm going to head over to Clarence's shop and give him the new specs. There was no answer when I called. Plus, maybe there's something I can do to speed things along. I definitely want to make it in under that thirty-minute window and get another hostage out of there."

"10-4. Sorry it won't be Moon, Sheriff."

"That makes two of us. I'll let you know when the bus is on the move."

Paulsen nods and picks up the bullhorn with her left hand.

As I walk to the end of the street to grab one of the extra vehicles from the Broken Rock station, Paulsen's voice echoes loud and strong down the laneway as she updates the armed crew about their new point of contact.

"**WHAT'S UP, CLARENCE?** How goes the remodel?"

"Not as easy as you might think, Sheriff. I've only got enough of this sheeting to cover half the windows on one side. It's gonna be hours before I get my hands on some more."

Resting a hand on his grease-streaked shoulder, I give it a squeeze. "Then I've got some good news, buddy. No curtains required. I cut a deal with the crooks to release another hostage if I get the bus there in under thirty minutes."

"Fine by me, Sheriff. I already rigged the gas tank. She looks full as can be, but there's barely two gallons in there! You can hop in and drive it over right now."

"Good to know. There are a couple of things I wanted you to do before you take it over. Shouldn't take you more than twenty to twenty-five minutes, if you're as good as they say." I gesture toward his massive collection of tools as I throw down the challenge.

Clarence tugs his beanie down over his ears and crosses his arms over his puffed-up chest. "Oh, you know I'm that good. What can I do ya for, Sheriff?"

Unfortunately, Alice and the White Rabbit come downstairs before Disco Donnie convinces the security guard to pay me a visit. With the time frame getting mashed down to thirty minutes, that doesn't give me much of a chance to figure out what the security guard's unfinished business might be.

The White Rabbit waves the tip of his handgun in the light cast from a cell phone. "Let's head back upstairs. And no more field trips without my permission. Understood, Alice?"

"Yeah. You bet, Ears. You're in charge."

We all head back to the main lobby.

To be fair, Donnie is talking the security guard's ear off, and as soon as I get to the top of the stairs Fred peeks around his frenemy's apparition to double-check the story.

Nodding as casually as I can, I hope to encourage the guard to trust me. Queenie was still at the back door when we passed. The Mad Hatter has a lock on the front door and windows, and the Cheshire Cat sits cross-legged on a desk, staring at the two seated hostages.

Hoping that the landline is being monitored by dispatch—or someone—I walk toward that desk and lean against it with my back screening the telephone and the dangling receiver.

The White Rabbit hasn't noticed the breach yet, so I attempt to get some potentially helpful information for the law enforcement officers camped outside. "Hey, did you find any ammunition for Hatter?"

The fuzzy white ears tilt sideways. "Why do you ask? You wearin' a wire?"

"Me? Wearing a wire? Like as an everyday accessory? I came into the bank to get some money for the register at my bookshop. I didn't know I was going to be a pawn in a robbery gone wrong." Bad choice of words.

"Hey, it hasn't gone wrong. We got our getaway vehicle on the way and we got our ticket out of town right here." He raises the gun toward my head.

"Then I'd advise you to be careful with that thing. If you mess up this ticket"—I wave a hand at my person—"more than the robbery is going to go wrong." Last time I popped off, I ended up in a zip tie. This time, he lowers the gun and nods. Apparently, I've made more headway than I thought.

"If they don't make it in under thirty, I'm taking out the one called Jeff." Rabbit waves his gun toward the other two hostages.

"Understood. Like I told you before, Sheriff Harper doesn't make promises he can't keep. The bus will be here. Don't worry."

Alice and Ears both nod.

Time to make one last attempt at gathering intel. "I'm trying to come up with the best order of loading onto the bus. When you guys come out of the bank, you're going to be targets. I was asking about Hatter's ammunition so we know who can take a strategic position, and who can't."

The fuzzy ears bob up and down thoughtfully. "I like the way you think, Mitzy. The Hatter's totally out. The spare shotgun shells were in the van. His gun is a prop at this point."

Dear Lord baby Jesus! I hope someone important heard that. "Got it. Then you better put him on me."

Alice's painted-on grin nods excitedly. "That's brilliant. The cops won't know Hatter's out of ammunition, and if anything goes down, the rest of us can return fire."

"You're packing, Alice?"

She pats the pocket of her apron, and I have to figure out a way to convey this information out loud. "You had a gun in the pocket of your apron this whole time? Wow! I never saw you pull it out. Nicely done."

She takes a mock bow and the White Rabbit checks the time on his phone. "They've got ten minutes, Mitzy. You better call."

"Sure. No problem." Pulling my phone out of my pocket, I tap speed dial for Sheriff Harper. There are several strange clicks and a disappointing ending.

"Deputy Paulsen for Sheriff Harper."

"Where's Erick?" That question wasn't for the gang of armed robbers, it was strictly for me.

"He went over to the garage to give Clarence the news to eighty-six the curtains. There was no answer when he called and he didn't want to lose any time. He put me in charge. What's going on?"

"They want an update. Time is running out. Is the bus on its way?"

Paulsen must put the call on mute, because the line goes silent. The gang fidgets, but in a moment she hops back on. "The bus is en route. When it arrives, send the exchange hostage out the front door, before you board."

"No problem. We'll send Jeff out. We're leaving Mr. Curb in the bank, and the Mad Hatter will have his shotgun firmly planted in my back when the rest of us get on the bus."

She scoffs.

"Hey, Paulsen, I know you're not too concerned about whether I make it out of this in one piece or not, but I'm under the impression that Erick is. So, tell your sniper to pull back. Nobody takes a shot at the crew. My life is on the line. You heard that, right? The Mad Hatter's double-barrel shotgun in the middle of my back. Can I be any clearer? Or do you need to call dispatch and have them play it back for you?" Ending the call with a huff, I shove my phone into my pocket with unnecessary force.

I hope they bought that performance.

The White Rabbit lowers his gun and nods. "I heard Smiley offer you a position on the crew. I'll double down on that. You got a real skill for negotiating. Compared to most women, you've got nerves of steel."

Pressing my lips together to stifle a smug grin, I nod in what I hope passes for humble acceptance.

He bought it.

Of course, the weak link in the chain is hoping that Deputy Paulsen can unravel my cryptic message and will review the dispatch tapes. If they're monitoring the call from Tilly's desk on a recorded line, they'll know that the gun in the middle of my back is empty.

Translation: they can take all the sniper shots they want.

With the few minutes I have remaining, I need to talk to Fred Clements. An otherworldly distraction would be mighty helpful. I hope Disco Donnie is smarter than he looks. "Hey, Ears, I know the whole ghost thing sounds weird, but I'd hate for them to throw some kind of monkey wrench into your final getaway."

Luckily, Donnie picks up what I'm laying down, and knocks over one of the gold stanchions holding a short length of velvet rope beside the empty customer queue.

The White Rabbit jumps and shakes his long ears. "Make it snappy, and Alice is gonna escort you down there."

"Copy that." Grabbing my puffy coat from the nearby desk, I gesture for Alice to follow me.

At the top of the steps, she hesitates and clenches my arm. "Mitzy?"

"Yeah, what's wrong?"

"This ghost is, like, really scaring me. Can you go down to the vault by yourself? I'll stay right here at the top of the stairs. Ears doesn't have to know."

I couldn't have planned this better—if I'd planned it. I'll promise to keep her little secret, and now I might get a favor in return. "Totally. I'm not thrilled about it myself. Um, I noticed you're not super into guns."

"Yeah, not even!" Alice rolled her eyes.

Now for my last-ditch play.

A couple weeks ago, Silas had instructed me to study an old tome containing barely readable essays on persuasive speech. I've slogged through about half of it, but I can't practice on Grams or Pyewacket. Technically, I could practice on Twiggy —but if she ever found out, she'd send me to join Ghost-ma in the "in between" without a second thought! No time like the present . . . "Alice, would you mind giving me your gun in case things go sideways down there?" I think I have the tone and pacing correct. Fingers crossed.

Once again, I can almost swear her plastic mask is capable of expressions. A wave of relief rolls off her. "OMG. I hate carrying a gun. I've never used one yet. In fact, you should just keep it. If something goes down when we're loading into that bus, I'm not going to be the one to, like, shoot back. You know what I'm saying?"

"Absolutely. No one has to know. We're cool."

She nods and hands me her gun.

"Thanks." I aim the gun at nothing as I creep down the stairwell toward the darkened vault. As soon as I'm past her sight line, I check the safety and tuck the gun into the back of my waistband—

hidden under my puffy coat. The naïve ingénue, Alice, might trust me, but I'm pretty sure the White Rabbit would frown on one of his hostages having a firearm.

As soon as I walk past the thick metal door, I feel a presence. "Mr. Clements, is that you?"

He barely shimmers in the darkness. "Donnie says you can fix things. Why should I believe him, or you?"

"Mr. Clements, I'm a very good friend of Silas Willoughby. He said the two of you passed many an evening over snifters of brandy and a backgammon table. I'm not sure how much you know about his extracurricular activities, but he believes in my ability to help earthbound spirits cross over."

It's as though someone slowly slides up a dimmer switch, and Fred's ethereal form glows with increased intensity. "You know Silas? Is that ol' dog still alive?"

"He is. He's probably going to outlive all of us." Oops, open mouth, insert foot. Obviously, he's already outlived Fred.

Lucky for me, Fred assumes the joke was intentional. As he laughs, his image solidifies before me.

"Look, Fred, we don't have a lot of time. Tell me what happened that day in the bank?"

He stares at me, and his apparition immediately dims.

"Listen, I'm not here to judge you. Donnie already told me his version, but I need to hear your side of the story. I can help you. I promise."

"It was a Wednesday, not that it matters. Every day was the same. Efficient staff, pleasant locals, and me locking up."

"But something different happened this Wednesday."

He nervously tucks his uniform shirt into his pants. "They came out of nowhere. There were five of them, just like today. There'd never been a robbery at the bank before, and I hadn't fired my gun in almost a decade. You know how it is. Nothing much ever happens in Pin Cherry."

I nod encouragingly and keep my opinions about Pin Cherry to myself.

"Well, that McElroy lady was beside herself. She had a real young babe at home, and she just wouldn't calm down. You know?"

I didn't, but for purposes of expediency, I nod and smile.

"They cleared out the cash drawers in seconds and were gonna force me to take 'em down to the vault. We turned to head toward the stairs, and Lindy made a break for the door. Donnie's friend . . . Of course, I didn't know him at the time, but Donnie and I have done our fair share of chewing the fat in the last fifty years. So now I know the guy's name was Tiny Tim. He aims his gun at Mrs. McElroy, and I reached down to grab my backup piece from my ankle holster." Fred pauses, pats his round belly, and shakes his head. "Now, I'm not as young or as svelte as I used to be, and it took me a second to get that gun and myself situated. But when I had him in my sights, I froze."

"What do you mean?"

"I couldn't do it. Couldn't pull the trigger. My brain was stuck in some kind of loop, you know? Well, Donnie saw me draw down on his buddy, and fired at me. When Donnie's gun went off, ol' Tiny Tim shot that poor lady. Donnie's bullet hit me and I collapsed to my knees. As I went down, I fired. I don't know what I was aiming at."

"But you missed Tiny Tim and shot Donnie instead."

"Sure did. I wasn't trying to get revenge for him shooting me, or anything like that. I wish I woulda shot Tiny Tim. At least I could've avenged poor Mrs. McElroy's death. I was just a damn coward. I've had to live with that every day." He turns away from me and he's barely a flicker.

"What's your biggest regret, Fred?"

"That I didn't take the shot on Tiny Tim. If I'd just taken the shot—"

"There's no way to go back in time. And there's no way to know if the outcome would've been any different. The bottom line is you helped us out to-day. You kept this gang on their toes, and, so far, all the hostages are safe."

"That wasn't me! That's Donnie. He always thought it was a hoot to mess with humans. Me? I just creep around in the shadows. Good for nothing in death, just like I was good for nothing in life."

Maybe if I come at this problem from a different angle, I can get Fred to end his pity party. "What happened after? Once you were a ghost?"

"Well, I saw that scoundrel Tiny Tim put his gun in Donnie's left hand. That way, Donnie would have both guns. The one that shot me and the one that shot Lindy. They laid the whole thing at his feet, just like Donnie said they would."

"Look, Fred, I'm going to help Donnie take care of his unfinished business, and I'm pretty sure that means convicting the right person of Lindy McElroy's murder. But for you, it seems like something different is needed. I think you need to be brave. I think you need to go upstairs and do whatever you have to do to make sure Jeff and Mr. Curb get out of this thing unscathed."

"What about you? Once you're on the bus, there's nothing I can do for you."

"You don't need to take responsibility for me, Fred. I've always been ten pounds of trouble stuffed into a five-pound sack. I promise you, if you make sure Jeff and Mr. Curb get out of this alive, I'll be back to help you cross over."

"Mitzy, come on! The bus is here!" Alice's nervous voice trickles down the stairwell and echoes inside the vault.

"They're playin' my song, Fred. Have we got a deal?"

He stands at the position of attention and pops a salute. "Yes, ma'am."

I run up the stairs, and Alice meets me halfway. "Any luck?"

"Not really. I hate to say it, but I think there's more than one angry spirit in this bank. The sooner we get out of here, the better. Now let's send Jeff out the front and see if Ears came up with the loading order for us."

She grips my arm as though we've been friends since elementary school, and we rush past Queenie, back to the main lobby.

The White Rabbit has the keys out and nods when he sees me. "We put Mr. Curb in his office, and we're about to send out Jeff. I decided you're gonna drive the bus. I don't want to take a chance on that sniper picking off one of my crew once we're through the alley."

"No problem. So what's the order?"

"You first, Hatter's got your back, then it's me, Alice, Smiley, and Queenie bringing up the rear."

"Understood. Do you want me to walk Jeff out, or just open the door for him?"

The White Rabbit strokes his long plastic whiskers and makes a low humming sound. "Go ahead and walk him out. That way, they know you're okay."

"Good plan. Come on, Jeff."

Ears unlocks the door and I reach for my phone. "Almost forgot. I need to let them know we're releasing a hostage." I wipe my hand comically across my brow, and the Mad Hatter chuckles.

Once I've prepped Deputy Paulsen, I push the door open and maneuver Jeff out onto the sidewalk.

The former blabbermouth staggers forward, and, once he stumbles into the street, a deputy from Broken Rock swoops in and escorts him off to the side. I turn and lift the back of my coat in the direction of Deputy Paulsen. I'm not sure whether she sees the gun tucked into my waistband, or what she'll think if she does, but every piece of information could matter.

The door closes, and Ears secures it.

I gesture to the lock. "Good thinking. We don't want them coming in behind us while we're loading onto the bus."

He nods his large ears and drops the ring of keys on a desk. The desk on the opposite side of the lobby from Tilly's. Looking away, I thank the powers that be that no one has noticed that receiver dangling off the side of her desk.

The White Rabbit holds his gun in the air. "Let's move!"

The five of us hustle toward the back door to join Queenie, who's carefully peering through the small crack between the door and the doorjamb.

"What's the story, Queenie?"

"All clear, Ears. The guy who dropped it off exited the alley that way. I didn't see him look up, or make any signals. I think they were telling the truth when they said they pulled back."

"Okay. Lineup."

I take the lead, the Mad Hatter behind me, and so on.

Slowly opening the door, I poke my head out and glance up and down the alley.

Hatter prods me with his shotgun. "Let's go. The longer we wait, the worse it's going to be."

Lurching forward, I head directly to the bus. Classic me, stumbles as I attempt to hustle up the deep steps. My knee bangs sharply into the metal edge and I hiss an unladylike expletive.

The White Rabbit shouts from the back, "What's the holdup?"

I scramble to my feet and slide into the driver's seat. Hatter takes the seat behind me. Alice and the Cheshire Cat head straight to the back, while the

White Rabbit and Queenie hunker down in the aisle about halfway between.

Ears shouts, "Let's go! Get this bus moving!"

I glance at the gas gauge, and can't believe it's full. I really thought Erick would pull a fast one on them, but I guess he didn't want to take any chances with my life. Shifting the beast into drive, I ease down the alley and wonder if anyone's going to take a shot at us.

For a brief moment, I can almost feel Erick's presence but it slips away. I really hope he listened to the dispatch tape. And that he got the clue about Canada. Man, do I want to see him again . . . to kiss his wonderful, pouty lips.

I love you, Erick.

And with that, I turn toward Main Street, head past the newspaper office, and wind my way back toward the scenic highway that encircles our great lake.

Canada, here we come.

CHAPTER 12

THE LUXURY MOTOR coach is easier to drive than I'd feared. My brief experience driving bobtail trucks for the plant nursery back in Arizona has come in handy. And I'm extremely grateful for a bus with an automatic transmission. However, now that we're out on the open road, my thoughts are wandering.

What's going to happen when we approach the Canadian border? If Erick figured out my not-so-subtle code referencing CC, his Canadian Mountie buddy, there's likely to be an armed reception. Since I'm sitting in the front seat, driving the get-away vehicle, there's a higher-than-average chance that their sniper will take me out first.

I've seen the movies. The sniper takes out the driver, the bus swerves, rolls, and skids to a crashing halt just before hitting the law enforcement barricade.

After doing more than my share of stupid things in my life, I've had to face my mortality more than once, but today has a sense of finality I've never felt before.

The energy of the crew is somewhat relaxed, now that we've officially gotten away and are outside the city limits. The Hatter's not even holding his shotgun on me anymore. Even though I knew it wasn't loaded, there's a sense of relief when the boom stick is removed from my right shoulder.

Glancing up into the mirror, I observe the gang. Smiley and Alice are sitting together on the left side of the bus. She has the window seat and has pushed her mask up to get a better view.

She's young. Much younger than I imagined. In fact—my psychic senses flicker back online—she's a minor. Great! Now I'll have to fight between my urge to save her and my need to see justice served. At least I got that gun out of her hands.

Right! I have a loaded gun. I could stop this bus, threaten them with my gun, and run away. Sure, that'd be the thing to do if I was looking to get an award for the world's shortest unsuccessful escape.

There are still three armed robbers on this bus, and my brief relationship with them has definitely taught me that the White Rabbit didn't come to play.

Ears and Queenie still have their disguises on and their guns drawn. Although, the ringleader's hold is way more relaxed than it was in the bank. "Hey, Mitzy?"

"What's up, Doc?"

Queenie and Hatter chuckle at my Bugs Bunny reference.

"You had a solid plan. I'm almost sorry we're going to have to hold you for ransom when we hit Canadian soil."

"Well, you could always let me go, and clear your conscience."

He laughs loudly and adjusts his pistol. "Nah, I don't want your sheriff to think we've gone soft."

At the mention of Erick, my heart sinks. I blew it. I had the world's perfect man, and I chose to keep my secrets rather than trust him fully. Now I'm going to die in a hail of gunfire and never have the opportunity—

The engine sputters. My eyes widen and I look into the mirror.

The White Rabbit is on his feet, walking toward me. "What gives? How much gas we got?"

"It's almost full. I swear. I told you, Erick's a straight shooter."

Before I can continue my defense of the sheriff,

the hairs on the back of my neck blast me with an intense tingle and my mood ring turns to ice as the scene reflected in the giant mirror above my head shifts dramatically.

The floor seems to explode! Carpet flies and metal clangs.

My foot comes off the gas without thinking.

The White Rabbit lurches forward and shouts, "Step on it!"

As though I'm watching an action film, Erick pops up from the floor, grips an open overhead compartment, and swings through the air. He lands two boot-clad feet directly in Queenie's chest as the man in glam attempts to get to his feet.

The Queen of Hearts goes down hard and the White Rabbit pulls his gun.

I can't return fire and drive this thing. But I can drive badly!

Swerving the bus back and forth, I knock Ears off his feet.

The Cheshire Cat shoves Alice into the restroom, pulls his gun, and aims at Erick.

Instinct takes over, and I yell, "Check your six, Sheriff!"

Erick spins and fires a round into Smiley's leg. The Cheshire Cat goes down grinning and drops his gun in the aisle.

The Mad Hatter stands helplessly with his

empty shotgun. But suddenly he's struck with a bolt of bravery. He pushes past Ears and aims the shotgun at the sheriff.

"Red light!" I shout at the top of my lungs and hope Erick has played the game.

He grabs the luggage rack, and I slam on the brakes. The Cheshire Cat's gun slides forward several feet, but not all the way to Erick. Ears and Hatter go down a second time.

The Mad Hatter struggles to get to his feet.

Grabbing the shotgun from Hatter, and using it like a bat, I crack him hard across the side of the head.

I left the bus in drive when I abandoned my post in the driver's seat. It's only idling, but the motor coach inches forward.

As the Hatter tumbles down the stairwell toward the folding door, I flip it open and drop a one-liner even Arnold Schwarzenegger would endorse. Plus, I deliver it in my best Arnold-esque accent, "Looks like this is your stop."

He falls out of the bus, onto the side of the road, and I quickly close the door.

Queenie's wig is askew, and he still hasn't moved.

That leaves an injured cat and an angry rabbit. Not my best day, but at least that evens the odds.

The White Rabbit fires, and Erick jerks backward.

"No!"

I pull the gun from my waistband and fire one into the rabbit's haunch.

When he grips his thigh and goes down, I bring my knee up hard into the side of his head and rip the ears off his murderous body.

He reaches for his fallen pistol. I take aim and shoot at his hand to discourage recovery.

Grabbing his gun, I stumble over him and kick the rabbit's filthy paw off my ankle as I lurch toward Erick.

"Erick! Erick!"

His eyes open, and he lifts his head.

"Don't try to talk. You've been hit. Do you have a radio? I need to call an ambulance."

He makes a fist with his left hand and knocks firmly on his chest. "Ceramic, Moon."

The surge of relief that floods through me is inexplicable. Whatever happens, whatever secrets he needs to know, I'm finally all in. I'm an open book.

As I attempt to embrace Erick, two things happen simultaneously. Someone grips a fistful of my hair, yanks hard, and drags me off Erick.

The Cheshire Cat slinks forward, dragging his injured leg behind.

"Don't move!"

My guns lie on the floor where I dropped them when I fell to my knees beside Erick.

The White Rabbit may not have a gun, but he slips an arm tightly around my throat as he offers his deal. "Drop your gun, Sheriff! You do exactly as I say, or I'll choke the life out of her right before your very eyes." His voice is unwavering, but I can sense the pain he's hiding beneath the surface. He has the upper hand now, but at least I put a bullet in his unlucky rabbit foot—well, leg actually.

Erick drops his gun and gets to his feet with his hands in the air.

I'm such an idiot! We had them on the ropes. My stupid emotions got the better of me. If I'd stayed focused and leaned into my extra senses, I would've known Erick wasn't hurt.

The Cheshire Cat moans loudly as he struggles to his feet and retrieves Erick's weapon. He presses the gun into the sheriff's back.

I don't know exactly how body armor works, but something tells me that a shot from close range is likely to cause some type of injury. Maybe not death, but something bad.

My lungs are screaming for air and things in my peripheral start to get blurry. I don't have a plan, and I'm pretty sure I ruined whatever plan Erick had.

The precise moment I'm about to give up hope,

my natural klutzdom and lack of attention to detail pays off big.

The bus, which has been slowly idling forward, now lurches off the road and plunges into the ditch.

Everything inside the bus goes topsy-turvy. Ears loses his hold on me, and I scramble to put some distance between us as I'm tumbling.

I hope the unexpected lurch is as fortuitous for Erick as it was for me.

Wedged between two of the high-backed seats, I hear a voice that makes everything right in the world.

"Tea party's over. We're all getting off the bus, single file. Mitzy will secure your wrists while I hold the guns."

Un-wedging my rear end from the narrow space between the seats is a daunting task, but eventually I get to my feet—flushed, but alive. Before a satisfied smile can even touch my lips, horror grips my face and nausea turns my stomach.

Alice must've crept out of the bathroom during the last round of shenanigans, and she retrieved Smiley's gun. Her hand is visibly shaking as she aims at Erick. "Look, Sheriff, I don't wanna hurt anyone. Just you and Mitzy get out of the bus. We don't need a hostage anymore. You can get off the bus, and, like, everything will be fine."

Erick doesn't lower his gun, or the pistol he retrieved from the White Rabbit. His eyes dart toward me and I shake my head, "No."

I hope he knows what that means, but, on the off chance that he didn't notice my subtle head movement, or has possibly misinterpreted the signal, I attempt to reach Alice. "Hey, you haven't done anything wrong yet. You didn't take any money at the bank, you didn't hurt anyone, and you actually helped me."

The White Rabbit grumbles. "You helped her, Alice? What the—?"

"Don't listen to him, Alice. You saw what happened at the bank. That ghost was the guy who robbed the bank in the 1970s. He's been haunted by what he did for fifty years. You remember what your Nan said? No unfinished business. Right?"

Her shaky hand lowers the gun a few inches.

I'm getting through. "Alice, if you put your gun down, I know Sheriff Harper will get you the best deal he can. He's fair. I promise you. And I'll pay for a lawyer, if you need one. I'll do whatever it takes. You're too young to ruin your life with one bad decision."

Ears makes a counteroffer. "One bad decision! Who are you kidding? She's been in the crew for over a year. We've knocked off forty-two local banks. There's no way you can prove she had nothing to do with any of this. If we're going down, she's going down."

Erick picks up my torch. "Not necessarily. She doesn't look like the mastermind of this gang. And if she turns state's evidence, I can get her immunity. But you better decide fast, Alice. I've got deputies running a thirty-second delayed pursuit. Once they get here, the deal is off the table."

Alice lowers the gun almost to her side. "What's immunity?"

Dear Lord baby Jesus! She might be younger than I thought. "Alice, immunity means you don't go to jail. You have a second chance. You can make things right."

She doesn't drop the gun, but she slowly collapses onto one of the high-backed luxury seats.

It's over.

I'm alive. Erick's alive.

We captured the gang with no loss of life, and I know how much that last part means to Erick.

CHAPTER 13

ONCE DEPUTY PAULSEN and the reinforcements arrive, the fear I held at bay for nearly four hours hits me like a tsunami. I thought I could make it to the ambulance, but—

The blue eyes smiling down at me are bursting with unspoken emotions. "Hey, you picked a weird time to take a nap, Moon."

I toy with the idea of faking amnesia—again—but that seems played out. "This is like the third time you've tried to send me off in an ambulance, Sheriff. Are you trying to tell me something?"

He inhales sharply, and his lips are on mine in a flash. "Just that I love you. And I'm glad there were no corpses today."

My heart stutters in my chest as the replay of

the bullet hitting him on the bus plays on repeat inside my head. "Me too. Hey, I need to tell—"

"Sheriff, the minor says she wants to cut a deal. We need you out here." Deputy Paulsen nods once in my direction.

My true confessions to Erick will have to wait. I return Paulsen's nod. When she lay on that icy sidewalk today and begged me to get them to send out her mom—well, that was the closest she's ever come to being human in my presence.

I take the blood pressure cuff off my right arm and assure the paramedic that I'm fine. He shakes his head, but lets me leave.

The scene is finale worthy. The sun is dipping into the west. Pinkish-orange light reflects off the drifting snow and softens the harsh flashing lights of the cruisers and emergency vehicles.

The gang, officially unmasked, stands in handcuffs under the watchful eyes of ten sheriff's deputies.

A tall deputy with intense brown eyes approaches. "Hey, I'm Boomer. You did a heckuva job today. I've seen a few of these hostage situations go south real fast." He offers his hand and I shake it firmly.

"Nice to meet you. I'm Mitzy Moon."

"Oh, trust me, I know. Harper asked me to take you into town. He's got to escort the minor back to the station and get her immunity locked down. He said he'll catch up with you in about an hour." Boomer gestures toward a Broken Rock vehicle.

My gaze lingers on Erick's back, but I know his duty to the citizens comes first. "Sure. Thanks." I wave, but no one sees.

Boomer kindly makes the drive in silence, and I thank him again when he drops me at the bookshop.

Grams is on me the second I crack the door. She's so close it feels a little like possession.

"Oh, Mitzy! Odell told me what happened. I've been frantic." She tries to hug me, but she's too freaked out to have any substance.

"I'm completely knackered. Can you give me some time to shower and get my emotions under control?"

"Knackered, sweetie?" She arches a perfectly drawn brow.

"Is that what I said? Weird. My mom used to say that at the end of a long day. Anyway, I'm gonna hop—let me rephrase—collapse into a steamy shower or maybe a bubbly tub and try to forget everything I ever knew about talking rabbits in Wonderland."

"If you insist, dear."

"I do." Stumbling up the circular staircase, I'm sort of aware of Ghost-ma's continued warnings and concerns, but mostly my brain is trying every trick in the book to forget that gunshot on the bus.

SADLY, MY DREAM of a quiet night confessing my psychic secrets to Erick is not to be. When I hit the medallion of twisted ivy and exhale as the bookcase door slides open—

Half the town is crammed into my bookshop, and Twiggy is passing pizzas around like she hasn't a priceless book care in the world.

All right, I guess this is happening. I dive into the fray and let the hugs and laughter wash away everything the water missed.

Gazing at all the faces of the people I love, crowded into my apartment and spilling onto the Rare Books Loft, my heart feels full. Erick and I have to tell and retell the story of our motor coach adventure until the muscles in my jaw hurt. However, the enthusiasm of our friends and family doesn't wane.

Stellen grabs a fifth slice of pepperoni and pineapple pizza and nudges Erick with his elbow. "Could you hear anything when you were inside that compartment?"

Erick smiles and leans back, resting his elbow on the settee. He's drawing his crowd in and waiting for his moment. "In town, the engine noise and the transmission shifting were pretty much all I could hear. Once Mitzy got the bus on the open road, I could pick up on footsteps and tone of voice. Couldn't really make out any words. But I knew there wasn't much gas in that tank—"

"That's another thing, Sheriff Harper. I was defending you to those crooks all day long! Telling them what a straight shooter you are, and then you sneak in with some underhanded gas tank thingamajig." Crossing my arms over my chest, I glare up from my seat on the floor and shake my head.

"Hold on. Hold on, Moon. Let's not be getting too high and mighty! You practically joined their gang. Writing up their demands, giving them the idea of a getaway vehicle, and carrying one of their guns!"

The room oohs and aahs in support of the sheriff, and I have to toot my own horn once again.

"Hey, you can't blame me for being persuasive. If it hadn't been for me, none of those hostages would've gotten out of there. And it's not like I gave them a great plan! I was sending them to Canada, for heaven's sake."

Rowdy laughter ripples through the crowd, and Odell raises his glass and calls out from his seat in the loft. "Three cheers to Mitzy Moon, the world's greatest criminal that never was."

Hip hip hooray!

Hip hip hooray!

Hip hip hooray!

I take a drink of my pop, that's right, just plain soda, and wish it were something stronger. But since we have a recovering alcoholic ghost and a couple of minors in our midst, I chose to take the high road.

Plus, I'm thrilled to see Yolo Olson snuggled next to Stellen. The petite, elfin-like creature, with lavender hair, violet eyes, and steampunk attire, has a wholly anime vibe. Luckily, her first year at college hasn't ruined her unique spirit. She's home for spring break and dressed to the nines. The assortment of buckles, straps, and gears connecting her one-of-a-kind garments boggles the mind. Stellen is obviously stoked to have her so near.

I sense my father has something to say, and my chest tightens when I think about how worried he must've been. Before he can make his move, Erick's mother beats him to the punch.

Gracie Harper gets to her feet, grinning like— well, like the Cheshire Cat. "Now, you all might think I'm biased, but I never doubted my Ricky for a second, you know. Ever since he could talk, he's been smart as a whip and twice as fast." She lifts her mug of coffee and beams with a thousand watts of motherly love. "Here's to the best sheriff Pin Cherry Harbor's ever had—remember to vote in

November—and the best son a mother could ever want!"

"Cheers!"

"Hear! Hear!"

Amaryllis and Tally dab at the corners of their eyes, and Grams is full-on ghost sobbing, but luckily I'm the only one who can see that hot mess. Technically, Stellen could see her—but he's only got eyes for one girl in the room.

"Mitzy! I would hardly call it a hot mess to show some genuine emotion. You could've been killed today!"

She sobs anew and swipes at the tears rolling down her cheeks.

Rather than interrupt the festivities, I opt to send Grams a thought message. *Sorry if I scared the resident ghost, Grams. I don't mean to take these risks. Somehow they just find me. And you can show your heartfelt emotions in any way you please. I love you.* And now, I have to wipe a tear from my eye.

Tally grabs her sister's hand and pulls Tilly to her feet. "Well, I'd like to thank Mitzy Moon, Sheriff Harper, and the whole lot of those law enforcement fellas for bringing my sister back to me in one piece."

Tilly curls an arm around her younger sister's shoulder and gives it a squeeze. "Gosh, you know you and Ledo couldn't survive without me."

Tatum raises her glass of cola and beams. "Here's to the best auntie in town!"

Everyone raises their glass, mug, or can, while I succumb to yet another telling of Erick's amazing *Bourne Identity* meets *Speed* meets *Taken* heroics on the bus to nowhere.

Rather than make a public spectacle, my father catches my eye across the room, lifts his glass and winks. We may have only been building a relationship for the last three years, but that tiny gesture speaks volumes to me. He trusts me. He admires me. He's thankful I wasn't hurt, and he'll move heaven and earth to keep things that way.

My brain is exhausted, my psychic powers are fading, and my body actually aches, but I have to take care of some serious supernatural business. A promise is a promise.

Slipping one arm around my kid brother and the other around his on-again-off-again genius girl-friend, I guide them down the curving left balcony of the mezzanine. Once we're out of earshot, I make my ask. "Hey, guys, I need to get the band back together."

For two brainiacs, they're not exactly doing the math. My clever quip is met with dull eyes.

"I have a couple ghosts to dispatch before— I mean, in the next twenty-four hours, and I could use some help."

Yolo bounces on her purple-boot-clad feet and grins. "A ritual?"

Chuckling, I shake my head. "I hope not. These two seem willing enough, but I have to figure out some details of their unfinished business."

Her shoulders sag and her long lashes droop. "Oh, just research then."

I lean in, as though we're in a huddle, and whisper. "We have to solve a nonexistent cold case and trace some crazy genealogy. Who knows what we'll uncover?"

That tidbit brightens her wide, eager eyes, and her happiness is immediately reflected on Stellen's face.

"Are you guys in?"

Stellen places his hand in the center and says, "Ghost Blasters assemble!"

Yolo instantly places her delicate hand on top of his.

However, I'm not convinced. "Ghost Blasters? For real? Is that the best you've got?"

He elbows me sharply. "It's a work in progress. Are you in or not, Mitzy?"

I place one hand under theirs and one on top. "Ghost Blasters for the win!"

We all giggle and throw our stacked hands in the air.

Stellen gets right down to business. "What's our first move?"

"I'll get the case files on the bank robbery that Disco Donnie was involved in—"

Yolo grips my arm and practically glows from the inside out. "Disco Donnie?"

"Not his real name. I'll explain everything tomorrow."

She claps and snickers. "That's lit."

My brother echoes her sentiment. "Yeah, totally lit."

"All right. Tomorrow I'll crack his case wide open, and you two will get all the info you can on Lindy McElroy. Deal?"

"Deal!" they reply in unison.

Turning to rejoin the festivities, I find that the fire of celebration seems to have burned itself out.

The energy of the party is dipping, but before the guests make their exit, Twiggy asks the question on many of our minds. "So what happens to the criminals, Sheriff Harper?"

"Things should be pretty open and shut. Thanks to the friendship Mitzy forged with the seventeen-year-old Alice Cooper." He raises his hand and waves off the questions. "Before anyone asks, it *is* her real name, and she's no relation to the heavy metal performer." Erick shrugs and grins playfully.

A light chuckle passes through the crowd.

"Anyway, she agreed to testify against the others. With her testimony, Mitzy's testimony, and the statements from the rest of the hostages, there isn't a prosecutor in the state who can't win this case. All the money was recovered, and the two injured members of the crew have been treated and released into our custody."

My father initiates a round of applause.

Erick waves for everyone to cease and desist. "I'm grateful things ended as smoothly as they did. Now, I appreciate all the support and the impromptu celebration, but I'm exhausted. So if you don't mind, I think I'm gonna have to call it a night."

You would've thought someone pulled the fire alarm. I've never seen a group of people clear out of an establishment so quickly. Before I can even figure out what's going on, Odell has offered to drive Gracie Harper home, and Grams is promising Erick and me all the privacy we can stand.

Amaryllis offers me a signature bearhug on her way out, and Stellen gives me a friendly punch on the shoulder.

In the span of five minutes, my bookshop goes from a bustling afterparty to an abandoned store.

"Excuse me, Sheriff, did you have some prearranged code word? I haven't seen a party clear out that fast since I was in high school and the cops showed up."

Erick grins and nods. "Now, why doesn't that surprise me?"

"Rude." Smiling, I kiss his lips lightly. "But you're not wrong."

He scoops his arms around me and pulls me close. "If loving you is wrong, Mitzy Moon, I don't wanna be right."

Sure, it's cheesy, but when it's whispered directly in your ear by the sexiest lips this side of the Mississippi . . .

Swoon.

CHAPTER 14

A SOMEWHAT FAMILIAR voice echoes over the intercom and wakes me from a deep slumber. The only words from the early morning message that register in my sluggish grey matter are *chocolate croissants* and *extra-large coffee*.

You don't have to tell me twice. My brain struggles to send the "move" message to my extremities.

"It's not like you to have a wake-up call, Moon."

Yikes! I'm only partially functional. Somewhere in the fog between dreamland and waking, I forgot I wasn't alone. A flicker of guilt hits me. It was too easy to postpone my big secret reveal and lose myself in celebrating Erick being alive last night. One more day couldn't hurt . . .

As I try to slip out of bed, Erick circles his arms around me and nuzzles playfully into my neck. His husky voice makes my skin tingle. "Where do you think you're going?"

"Erick Harper! There are children just outside that door. Get up and make yourself presentable. And . . . act like you slept on the couch."

His laughter fills the room as I rush into the bathroom to splash cold water on my face and drag a comb through my white haystack of a hairdo.

While I'm in the closet selecting today's perfect T-shirt, a fully dressed Sheriff Harper peeks into the room I've nicknamed *Sex and the City* meets *Confessions of a Shopaholic*. His gaze travels around the vast space and stops on the T-shirt in my hands. "*Cute but Psycho*. It's like you have these things custom-made."

I whip the T-shirt at him as though it's a wet towel in a locker room. "Rude!"

He dodges, chuckles, and heads for the door. "But I'm not wrong. If you and your Nancy Drew squad take a break later, let me know. I can meet you at the diner for lunch."

As he reaches toward the medallion that serves as the opening mechanism for the sliding bookcase door, I wave my hands and call out. "Hold on."

Erick turns toward me and grins.

I hustle across the thick carpet and slip into his arms one last time. He leans down and kisses my lips with an intensity that causes my heart to stutter.

"That was—"

He gently strokes the hair back from my face. "Just something to remember me by."

"Yeah, that should do the trick." I swallow and gasp for air.

Sheriff Harper reaches out, presses the plaster circle of twisted ivy, and we wait hand-in-hand as the bookcase slides open.

Yolo and Stellen look up from the table where they've laid out an impromptu breakfast spread.

She winks at me and Stellen blushes a bright fuchsia.

Erick heads across the loft, but before he makes it to the wrought-iron spiral staircase, my brain finally kicks into drive. "Hey, we need the case files for that bank robbery in the '70s. I need to figure out how to get Disco Donnie off the hook."

His brow arches. "Disco Donnie?"

"I'll explain it all later. Can I send Twiggy over to the records office?"

He dips his head in that way that insinuates he's doffing a cap, and smiles. "I'm sure Wayne will be only too happy to hand over whatever she needs."

Ignoring his poke at Twiggy's extracurricular relationship, I calmly reply. "Thank you, Sheriff."

Disappearing down the staircase, his low chuckle echoes softly through the still morning air as he steps out the side door and heads to the station.

Yolo pushes the lovely pink box of pastries toward me and points to one of the large coffees. "I think you only take cream, right?"

"Well remembered."

"I can't really take the credit. Stellen's totally the best brother ever. He knows all kinds of stuff about you."

Since my mouth is already full of chocolate croissant, I'm unable to make a comment. But I shrug and take a long, delicious sip of my black gold.

While I continue to shove flaky treats into my mouth, Stellen makes notes on his phone. "So what's the plan, Mitzy?"

"I'll go over the case files, and you two will head to the library and find out all the deets on Lindy McElroy. I mean, her survivors. We have to figure out this unfinished business and get those earthbound spirits out of the bank today."

Yolo wipes her perfect strawberry mouth with a paper napkin and adjusts her purple, crushed-velvet top hat—complete with steampunk goggles. "If it's a crime scene, isn't it closed for the investigation? How are we gonna get back into the bank?"

I gesture in the direction of my boyfriend's recent exit. "Let me take care of that part. You guys get over to the library as soon as it opens and talk to Pyrrha, the reference librarian. She's well acquainted with Silas and will hopefully be in the mood to do us some favors."

Stellen pushes his bottom lip between his teeth with his finger and bobs his head slowly up and down as he chews his lip. "First, we need to find out the date of the robbery. Then we can find Lindy's obituary. Once we know about the survivors, hopefully we can track one of them down."

I nod my head in agreement. "We know she had a child. Let's hope that child married and had a child of his or her own. If the line ended with Lindy's offspring, we might not be able to get Fred Clements the closure he needs."

"Fred?" Yolo and Stellen question the name in unison.

I give them a crash course on the Pin Cherry Harbor Bank & Trust ghosts as I walk them to the side door. They head out to see what time the library opens, and I place a call to Twiggy. She must be feeling generous after I risked my life attempting to get the drawer money yesterday, because she quickly agrees to stop by and get the files from Wayne. Now I just need to—

"RE-ow." Feed me.

"As you wish, your furry highness." When I turn to make good on my promise, Pye runs in front of me, and plunks into an irritated roadblock position. "What's up, son? I thought you wanted food."

"Ree-oow." A gentle reminder.

"Oh! That's on me. Of course you deserve praise before sustenance." Bending, I scratch his broad head, and he offers me a rare opportunity to stroke his neck below his powerful jaw. I am honored and unnerved. "You tried to warn me about the rabbit robbing the bank and I missed the clue. However, for future reference, Mr. Cuddlekins, a plush toy isn't a great deterrent. Next time try knocking an armed-robbery-themed book off the shelf."

"Ree-OW!" A warning punctuated by a threat.

Pulling my hand back, I swallow loudly. "You're right. I should've made better use of my abilities and figured out the helpful clue. It's all on me."

He squeezes his eyelids closed, over his all-knowing golden eyes, and I swear he's grinning.

While I'm feeding Pyewacket his favorite sugary children's cereal, Grams floats into the back room, carrying a list in her ethereal hands.

"What's that, Grams?"

My voice seems to break her out of a trance and

all color fades from her image. For the first time since I met her, she turns white as a ghost.

Ghost-ma's surprise is immediately replaced with giggles. "Oh Mitzy, you're such a hoot! White as a ghost." Her laughter tinkles like fairy bells.

"No thought-dropping, Isadora. What's that piece of paper in your hand?"

Guilt quickly replaces surprise. "This? It's nothing. I must've left something in the—" Without finishing her sentence, she vanishes through the wall. Paper and all!

"Now that's definitely new." If she'd stuck around for a minute, I could've asked her about the robbery, but the less time I spend around her, the better. I can only get away with the "blank mind" trick for so long. Eventually, I'll mess up and she'll discover I'm onto her big plans. The last thing I want to do is ruin all her hard work. I mean, the hard work of her minions!

Drifting up to the loft, I run through my flimsy plan. If there's any trace of Lindy McElroy, my junior super sleuths will find it. Stretching my arms wide as I yawn, it's hard to ignore how much I've come to rely on friends and family. Something I never thought I'd have the chance to do. When I was bouncing between foster homes, mourning the loss of my beautiful mother, I never imagined relying on anyone. Every time I had to defend myself or run from trouble, I was alone. Me against the world. That's how I thought it would always be. Ever since I arrived in almost-Canada, the universe has tossed me one surprise after another.

Despite all the good things happening in my life, there's a deep dark part of me that worries it's all too perfect. That shattered eleven-year-old girl that had to face life without a mother is still waiting for the other shoe to drop. Why do I have such a hard time believing I deserve good things?

SLAM!

The heavy metal door from the alley bangs closed and startles me from my reverie.

"You gonna come down and get your box of goodies, kid? Or are you waiting for an engraved invitation?" Twiggy's cackle bounces off the tin-plated ceiling and puts me in my place.

"Coming!" I circle down the steps, climb over the "No Admittance" chain hooked at the bottom, and nearly make a clean break. My toe catches and throws me off balance. As I hop forward, flailing my arms like a windup bathtub toy, Twiggy drops the box at my feet and slaps her hand on her dungarees. "Never gets old. I keep thinking it will, but it never does." And with that, she turns and heads into the back room.

I catch myself on the end of the bookcase just in time. "Thanks, I think."

She calls out from the back, "I should be the one thanking you."

"True." After a quick time-space calculation, I have to ask, "Hey, how did you get this evidence so fast?"

There's a sinister chuckle, followed by a vague explanation. "Let's just say I happened to be 'in the room' when Wayne got the call from the sheriff this morning. Wayne offered me a ride to work, and when you called me, we made a little stop on the way."

"Must be nice to be dating a guy with connections."

"Says the gal dating the sheriff." She guffaws at her own joke while I scoop up the evidence box and head upstairs.

Inside the apartment, I clear the coffee table and start reviewing Donnie's case.

A two-page police report.

Three witness statements—all equally vague.

Three confessions that name Donald Whitely as the leader of the gang and mastermind of the robbery.

Then the final nail in the coffin. Tiny Tim's confession. He claims to have tried to stop Donnie from shooting the innocent civilians, but he was too late. Tim blamed both murders on Donnie.

It really was open and shut. My dad's case was

eighteen or nineteen years old when I started digging through it, and we had five boxes of evidence. One box, even for such an old case, seems a little slim.

Clearly, the cops simply recorded exactly what they were told, pinned the murders on Donnie, and the rest of the crew got off easy.

Tim Rosacker, a.k.a. Tiny Tim, served almost five years, but that was the longest sentence by far. The names of the other gang members mean nothing to me. Donnie didn't mention them in his story, and, as far as I know, they only played a part in the armed robbery.

Opening the notes app on my phone, I type up a list of their names. Adding Tim Rosacker at the end, the hairs on the back of my neck tingle and my mood ring burns when I type his alias.

The image in the smoky mists of my antique mood ring shows a baby. I'm not sure what that—

Tiny? Baby?

He was the youngest!

I'm already dialing Erick as the thoughts tumble through my brain. If there's a chance any of these guys are alive—

"What's up, Moon?"

"I'm going through the files from that bank robbery case. Can you run the names of the other guys in the crew and tell me who's still kicking?"

"Sure. Shoot."

We run down the names, and the first three are deceased. Two were repeat offenders who died in prison, and one died of a heart attack eight years ago.

"The last name on the list is Timothy Rosacker. What have you got?"

There's a pause while Erick types the query into his database, and I dig through the remaining contents of the box. We seem to discover our leads simultaneously.

He enthusiastically calls out, "Rosacker's alive." While I shout, "The guns!"

Erick's voice tightens with concern. "What guns? Does someone have a gun? Are you—?"

My brain finally acknowledges the convict update. "Wait, did you say he's alive? Tiny Tim? Where?"

There's a strange pause, and the sheriff seems to be waiting for something.

"Oh, sorry. I found the guns in two evidence bags at the bottom of the box. But you go first."

"Tiny Tim lives in Gooseberry Falls, in an assisted living facility."

"Erick, I need you to dust this gun for prints— actually, both of the guns."

"What are you hoping to find?"

He didn't say no. Let's all remember that. "I'm

hoping that Tim Rosacker's prints are on his gun. If Donnie's story is true, and Tim placed the second gun in his left hand as Donnie was dying, then Tim didn't have time to re-fire it. There's no evidence in the file that indicates anyone checked Donnie for gunshot residue."

"They had a dead bank robber with two guns in his hands and a local young mother murdered in the prime of her life. There had to be a lot of pressure to close the case fast. I don't think anyone did any investigating above and beyond."

"I understand, Erick. But I'm hoping Tiny Tim's print is still on the trigger."

"Drop those evidence bags in your purse and meet me at the diner for brunch."

"Copy that. But you know I don't carry a purse, right?"

He chuckles. "I'm sure you can find something in that endless closet of yours."

"Touché. I'll text the B-team and see if they have anything."

I can't risk losing one of Grams' vintage bags at the crime lab, so I grab a black paper bag with a gold ribbon from the bookshop and drop both guns inside.

Slipping the loaded bag over one arm, I text Yolo and Stellen as I walk toward the diner. Their reply pings back:

"might have something big 👍 no time 4 food"

I keep my response short and sweet. "No problem."

As I slide my phone into my pocket, I can't help but finish the text—in my mind: that means more Sheriff Too-Hot-To-Handle for me.

ERICK DEFINITELY HAD a few minutes head start, because as soon as I walk through the door, Odell strides out of the kitchen with two breakfasts and meets me at the table. "Good morning, Mitzy. Robbed any banks lately?"

"Hilarious, Gramps. Not yet, but the day is young." Ever since I discovered he's my biological grandfather, I've been mentioning it every chance I get.

He chuckles under his breath and slides the food onto the table. Erick offers me a welcoming smile as Odell glances at the gift bag in my hand. "Who's the present for?"

A sly smile creeps across my face as I lean the bag toward him and open it wide.

Surprise grips his lined face, but only for a second. The shock evaporates, and he places a weathered hand on my shoulder. "Have I told you how happy I am to know you're working for the good guys?"

Pushing the bag of weapons toward the sheriff, I pat Odell's hand. "You don't have to thank me, Gramps."

He shakes his head and mumbles, "That never gets old." He raps his knuckles twice on the silver-flecked white Formica and disappears into the kitchen.

Erick is working on a large bite of blueberry pancakes, but pauses to peek into the bag. "What are we going to do if we find this Tiny Tim's print on the other gun?"

"Hey, it's my job to get ahead of the investigation, not yours."

He nods and licks a drop of syrup from his lip.

What I wouldn't give to be that syrup. Memories of his passionate kiss this morning draw me into my inner world of daydreams.

"Mitzy? Oh, Mitzy Moon. Did I lose you?"

"What? I wasn't doing anything."

His blue eyes sparkle, but he lets me off the hook with a subject change. "Seems like you're pushing for a field trip."

After shoving some perfectly browned home fries into my mouth and washing them down with my favorite go-go juice, I wipe the corners of my mouth like a dainty princess. "I was hoping I could come to the lab with you. That way, *when* we find the fingerprint, we can head straight to Gooseberry Falls." I smile invitingly and bat my eyelashes.

"Wow. You're really laying it on thick. Why is it so important to deal with these ghosts today? They've been in the bank for over fifty years. Why can't they just stay there, like your grandma at the bookstore?"

"I'm glad you asked that, Sheriff. I can honestly say I don't know. Fred Clements may remain timid, but something about spirits bound to this plane, against their will, being prone to dark rages bothers me. Plus, there's the fact that I gave Disco Donnie my word." Taking a hesitant sip of my coffee, I wait for Erick's comment. None arrives, so I up the ante. "Plus, Donnie said if I didn't keep my word, he'd make sure Tilly paid for it. He may be remorseful about what he did back in the '70s, but I definitely don't want to put Tilly in the ghost crosshairs of a known murderer."

Erick finishes his breakfast, takes a long sip of coffee, and carefully wipes his mouth. "Then I suppose the mountain of paperwork on my desk will have to wait. And what story will I be giving my deputies—assuming we find what we need, and I have to escort you into the bank later today?"

"Well, I think we've used the one about how it helps me remember the sequence of events if I can be inside the venue—or something like that. If it ain't broke, don't fix it."

He shakes his head, and his shoulders slump in defeat. "At your service, Miss Moon."

It doesn't take me long to power through the rest of my breakfast. I bus our dishes and accept a thank-you hug from Tally.

"Ledo said to tell you he was sorry he couldn't make it to the celebration last night. He had an emergency surgery on a guinea pig. But he wanted me to tell you he's glad you're all right."

"No worries. There were too many people as it was—but it was really nice of everyone. Tell him thanks for me." Good save, if I do say so myself.

Tally smiles brightly and nods. Heading toward the door, I sigh with satisfaction and wave to Odell.

Erick hurries ahead to leave instructions for his deputies while I wait by the car with my sack of pistols.

Sheriff Harper opens the passenger door on his cruiser for me. I drop onto the seat and ogle him as he walks around to the driver's side.

It's a short ride, and I'm too full to make conversation.

The lab has significantly tighter security than

the sheriff's station. I have to sign in, show my driver's license—

"You still have your Arizona driver's license?"

I gaze up at Erick like he's crazy. "Of course. It doesn't expire for like thirty years. Why would I get a new one?"

"Because you don't live in Arizona anymore."

"Sure, but I'm still in the United States of America, right? I'm a licensed driver in one of those 'united' states. My license is valid."

He reaches out and takes the license from the clerk when she returns from the copy machine. "I'll be hanging onto this, Moon. In exchange for these series of favors, I'll expect you to get a proper driver's license."

I'm in no position to argue with the man holding my permission to drive. However, I withhold verbal agreement and glare at him instead.

The clerk slides a visitor badge through the curved opening at the bottom of the window. I accept it and clip it to my T-shirt.

Erick leads the way to the lab, and a young redhead in a lab technician's coat smiles broadly when she sees him. "Sheriff Harper! Great to see you. Glad I'm working today. How can I help you?"

Easy, girl. This man's spoken for. I'd hate to have to body slam her before she tests these guns for prints.

"Roxy, I'd like you to meet Mitzy Moon. She's assisting the department on a case."

She offers her hand, but I'm still having a little pout, so I respond with a curt nod and a plastic smile.

Her arm drops to her side as Erick reaches into my gift bag and extracts the two firearms. "I need you to dust both of these guns for prints."

She picks up a tray and places both bagged guns on it. "A Colt Super .38 and a Saturday night special, or MP-25, if I'm not mistaken."

Erick smiles warmly. "You know your guns, Roxy."

Her cheeks pinken, and she stares at the tray. "Looking for anything in particular?"

He shakes his head. "I'd rather you take your best pass and see what you get. I trust your instincts."

Oh, he trusts *Roxy's* instincts, does he? Meanwhile, he's nailing me to the wall for every hunch I get. I'm definitely gonna be waiting in the parking lot for this chick.

"Hey, is something wrong?" Erick places a hand on my shoulder.

"No. Why?" My eyes dart toward the floor.

"That look on your face—"

"Oh, it's nothing. I was thinking about something else."

He lifts an eyebrow and nods in a way that says he's not buying what I'm selling.

Despite her unnecessary overtures toward my sheriff, even I have to admit that Roxy has got skills. She's processed both guns and uploaded two sets of fingerprints to check against the AFIS database in less than twenty minutes.

Pin Cherry Harbor may be the town that tech forgot, but this lab makes up for all those deficiencies. Erick and I stand behind the tech as she tags the loops and whorls. While the computer searches for matching markers, she returns to her work area and picks up a clipboard. "Sheriff Harper, what case am I billing this to?"

I hope my gulp isn't audible.

Sometimes I forget what a cool customer Erick can be. "Let's bill it to community service, Roxy. This legwork ties into a cold case that hasn't officially been reopened."

She smiles and winks as she makes a note on her clipboard.

A wink? Oh man, I'm definitely going to have to do something about this. "Erick, did you say you're bringing dinner to my place tonight?"

That got her attention. Her ink pen stutters to a stop on her little form and my psychic senses detect she's holding her breath.

Erick leans back and scrunches up his face.

"Did I say that? Man, I must've been high on blueberry pancakes. I don't remember that. But I'm happy to pick up whatever you want. Angelo and Vinci's? Or are you in the mood for Chinese?"

Bless his innocent little heart. He has no idea there's a Battle Royale happening right in front of him. However, I'm not going to miss my opportunity to land the killing blow. I slip my arm through his and lean toward him with a cheesy smile. "Why don't you surprise me? You know what I like."

Roxy drops her pen.

My gentleman of a boyfriend moves to retrieve it, but I manage to get one of my sturdy hips in the way—accidentally.

She picks up her own pen and finally returns to the computer. "I'm afraid nothing is coming up as a match in AFIS. There was one set of prints on the Colt Super .38, and the same palm print was on the Saturday night special."

Erick extracts himself from my needy grasp and steps toward the screen. "What about the other set?"

"Same result. No match. The other set of prints was only on the Saturday night special. Specifically, the magazine release and the trigger. Any other prints were obscured by the smudged palmprint."

Now she has my attention. "Did you say the trigger?"

"That's correct. There was only one print there. And it was not a match for the prints on the Colt Super .38."

Bingo. Yahtzee. Full House. That proves Donnie was telling the truth. "Why aren't the prints coming up? We know the suspects were involved in a robbery."

Erick intervenes. "AFIS was established in the '90s. Tim Rosacker must have gone straight before that, which means his prints were never uploaded. Sorry, Mitzy. Looks like a bust."

I place a hand on my hip and widen my eyes. "Not entirely. It just means we have to make the drive to Gooseberry Falls."

There's a strange sense of satisfaction emanating from Roxy. She must assume we're fighting. Poor woman. She has no idea how our relationship works.

"Thanks for getting this processed so quickly, Roxy. You're definitely one of the best techs we've got."

Her zeal returns, and her whole face lights up with a smile. "Thanks, Sheriff Harper." She returns the guns to the evidence bags and Erick puts them in my flimsy gift bag.

We say our goodbyes and head out to the patrol car. No sooner has he started the engine than he launches into an inquest of his own. "So, was that a catfight I just witnessed?"

"I'm sure I have no idea what you're talking about." I cross my arms and stare out the passenger window.

"Okay. It seemed like you were eager to let Roxy know about our relationship, even though you usually have a thing about public displays of affection."

I have a thing? The nerve of this guy. "Fine. I didn't like the way you were calling her *Roxy* and talking about how you trust her instincts. I never get anything but grief from you about my hunches."

His smile falters. "Former Deputy Roxborough is happily married. You've got nothing to worry about. She worked with us for about six months and picked up the nickname before she got accepted to medical school and took the ME track. She's just friendly and good at her job. And as far as your hunches go—"

"Never mind."

He reaches across and places a hand on my knee. "There's more to your hunches than instinct, Mitzy. We both know that."

My post-ordeal guilt has lessened. If he thinks he's going to trick me into having this discussion in the middle of an investigation, he's wrong. Time for a classic left-field question. "If it turns out that Tiny

Tim is the one who actually killed Lindy McElroy, are you going to make an arrest?"

He withdraws his hand, and my extra senses feel a subtle energetic wall rise between us. "I'm not sure. As of right now, we don't have much to go on. A ghost story and a fingerprint that doesn't match anything in the database."

We make the rest of the drive in silence, and when we walk into the facility in Gooseberry Falls, a quick flash of Erick's badge provides instant access to Tim Rosacker's room.

As we head down the hall, the nurse mentions Tim is suffering from lung cancer and other complications resulting from a lifelong smoking habit. She pushes open the pale-peach door and gestures toward the occupant.

The elderly man hunched over in his easy chair hardly looks like a murderer. However, I believe Donnie's story. The only thing left to do now is figure out a way to make Tim Rosacker confirm those details.

CHAPTER 16

THE MAN SLUMPED before us may bear no resemblance to my fantasy image of the infamous Tiny Tim, but that doesn't stop his old heart from racing when he catches sight of Erick's uniform. "What can I do for you, Officer?"

"It's sheriff. Sheriff Harper. My friend and I just came to chat with you. I hope that's all right?"

Erick offers me the chair opposite Tim, as he casually stands and introduces me. "This is Mitzy Moon. She owns a bookstore in the town of Pin Cherry Harbor. Have you heard of it?"

Tim shakes his head no, but the spike in his pulse and the rapid breathing say otherwise.

I need to build some rapport with this man before I hit him with my questions about Lindy McElroy's murder. Perhaps a loose link to his past will do the trick. "I'm Shelly's great-granddaughter. You might've known Shelly."

His foggy eyes lock onto me with crisp clarity. "Shelly and I never had any daughters, granddaughters, or great-granddaughters. She had a stroke and died nine years ago. I don't know what you're playing at, but I'm not interested." He reaches toward the call button with his right pointer finger, and my psychic senses kick into hyperdrive.

I strike like a cobra, and grab the remote from his chair, careful to put my fingers on the sides and avoid the buttons. "Erick, pull a print off this." It's a total bluff, but I hope my whip-smart boyfriend can play along.

Tim attempts to rise from his chair, but I lift my hands and wave him back. "Look, Tiny Tim, I tried to do this the easy way, but it looks like that's not your style."

At the use of his old gang handle, Tim's entire energy shifts from doddering old man to defensive, dangerous murderer in hiding. "Who sent you?" His voice has the rasp of illness and the chill of fear.

"We'll get to that. What I'd like to know is how you ended up marrying Donnie's old lady?"

At the mention of his dead friend, Tim's eyes widen. "Who are you?"

"You answer my question, and I'll answer yours." I lean back in my chair and cross my arms.

Tim's mouth works back and forth for a few moments while he considers my offer. Lucky for me, he bites. "Shelly was real upset after that cop whacked Donnie. I was there for her, you know?" He coughs and pats his chest.

I nod.

"One thing led to another. It was all innocent enough."

"So you're telling me that framing your best friend for murder, and blaming an entire bank robbery on him, is innocent?"

Tim narrows his gaze. "Your turn."

"Fair enough." Taking a deep breath, I launch into my tale. I choose to go with the idea that I'm a medium that happened to bump into Donnie's ghost while conducting business at the bank. No need to drag out the whole botched robbery story.

Tim leans forward, one gnarled hand grasping the other. "You expect me to believe you were talking to Donnie's ghost? Get outta here."

"I'm not leaving until I get what I came for, Tiny Tim. I know that security guard was going to shoot you. He hesitated, and that gave you the opportunity to kill Lindy McElroy. The guard went down, and he got one shot off. His crazy shot missed you and nicked Donnie's femoral artery. As your friend bled out in the middle of that bank, you pressed your gun into his left hand."

Tim's eyes grow wider with each sentence.

"Then you and your crew walked out of there, called Donnie the ringleader, and let him take the rap for two murders. How am I doing so far?"

A deep cough rattles his chest. He shakes his shoulders and wrings his hands. "It's what we talked about. Everyone knew the drill. Donnie shoulda made his shot count. It's not my fault that guard got one off before his ticker stopped."

"Maybe not. But it is your fault Lindy McElroy is dead. Leaving her child motherless. That is your fault."

Tim leans back in his chair and hangs his head. The fog creeps back over his eyes and I can sense that he's lost in a memory. Good. Let him play through that scene in his mind a few times.

I'm sure his confession will never be admissible in court, but I need to hear him say it nonetheless. Picking up his apple juice, I trace the truth runes Silas taught me into the liquid. "Here, Mr. Rosacker, maybe this will help that cough."

His hands shake as he places the straw between his lips, but he takes a long pull of the liquid.

I set the cup back on the tray beside him and glance toward Erick.

He's tapping out a text on his phone, and I wait for him to finish.

"Erick, were you able to send a photo of the print to Roxy?"

He looks at me, arches an eyebrow, and picks up the call button remote. As he wiggles it back and forth it all clicks into place, and he grins with satisfaction.

Before he says anything, I know I'm on the right track. "Sheriff, can you read him his rights and record his confession?"

Erick walks hesitantly toward Tim. "What makes you think he's going to confess?"

As much as I hate to say it . . . "It's a hunch."

Sheriff Harper informs Tim Rosacker of his Miranda rights and presses record on his phone.

Now it's my turn to finish what I started. "Tim Rosacker, a.k.a. Tiny Tim, what role did you play in the bank robbery that ended in the death of Lindy McElroy?"

Tim turns toward me, and I can feel the struggle within him.

"State your name for the record." I point toward the recording device in Erick's hand.

"Timothy Ernest Rosacker."

"Were you involved in the robbery at the Pin Cherry Harbor Bank & Trust in 1975?"

"Yes, I was." He presses a rheumatoid arthritis crippled hand to his throat and his eyes dart left and right.

"Please walk me through the events of that day."

Tim attempts to circumvent the scene I'm most interested in by supplying tons of unnecessary details leading up to the robbery.

"Tell me about the woman who kept mentioning her child."

He struggles to press his lips together, but the alchemy has done its work. "There was this broad. She kept going on about her kid. We were almost clear when Lumpy said the cops were on the move."

"And what happened next?"

"We needed to get the cash from the vault. Everyone just had to sit tight for a few more minutes. Two of the guys were taking the rent-a-cop downstairs, and that dumb chick made a break for it." His hands clench into weak fists.

"This would be the woman you came to know was Lindy McElroy?" Erick's voice surprises me, but I understand his need to establish the correct identity of the victim.

Tim nods. "Yeah, that's what they said in court."

Erick moves the recording device closer to Tim. "Did you shoot Lindy McElroy, Mr. Rosacker?"

His swollen knuckles whiten, but the runes

compel him. "Yeah. Yeah, I did. All right? She was going to mess everything up."

Erick glances toward me and continues. "And then what happened?"

"Donnie fired one into the guard, and the guard went down. The gunshot scared me and I fired at the broad."

"You mean, Mrs. McElroy?"

"Yeah, McElroy." His voice is soft and almost remorseful. "But like she said"—he gestures toward me—"the cop got one off. He hit Donnie real bad." Tim gazes out the window and continues. "I ran over to him, you know? I tried to get him up, but he was bleeding so much. He said he wasn't gonna make it. He said we should go with the plan."

Uncrossing my arms, I angle toward him. "So instead of applying pressure to your friend's wound and waiting for help to arrive, what did you do?"

"I shoved my gun into his left hand. His lights were going out. We had to stick to the plan."

Erick finishes the interrogation with one final question. "Mr. Rosacker, is it your testimony that you killed Lindy McElroy and placed your MP-25, also known as a Saturday night special, into Donald Whitely's left hand?"

Tim drops his head into his hands and rubs his face. "Yeah, I did it. I shot the lady, and I set up my buddy. I did it all." He leans back in his seat and moans. "But I learned my lesson. I went straight. I took care of Shelly and the boys, and I never put my toe over the line again."

Erick stops the recording on his phone and sighs heavily. "I don't think Lindy McElroy's widower or her child would find much comfort in those words."

I recognize a good exit line when I hear one. So, despite my lingering curiosity, I get to my feet and follow Erick out of the small room, which is somehow drab and cheery at the same time.

The road to Pin Cherry unfolds ahead of us. "So what happens next, Sheriff?"

He twists his hands on the steering wheel and sighs. "I'll take the confession and the fingerprint evidence to the district attorney, but without a pressing need to reopen such an old case, I'm not sure they'll make a move on Mr. Rosacker."

"Well, I think it sucks that he got away with murder."

Erick takes his eyes off the road for a moment and gazes at me. There's a deep sadness swirled with compassion. "You saw him, Mitzy. He's a broken man. He lost everything he ever cared about and is being consumed by a disease of his own making. There may not be a murder conviction on his record, but he's definitely serving a life sentence."

I can't argue with that. Erick is a lawman, but he leads with his heart, not his gun.

He reaches across and rubs his hand on my knee. "What about your side of things?"

"My side of things? What do you mean?"

Erick chuckles for the first time on the return drive. "The ghost side."

"Oh, that! I'll tell Donnie about the fingerprint and play the confession for him. If that doesn't take care of his unfinished business, I don't know what will."

"What about the other one? The security guard."

"Hmmmm. I better check in on the junior sleuths. I'm hoping they've come up with something I can use on that front." Sliding my phone from my pocket, I fire a text off to Stellen and Yolo.

There's no response.

I know for a fact that humans their age are never without their cell phones. Maybe they have their phones silenced since they spent the day in a library. Quickly swiping to my speed dial list, I tap Stellen's name.

He answers on the first ring, but his voice is hushed.

Before I can ask any of my pressing questions, he offers me a vague stall tactic and promises more when he sees me at the bookshop.

Erick's voice is filled with concern. "That didn't exactly sound good. Are the kids okay?"

"Stellen was being super sketchy. He said what they found is bigger than any of us could've imagined. They're waiting at the bookstore, so I guess we'll find out in a few minutes."

The sheriff swallows up several miles of the road in silence. "Then what?"

"Assuming what they found is useful, we'll need access to the bank tonight. I want to get this ghost business handled ASAP. I don't want any of this weird energy hanging around on my birthday."

There's a pulse of nervous excitement from the driver's seat, and I quickly prepare to hide my knowledge of the surprise party.

"That's the first time I heard you mention your birthday this whole week. Do you have plans with your family?"

Here goes nothing. "Nothing official. I mean, I'm not even used to celebrating, you know? I'm sure Amaryllis will make a cake, but other than that, it should be pretty casual."

Laughter erupts from his throat, and he steadies himself on the steering wheel as he catches his breath. "If there's any way you can carve out an hour or two for your current boyfriend, amidst those casual plans, I'd appreciate it."

Stealing a quick glance at his smug expression, I can tell he's mostly fooled by my performance. "Sure. Shouldn't be a problem."

The sparse lights of Pin Cherry loom into view, and within minutes we're parked in the cul-de-sac at the end of Main Street.

I'm pleased I chose to wear my special key today. As we approach the front door, I pull the chain from around my neck and hold the large brass key, with its unique triangle-shaped barrel, in my hand. One more of the special things that link me, inseparably, to this town.

Pushing the key into the lock, I twist it three times and feel the door and the store beyond opening. Even though Stellen let himself in through the side door, the bookstore isn't officially "open" until I unlock this portal.

Thundering footsteps greet us. Stellen is in the lead, and Yolo lags, lost in thought.

"Hey, guys, what did you find? I can't believe you are being so mysterious."

Stellen grabs my arm and tugs me forward. "Come on. I'm going to let her tell you."

Erick steps into the circle and Yolo bounces on her toes as she adjusts the lapel of her deep-brown brocade waistcoat. "I'll start at the beginning. That's the only way any of it will make sense."

We nod, and she continues.

"Lindy McElroy was survived by her husband and three-year-old daughter, Rosa. Lindy's husband died less than a year later, and Rosa ended up in foster care."

A stabbing pain hits my heart. At least I was eleven when I got dropped into the system. I could speak and ask questions. A three-year-old. How awful.

Yolo continues. "We lost the trail for a bit after that. But Pyrrha was totally on it. She knew about a church that helped with a lot of placements at that time. That contact turned us on to some records that led us to Rosa's placement. She was eventually adopted, and the new family kept her name."

I place a hand on her shoulder and give her an encouraging squeeze. "That's good."

"Yeah, but Rosa was uber troubled and had some run-ins with the law. She ended up pregnant at sixteen and—" Yolo tears up, but her perfect eye makeup withstands the salty drops. "—Rosa died in childbirth. I guess the family was, like, totally ashamed, and they gave the baby up for adoption. We had to go over to City Hall to find the name of that baby, but Pyrrha and the city clerk are Bunco pals, so she was really helpful."

Shaking my head, I offer up my amazement. "You guys must have been working some kind of magic. I've never seen the city clerk be helpful to anyone!"

Yolo nods and bounces on her toes again. "So

the baby's name was Emily, and—" She reaches out, squeezes Stellen's arm, and nods for him to pick up the story.

He rubs her hand and takes up the tale. "It seems like bad luck just ran in the family. Emily also got pregnant at sixteen, and she abandoned her baby on the steps of the Lutheran Church."

Erick groans and crosses his arms. "I wish we had better support for people who find themselves in these terrible situations."

Rubbing my hand on his arm, I nod my agreement. "So, is that where the trail ends?"

Yolo regains her composure and picks up the story. "The pastor at the church had been counseling a couple who'd suffered a recent miscarriage. He knew how badly they wanted a child, and he held a lot of sway over social services, because of the many placements credited to his church."

My psychic senses flutter and the mood ring on my left hand burns. It takes all the willpower I don't have to resist spoiling the end of Yolo's tale.

She grabs Stellen's hand for courage and finishes. "There was a note in the basket. The baby's name was Yolonda McElroy. Last year, right after I graduated, my parents told me the story of how I'd been abandoned on the steps of the church. Before that, I never knew I was adopted. Maybe I might have suspected, but I never knew. They thought it was the right time to tell me. And now—"

I wrap my arms around her and squeeze. "I'm so glad the Olson's adopted you, Yolo. Their love broke your family's curse. You're brilliant, and you're gonna achieve amazing things. I'm so happy you were home for this case."

She cries into my shoulder and squeezes me hard. "Me too. Me and Bricklin will be indebted to you forever."

Loosening my arms, I tilt her back and stare down into her tiny pixie face. I can't help but love her like a little sister. "You and your adorable dog don't owe me anything! As far as I'm concerned, you're part of the family. We take care of each other."

Erick pulls us all into a group hug before getting our mission back on track. "Sounds like we have everything we need to take care of these ghosts. I'm no expert, but should we head over to the bank, Mitzy?"

"Yeah. Ghost Blasters assemble."

Stellen laughs and shakes his head. "On second thought, that's not a great name. We're not really blasting anything. We're kinda sending them where they're supposed to be, right?"

Yolo and I nod in unison. She offers her suggestion. "What about Spirit Senders?"

Chewing the inside of my cheek, I nod once. "I think you guys are on the right track. Maybe Ghost Questers?"

That name brings a hearty round of laughter.

"How about we table the naming decision until after we complete this mission?" Erick gestures toward the front door, and none of us argue.

As we reach the exit, a shimmering glow approaches. Stellen and I turn.

Grams sparkles into being and places an ethereal hand on each of our shoulders. "Good luck, Ghost Guides."

Grams for the win.

CHAPTER 17

ERICK MARCHES UP MAIN STREET to retrieve a
key to the bank, while the three Ghost Guides slink
down the alley and wait at the rear door. Even
though Yolo can't see ghosts, she's an honorary
member on account of the séance she took part in—
but that's another story.

Excitement hums in the air like electricity
down a power line. By the time the sheriff arrives,
Stellen and Yolo are beside themselves.

Sheriff Harper slips the key in the lock, but
before he opens the door, he turns toward us.
"You guys made a believer out of me with the
whole ghost of Isadora thing, but this is my first
time taking part in a send-off. I'm officially
putting Mitzy in charge, but if things take a bad
turn, I'm getting all of you out of there whether

this ghost business is finished or not. Understood?"

"Copy that." His total "dad" vibe is kind of adorable.

Stellen and Yolo mumble their acceptance, but it's easy to tell that they're in it to win it.

We step inside the bank, and Erick moves toward a light switch. I grab his hand. "It's better if we leave the lights off. Use a flashlight if you have to, but I think there's enough light from the security fixtures and the exit sign."

"10-4."

We make our way to the lobby, and I motion for everyone to sit in a circle on the floor. "Donnie? Donnie, it's Mitzy. I kept my promise."

The first apparition to appear is Fred Clements. His aura has grown a little brighter than it was during the robbery, and I'm sure it has something to do with the faint hope he now carries.

Stellen points, and Yolo and Erick turn to stare at the empty air.

Taking my job as an afterlife interpreter seriously, I take the lead. "Fred, can you find Donnie for me? I think he's going to be happy to hear what I found."

The security guard nods solemnly, and his ethereal shoulders sag.

"Don't worry, Fred, I didn't forget about you.

I'm saving the best for last."

He glows brightly and vanishes.

Erick looks at me and shrugs.

"Fred Clements went to find Donnie. It seems like we need to take care of Disco Donnie's business first. I'm no expert, but that's what feels right."

My supportive boyfriend reaches over and squeezes my hand. "Then I'm sure it is."

Whatever else happens tonight, I have to admire the willingness of this logical military man. He was unceremoniously dumped into the world of the paranormal, and he's done a heckuva job playing catch up. Maybe he could handle the rest of my story—

"Mitzy! So you're more than just a stone cold fox, eh?"

Stellen's eyes widen. He can see ghosts, but he can't hear them. However, with Disco Donnie, a visual is all you need. My stepbrother looks at me and grins from ear to ear.

"Let me make some introductions. Donnie, this is Sheriff Erick Harper, Stellen Jablonski, and Yolo Olson. Everyone, meet Donnie."

He moves around the circle, patting everyone on the shoulder with his shimmering hand. Yolo and Erick jump significantly, but Stellen gives Donnie a big thumbs up when he reaches the end of the circle.

Donnie floats upward, adjusts his huge collar, and shakes a finger at me. "You didn't tell me the kid sees ghosts. Can he hear me too?"

"No, Stellen sees ghosts, but doesn't hear them —yet. Who knows what will happen with practice?"

Donnie slides a thumb along his chin. "That's right. I like your attitude, babe."

"Let's get down to business, Donnie. I promised you I'd get to the bottom of things and help you finish your unfinished business."

He sinks toward the ground, and it almost looks as though his platform shoes are touching the floor. "Yeah, chicks say a lot of things. Did you really come up with anything?"

"This chick doesn't make promises she can't keep, Donnie."

The unnecessary chuckle from the sheriff to my right will have to be ignored, for now.

"I pulled the old case files, and the sheriff here had both guns fingerprinted. Turns out the only print on the trigger of that MP-25 was Tiny Tim's. There's no way you pulled that trigger."

The ghost of Disco Donnie flickers and he presses both hands on his stomach. "I told you! I wasn't lyin'." He flickers again. "Geez, I feel funny."

"It gets better, Donnie. We found Tiny Tim, and I got him to confess." It seems like mentioning

Shelly would be counterproductive, so I leave that tidbit to be lost to the ages.

"That son of a gun is still alive? Wow. He used to smoke two packs a day."

"Trust me, Donnie, that bad habit caught up with him." Gesturing toward Erick, I point to his phone. "Sheriff Harper, can you play the confession?"

He pulls out his phone, scrolls through the recordings, and plays the confession for Donnie.

As Disco Donnie listens to the raspy, aged voice of his once friend, his eyes get a little misty. He nods in agreement with Tim Rosacker's version of events as the recording plays. Thankfully, the locked-on sheriff noticed me leaving Shelly out of my version of events, and pauses the track before Tim makes his last declaration of doing right by Shelly and the boys.

Donnie's already fading fast by the time we reach the end of the recording.

"It's time for you to let go, Donnie. You've been cleared of Lindy McElroy's murder. And you and Fred made your peace a long time ago. You can finally let go. I hope you got people waiting for you on the other side."

The film-school dropout in me swells with pride as I watch the darkened bank transform into a 1970s discotheque. The mirror ball on the ceiling twirls and the sparkling shards of light meld with Donnie's spirit as he fades out to take his last boogie on the disco 'round.

Oh yeah.

Fred watches from the shadows as Donnie disappears beyond the veil. His hope dares to bloom and he drifts forward. "Do you think you can really help me?"

Turning toward the spirit of the security guard, I keep my answer honest but hopeful. "In the end, it's up to you, Fred. Let me tell you what we uncovered."

Our small group settles in for the next stage of our operation. Stellen is kind enough to bring Yolo and Erick up to speed, while I prep Fred.

"Fred, have you ever heard of the butterfly effect?"

He floats aimlessly, as he searches his fading memories. "Is it a book?"

"No, well, I don't know. They did make a movie, so anything's possible. It's a concept that originated from Chaos theory. The butterfly effect refers to the interconnectedness of everything on our planet. The theory loosely means if a butterfly flaps its wings in the Amazon, it can trigger a sequence of events that could eventually lead to an avalanche which could kill a skier in the Rocky Mountains."

Fred shakes his head. "That sounds pretty far-fetched."

"Maybe, but the idea that every action has a re-action that technically causes a chain of events to occur isn't that hard to believe, is it?"

He wags his head back and forth. "I s'pose not."

"What I'm getting at, Fred, is that you blame yourself for Lindy McElroy's death because you hesitated that day in the bank."

He zooms toward me and shakes his finger adamantly. "It is my fault. I did hesitate. If I'd shot that Tiny Tim, Lindy McElroy would still be alive."

Shrugging my shoulders, I lift my hands and sigh. "Possibly. Although, you could have missed, and Tiny Tim would've shot her, anyway. The bottom line is, we don't know what could've happened. We only know what did happen. But your actions put something in motion. An entire sequence of events in the McElroys' lives."

Yolo presses her hands together and swallows hard.

Part of me wants to lay out every piece of the puzzle, but my brief experience with Fred leads me to believe he'll get bogged down in the negativity and not see the good. I think this is a situation where it's better to skip ahead. "I want you to meet someone, Fred."

His eyes trace the faces of everyone in the circle, and I gesture for Yolo to get to her feet.

Stellen pats her leg supportively. She stands and looks left and right.

"Yolo, Fred is right there, just behind Stellen."

She smiles and turns toward what she sees as an empty space.

"Fred Clements, I'd like you to meet Yolonda McElroy Olson. She's the great-granddaughter of Lindy McElroy."

Fred's heavily lidded eyes widen and his apparition glows the brightest I've seen yet. "Lindy's kid did okay?"

Not really the point, and I'm not about to get Fred sidetracked. "Things ended up exactly as they were supposed to, Fred. Yolo is a brilliant scientist and a genius inventor. She graduated from high school early and got accepted into a special program at MIT. For all we know, she could be the person who discovers time travel."

Yolo turns toward me and raises one fingerless-gloved finger. "Technically, time travel has already been discovered. Particle theory . . . Well, not to get sidetracked. The point is, we need to perfect the calculations of space travel so that when we move molecules through time, we can predict the space where they will land."

The rest of us exchange confused glances, and I

reply. "I'll take your word for it, Yolo."

She covers her perfect little mouth with one hand and nods. "Got it. Not really the point of your speech."

"What I'm trying to say is that Yolo was adopted by a loving family who was grateful for a child. They created this beautiful environment for her to be the best version of herself. Your hesitation in the bank over fifty years ago resulted in this. I know you carry guilt for what happened, but can you see another side of it now?"

Big salty ghost tears are rolling down Fred's ruddy cheeks. "I still feel like I need to apologize to her."

"All right. Stellen, can you help Yolo connect with Fred?"

Stellen gets to his feet, steps behind Yolo and lifts both of her arms toward the approaching specter.

"Now, Fred, go ahead and take hold of Yolo's hands."

He gently grips her fairy fingers in his meaty paws, and she shivers. "It's a pleasure to meet you, Yolonda McElroy Olson. So sorry I wasn't able to save your great-grandmother. But you turned out to be a lovely woman. If I manage to make it to the other side, I'll be sure to tell her just that."

I jump in as an afterlife interpreter and share

Fred's heartfelt message with Yolo. The ghost bumps on her arms dissipate as she sinks into his ethereal grasp. "Fred, I can't technically see you, but I can feel you. And I want you to know, I forgive you. I forgive you, and I want you to tell my great-grandmother that, too."

Now everyone's crying. Even Erick has to wipe an errant tear from his cheek.

A vast green meadow opens behind Fred. A golf cart pulls up, driven by a man I don't recognize —but who bears a strange familiarity.

"Fred, I think that's your ride."

Fred reluctantly drops Yolo's hands and turns in the direction I'm pointing.

"Jed Willoughby? Is that you? I haven't seen you on the links in a month of Sundays."

"Come on, Fred. You're late for your tee time."

Fred takes a step toward the waiting cart, but turns and glances over his shoulder. "Thank you, Mitzy Moon. I never thought I'd see this day."

Swiping at my traitorous tears, I swallow hard. "You keep a backgammon table warm for Silas Willoughby. I'm sure he'll outlive me, but eventually he'll be joining you."

Fred's eyes brighten, and he laughs with the lightness of an unburdened spirit. He slips into the golf cart.

The vision, and Fred Clements vanish.

CHAPTER 18

It's been a long and exhausting day. My need for peace and quiet supersedes my desire to hang out with Erick—or spill secrets. Stellen offers to give Yolo a ride home, and Erick and I head toward Main Street. He walks me to the corner and kisses me goodnight before returning to the station.

Don't get me wrong, it's a great kiss. It definitely makes me reconsider my choices, but in the end the exhaustion trumps the tingles.

The night air is icy, but now I can't bring myself to head inside. As tired as I feel and as much as I love Grams, I need a little break from ghosts right now.

Pulling up the zipper on my puffy jacket, I head down the embankment toward the thawing shores of our great lake.

Tomorrow is going to be a lot. I'm looking forward to celebrating my birthday with my wonderful family and what I'm sure will be many new friends. However, part of my heart longs for the simplicity of eating cake in bed with my mother.

They say time heals all wounds, but I haven't found that to be true. Time dulls the pain and changes the perspective, but the gash that was left in my heart when Coraline Moon was taken from me will never truly heal. I don't think I can handle all of tomorrow's hype on my own.

Without a conscious awareness of my actions, I see my phone in my hand, and a welcome voice pours from the speaker.

"Good evening, Mitzy. I hope the lateness of your call is not cause for alarm."

"Silas. It's so good to hear your voice. It's been the craziest day."

He gently coaxes the details from me and offers touches of wisdom and encouragement as needed. "I'm pleased you were able to help Mr. Clements. His spirit deserves peace."

"I agree. I think everyone can use a little peace every now and then."

"And is that the true purpose of your call, Mizithra?"

Uh oh, formal name territory. He's onto me. "I knew you'd get to the heart of the matter sooner or later, Silas. I'm sure you're aware of the grand festivities Grams has planned for tomorrow."

He harrumphs and chuckles softly. It's easy to picture him smoothing his mustache with a thumb and forefinger. "Your grandmother's spirit is not easily contained. She has gone to a great deal of effort and I hope you will enjoy yourself."

Wrapping my arms around my knees, I shudder in the face of the frozen lake's gaze. "I want to. I actually want to. I just don't think I can take all of that energy. You know what I mean? I kinda want to seal myself off from all the psychic hits and unwanted extrasensory information."

"I understand perfectly. Allow me to offer a solution."

A sense of relief seeps into my shoulders. "Thank you, Silas. I knew I could count on you."

"It is not I on whom you shall count. In this matter, you must perform the technique on yourself. You must never give your power away. You may choose when to use it or when to turn down the volume, but you must never allow another person to control your gifts."

There's a deeper message in there somewhere, but the weight of the day is tugging at my eyelids. I have no interest in delving into the depths of this lesson. "I understand. What should I do?"

"Get to your feet."

How does he know I'm sitting down? No time for that. I'll skip that question and stand. "All right. I'm ready."

"Place your right hand in front of your body, just below your belly button. Turn your palm up as though you're scooping something."

"Got it."

"Now scoop your right hand slowly upward all the way to the top of your head, slowly inhaling. As your hand moves, visualize closing the receptors in your body by choice. Remain in control. You are consciously making this decision."

As my hand moves upward, something shifts. "I feel something."

"Well done. Perform the movement two more times, using the same visualization each time. After the third motion is complete, you may say aloud, if you wish, 'It is done.'"

I repeat the gesture, as I've been instructed, and when I finish I say aloud, "It is done."

"You should be ready to face the day tomorrow with renewed inner strength. I look forward to my part in the momentous occasion's busy schedule."

As I'm about to end the call, a sudden concern pops to the forefront. "Wait, how do I turn it off? Or am I turning it back on?"

"Ah, yes. Simply reverse the motions and visualize yourself opening up to all the messages the universe has to offer. Once again, you are in control of the flow. You are not the tool, you wield the tool."

"Thank you, Silas. Thank you for taking my call. I'm sorry to have bothered you so late at night."

"Your calls are never a bother, Mizithra. Sleep well, and I wish you the happiest of birthdays."

My attempt to sneak into the bookstore via the alley door is a double epic fail.

"Ree-ow." Soft but condescending.

"Mitzy! We've been worried sick! What happened at the bank?"

Crouching down to scratch Pyewacket between his black-tufted ears, I feel calm flowing over me. "It's nice to see you guys. It has been THE craziest day. Follow me upstairs and I'll tell you as much of the story as I can before I crash out."

Our strange animal-human-ghost trio meanders up to the apartment. I barely have the energy to take off my coat. Tonight is definitely going to be a "sleep in my clothes" kind of night.

I share the highlights of the story with Grams, and drift off to sleep as she's singing my praises.

"Oh Mitzy, I'm so proud of you. You really helped—"

. . .

A SPARKLE OF SUNLIGHT dances across my eyelids a moment before a hungry caracal head butts me.

"Easy does it, son. I'm awake. I'm awake. Give me a second to take care of my human business, and I'll pour your Fruity Puffs. Deal?"

"Re-ow." Thank you.

As I stumble down the spiral staircase, Grams zooms up to greet me. "Happy birthday! I wanted to be the first."

"Well, technically, Silas wished me a happy birthday last night, but that was before midnight, so I suppose it doesn't count. I'll give you the official title of first birthday wisher."

She claps her hands as though it's an actual contest. "You better jump in the shower. Odell slipped a note under the door and he's planning to have breakfast with you this morning. I'm sure you'll want to look your best."

"I'll agree to wash my face and even comb my hair, but there's no way I'm taking a shower before breakfast. We'll deal with that when I get back. I assume you'll have an outfit laid out for me?"

She places a bejeweled hand over her mouth and giggles. "I'll see what I can do."

Filling Pye's bowl, I complete my task and back away. While he indulges in one of his favorite pastimes, I trudge upstairs and drag a brush through my hair.

Yesterday's T-shirt will have to do. Throwing on my jacket, I attempt to escape before Grams can scold me.

No such luck.

"Honestly, Mitzy. You have a closet literally overflowing with gorgeous couture. You could at least put on a fresh shirt."

"I'll be back soon, Grams. And then I'm all yours. You can dress me up like a little dolly and tell me to do whatever you want with my hair. Just let me enjoy my birthday breakfast in peace, all right?"

Her aura practically bursts with joy. "Oh, all right. I'll see you soon."

When I walk into the diner, Odell offers me a spatula salute through the orders-up window. And Tally's smile beams brightly as she brings two cups of coffee to the table, while Odell follows with our breakfasts. He's made me my favorite, of course. But I'm eager to discover what's on his plate.

"Chicken fried steak, two eggs over easy, and a side of whole wheat toast. Good to know, Gramps."

He winks and smiles. "Happy birthday, Mitzy. Or should I say, world's greatest granddaughter."

I offer a formal nod. "I'll accept the title."

He chuckles and we both dive into our delicious fare.

Odell wipes the corner of his mouth with a thin paper napkin and gazes across the table. "So, how long have you known?"

I attempt to paint my features in a portrait of innocence, but there is no fooling Odell. "I mean, I think I've known the whole time."

He lifts his mug in a toast. "Here's to some of the best acting I've seen since Myrtle Isadora herself."

"I hope so. I really didn't want to spoil her fun."

"Don't worry, many have tried, none succeeded. When Myrtle Isadora gets her mind on something, come hell or high water, there's no changin' it."

We clink our mugs and enjoy a humorous toast at my grandmother's expense.

"I'm not sure what part you played in all of it, but thanks. It's my first actual birthday party since—"

A strong hand reaches across the table and lovingly pats my fingers. "Happy to do it. I'd do anything for you. You know that, right?"

The protection that Silas taught me last night is doing its job. I can sense the tenderness in Odell's comment, but it doesn't hit me in the gut as hard as I know it usually would. Good news. I might actually make it through this day in one piece. "Thank you. You know I'd do the same for you."

Breakfast ends too soon. I give Odell an enormous hug before reluctantly returning to the book-shop to take my role as Ghost-ma's plaything.

THERE'S NO DENYING the rejuvenating proper-ties of a luxurious steam shower and eucalyptus-scented bath products. By the time I towel off and rake my fingers through my wet hair, my worries are soothed and I'm ready for anything Grams is going to throw at me.

"Good! Get your rear end in that closet and be prepared for a fashion show!"

Blerg.

"I gave you three options, which I think are quite reasonable considering how excited I am about this day." Ghost-ma hovers eagerly above her selections.

"You and I have very different definitions of reasonable, Isadora."

Grams flits about the closet like the fairy god-mother she is. "Start here!"

The first contraption I'm forced into makes me look exactly like a giant blob of cotton candy with a head stuck on top.

"It's lovely!"

"Gimme a break. The only person who would think this is lovely is a sugar-addicted toddler. I'm sorry, Grams, but it's a hard pass."

"All right. On to the next one!"

I extract myself from the frothy gown and pick up a slinky red number. This dress is less grandiose, but, in my opinion, it leaves far too *little* to the imagination.

"Nonsense. You have a dashing figure. There's nothing wrong with flaunting it." She circles around me like a hyperactive judge at a dog show.

"Once again, I don't share your opinion on the flaunting front. Plus, it's not exactly warm outside. I realize all of you almost-Canadians think that anything above freezing is suntanning weather, but I'm not there yet." I peel off the *Lady in Red* wardrobe and wait for further instruction.

"Well, I guess we're down to the last option. Looks like you'll be wearing this one, whether you like it or not."

"Don't get ahead of yourself, Isadora." Lifting the hanger and scanning the last item, the nicest thing I can say about the final selection is that it has pant legs. "A jumpsuit? What am I, five?"

"Jumpsuits are the height of fashion. That was custom made by one of the finest designers in New York City. Give it a fair chance." Grams zips me up in the back and I tug at the puffy shoulders.

"It seems a little frou-frou."

"It's called style, dear. Get on board."

Turning back and forth in front of the full-length mirror, there is something nice about the way the tapered pants give the illusion of long legs. I'm not entirely sure I'm in love with the bright-red hue of the fabric or the pin-cherry-printed top, but as I gaze at the empty padded mahogany bench in the center of my enormous closet, I'm out of options.

"Don't you just love it?"

"I don't. It seems a bit snug, and the pants are too long."

"Hardly! Slip into those silver heels I selected."

Of course, I forgot the *pièce de résistance* to any of Ghost-ma's getups: heels!

"Now, Mitzy, I know ten women who would—"

"I know, I know. Ten women who would kill to wear these shoes for five minutes."

Grams crosses her arms and her coral lips purse into a pout. "Well, it's true."

I buckle on the strappy silver shoes and twist in front of the mirror. I feel silly, but I look nice. And it is my birthday.

"You look fantastic. And you deserve to feel like the Pin Cherry princess on your birthday!"

"Grams! Get out of my head. Just because I'm allowing you to pick out my outfit, doesn't mean I'm allowing you to pick my brain."

She giggles wildly. "You're such a card!"

"Well, it looks like the clothing dilemma has been solved. Now what?"

"Let's get that hair blown out and shining like the moon." She snickers at her own clever quip. "And, you absolutely have to wear some makeup today."

Once I've carried out the orders of my other-worldly master, an unexpected arrival catches me off guard.

Twiggy's voice crackles over the intercom. "Hey, kid, you've got a fan club or something waiting for you."

My thoughts jump to the ragtag bunch of snow-mobilers I met last winter, but that definitely doesn't make sense.

"Time to head downstairs, sweetie. Let's get your party started."

"One last thing." Hurrying to the jewelry box, I slip out the dreamcatcher necklace that belonged to my mother and clasp it around my neck. She may be gone, but at least she'll be with me in spirit.

Grams sniffles and dabs at her eyes. "Oh, Mitzy."

I swallow hard and stuff down all the feels. "Let's do this."

WALKING ACROSS THE LOFT, I take a moment to catch my breath and center myself. Today is about fun. It's important to keep a positive attitude and go with the flow.

"That's the spirit, dear."

"Grams!" There's no point wasting my breath. I head downstairs and it's hard to admit, but I'm pleased when I watch Erick's mouth drop open and his eyes widen with anticipation. "Wow! You look amazing."

I stop just before the "No Admittance" chain and twist left and right. "Thank you. I've been dressed by the best ghost stylist in all of Pin Cherry."

Stellen and Yolo get a chuckle from that comment, but Erick is still admiring the merchandise.

Rather than tempt fate, I unhook the chain, hurry to the bottom step, and hook it back up again before the alarm can sound. "So what happens now?"

Erick pulls a piece of paper from the back pocket of his "just right" jeans and fans it in the air. "Maybe you should take a look at this."

He hands me the 3 x 5 card and I read it aloud.

> "Come to the one place where
>   wheels repair
> All kinds of legs, fins, and beaks
>   with flair."

"What is this? A riddle?"

Yolo bounces up and down on her toes and adjusts her festive bandolier. Rather than ammunition, her steampunk version holds candies, lip gloss, and small tools. "It's a scavenger hunt!"

"Oh, I get it now. We have to solve the riddle to get the next clue?"

Stellen smiles. "You got it, sis. What's your answer?"

I read the riddle silently a couple more times, and then it hits me. "Wheels! Like on a wheelchair. It's gotta be Doc Ledo. Let's head over to the veterinary clinic."

Erick leads the way and we all follow him out to his Nova parked in the alley.

As per usual, he drives his personal vehicle with far more abandon than his police cruiser. Speed limits may be stretched or possibly broken, and brakes are only used as an afterthought. We arrive at the vet's office in record time.

The four of us rush through the front door, full of giggles and energy.

Doc Ledo rolls out from the back room and offers a wave. "So the game is afoot, eh?"

We return the wave, and Stellen replies. "Yep. Mitzy figured out the first clue, no problem. Do you have the next one for us?"

He crosses his arms and shakes his head. "I was instructed to offer no assistance. The four of you are used to solving mysteries, right? You better get crackin'."

Our shoulders sag and we look at each other in confusion. I sum up our conundrum. "So we don't just have to solve the riddle. We have to figure out where the next clue is once we get to the place the riddle takes us?"

Doc Ledo nods. "That sounds about right. I wish you luck. Gotta get back to work." And without further ado, he wheels into the back and leaves us unaided.

"Since it's Mitzy's birthday, let's assume all the

clues will have to do with her." Erick shrugs his shoulders and we all nod in helpless agreement. "So, how many times have you been here?"

Chewing the inside of my cheek, I rifle through my memories. "Quite a few times. Pyewacket is always getting himself into trouble."

Stellen chuckles. "Accurate."

Yolo raises her hand, as though we're in a classroom, but proceeds without waiting to be acknowledged. "Maybe it has to be something important. Not just a routine visit. How about the first time you were here?"

When the memory of Pyewacket taking a bullet for me and my father hits me in the gut, I'm glad to be feeling that memory through a filter. Once again, I'm thankful for the protection Silas taught me last night. "Wow, I can't believe I almost forgot about Pye getting shot."

Erick nods excitedly. "That's right. You insisted on staying at the animal hospital with your cat, like a freaky cat lady."

I punch him playfully on the arm. "Hey, that cat saved my life. I'm sure if your precious little potbelly pig, Casserole, had done something like that for you, you would've followed him to the ends of the earth."

He nods. "Precious Casserole, God rest him."

Stellen waves his hands eagerly. "That's gotta

be it. Focus up, everyone. If Pyewacket was shot, there must've been a surgery and recovery. If you were staying with him, maybe the clue is in the recovery room."

Yolo squeezes an arm around Stellen's shoulders. "Dude! You're onto something!"

We all rush toward the hallway, and Stellen, who interned at this clinic, leads the way.

Outside of the recovery room, there's an envelope taped right below the placard.

Stellen pulls the envelope from the wall and hands it to me. "We found it. Read the next clue!"

It's fun. I'm allowing myself to be swept up in the moment. I wish my mother could be here, but I'm lucky to have such a wonderful group of friends to share this special day with me. Time to let the past drift away and enjoy everything that's special about the here and now. Opening the envelope, I fan the next clue and wink at Erick. "You ready, Sheriff?"

He winks back and claps his hands. "I was born ready, Moon."

As I read the second clue aloud, my face shifts to an unbecoming shade of red, which closely matches the pants portion of my pantsuit.

"You once stormed a tin castle
within our walls,

*In an effort to escape the law's
eyeballs."*

"A tin castle?" Erick shakes his head. "There aren't any castles in Pin Cherry. Do you think we have to drive out of town?"

Stellen and Yolo offer a few suggestions while I dwell in embarrassed silence. Finally, all eyes turn toward me.

"I know that look, Moon. Spill." Erick crosses his arms in that yummy way that makes his biceps bulge, and I'm powerless to resist.

"I don't know how you guys got this information, but there was this one time at the grocery store when I had a little run-in with Deputy Paulsen. After I dropped a really solid burn, and I wanted to get out of the store before she could think of a comeback . . . I was running kind of fast down one of the aisles, and I turned and slammed right into a tower of cans. I hit the ground. The cans hit the ground. It was mortifying."

Everyone enjoys a hearty laugh at my expense.

Erick raises his hand in the air to ignite the charge. "To the Piggly Wiggly!"

Once we reach the store, I'm forced to access a quick psychic replay to see if I can find additional clues.

"Where was the tower, Mitzy?" Yolo gently asks.

"It was right up front. You know, one of those holiday endcaps."

"What was in the cans?" Stellen leans forward eagerly.

"I think it was pumpkin."

We race to the baking aisle and crouch down in front of the pie fillings. There, below the cans of pumpkin puree, is another telltale envelope.

Yolo squeals with excitement. "We found it!"

She pulls the envelope from the shelf and hands it to me. But I wave it away and point to her. "No. You found it. You read this one."

Yolo opens the envelope, fans the card dramatically, and clears her throat.

> *"All these words are taken without*
> *pay,*
> *But none are stolen or given away."*

I can't make heads or tails of it. "Words without pay?" The four of us exchange shrugs.

"Could it be the newspaper?" Erick offers his idea, with little conviction.

Shaking my head, I sigh. "No. Reporters are paid for their stories, and people have to buy newspapers. So the 'without pay' part doesn't apply."

Stellen lifts his finger. "If people don't pay, but they don't steal and they aren't given, how do they get the words?"

My eyes sparkle with excitement. "I've got it! The library! People check out the books. They don't steal them or buy them."

Erick gestures toward the front door of the Piggly Wiggly. "Back in the car, everyone."

I argue for a stop off at the patisserie for a flaky pastry recharge, but the team is too excited to entertain a distraction. Yolo offers me one of her candies as a consolation prize.

You know me—of course I take it.

The four of us run up the steps and burst through the front door, but as we stand in the vast atrium, the sheer weight of our search dampens the spirit.

Yolo says what we're all thinking. "It could be anywhere. I wouldn't even know where to start."

Erick paces in front of the entrance.

Yolo bounces on her tiptoes and taps a finger on her bottom lip.

Stellen and I lock eyes, as though some step-sibling mind meld can save us.

Wait, it's actually working.

Stellen smiles, and his green eyes twinkle. "It's all about you, right, Mitzy?"

I nod.

"So your foundation rebuilt the entire library after the tornado, but you added a special wing for curated displays."

"You're right! Let's start there."

We hurry toward the displays, and, as we pass through the entrance to the Duncan-Moon exhibit hall, my heart fills with pride. There's a lovely display honoring my grandfather, Cal Duncan, and his contribution to the railroad industry in Pin Cherry Harbor. One of my grandmother's wedding gowns is lit up like a Christmas tree, and there's a lengthy explanation of her many philanthropic ventures in the community. But when I see the one-of-a-kind flapper dress that used to reside in my apartment, glittering in its newfound home, my heart skips a beat.

One of my favorite ancestors, Sidney Jensen, left her mark on history. The first female jazz saxophone player, and quite a femme fatale in the 1920s. She fell in with the wrong crowd when she became a gangster's moll, but I happen to know the ghostly end of that story, and it warms my heart to see this memorabilia.

"The saxophone! I don't know why, but I think it might have something to do with that instrument."

My three teammates turn, and we carefully approach the display. The saxophone hangs on a stand inside a glass case. No envelope is visible.

Yolo pats my shoulder. "It was a good idea."

Erick drops to the ground, rolls onto his back, and slides under the display like a mechanic on a creeper. "Found it."

We all clap.

He rolls out and hands me the envelope.

"New rule. Finders keepers. You found it, you read it."

Erick opens the envelope, scans the card, and chuckles.

> *"Here you were once arrested for*
> *being a fake.*
> *A few donations and a speech cut*
> *you a break."*

He flashes his eyebrows. "Do you remember?"

Stellen steps forward and grabs my arm. "I remember. It was that day you came to the high school and pretended to be a student from the community college. You defended me when they picked on me in health class." His voice catches in his throat, and his eyes glisten with emotion.

Bumping my shoulder against his, I grin. "Yeah, I felt like crap when my cover was blown and the sheriff tossed me in cuffs."

Erick throws his hands in the air. "How am I coming out of this thing the bad guy? You were impersonating a teacher at a high school!"

"I was on a case, Sheriff."

Stellen throws an arm around my shoulders. "I'm glad you got arrested that day, sis. I had no idea how things would turn out between us. But I knew you were good people."

My cheeks flush with color. "Aw, shucks."

Erick shoves the envelope in his pocket. "Looks like we're off to the high school, gang."

The high school has played a role in several of my investigations. But since Stellen brought back the memory of my first visit there. I might know where to start our search.

Once inside, I share my theory with the crew. "Since the clue has to do with the first time I was at the school. I think we should start in the nurse's office. She was the person I was shadowing when I was pretending to help with the health classes."

We head into the nurse's office and begin searching randomly.

Yolo stops, tilts her head to the side, and points. "Those computers are new. Were they part of your donation?"

I rush toward the shiny new screens. "They were!" Searching around the new computer, I find the envelope taped to the back of the computer screen. "I finally found one!"

They all gesture for me to rip it open.

> *"This is the place where you took a*
> *risky cheap shot.*
> *It was almost as though you wanted*
> *to get caught."*

"Um, this is gonna be tough. People tell me I take a lot of risks."

Stellen nods. "That's actually true."

"Rude."

Erick rubs his hands along his jaw. "I can really only think of one cheap shot that resulted in you getting caught."

My eyes widen. "Oh. Yeah. Sorry about that. Again."

Stellen and Yolo gaze back and forth between Erick and me, and Yolo asks, "What are you talking about, Erick?"

He sucks air in between his teeth and shakes his head. "Mitzy was working undercover as a bartender at Final Destination. Before I knew what she was up to, I came in and saw her there—in a wig. To keep me from blowing her cover, she punched me in the face."

Stellen and Yolo gasp simultaneously. "What did you do?"

I throw my arms in the air and wave wildly. "Let's not get sidetracked, gang. We have our next clue. We know we're going to Final Destination. Load up."

The junior sleuths continue to mumble as we head back out to the Nova.

As soon as we walk through the creaking front door of the town's only dive bar, Lars shouts a hello and points to the minors. "For the record, Sheriff, they came in with you."

Erick nods and waves the owner's worry away with a quick gesture. "Absolutely. We're just here to find a clue in this crazy scavenger hunt."

Lars puts both of his large hands on the bar and takes a deep breath. "Well, you won't get any help from me. Or at least that's what I was told."

Leaning one elbow on the bar, I smile up at him. "And nobody crosses Twiggy. Right?"

He nods firmly. "Darn right."

Stellen circles the pool tables, grabs a handful of stale bar mix, and munches on it while he thinks. "Where did the, um, incident take place, Erick?"

Erick walks toward one of the barstools. "Right here."

Yolo rushes forward and feels around underneath the seat.

I step toward the action. "Incorrect, Sheriff. You were sitting on this stool." I reach underneath and secure the envelope. Waving it back and forth to the rest of the crew, I announce, "That's two for me."

Stellen leans in. "Yep. Read it."

> *"Ancient narwhal tusk and a deadly*
> *rival.*
> *Your study group was a means of*
> *survival."*

The mention of the narwhal tusk brings a sick swirl of nausea to my stomach. Anytime a memory of Rory Bombay surfaces, it's decidedly unpleasant.

Erick sees the look on my face and places a comforting arm around my shoulders. "Don't think about the bad stuff. Just think about what the clue means."

"Copy that. I guess it's probably the community college. Since it mentions the study group, that must refer to the students. And I was pretending to be a student there at the time."

Stellen chuckles. "Again? You pretended to go there twice?"

I shake my head. "You're such a little brother."

He smiles proudly. "Okay, let's all go to college."

Erick drives us over.

Locked. Closed for spring break. We got lucky at the high school. There was a crew there repainting the hallways. No such luck at Birch County Community College.

Yolo sidles up next to me and points to her bandolier.

A thrill and a giggle grip me. "Sheriff, you better look the other way."

Erick scrunches up his face, but it only takes him a second to clock our intentions. "I'm not involved."

"Copy that."

Yolo hands me a tension wrench and a rake—I won't even ask why she has them—and in less than a minute, I'm in. Thanks must be offered to my horrible foster brother, Jarrell. He did teach me a few useful things amidst all the cons.

"Looks like this door is open." I announce my "find" loudly, and Erick reluctantly follows us into the administration building.

After a few dead ends, I mention that the case was the one where the professor was murdered. "I bet it's in Professor Klang's old office."

Since I'm the only one who knows where that is, I lead the team. As we round the last corner, Yolo rushes ahead and snatches the envelope tucked under the nameplate of the new professor. "That's two for me, too!"

I offer her a wink. "Great minds. What can we say?"

She giggles and pulls out the clue. "It says this is the final clue."

> *"Now, back to the place where it all*
> *began.*
> *A ghost, a cat, and cranky human."*

Four voices unite, "Bell, Book & Candle!"

CHAPTER 20

INSTEAD OF DRIVING STRAIGHT BACK to my book-shop, Erick parks in the small parking lot beside the Duncan Restorative Justice Foundation. Weird, right?

"Is there a reason you parked so far away from my store, Sheriff?"

He purposely avoids my gaze, mumbles something unintelligible under his breath, and hops out of the car. He circles around and opens my door while Stellen and Yolo wait for me to slide the seat up so they can tumble out of the back.

There is an eager anticipation humming through my cohorts.

Fine. I'll let sleeping dogs lie.

As we round the corner onto First Avenue, my

father and Amaryllis race down the front steps of the foundation and look as though they've seen Sasquatch when they spot me on the sidewalk.

"Mitzy! How's my favorite daughter?"

Amaryllis rushes toward me, unzips my coat, and lifts my arms up. "The jumpsuit is gorgeous! I couldn't quite picture it from Isadora's written description, but it really is breathtaking."

A round of happy birthdays and hugs follows their hurried comments. When I move to continue toward the bookshop, Amaryllis scoops my arm into the crook of her elbow and squeezes. The gold flecks in her eyes catch the late afternoon light, and big auburn curls poke out from beneath her stocking cap.

"All right, what are you guys up to?"

My father dons his best poker face. "Up to? Can't a father wish his daughter happy birthday?"

The awkward silence is interrupted by the strains of a famous '80's song. Amaryllis claps her mittened hands together and tugs me forward. "It's go time!"

As we surge forward, the chorus of "Hungry Like the Wolf" echoes down the street.

Pointing toward the ruckus, I ask, "So, it sounds like there's a DJ. Will there also be a dance floor?"

My posse giggles, and when we reach the

corner of First and Main, my eyes nearly pop out of my head. Apparently, the scavenger hunt was a total decoy. While we were away, an enormous tent popped up. The sounds of music, laughter, and several luscious aromas are wafting from within.

"How in the world? It would've taken like a hundred people to get this together while we were gone."

Biker boots stomp out of the tent, and Twiggy shakes her severe grey pixie cut. "Try two hundred, kid. Your grandmother spared no expense."

And with that, she holds open the door of the beautiful tent and ushers me inside. A forest of sparkling trees, spaced between quite necessary propane heaters, illuminate the tent that engulfs the entire cul-de-sac next to my store.

"It's gorgeous! It's like a fairy wonderland." My gaze is drawn to the live band—not a DJ. "Wait! Is that Duran Duran?"

Twiggy puts a firm hand on my shoulder. "Not exactly. After their sixth refusal, Isadora got me onto finding a cover band. It's as close as I could get to the real thing."

Erick takes my hand and pulls me to the dance floor. "Is this one of your favorite bands or something?"

A warm memory floods in. "Not really, but I told Grams a story about one of my favorite memories of my mother. I had the chickenpox, and she had to take a couple days off work, from both of her jobs. Which now I know must've been very hard on us financially. At the time, she never let on it was any problem. She got out an old stack of records, and she played her Duran Duran album over and over—dancing all silly to keep my spirits up and distract me from itching. I'm sure she played music from other bands, but this was the one that stuck." A tear springs to the corner of my eye. "Grams thought of everything."

Erick turns me to the left and points to the roof of the tent. "She really did."

The side of the tent facing the bookstore has a clear plastic roof. I'm sure people will assume it's so we can dance under the stars, but as I gaze through the 6 x 6 windows on the side of the bookshop. My heart melts with love. Grams is blowing me kisses through the slumped glass window pane.

Without thinking, I wave like an idiot and blow kisses back.

Tally approaches to wish me a happy birthday. "Who are you waving at?"

"Oh, no one. I just thought that bird was looking at me."

Erick pokes me in the side. And I immediately giggle.

"Well, happy birthday. Odell will be here any

minute. He's closing the diner early today in honor of your birthday."

"Wow. Almost feels like a national holiday."

She chuckles. "As far as he's concerned, it is."

Before I get caught up in admiring the doppel-gänger Duran Duran band, Erick steers me toward the buffet. "You better eat something. I understand your grandmother made an exception to her no alcohol policy, after significant pressure from Twiggy. And, if I know you, there'll be a lot of champagne heading downstream. You better get a base going."

Pushing up to my tiptoes, I plant a kiss on his cheek and wipe away the smudge of red lipstick. "You're not wrong."

Anne, from Bless Choux patisserie, is manning the buffet table. "All of your favorite desserts are stacked around your three-tier chocolate cake with salted-caramel filling and *dulce de leche* buttercream frosting."

I lean across the table and smile foolishly. "Have I told you how much I love you?"

She giggles and blushes. "Don't mention it. I was happy to do it."

"So what do we have here in the savory section?"

She walks us through the delectable options. "These are potato and cheese pierogies. Here is my interpretation of Far-East spiced meat pies, and these are macadamia nut and panko bread crumb coated John Dorys." She leans toward me and whispers, "It's fancy fish."

"Sounds great to me."

She moves down the buffet and introduces the various starchy side-dish options. "Orange and almond risotto, dauphinoise potatoes, and cheesy riced cauliflower."

There's a selection of vegetables, which don't really grab my interest, although the roasted Brussels sprouts with bacon are tempting.

"At the end, you'll find pumpernickel rolls, pull-apart buns, and a braided caraway loaf."

My mouth is watering, and I feel like one plate won't be enough. "You thought of everything."

Erick grabs a plate. "If you ask me, that's enough talking. Let's get to eating."

No one has to ask me twice. We pile our plates and grab a table beside the temporary dance floor. The tent is filling up, and well-wishers pass by the table every few seconds. I recognize most of the faces, but I can only produce names for a handful. Grams definitely invited everyone. Even though my list of acquaintances could barely fill a page—let alone an enormous tent.

The music rocks on, and Erick drags me onto the dance floor several times.

I even have to do something called a "chicken dance." Which is exactly what it sounds like.

Eventually, the Duran Duran wannabes play happy birthday, and Amaryllis serves up the delectable cake.

Just as I'm about to breathe a sigh of relief, a spotlight spins toward the crowd and nails me like an escaping convict in a silent movie. I reach for Erick's hand, but he's nowhere to be found.

A voice calls from the stage. "Ladies and gentlemen, please put your hands together for Sheriff Erick Harper." The Simon Le Bon lookalike hands the microphone to Erick as he steps into a second spotlight.

Oh no, what's happening? Is it what I think it is? Am I ready for this?

"Mitzy Moon, please join me on stage."

My feet are frozen in place.

Erick eggs on the crowd. "Let's give her a little encouragement, folks. You all remember how our Pin Cherry Princess likes to avoid the spotlight." The spotlight operator flicks the bright beam off and on, and the crowd roars with laughter.

I guess I better get up there. The longer I wait, the worse it's going to be.

As I move toward the front, applause erupts throughout the tent.

When I reach the stage, Silas steps from the shadows and offers me a hand up the steps. I search his face for some clue as to what is about to happen, but he offers no hint.

Erick takes my hand and walks me to the center of the stage. "Well, Miss Moon. It's no secret how much you've helped the sheriff's department since you arrived in town."

My sense of humor defense mechanism is kicking in, and I can't stop myself from pulling the mic my direction. "Was that before or after you accused me of murder, Sheriff?"

The crowd's boisterous laughter bolsters my courage.

Erick comically hangs his head, but takes back the microphone. "I think it was the first time I laid eyes on you in the diner."

Oh dear. This is taking a turn, and I can't breathe.

He smiles out at the crowd. "Most of you probably think this is long overdue, but you all know me. Sometimes I can be a slow learner."

Another round of chuckles.

He reaches into his pocket with his right hand and pulls out a small flat box.

It's not the ring box I imagined, but who am I to judge? Let's see what he picked out.

Erick pops the box open toward the audience, and doesn't get on one knee.

I have to say, I'm a little disappointed. I've known him to be more chivalrous and romantic.

"Mitzy Moon," he turns the box toward me, "I'm making you an official honorary deputy of the Pin Cherry Harbor sheriff's department."

There's a moment of confusion in the crowd, but Amaryllis leaps to her feet clapping and everyone follows suit.

Confusion, mixed with disappointment, clouds my brain. I take the box, and I hope I smile, but when my ears hear the rest of his speech, I pray it's all a bad dream.

"Ladies and gentlemen, the Federal Bureau of Investigation has taken note of the work our sheriff's department has done with the help of civilian liaisons. I'll be heading to Quantico, Virginia, to lead an eight-week seminar assisting the Bureau in utilizing civilian liaisons to a more effective level. In exchange, I'll be involved in some training exercises, and our sheriff's department will receive some much-needed tech upgrades. However, your sheriff will get to be an instructor for several weeks. I'll leave you in the capable hands of acting Sheriff Paulsen and honorary deputy Moon, and I look forward to getting back to work with renewed purpose when I return."

The sound is fading from the room. All I can hear is a dull ringing. Someone takes my hand and leads me off the stage. A surge of excited citizens swarm around Erick, and I drift, alone, toward the tent's exit.

As soon as I pass through the front door of my beloved bookstore, the waterworks let loose. I fight to get my shoes off and abandon them in the stacks.

Running up to my apartment, I pull the candle handle and race inside. "Grams! Grams! Did you know he was going to do this? I can't believe you wouldn't tell me."

She swooshes from the window to my side. "Let me see the ring, sweetie!"

"Ring? What are you saying? It's a stupid deputy's badge. Something you'd give to an eager child."

I attempt to hand her the box, but it falls through her ethereal hand and hits the floor.

No one picks it up.

Sinking onto the settee, I sob into my hands.

"Deputy? It's not—"

I moan and echo her sentiment. "No, it's not."

Even with the protections in place, my heart aches, and my stomach is tied in knots.

The bookcase slides open behind me, but I refuse to turn.

"Isadora, if you're here, can we have a minute?" Erick's voice is soft and pleading.

Grams pops out of existence and he drops onto the settee next to me. He grips my hand and squeezes hard. "Hey, what's wrong?"

"What's wrong? Are you serious? You call me up on stage in front of the whole town, at my birthday party. Then you pull a box out of your pocket and make me an *honorary deputy*. What do you think is wrong?"

He drops my hand, heads into the bathroom, and retrieves a box of tissues. As I wipe my eyes, he explains. "Look, it wasn't a setup. I honestly thought you'd get a kick out of it. You're always teasing Paulsen about how you do her job better than she does, and the two of you will have to work together while I'm gone."

My chin shoots up and I stare daggers into his blue eyes. "Yeah, that's another thing. When were you planning on telling me?"

He squeezes my hand and shakes his head. "Hey, I know I took the coward's way out. I didn't want to tell you when we were kinda fighting. I didn't want to tell you after the whole bank heist scare—"

"I thought you were gonna propose, Erick. I feel like an idiot." I blow my nose loudly and throw the tissue on the floor.

He slips an arm around my shoulder. "Hey, we said no surprises. Remember? I promised you that we would make that decision together, and it doesn't seem like you're ready."

I clench my jaw, but I can't argue with his logic.

"It seems like you've got a lot of things to think about. We can't be partially together. You need to decide if you're ready to trust me completely, and this opportunity seemed like a sign. To me, I mean. You'll get some space, and you can think about what you want in your life."

My gaze drops to the floor, and I suck in a ragged breath.

"Hey, everyone doesn't have to be married to be happy. And you don't have to share all of your secrets with me if it doesn't feel right. But I did a lot of thinking after the FBI offer came in, and I don't think I can be in a relationship where I only get to know a piece of my partner. I need my partner to trust me with her whole heart. Hopefully, this time apart gives you a chance to think about things—with no pressure. I'm not going anywhere—"

My voice is raw and angry. "False. You're going halfway across the country. For two months!"

He scoops me into his arms and kisses the top of my head. "What I mean is, my heart isn't going anywhere. I love you, Mitzy Moon. And I'm ready to give you every part of myself. But I'm also willing to give you the time to decide what you really want. I'd never force your hand."

I sigh and soften my tone. "When do you leave?"

"Tomorrow."

My eyelids jerk open, and there are no words.

He wipes a tear from my cheek and smiles in that way that melts my heart. "I didn't want to spoil your birthday by telling you before . . . Then, time kinda ran out."

Before I can protest, his lips are on mine, and I'm lost in a swirl of confusing emotions.

The good news: Ghost-ma planned the most amazing birthday party—ever! Plus, she surprised me beyond belief. Kudos to Grams.

The bad news: The other shoe dropped. Erick finally got tired of my coquettish games of evasion. It's time for me to face the music or fire the orchestra.

In other news: Don't tell Grams, but I think her serenity prayer is exactly what I need right now. I can't change the past, but if I can find the courage . . . There's still a chance to take the world as it is.

He's leaving town. He's not leaving me. He promised that his heart isn't going anywhere.

One day at a time. That's all any of us can handle.

. . .

End of Book 18

~A NOTE FROM TRIXIE

I know! I know! I can already see the emails. LOL! As Erick would say, "Sit tight." Mitzy Moon (*and Sheriff Too-Hot-To-Handle*) will be back in Book 19, and your heart will start beating again—I promise. I'll keep writing them if you keep reading . . .

The best part of "living" in Pin Cherry Harbor continues to be feedback from my early readers. Thank you to my alpha readers/cheerleaders, Angel (*who was furious with me*) and Michael (*who buried his rage*). HUGE thanks to my fantastic beta readers who continue to give me extremely useful and honest feedback: Veronica McIntyre and Nadine Peterse-Vrijhof (*also slightly miffed*). And big "small town" hugs to the world's best ARC Team – Trixie's Mystery ARC Detectives!

My fantastic editor Philip Newey definitely

sent me back to the drawing board on a critical scene. Thanks to him, I avoided a giant time fumble. I'd also like to give buckets of gratitude to Brooke for her tireless proofreading! (*Despite her jam-packed schedule.*) Any remaining errors are my own.

As usual, I turned to Morgan for gun facts, as well as various bus-related tidbits.

FUN FACT: One of my most prized books is an oversized, illustrated *Alice in Wonderland* from Grosset & Dunlap circa 1958.

My favorite line from this case: "If loving you is wrong, Mitzy Moon, I don't wanna be right." ~Erick

I'm currently writing book nineteen in the Mitzy Moon Mysteries series, and it's going to have a satisfying mystery and a hilarious switcheroo. Mitzy, Grams, and Pyewacket got into plenty of trouble in book one, *Fries and Alibis*. But I'd have to say that book three, *Wings and Broken Things*, is when most readers say the series becomes unputdownable.

I hope you'll continue to hang out with us.

Trixie Silvertale (March 2022)

Once you're in the Club, you'll also be the first to receive

updates from Pin Cherry Harbor and access to giveaways, new release announcements, behind-the-scenes secrets, and much more!

Scan this QR Code with the camera on your phone. You'll be taken right to the page to join the Club!

Mitzy Moon Mysteries 19

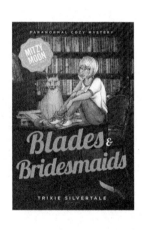

A simple canoe trip. A deadly eco-warrior. Will our psychic sleuth be up a creek without a paddle?

Mitzy Moon is a dry land kinda gal. Never in her life has she wanted to take an extended adventure in a tippy canoe. But when her newly engaged cousin calls for help, she'll have to put her faith in a snippy rival or risk losing everyone...

With a militant environmentalist stalking the bride-to-be and her maids on a camping trip, Mitzy is stuck with only mean-girl Deputy Paulsen as backup. After last-minute advice from Ghost-ma and her feisty feline, she heads deep into the wilderness to find the missing girls—with nothing but a tent and a flimsy plan.

Will Mitzy chance spilling her secrets, or turn turtle and transform the pending nuptials into a funeral?

Blades and Bridesmaids is the nineteenth book in the hilarious Mitzy Moon Mysteries paranormal cozy mystery series. If you like snarky heroines, supernatural intrigue, and a dash of romance, then you'll love Trixie Silvertale's cunning conundrum.

Buy *Blades and Bridesmaids* to recycle a killer today!

Grab yours!
readerlinks.com/l/2346664

Scan this QR Code with the camera on your phone. You'll be taken right to the Mitzy Moon Mysteries series page. You can easily grab any mysteries you've missed!

THANK YOU!

Trying out a new book is always a risk and I'm thankful that you rolled the dice with Mitzy Moon. If you loved the book, the sweetest thing you can do (*even sweeter than pin cherry pie à la mode*) is to leave a review so that other readers will take a chance on Mitzy and the gang.

Don't feel you have to write a book report. A brief comment like, "Can't wait to read the next book in this series!" will help potential readers make their choice.

Leave a quick review HERE
https://readerlinks.com/l/3315395

Thank you, and I'll see you in Pin Cherry Harbor!

This is Isadora "Grams" Duncan's non-alcoholic version of the glögg that is popular at the Northern Lights Yuletide Extravaganza!

This warming beverage can be served with an orange slice (candied or fresh), and a cinnamon stick or even a festive star anise. Add a of dollop whipped cream for an extra festive touch.

Yuletide Extravaganza Mulled Cider Recipe

Ingredients

- 2 cups cranberry juice, unsweetened if you prefer
- 84 ounces apple cider
- 1 orange, studded with whole cloves (approx. 15-20)
- 1 cup water
- 1 granny smith apple, cored/sliced
- 3 cinnamon sticks
- 2 star anise
- ½ cup brown sugar or Sukrin gold

Directions

1. Mix cranberry juice, cider, and water in large saucepan or crock pot.
2. Add brown sugar (or Sukrin gold) and stir to dissolve.
3. Add apple slices, clove-studded orange, cinnamon sticks and star anise.
4. Bring to a boil and immediately turn to low. Simmer for 4 hours.
5. Serve in glass mug.
6. Garnish with a dollop of whip (for an extra touch) and a slice of candied orange peel or fresh orange slice, if desired.
7. Makes 13 servings.

Heists and Poltergeists: Paranormal Cozy Mystery

Blades and Bridesmaids: Paranormal Cozy Mystery

Scones and Tombstones: Paranormal Cozy Mystery

Vandals and Yule Scandals: Paranormal Cozy Mystery

More to come!

MAGICAL RENAISSANCE FAIRE MYSTERIES

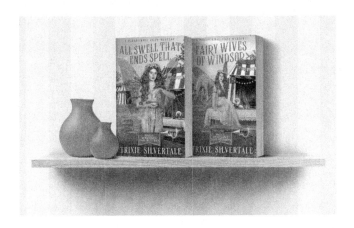

Explore the world of Coriander the Conjurer. A fortune-telling fairy with a heart of gold!

Book 1: **All Swell That Ends Spell** – A dubious festival. A fatal swim. Can this fortune-telling fairy herald the true killer?

Book 2: **Fairy Wives of Windsor** – A jolly Faire. A shocking murder. Can this furtive fairy outsmart the killer?

You can join Sydney Coleman and her unruly ghosts, as they solve mysteries in a truly haunted mansion!

Book 1: **Moonlight and Mischief** – She's desperate for a fresh start, but is a mansion on sale too good to be true?

Book 2: **Moonlight and Magic** – A haunted Halloween tour seem like the perfect plan, until there's murder...

Book 3: ***Moonlight and Mayhem*** – An unwelcome visitor. A surprising past. Will her fire sale end in smoke?

USA TODAY Bestselling author Trixie Silvertale grew up reading an endless supply of Lilian Jackson Braun, Hardy Boys, and Nancy Drew novels. She loves the amateur sleuths in cozy mysteries and obsesses about all things paranormal. Those two passions unite in her Mitzy Moon Mysteries, and she's thrilled to write them and share them with you.

When she's not consumed by writing, she bakes to fuel her creative engine and pulls weeds in her herb garden to clear her head (*and sometimes she pulls out her hair, but mostly weeds*).

Greetings are welcome:
trixie@trixiesilvertale.com

BB bookbub.com/authors/trixie-silvertale

f facebook.com/TrixieSilvertale

O instagram.com/trixiesilvertale

Printed in Great Britain
by Amazon

28161136R00443